New York Ti
JACI BURTON

"Burton is a master at sexual tension!" —*RT Book Reviews*

"This sexy and sizzling-hot story will leave you breathless and wanting more." —*Fresh Fiction*

New York Times Bestselling Author
CARLY PHILLIPS

"Carly Phillips has me addicted!" —*Joyfully Reviewed*

"Phillips's characters are always believable, and I think that's what makes her books keepers." —*Fresh Fiction*

National Bestselling Author
JESSICA CLARE

"Clare's sizzling encounters in the great outdoors have definite forest-fire potential from the heat generated." —*RT Book Reviews*

"Sexy and funny." —*USA Today* Happy Ever After Blog

National Bestselling Author
ERIN McCARTHY

"One of the romance-writing industry's brightest stars." —*Romance Reviews Today*

"Readers won't be able to resist McCarthy's sweetly sexy and sentimental tale." —*Booklist*

HOT
SUMMER NIGHTS

**JACI BURTON
CARLY PHILLIPS
JESSICA CLARE
ERIN McCARTHY**

B

BERKLEY SENSATION, NEW YORK

THE BERKLEY PUBLISHING GROUP
Published by the Penguin Group
Penguin Group (USA) Inc.
375 Hudson Street, New York, New York 10014, USA

USA | Canada | UK | Ireland | Australia | New Zealand | India | South Africa | China

Penguin Books Ltd., Registered Offices: 80 Strand, London WC2R 0RL, England
For more information about the Penguin Group, visit penguin.com.

HOT SUMMER NIGHTS

A Berkley Sensation Book / published by arrangement with the authors

Berkley Sensation Books are published by The Berkley Publishing Group.
BERKLEY SENSATION® is a registered trademark of Penguin Group (USA) Inc.
The "B" design is a trademark of Penguin Group (USA) Inc.

For information, address: The Berkley Publishing Group,
a division of Penguin Group (USA) Inc.,
375 Hudson Street, New York, New York 10014.

ISBN: 978-0-425-26339-6

PUBLISHING HISTORY
Berkley Sensation mass-market edition / July 2013

PRINTED IN THE UNITED STATES OF AMERICA

10 9 8 7 6 5 4 3 2 1

Cover photo of Couple on Beach by Walter Zerla/Getty Images.
Cover design by Annette Fiore DeFex.
Interior text design by Kelly Lipovich.

ALWAYS LEARNING   PEARSON

HOPE SMOLDERS

JACI BURTON

CHAPTER ONE

Despite the five or six little kids trailing behind her, Will Griffin noticed the woman. How could he not? Great legs drew his eye every time, and hers were outstanding.

This woman had dark hair pulled back in some kind of messy ponytail, a rainbow-colored straw hat, and the ugliest swimsuit cover-up thing he'd ever seen.

Not the typical kind of body you saw walking past the glass in the workout room at Hope's community gym.

Maybe that's why she'd caught his eye. The kids all squealing with delight as they made their way to the pool might have been the ones who'd drawn his attention at first, but their leader, with her sexy legs peeking out the bottom of that ugly-as-hell cover-up, kept his attention after that.

Plus, he was sure he knew her. Her straw hat was pulled just low enough, and she kept turning her head away from the glass so he couldn't see her face.

Was she doing it deliberately?

He hadn't yet started his workout, so he detoured from

the gym area where he'd been headed and made a beeline toward the pool.

He hit the men's locker room and grabbed a towel.

"You gonna do some laps, Will?"

He stopped and turned to look at his friend, Hope police officer Luke McCormack.

"Hey, Luke. Get off late today?"

"Yeah. We had a fender bender up at the high school after the basketball game. With injuries. Took a while to clean that one up."

Will grimaced. "Is everyone all right?"

"Yeah. Injuries were minor, but that one left me tense so I figured I'd get a workout in. Are you going for a swim?"

Following a woman with kids probably wasn't the best of ideas. "Actually, I thought I saw someone I know."

Luke grinned. "Now that you're off nights, you're probably going to see a lot of people you know."

"You're right. Are you heading into the weight room?"

"Yeah.

His gaze lingered at the door to the pool. "I'll meet you on the treadmills."

"Okay. Later."

After Luke left, Will pushed open the door to the pool area and was instantly hit by the pungent smell of chlorine. The squeals of kids echoed throughout as children splashed and played at the shallow end while adults did laps.

He searched for the woman in the straw hat, but didn't see her. Ah well, probably best he not act like a stalker anyway. He closed the door and headed to the weight room.

Jane Kline realized she hadn't carefully thought out this idea. When she'd originally agreed to take on a part-time job doing day-care duties at the community center gym, she figured she'd hide out in the day-care room while the rest of the hard bodies got their groove on in the workout areas.

She could play with the kids and make some desperately needed extra money.

What she hadn't counted on was the manager asking her to take a few of the kids for a swim, which meant she'd have to walk down the hall toward the indoor pool, and that meant crossing right in front of the glass wall that separated her from said hard bodies huffing and puffing on bikes and treadmills while she toted herself, five six-year-olds, and about ten pounds of excess weight that she kept meaning to take off. But between getting divorced, teaching during the day, and dealing with her own two kids at night, there just didn't seem to be enough time for diet and exercise.

One would think the post-traumatic divorce stress over the past two years would have caused the weight to drop off, but all it had done was make her crave cookies, donuts, and chocolate. Oh, and pizza. She really liked pizza. So did her kids, and since they were currently without a father, how could she deny them pizza?

But there was no avoiding that glass wall of shame, so she got the kids she was responsible for—including Tabitha, her five-year-old—ready for the pool. She changed in the back room of the day care, then threw her not quite white anymore and kind of holey cover-up on over her swimsuit and tossed the straw sun hat on over her hair, which was a wreck and slightly lopsided. But hey, it worked. She pulled the brim down low. Hopefully none of the residents of her small Oklahoma town would even notice her.

No such luck. They didn't even make it twenty feet.

"Jane. I didn't know you were working here."

"Hi, Jane. So great to see you. Are you here to work out?"

"Oh, Jane. Are you heading to the pool for a swim?" the last one asked with a quick glance in the general direction of her thighs, which no doubt carried much of her pizza weight.

She acknowledged them all with a quick smile and told them she was working and, oh gosh, she had to monitor the kids. Then she stepped up her pace, refusing to even glance to her left where the whirring sound of cardio burn shamed her.

"Mommy, you look funny in that hat."

"Thanks, Tabby," she said with a tight smile as they walked along, calling attention to themselves as the kids chattered noisily.

Maybe when she had some free time she'd make use of one of the fringe benefits of working at the center—namely the free gym membership.

Sure. Free time. What was that? She'd long ago lost any comprehension of the word "free." But whatever it took to keep the roof over her kids' heads was worth it, so she carried on conversation with the kids and led them to the pool, took off the sun hat, and jerked off her cover-up, refusing to acknowledge her cellulite as she climbed in the water, six screaming five-year-olds cannonballing in all around her.

Good thing she didn't have much of a hairstyle going anyway, since she was immediately drenched. She swept her hair out of her face.

"Okay, kids," she said, counting her charges so she could keep track of them. "Remember, we have to stay in the shallow end."

The kids swam and played and burned off the excess energy that had driven everyone crazy in the tiny room they used for the gym day-care center. After about thirty minutes, Jane rounded them up, dried them off, and led them toward the day-care room, her cover-up clinging to her wet suit as she was once again forced to walk past the glass wall. Only this time she couldn't help but take a quick glance.

Ugh. The place was packed with sweaty, firm bodies, a lot whom she recognized.

Unfortunately, while she was glancing in the direction of the glass wall, she wasn't paying attention to where she was going, which sent her crashing into the chest of one of the gym patrons.

"Oof. I'm so sorry."

She heard a deep male laugh, and strong arms shot out to steady her, giving her a brief glimpse of very strong, very toned biceps.

"Are you okay?"

She kept one eye peeled around him to see the kids all scurry back into the day-care room. "I'm fine. Sorry again." She was about to dash away when he said her name.

"Jane?"

She lifted her gaze and was blasted by melt-your-panties whiskey brown eyes, dark hair closely cropped, a strong jaw, and a smile she knew all too well, though she hadn't seen Will Griffin in a while. He worked nights on highway patrol, and she worked days, which meant they didn't run into each other often. And that suited her just fine, since he'd been best friends with her ex-husband, and seeing him reminded her of things she really didn't want to be reminded of.

Like good-looking men. And getting dumped.

"Oh. Will. Wow, it's been a while. Wish I could hang out and talk, but I have kids I need to watch over, so I can't. Great seeing you again."

She started to walk away, but he grasped her wrist. "Wait. What are you doing here?"

"Oh, uh, I'm working at the day-care center here."

His brows shot up. "A new job? You're still teaching, aren't you?"

"Yup. Still do that, too. Gotta run. See you later."

Or, never. Hopefully. She looked like a wet basset hound, while Will had always been hot. And built. And as sexy as any man she'd ever known.

Of course she'd once thought Vic was hot and sexy, and look where that had gotten her. Divorced, with two children, a mortgage, and flat broke.

Never again would she let a hot body and bedroom eyes seduce her. She was a lot smarter now.

Though her rapidly beating pulse and all her feminine

parts hadn't gotten the message. They were screaming at her that she hadn't been with a man since she'd been abandoned by her husband two years ago. She hadn't even gone out on a date.

Too bad. There were things high on her priority list, like making sure to keep a roof over her children's heads, and keeping everyone fed.

Not dating. Or having sex. Those weren't essentials. And right now, all she could afford to think about were essentials, so her thrumming body could just go to hell.

Will Griffin stood in the hallway, too surprised to even move as Jane hustled away after a trail of small kids, her daughter, Tabitha, one of them.

No wonder he'd recognized the great legs earlier.

He blew out a breath, guilt knotted up in his stomach. He should go by Jane's house more often, should have made it by regularly when he'd known for sure Vic wasn't coming back. But it had been awkward then. Still was. What was he supposed to say? Sorry? Not that it was his fault his former best friend turned out to be such an asshole. But he could have offered to mow her lawn or help her out in some way. Instead, he'd stayed away, figuring the last person she needed to see was someone she so closely tied to her deadbeat ex-husband.

And now, two years later, he still wasn't any better at making conversation with her or seeing her. The distance between them was as wide as the Grand Canyon. They all used to be close—him and Vic and Jane. That changed somewhat when he and his girlfriend Chelsea had broken up, but Jane insisted nothing would change just because Jane and Chelsea were best friends. He'd appreciated their friendship, but he hadn't turned out to be such a good friend after all, had he?

No sense gawking after shadows of the past when there

was nothing he could do about it now. Jane obviously wanted nothing to do with him.

He'd come out to get a sports drink after his treadmill workout, so he wandered over to the vending machine, grabbed one, then used his key card to get back into the workout room, deciding he needed to lift some weights and ease some of the tension this day and seeing Jane had dropped on him.

He caught sight of Luke on the weight bench and wandered over there. He warmed up with some lighter weights, then laid down on the bench for the heavy stuff.

Luke came over. "Want me to spot you?"

"Sure. Thanks."

He went three sets, then racked the bar with Luke's help. When he added another twenty-five pounds to each side, Luke cocked a brow.

"Sure you're up for that?"

"Trust me, I need the challenge."

"Okay, buddy. I'll hang on to the bar for you in case it comes crashing down on your chest."

"You're so funny. I think I can handle it."

Will slid onto the bench, determination setting his lips in a grim line. As he lifted the bar out of the rack, his arms shaking from the added weight, he realized he deserved this punishment for not being there for Jane, for not recognizing how Vic had been self-destructing in front of him.

Maybe he just hadn't wanted to see it.

"Eleven, twelve," Luke said, racking the bar. "Though I think I had to do the last one mostly by myself."

Out of breath, his arms wobbling like overcooked spaghetti, Will grabbed his towel and swiped it over his face. "Yeah, you probably did."

"Why the punishment? You hand out too many tickets on the highway today and feel guilty?"

Will choked out a laugh. "I never feel guilty about that."

"Did you sleep with some girl then dump her?"

"Uh, no."

Luke came around and faced him. "Then what is it?"

"Nothing, man. Just a rough day and I needed a push."

"Well, if there's something you want to get off your chest, you know I'm always here for you. Even if you are highway patrol and I'm local law enforcement. I mean, I can forgive you even that."

Will snorted. "Gee, thanks."

Luke gave him a wink. "Hey, nobody's perfect, man."

Yeah, Will was definitely not perfect. Far from it. In fact, in some areas he was a downright failure.

But maybe he could fix that.

CHAPTER TWO

"**I** hate broccoli."

Jane inhaled a deep breath and let it out, then turned and faced her eight-year-old son, Ryan, with a smile on her face. Always approach everything with a smile, right?

"Broccoli's good for you."

They were eating dinner at Bert's, one of her favorite diners in town. It had been a rough day, and she just didn't have it in her to cook a meal and spend the evening inside with the kids. She needed to be around the presence of other adults.

Ryan stared at his plate, grimaced, and pushed it away. "Doesn't mean I have to like it."

"I love broccoli, Mommy," Tabitha said. Always the pleaser, she took a big bite and chewed and tried her best not to make a face. She even smiled through it.

Yeah, Tabitha hated broccoli, too, but she'd do anything to make Jane happy. Even eat broccoli.

"There's a two-week camp coming up next summer," Ryan said. "Chris says it has archery and canoes and swimming in the lake and hiking. I was wondering if I could go."

Jane frowned. Chris's parents owned one of the car dealerships in town. They had money. Jane did not. This camp wasn't going to be free. She sensed disappointment ahead for her little boy. "Do you have a brochure?"

"Yeah." Hope glimmered in her sweet boy's brown eyes, and he fished it out from his backpack, no doubt with a sales pitch already planned. Her kid was nothing if not prepared when there was something he wanted. He was a lot like his father in that respect.

He handed it over. "They have lots of activities, Mom, and the counselors are all trained in CPR and first aid. Most of them went to the camp when they were my age. Isn't that cool?"

Jane couldn't help but zero right in on the cost. She swallowed, hard. No way could she afford it. She was stretched thin enough on her budget as it was, and trying to locate Vic to pay his back child support was harder than trying to find a dress that didn't make her butt look big.

Might as well rip the Band-Aid off rather than give Ryan false hope. She looked up at him and gave him a smile that she prayed showed him how much she loved him. "It looks awesome, sweetie. But it's a little too much money, and you know how things are."

His hopeful smile died. He looked crushed, and her heart ached at his disappointment as he gazed down at his plate and pushed the broccoli around with his fork. "Yeah. It's okay. I understand, Mom."

That was the problem. He did understand, and he still loved his father, still hoped his dad would show up at his ball games. Or just show up.

Part of her wished he would, too, that he'd get clean and come back—at least for his kids. What she had with Vic was over, but his children needed a father, the kind of father he used to be, not the one he'd become when he'd spent every day so drunk and high that he could barely remember his own name.

But it was times like this she was so angry at Vic that if he showed his face right now she wasn't sure what she would do. Likely lay him flat for running out on his children and leaving them wanting things they couldn't have, things she couldn't give them.

Damn him.

"Hey, kids. I have all this extra chocolate cake and I thought—wow, the place is kinda empty tonight, and if there aren't enough people eating dessert, I'm gonna have to throw it away. I thought maybe you could take it off my hands."

God bless Anita, who was her favorite waitress and a good friend. Divorced three times and with two grown sons, Anita had been her lifesaver. They'd had a few heart-to-heart talks about lousy husbands. And Jane knew that cake wouldn't end up on her check tonight.

Ryan had a sweet tooth that rivaled any kid in town, and Anita's offer distracted him from his disappointment. His eyes widened. "Oh, cake. Can we have cake, Mom?"

She'd deal with the sugar high for hours and it would be hell to get the kids to bed tonight, but it would be worth it. "Of course you can have cake. Thanks, Anita."

Anita winked and shoved her pencil into the wild mass of streaked blonde and brown hair piled on top of her head. "No problem, honey. Kids, go have Charlotte serve up that cake for you at the counter."

The kids scrambled off. They loved sitting at the counter, where Charlotte, Bert's wife, would serve them cake, no doubt with a dollop of ice cream on the side.

"Thanks again," she said as Anita filled a cart with their empty dishes.

"You looked like you could use a ray of sunshine today."

She hated that it showed on her face. "Oh, I'm fine. I just hate saying no to the kids."

Anita laughed. "It's a good word for them to learn. Teaches them that not everything in life is free."

"I know that, but I haven't been able to do anything special for them since Vic left. And Ryan wants to go to this fancy summer camp and I just can't afford it."

"Yeah, well, that's Vic's fault, not yours." She punctuated the statement by tossing the utensils viciously into the cart.

"But my kids still adore their father."

Anita gave them a look over her shoulder. Tabitha and Ryan were busily scooping from the bowl of ice cream Charlotte had given them and paying zero attention to their conversation.

"They'll get over that when they're older and realize how much he piled on your shoulders."

"I got the great end of the deal," Jane said with a smile. "I got them."

Anita squeezed her arm. "You sure did, honey."

Charlotte came over. She was a slight, just a bit over five feet tall woman with short gray hair, but she was formidable and ran Bert's like a drill sergeant. She was also one of the sweetest women Jane had ever met. She slid a bowl of chocolate ice cream in front of her. Jane didn't know what she'd do without Bert's as a refuge.

"Some for you, too, sweetie," Charlotte said.

She lifted her gaze at Charlotte. "Thanks. I needed that."

"Figured," Charlotte said with a wink.

Alone at the table, Jane inhaled and took a bite of the ice cream, then sighed, realizing this wasn't going to do much to thin her thighs.

Then again, today she didn't much care.

"Did you hear that Emma Burnett is back in town?" Anita took a seat across from her. It was a light crowd at the diner, and they'd come before the typical dinner rush anyway.

Jane was glad for the company—and some town gossip.

"No. Really?"

"Yes. She bought out Doc Weston's veterinary practice and is reopening it."

Jane smiled, happy to be talking about someone else for a change. "That's great news. Gosh, I haven't seen Emma since . . . high school, I guess. It's been a really long time."

"Yeah, she left town for vet school and then some job somewhere else and hasn't been home much. I know she popped in here now and then during breaks from college, but we sure haven't seen much of her over the years."

"You're right about that. Come to think of it, I don't know that I can remember the last time she was back in Hope."

Anita nodded. "Anyway, that's all I know. Now she's back and prepping the clinic to reopen."

"That's good news for Hope. Since Dr. Weston retired, everyone with animals has only had one clinic to go to. I can't wait to see her. I'll be sure to drop by once the clinic opens."

"The Burnett sisters sure pulled a disappearing act, didn't they?" Anita asked.

Jane frowned, then nodded. "Oh, that's right. Emma's little sister, Molly, left, too, didn't she? I didn't know her all that well because she was a few years younger than Emma and me."

"Yeah, she hightailed it out of town even before Emma left. No idea what happened to her."

"Huh. Me, either." She hadn't thought about the Burnett sisters in a long time. She and Emma hadn't been best friends in high school, but they'd hung out in the same circles.

After dinner, Jane and the kids took a walk to the community park. Tabitha liked the playground there and Ryan fed the ducks, at least until he found a few of his friends and a game of football ensued.

Her little boy was growing up. He was so tough and was trying so hard to be the man of the house. But he was still only eight years old, and underneath the tough-kid exterior was a vulnerable little boy who'd been hurt when his daddy, his hero, had abandoned him.

Fortunately, he loved his sports, and that kept his mind occupied. She wished she could send him to that ridiculously expensive camp this summer. But there was no sense wishing for things that weren't going to happen.

Glad Ryan had an outlet for his excess energy, Jane took a few minutes to stretch out on the playground bench, take a couple deep relaxing breaths, and exhale.

At least she had a job. And now another job at the health club. She'd also applied to teach summer school, since positions were at a premium and you had to apply early. Maybe she could afford a few extras for the kids this summer.

Maybe.

Tabitha played with Karen Redmond's daughter, Heather, and Karen stood watch over them like a hawk. Ryan was deeply involved in a football game, with other parents supervising, so she tilted her head back and closed her eyes for just a second.

"Jane?"

It must have been more than a second because she felt disoriented, like maybe she'd allowed herself to fall asleep. She blinked and opened her eyes to find a sweaty hunk of beefcake standing in front of her. She shielded her eyes from the setting sun, unable to make out his face until he moved out of the shadow of the sun.

Will. Again? Why was she suddenly running into him a lot when she rarely ever saw him?

"Oh. Will. Hi. What are you doing here?" Other than catching her napping when she should be watching her kids. She made a quick search. Tabitha was still screaming down the slides with Heather, and Ryan had the football tucked under his arm, his buddies going all out to try and tackle him.

And she'd been passed out on the bench.

Wasn't she just mother of the year?

"I was taking a run in the park, saw you sitting here."

"I sure am seeing a lot of you lately."

"I switched from nights to days."

"Oh. Right. I heard about that."

His lips curved. "Of course you did. Is there anything in this town that isn't broadcast somewhere?"

"No. There's a daily gossip update via social media. You can't have secrets in Hope. Don't even try. We even know what brand of toilet paper you buy via our spies at the grocery store."

He laughed. "I'm going to assume you're kidding about that."

She arched a brow. "Am I?"

"Now that's a scary thought." He looked around. "Are the kids in the playground?"

"Yes. Over there," she said with a nod of her head, grateful she'd been wearing her sunglasses so maybe he wouldn't notice she'd been asleep.

He turned and she took a moment to check out his muscles, lean body, and long legs. Did the man have to be tanned and in such great shape? She wanted to not be in her yoga pants and a T-shirt, both more than a few years old. She'd just tossed the outfit on for the walk and now she looked down with a critical eye. The yoga pants were faded, but supremely comfortable, because really, once she got home, who cared? It wasn't like she was trying to impress anyone.

And she sure wasn't trying to impress Will.

"Wow, the kids have gotten so big. Ryan looks a lot like Vic."

Her gaze wandered over to where Ryan was dashing for some imaginary end zone, a wide grin on his face. She smiled wistfully. "Yes, he does."

Will took a seat next to her. "Have you heard from him?"

"From Vic? No."

"At all?"

"No."

"I'm sorry, Jane."

She shrugged. "I'm over it."

"I'm sorry for not coming over, too."

Coming over? Why would he want to do that? "My family isn't your responsibility. It's Vic's."

"Still, I could have been there to help you through this. I guess I thought maybe you wouldn't want to see me, that I'd remind you of what you lost."

She frowned. "That's ridiculous. You had nothing to do with him leaving."

"But he and I were best friends. I should have seen it coming."

She let out a very unladylike snort. "I was married to him. I lived with him every day. I shared his life. And I didn't see it coming. Neither did his parents. So unless you're some kind of psychic, I don't think you had an edge on knowing he was going to abruptly check out of marriage and fatherhood without letting anyone know."

Will stared out over the playground. "I know it's been two years, but I still can't believe he just up and disappeared without a word, that he hasn't contacted you."

"Oh, we were in contact through his attorney—at least long enough for him to sign the divorce papers."

"Maybe he figured he was so screwed up that he was doing you a favor."

"Some favor," she said with a laugh. "Leaving me and the kids and then disappearing so well I can't find him in order to get him to pay child support."

"Jesus." Will shoved his fingers through his hair and looked down at the ground. "I had no idea it was that bad."

Wasn't she a brilliant conversationalist? She could bring down a chat in three seconds flat. God, how depressing could she be?

She stood. "It's not that bad, Will. The kids and I are doing just fine." She hollered for Tabitha and Ryan, then turned to him. "Great to see you again."

Will's gaze was intense as he stood and came to stand beside her. "You don't have to go, Jane."

"Yes, I do. It's late and it's getting cool out here. I have papers to grade and the kids have homework. I'll see you around."

She gathered up the kids and headed down the street before she poured out her heart and soul and wept on Will's shoulder, the absolute last thing she wanted to do.

She was strong, and a survivor. She hated those looks of sympathy and pity from anyone, especially Will.

Her life was just freaking fine.

Will watched Jane wander down the street with her kids. She held Tabitha's hand, and Ryan was walking backward, talking nonstop to her about something.

Will had said something wrong, because she'd looked hurt or pissed off and she couldn't wait to get away from him.

Maybe because she didn't like talking about Vic and the divorce. Either way, he made a mental note to look forward, not back, the next time he saw her.

He knew he'd woken her up when he'd come upon her on the bench. She was likely exhausted. He wondered how long it had been since she'd gone out and had some fun. Had she even been out at all since the divorce? Or had she been so focused on rebuilding her life with the kids and making sure their needs were met that she hadn't been meeting her own?

He might not be able to do anything about her sonofabitch loser of an ex-husband, but he could definitely do something about her having some fun.

CHAPTER THREE

Two algebra classes in a row always made her brain tired, but Jane lived for math, even if her students didn't jump for joy over quadratic equations.

Her next class was basic math, so she'd get a breather, though she had a couple kids in this class who needed one-on-one help. They were skating the edge of failing and she'd be damned if she'd let that happen.

If a kid didn't give a crap, she'd work with him or her and try to explain what it would mean to fail her class. She'd push and prod, and often, the kid would come around. Sometimes it wouldn't matter, and no amount of cajoling and notes and phone calls home to parents would change the kid's attitude. And attitude was so prevalent in this age group, where hormones came into play. There was so much to juggle at the early high school age. Boys and girls noticed each other, so you had burgeoning sexuality to deal with along with surging hormones.

So fun.

But God, she loved these kids, this awkward age she

remembered so well from her own years in the gawky teens.

It hadn't gone so well for her, so she tried her best to pave the way for those not born with perfect genetics.

After she went through the work with the entire class, she worked with Susie and Robert. Robert was more amenable to the one-on-one instruction. Susie was the balker. She was in foster care, her dad had never been in the picture, and her mom was in and out of jail for drugs. Jane's heart went out to Susie, who hadn't had an easy life since birth. Born addicted, she had some learning disabilities, but the kid was tough. Jane was determined to see her make it, despite all the strikes against her. She gave Bobby a worksheet and went through the simple math problems over and over again until Susie was frustrated.

"You want to pass this class, don't you, Susie?" she asked.

Susie just shrugged a shoulder, affecting her typical "I don't care" attitude as she stared at the worksheet.

"I think you're really smart and you can do anything you set your mind to do."

"I'm not smart," she whispered. "I'm stupid."

Jane so wanted to fold this girl in her arms and give her a huge hug. "You *are* smart. You have to work harder than anyone else in this entire school, so that means you're smarter than any of them."

Her dark eyed gaze lifted to Jane's. "Yeah?"

"Yeah. So let's show them all how smart you really are. And how tough you are. Don't fail."

She saw the tears of frustration shimmering in Susie's eyes. "I'll try."

"That's all you have to do." Jane leaned over the worksheet and went over the math problems again. By the end of the class, Susie had gotten them all right. It felt like a triumph. Jane sent another worksheet home with Susie with a note to her foster parents to work on it with her, along with praise for how well she was doing.

It was all she could do, but she knew Susie had a good foster family. They'd work with her.

Her fingers were crossed.

After school, she went and picked up Tabitha and headed to the community center to work at the day-care center. Her dad was going to pick up Ryan and take him to baseball practice.

She wouldn't have survived the past two years without her parents' support. They'd pitched in when needed to run the kids to sports or dance if she had to go in an opposite direction. She tried not to lean on them too much, but frankly, she'd have drowned without them.

Tabitha loved the day-care center, so it was no hardship to bring her along. Several of her friends' parents worked out at the community center, so she got to play for a few hours while Jane watched the kids. At least this afternoon there wouldn't be any swimming involved and she could hide in the day-care room and not have to parade past the hard-body room.

She traded with Marisol, the other person on duty at the day-care room, checking kids in and out and alternately playing with them. They ranged in age from eighteen months—the minimum age they'd accept—to five years, Tabby's age. After that, the parents were on their own, which was why she couldn't bring Ryan.

Another reason she adored her parents. She needed this extra money, as paltry as it was, but working here a few days a week after school would help.

"Hey, Jane."

She stood at the doorway, which had a door that partially opened from the top only. The bottom half of the door remained close to discourage runaway kids. She had just checked out one of the kids so she was initialing the departure.

She raised her gaze when her name was called, thinking it was the father of one of Tabby's friends.

It wasn't. It was Will, whom she hoped she wouldn't run into again. He made her senses go haywire, and made her remember things she hadn't had in a very long time.

Things she shouldn't want.

"Oh. Hey, Will."

"I thought I saw you come in right before me."

Her hair was half pulled out of her ponytail since she'd been holding baby James and he was a hair puller. And then he'd wiped his jelly snack all over her left breast. She looked a mess. Once again, Will had on a sleeveless tank and gym shorts, and was tanned, muscled, and gorgeous.

Sometimes life just wasn't fair.

"Yes. Working again." She turned to see if she needed to make a hurried exit, but there were only three kids in attendance at the moment. Baby James was down in the porta-crib for a nap, and Tabby and her friend were being entertained by Marisol, so Jane was out of luck.

"You stay busy, don't you?"

She offered him a smile. "You have no idea."

"Where's Ryan?"

"My dad took him to ball practice."

"Yeah? I'd like to watch him play sometime."

Ryan would adore that. Which meant it would never happen. The last thing she needed was for Ryan to attach himself to some male that he'd use as a substitute for his father. "Yeah. Sure."

"I was wondering if you'd like to come out with me sometime."

She blinked several times, certain she hadn't heard him right. "Excuse me?"

His lips curved and, oh, God, when he smiled he looked even sexier. If that was possible. "You're going to make me ask it again?"

"I'm not sure I understood what you said."

"Okay, then I'll say it again. I'd like to go out with you. I'd like you to go out with me."

"You want to go out with me? Why?"

Two parents had suddenly shown up in line behind him. Will turned around. "Maybe this isn't the best time. What time to do you get out of here?"

"Uh, six thirty."

"I'll come to your house and bring a pizza. We'll talk about it then, okay?"

"Uh, wait, Will."

But he was already gone.

Come to her house? Bring pizza? Was he insane?

And he wanted to take her out?

She was living in some kind of alternate universe, because surely that hadn't just happened.

A guy like Will Griffin did not go out with a woman like Jane. She had issues. Her life was a nightmare. He was single and gorgeous. She had two children.

And apparently he was coming over for pizza tonight. At which time she'd set him straight.

Okay, so maybe he'd hustled her, but Will figured Jane's life was all about being busy with her kids and her jobs, and if he didn't, she'd never say yes.

She still hadn't said yes, because he hadn't given her a chance to. But he did pull into her driveway with an extra large pizza at seven fifteen. And her car was visible in the garage, so she hadn't shut the garage door and turned off all the lights, pretending she wasn't home.

It was hot as hell, like a typical late August in Oklahoma. And her lawn needed to be mowed and weeded, he noted as he walked toward the front door. She probably did all that herself, too.

Mentally calling Vic a list of very unkind names, he rang the doorbell.

Ryan answered the door. He looked up and studied Will, as if deciding whether or not to let him in.

"Hey, Ryan."

"You're Will. I remember you. You used to be friends with my dad."

He smiled. "I remember you, too."

He opened the screen door. "Mom said to let you in. That you'd have pizza. She's in the shower. One of the babies at the gym barfed on her. She smelled really bad."

He laughed as Ryan led him into the kitchen. "Is that right?"

"Yeah," Tabitha said, taking his hand as he got into the kitchen. "I'm Tabitha and I'm five."

"Hi, Tabitha. I'm Will."

"Mom got barfed on."

"So I heard."

"I mean really bad," Tabitha said. "And we had to ride in the car with her the whollle wayyyy hommme." She scrunched her nose and rolled her eyes.

"You poor kids. I'll bet it was awful."

"You have no idea," Ryan said. "I thought I was gonna barf, too."

"Can we not say barf anymore, kids? We have a guest who was nice enough to bring us dinner. Let's try not to ruin his appetite."

Jane came out of her room and Will's breath caught. Her hair was wet, long brown strands laying damp against the dark blue T-shirt she wore. Her capris hid those great legs, but God, when she came close she smelled like something sweet—something he wanted to lick. When she passed by, he said, "You smell really good."

She stopped, paused, and turned to look at him. "Uh, thank you."

"Yeah, not like barf anymore," Ryan said.

"Ryan," she warned. "Why don't you get the plates out?"

"Okay."

"Tabby, you're on napkins and utensils."

"You mean we have to eat pizza with a fork?" She screwed

up her nose as she looked at her mom, her blue eyes and dark hair making her look so much like Jane it was uncanny.

"No, but just in case someone else wants to."

"Okay."

"Sorry about that," Jane said. "I had an unexpected crisis at the gym, as my kids have no doubt informed you in more detail than you'd like."

He laughed as they made their way to the dining room table. "It's okay. I'm used to gory detail in my job."

"What's your job?" Tabitha asked as she laid the utensils on the table.

"He works for the highway patrol," Ryan answered.

Will grinned. "You remembered."

"Yup."

"What's the highway patrol?" Tabby asked.

"It's like a police officer, except I'm in charge of the highways. So if someone's driving too fast or there's an accident, I take care of it."

"Oh. That's neat," Tabitha said. "My daddy used to build the highways, until he got hurt on his back."

"I know, Tabby," Will said. "I was a really good friend of your daddy's."

Her eyes widened. "Do you know where he is? We can't find him."

"I'm sorry, baby. I don't. If I did, I'd sure do my best to bring him home to you."

She nodded. "Yeah, nobody can find him. It makes Mommy sad."

Jane looked to Will, then over at the kids. "Hey, how about some pizza?"

"I also brought cinnamon sticks for dessert," Will said, hoping to deflect the somberness with dessert.

"I love cinnamon sticks," Tabitha said. "They're sugary goodness."

Will laughed. "That they are."

They ate and Jane went through her obvious routine of asking them about their day at school. Will sat back quietly and listened. She was very good with the kids, knew how to ask the questions so she'd get actual answers other than "fine" or "nothing." She also engaged Will in the conversation, asking him about his day.

"Did you give out a lot of speeding tickets today?" she asked.

"I gave out a few. I had to assist in some traffic realignment, so that took up part of my day."

"What's that?" Ryan asked.

"Sometimes during road construction, they have to shift the way the highway goes, and it changes all of a sudden, so my job is to alert the traffic by parking my car and turning the lights on my cruiser so people driving by know there's a change in the way the road is going to turn."

"Oh, so there's no accident because people are used to a road going a certain way, and then suddenly it isn't," Ryan said.

"Exactly."

"That's probably pretty boring," Tabitha said.

"Sometimes, but it's part of my job, so I have to do it."

Ryan nodded. "It's like school. Some of it's fun, and some parts aren't, but you gotta do it no matter whether you like it or not."

Jane's lips curved. She was hot when she gave that half smile. And he probably shouldn't be thinking that in front of her kids.

After dinner, the kids were sent to their rooms to do homework, and he and Jane sat in the living room.

"How are your parents doing?" Jane asked.

"They're great. Enjoying retirement in Florida."

"I'll bet visiting them is nice."

"It is, when I get a chance to go down there. But they're happy and Dad loves the condo. He says he doesn't miss mowing the lawn."

She laughed. "I'll bet. It's not one of my favorite things, either, as you can probably tell from the prairie in my front yard. I really need to get to that."

"Well, you do have a lot on your plate."

"Speaking of plates, thanks for bringing pizza tonight. You didn't have to."

He noticed she shifted the topic when he brought up how overwhelmed she was. "You're welcome. I wanted to. Normally I go home to my empty apartment. Trust me, this was way more fun."

"Oh, sure it was."

He shifted on the sofa so he was fully facing her. "You think I'm lying? You have great kids, Jane. Very polite and animated and fun to talk to. You should be proud of them."

She looked down for a second, then back at him. "Thank you. They're everything to me. My whole life. Which is why I can't go out with you."

He cocked a brow. "You can't go out because of your kids?"

"I have to see to their welfare."

"Not twenty-four hours a day, seven days a week. What about your welfare?"

She swallowed. "There'll be time for me. Someday."

He grasped her hand, and the surge of electricity between them hit him hard. He didn't know if Jane felt it, but judging from the way her eyes widened and her lips fell open, he'd say she did.

"Someday is now, Jane. It's been two years. It's time you get out and have a little fun."

She inhaled and let it out on a shaky sigh. "I shouldn't."

"Give me a good reason why not."

She opened her mouth, and before she could object, he swooped in and took her mouth in a kiss he'd been thinking about ever since he first saw her walking down the hall in that stupid hat, her gorgeous legs peeking out of that hideous swimsuit cover-up.

She tasted like lemonade and cinnamon, and he knew her kids were just down the hall, but he wanted to delve deeper. He slid his tongue inside, and she moaned, clutching his shirt as if she was going to fall right off the couch if she didn't hold on to him.

Oh, yeah. He liked that response, liked the taste of her, the softness of her body as she yielded against him. He wanted a lot more of this, wanted to put his hands on her, but resisted, because if one of the kids—

"Hey, Mom?" Ryan called from his room.

Like someone had thrown cold water on them, Jane shoved away from him at the sound of Ryan's voice. She looked down at Will, regret and desire in her eyes.

"Yeah, sweetie?"

"I need help with this math."

Despite the hard-on raging against the zipper of his jeans, Will stood. "That's my cue to get out of here."

Jane stood, too, and met his raging erection with her heated gaze. She finally met his gaze with a look of regret. "I'm sorry."

"I'm not." He hauled her into his arms for another kiss, brief but just as damaging as the first. And just like the first, she gave as good as she got, kissing him with a pent-up fury that he knew, once burst, would be explosive. "It's going to be a painful walk to my car."

She licked her lips. "Thanks again for the pizza."

"Thanks for letting me come over."

She walked him to the door.

He turned. "Jane?"

"Yes?"

"Do you have a phone?"

"Yes. Of course."

He pulled his out. "What's the number?"

She gave it to him. He entered it into his and smiled. "I'll call you for that date."

She seemed hesitant, then nodded. "Okay. Good night,
Will."

"'Night, Jane."

He walked out, uncomfortable, hard, and grinning.

CHAPTER FOUR

"**Y**ou're going out with Will Griffin?"

Jane looked around. "Shhh. I didn't say that. And I don't want anyone to know."

The one thing Jane knew about the teacher's lounge at the high school was that it was the worst place to tell anyone anything, because teachers were the most horrible gossips in town. And in Hope, once word got out about something, everyone knew.

But Jane had to tell someone, and who else but her best friend, Chelsea, who coincidentally used to be Will's girlfriend.

"I wasn't going to tell you at all, considering your history with Will. I wasn't sure how you'd feel about it."

Chelsea waved a hand at Jane. "Don't be ridiculous. Will and I were ancient history three years ago. And we're still friends, so it's not like I'd hate you for going out with him. Hell, you need to go out with someone."

"Come on. Do I look that desperate?"

"No. And that's the problem. You look resigned to your

fate, like you don't deserve to go out. And that's just sad, Jane. When Will and I broke up, did I sit at home and waste away?"

Jane laughed. "Hardly. But you're a stacked redhead and you're never lacking for offers. Besides, you broke up with him."

"Hey, we dated for a year. It hurt when we broke up. But we never saw each other. He worked nights, I worked days, and I like a social life now and then. It didn't mean I didn't care about him, you know."

"I know, and I'm sorry. I didn't mean to make light of your breakup. I remember how hard it was on you. I know you cared about him."

"I did. But it was nothing like you and Vic, and I realize that. I wasn't left by a husband, and I don't have kids. It's not the same thing at all. But even if it was, that doesn't mean I'd have to stop living. You might be a mother, and yes, that's a priority for you, but you're still a woman, Jane. You have needs."

Chelsea emphasized the "needs," and after last night's kiss, those needs had been reawakened. Boy had they ever been reawakened. She'd lain awake practically all night, sweating and flopping around on her bed, her body tingling in places it hadn't tingled in a long time.

Even before Vic had left, there'd been no sex. He'd been too busy boozing it up and hanging out with his drug buddies all night long, and she'd spent all her time worrying about him. When they'd been together, there'd been arguing. She'd gone so long without a man she'd forgotten what it was like to be held and stroked and—made love to.

"I've probably forgotten how to do it," she said to Chelsea.

Chelsea laughed. "I don't think you forget how to have sex, but trust me, if you need instruction, Will's very good at it."

"This is bizarre, talking to you about having sex with someone you've had sex with."

"Like I said, honey. Ancient history."

"Apparently not, if your memories are vivid."

"Hey, a girl never forgets great sex." Chelsea waggled her brows.

"If it was that great, why don't you start seeing him again, now that he's working days?"

Chelsea shrugged. "He was great and all, but we're just not a match. We're better as friends. I can definitely see the two of you together, though. There's a tender side to him that matches well with you."

Jane picked up a carrot and mulled it over while she munched.

"Maybe I should take a walk on the wild side."

"Now you're talking," Chelsea said.

The lunchroom had cleared out, so Jane felt freer to talk. "Just one good orgasm and I'd be good for a year or two."

"There you go."

She thought about it for a minute. "Then again, maybe he just wants to take me to a movie."

"Honey, the way you described that kiss? I don't think 'just a movie' is what Will has in mind."

Jane smiled. "Maybe not."

"So that's a yes?"

"Yes. As soon as I lose ten pounds. Because no man is going to see me naked the way I look now."

"Jane," Chelsea said, giving her a hard stare. "You're hot and curvy and you have legs a mile long. You've always been way too harsh on yourself. I'm going to give you an assignment. Tonight, get naked and stand in front of your mirror and tell yourself how lush and gorgeous you are."

Jane laughed. Chelsea didn't.

"You're kidding, right?

"Nope. Do it. Tonight."

"I do not look at myself naked."

"Why the hell not?"

"Because . . . because it's stupid."

"It is not. Every woman should look at herself naked and tell herself how gorgeous she is. Pick out your good points and highlight them."

Jane stared at Chelsea, who had the most beautiful red hair that didn't come from a salon, the most gorgeous breasts that any human—man or woman—could appreciate, and a tight, toned body that Chelsea worked on with yoga. Of course she had no problem looking at herself naked. Jane, on the other hand?

"I don't think so."

"I do think so. You just haven't looked at yourself in so long, and haven't had a man appreciate that beautiful body of yours in so long, that you're picking out imaginary flaws. Tonight that ends. Get naked. Do inventory. And tell yourself that you're beautiful. Because you are. Obviously Will thinks you're hot or he wouldn't have been kissing you last night."

"I'm . . . mushy."

"You are not. You run around like crazy after those kids and at school. You get more exercise than the average woman. I think when you give your body a critical look, you might be surprised."

"I think I'll be depressed."

Chelsea huffed out a frustrated breath. "Do it. That's an order."

She sighed. "Fine."

"And when Will calls you for that date, you say yes."

She would, but she still wasn't sure about the sex part.

When she got home that night after working at the gym, something was different, but she couldn't put her finger on what it was.

"Did you hire someone to mow the lawn, Mom?"

Leave it to Ryan to figure it out. Someone had mowed the lawn. And weeded, too.

"Uh, no, I didn't."

So, who had? She hustled the kids inside and asked Bill Doughty, one of her neighbors, thinking he'd probably gotten tired of her extra-long grass. She'd meant to get around to mowing it, but it was her least favorite chore and she always left it 'til last, which only made it harder to mow. She knew that, of course, but she still procrastinated.

Bill said he hadn't done it, but he told her Will Griffin had come by with his mower and weed eater on the back of his truck and had taken care of it this afternoon. Then Bill's wife, Claire, had come outside and asked if Will was Jane's new boyfriend.

Jane had smiled politely and thanked them for letting her know. She wasn't about to give Claire, a very nice woman but one of the worst neighborhood blabbermouths, any information.

She fed the kids, they did homework, and after they went to bed, she graded papers, took a shower, then opened her closet door where she hid her full-length mirror.

This was stupid. She rarely looked at herself naked. Typically after she showered she slathered on lotion, always trying to avoid catching sight of herself in the bathroom mirror. She knew what waited for her there—disappointment. After Vic left, she'd stopped caring what she looked like because there was no one around to impress.

But Chelsea was right. It was time to take a critical look at her body, especially if lean and muscled Will was possibly, maybe going to be touching it.

The thought made her squeeze her eyes shut and cringe. She was thirty-two years old. She'd had two children. Will was single and no doubt used to smooth, unmarred bodies that hadn't delivered two babies.

Yikes.

Might as well get this over with. She hit the big light and threw her eyes open.

Wow. She desperately needed a haircut. That was a mess.

And her eyebrows had nearly reached unibrow status and
were in desperate need of waxing. Taking a glance south,
she realized other parts of her could use a waxing, too.

Ugh. Being single and without a man had definite advan-
tages. Dating required grooming. Making a mental note to
call her hairdresser, Phoebe, for an appointment tomorrow,
she took a deep breath and continued the self-perusal.

Breasts—full and not too saggy, yet. In fact, since she
frequently lugged around heavy textbooks and Tabby still
liked to leap into her arms and be held and carried, she had
good shoulders and strong arms and her boobs were still in
really good shape. Yay for perky boobs! Though there were
stretch marks there, because she'd breast-fed. She was proud
of those marks, as well as the ones on her stomach.

She splayed her hands across her belly, remembering
being pregnant with both her kids. She smiled and she defied
any man who didn't appreciate the work she'd gone through
bringing her children into the world.

Her waist was indented, her hips swelled out nicely,
and—what do you know about that? Chelsea was right,
she thought, as she turned this way and that. She was
tall, so she had long legs. Long, still shapely legs. She still
thought her thighs were a little on the thick side, but screw
it. She turned to the side and decided her butt was nicely
rounded. And bigger butts were the in thing now, weren't
they?

If a man couldn't appreciate her body, he could shove it.
It wasn't as bad as she'd thought, and maybe she needed to
start dressing better to appreciate it. It was time to do a little
shopping—at Goodwill, which often had killer clothes at
bargain prices. People threw out awesome clothes that they
barely wore. She might not have a lot of money, but she knew
how to shop.

Determined to get a haircut, a wax, and find clothes that
actually fit, she felt a lot better as she climbed into bed.

But there was something she needed to do first. She grabbed her phone and dialed Will's number.

"Hey," he said when he answered on the second ring. "What are you doing?"

"Sitting in bed. I wanted to thank you for mowing my lawn. Why did you do that?"

"Because it needed mowing and your current schedule doesn't seem to allow enough time to fit that in. I have a lot more spare time than you do."

"I was going to get around to doing the yard work."

"I'm sure you were. But now it's done, and that was my outdoor sweaty exercise for the day so, actually, you were doing me a favor."

She smiled. "In that case, you're welcome."

"Did you have a good day today?" he asked.

She loved that he cared enough to ask. "It was all right. As exciting as math can be."

"I never had math teachers as pretty as you. Mine were all old, with gray hair and pinched expressions on their faces, like their shoes were too tight."

"I'm certain you're exaggerating. Most math teachers are gorgeous and sexy."

He laughed. "Clearly I went to the wrong school."

"Clearly."

"So did you think about that date?"

All she'd been thinking about was that kiss. And she wanted more. "A little."

"How about Saturday night?"

That would give her plenty of time to take care of her hair and eyebrows and . . . other areas, and do some shopping and beg her parents to watch the kids. "Uh, okay. Sure. Thank you. Are you sure you want to go out with me?"

"Jane. I really want to go out with you. How about I pick you up at six thirty?"

"All right. I'll see you at six thirty Saturday."

"You'll probably see me before then, but we have a date Saturday night."

Her heart did a ridiculous flutter in her chest. "Okay. Good night."

"Good night, Jane. Try to dream about me tonight."

She hung up and laid her phone on the nightstand, feeling a little dizzy and giddy and utterly too old to feel like this.

She slid down in the bed and pulled the sheet up, then wiggled her toes and stared up at the ceiling.

He made her smile. No man had done that in a very long time.

CHAPTER FIVE

Tabitha and Ryan were thrilled to be spending the night at their grandparents'. Since Jane rarely leaned on her parents, the kids didn't get to stay over all that often, something her parents complained about, and so did the kids. But she felt like she needed to take responsibility for her children and not dump them on someone else. It was bad enough their father left them. The last thing they needed was to feel abandoned by their mother.

"You know you're being ridiculous about this," her mother said. "We love having the kids."

"I know you do. But they're also my responsibility, Mom."

Ignoring the inevitable argument, her mom said, "So . . . a date?"

Another reason she hadn't wanted her parents to watch the kids tonight. She'd known this discussion was going to come up, and she didn't want to talk to her mother about Will. Jane had originally wanted to tell her mother she just needed a night out on her own, but if anyone saw them together, by Monday her mother would know and then Jane would be in trouble for the lie of omission, so she came clean.

Then she'd planned to pick up the kids after her date, but her mother had thought it a better idea that the kids spend the night.

"Are you certain this is okay?" Jane asked.

"Of course. We love spending time with the kids. Besides, you might see some action," her mother said with a wink.

"Mom. Honestly." Jane had blushed ten shades of crimson, even though she'd thought of nothing but seeing Will naked for the past three days. Not that she'd admit that to her mother.

"What?" her mother asked. "You've been living like a nun since Vic left you. It's high time you have some fun. And some sex. Will Griffin is a great guy. And hot. If the opportunity presents itself, jump his bones."

"I am not having this conversation with you, Mom," Jane said, then ran outside where her father was entertaining the kids in the pool. She kissed them all good-bye and dashed out the door so she could go home and get ready for her date.

She'd dropped the kids off plenty early so she'd have time to decide what to wear. She'd had the waxing thing done a couple days ago. Today she'd gone to get her hair cut and Phoebe had insisted her hair was drab and she needed highlights. She'd argued that brown hair was brown hair and there wasn't much one could do to make it better. Besides, she couldn't afford a fancy new hairstyle, but Phoebe had given her a discount and she relented. The highlights were subtle and gorgeous and really made a difference, brightening her face. Or maybe that was the eyebrow wax, which made her eyes seem rounder and made her green eyes brighter. She had no idea. She only knew she felt better.

But now she had to decide what to wear. She'd chosen three dresses, but she needed Chelsea's help. She called, and Chelsea had told her she'd been prepared for the phone call and had known Jane was going to need her. She came right over and perused the outfits Jane had selected.

"Seriously, Jane?" Chelsea asked. "These are the dresses you bought?"

Jane looked at the bed where she'd laid out the dresses. "Well, yes. What's wrong with them?"

Chelsea sighed. "Girl, when was the last time you dated?"

She wrinkled her nose and did the math. "Thirteen years ago?"

"Ugh. I thought this might be a problem. You've forgotten how to be sexy. I brought a few things."

"Chelsea, wait," Jane said, but Chelsea had already left the room. She came back a few minutes later with an armload of skirts and tops and stuff that Jane could already tell wouldn't fit her and were going to be way too short.

"I can't wear those."

"Sure you can." Chelsea looked at Jane, then at the pile she'd tossed on the bed. She picked up a sinfully short champagne-colored skirt adorned with sequins and feathery thingies. "Try this one."

Jane backed away like the skirt had a communicable disease. "I don't think so. I mean, yes, I'm single, but not the same type of single as you, Chelsea. I do not have your slender legs or your fantastic ass."

Chelsea grinned. "You think I have a fantastic ass?"

Jane rolled her eyes. "Is this really 'admire Chelsea' night?"

Chelsea shoved the skirt at her. "You're right. We'll sing my praises another night. Put the skirt on, Jane."

She grabbed the skirt. "Fine. But if you laugh at how ridiculous I look in it, we're no longer friends."

"And take this top and put it on, too. And these shoes."

Horrified, Jane rolled her eyes. "I really hate you."

"You won't when you see how rockin' hot you are in this outfit."

Dubious that she'd even be able to get the skirt on over

her hips, she dropped her robe and pulled the skirt up. Surprisingly, it fit. So did the superslinky peach silk sleeveless top that fell over her skin like a waterfall.

"Don't forget the shoes."

"I can't walk in those."

"Will can help you walk."

Jane laughed, but climbed into the ridiculously high heels. "I feel six feet tall in these things."

"But your legs are amazing. Now turn and look at yourself in the mirror."

She did, gasping at the transformation.

She looked stunning. She had to hold on to Chelsea to twist and turn to see her body, but she had to admit, she was a sex goddess in this outfit. Her legs did indeed look amazing. The skirt brushed the tops of her thighs, and the draping of the top made her look superskinny. It also revealed a ton of cleavage.

"Wow."

"I know, right?" Chelsea said, grinning.

"This is a gorgeous outfit, Chelse," Jane said, turning to her. She slid off the heels. "But it's so not me."

"Ah, well. I figured that. But I wanted you to realize how utterly gorgeous you are."

"Point taken." She grabbed Chelsea and hugged her. "Thank you for that."

She ended up choosing a black and white striped skirt that rested on her hips and hit just above the knee, along with a black tank with a cutout in the back. Slightly subdued, but also sexy. She also decided on the new black wedge heels she'd bought that weren't going to give her a nosebleed.

She was pleased with how she looked and Chelsea pronounced her drop-dead gorgeous, fresh, and sexy, which was good enough for her.

Chelsea hightailed it out of there about fifteen minutes before Will was due to arrive, leaving Jane enough time to ponder jewelry and touch up her makeup, which she'd left minimal, but she did add some lip gloss just before he rang the doorbell.

Her stomach tightened and she took a deep breath, smoothed her skirt, and went to the door.

He took her breath away in dark jeans and a button-down, long-sleeved shirt with the sleeves rolled up.

"Hi," she said.

He was staring at her, and when she spoke, he jerked his head up. "Hey. You look gorgeous."

She smiled. "Thank you. I wasn't sure where we were going."

"You're perfect for where we're going. Unless you just want to stay in."

Her smile died. "You want to stay in?"

He laughed. "No. I was joking." He held his arm out for her. "Let's go, Cinderella. Time for your night out."

She felt like Cinderella. She was going out on a date tonight.

"Do you like Asian food?" he asked after they were in the car.

"I like any food that doesn't come with a dressed-up character and Skee-Ball afterward."

He laughed. "You're in luck, then, because none of that tonight."

He hopped on the highway and they headed into Tulsa. She didn't get to Tulsa all that often, unless for some reason she needed to go to the mall, which was typically only to do Christmas shopping. So when he took her to Utica Square and pulled in front of P.F. Chang's, she figured this was going to be the best date she'd had in a very long time.

Okay, so it was the only date she'd had in a very long time.

"Will this work?" he asked.

"It totally works. Thank you."

He laid his hand on the small of her back and led her inside. She'd forgotten what that felt like—to have a man put his hand on her. It was just a light touch, really, but what it signified meant so much. It was a stamp, a "hey, we're together" kind of thing.

She was being silly. It meant nothing. They were having dinner. He felt sorry for her because she'd lived like a nun for the past two years. She should stop reading anything into this.

Except there'd been that kiss.

The dark atmosphere inside was nice, but there was nothing romantic about P.F. Chang's. On a Saturday night, the place was bustling with activity. Will, being a smart guy, had made reservations, so they were quickly shown to their table, a booth against the wall.

Their waitress appeared right away with their menus and said she'd be back in a few to take their drink order.

Will perused the menu, while she stole glances at him. When he peeked at her over the top of his menu, she quickly looked down.

"What are you thinking about in terms of a drink?"

She had no idea. Normally when she went out, it was Chuck E. Cheese's or Incredible Pizza, where there'd be a buffet or games for the kids to run and play. Drinks consisted of soda. This was a grown-up menu, and she didn't take her kids to grown-up restaurants. One, because they cost too much and it was a waste of money she didn't have, and, two, because those kinds of restaurants weren't fun for her kids.

"Uh, I have no idea. As you can imagine, I don't get out much."

He gave her a lopsided smile, and her stomach tightened. Really, all she wanted was to kiss him again. Nothing like a one-track mind.

"How about some sake?"

"Sure. That sounds great."

When their waitress came back, he ordered for both of them.

"Are you hungry?" he asked.

"Starving, actually." She'd been so focused on getting ready for the date, she might have forgotten to eat much today.

"Good. How about an appetizer? Their lettuce wraps are good."

"Sounds fantastic." At the mention of food, her stomach grumbled. Yeah, she definitely needed to eat, especially if she was going to be drinking. She was a lightweight in the alcohol department, so getting food into her was paramount if she was going to stay sober.

The waitress brought their sake and Will ordered the appetizer.

"Would you like to order dinner now, or wait a bit?" the waitress asked.

Will looked to Jane. "Oh, I didn't look at that yet. Sorry."

"We'll wait," he said to the waitress, who left.

"I guess I should figure out what I want to eat."

"There's no hurry, Jane. We're not on a schedule here. Just sit back and enjoy your drink."

"Right. I'm so used to my life being scheduled. Eating out with the kids typically means arguments and me wanting to get home as soon as humanly possible."

He laid his hand over hers. "Not tonight. Relax."

The contact was electric, the zing from his hand over hers shooting through her nerve endings and hitting all those sweet spots that hadn't been touched in a very long time. She took a hard swallow of sake, her eyes watering.

"Wow," she said, glad she had a glass of water at the table to wash it down with.

"It's kind of strong," he said. "You might want to sip it."

"Now you tell me." But she did sip after that, and she liked the flavor. "I've never had sake before. It's interesting."

"Sake and beer are good together, too. Some night when we have a designated driver, I'll get you toasted on it."

"Hey, I'm not the one who's driving."

He signaled the waitress and ordered an Asian beer and another round of sake.

Her eyes widened. "I was joking, you know."

"I'm dead serious."

She arched a brow. "You would get me drunk?"

"In a heartbeat. Easier to take advantage of you that way."

As if the sake hadn't already made her sweat, his words sent her up in flames. "I . . . see. You're going to have to go a little slower, Will. I'm out of practice."

He smiled at the waitress as she brought the beer and sake along with their lettuce wraps, then he turned his attention back to Jane. "I don't know about that. Seems to me you're doing just fine."

She took a sip of the beer, also surprisingly good. Probably a little too good, because she started to feel the buzz. "Just stop me if I start to strip off my clothes and climb up on the table to dance."

"Duly noted. Here, have some food." He scooped some chicken onto a piece of lettuce, rolled it up, and slid a plate across the table in front of her.

She didn't want to eat. She wanted this nice, relaxed feeling to continue and didn't want the food to ruin it. She hadn't felt this way for a long time. And she had no kids around, no responsibilities, didn't have to worry about Ryan and Tabby arguing or throwing things and talking too loud or wanting to go play a game. She could sit back and have an adult conversation. When was the last time that had happened?

Chelsea was right. She deserved this. But she also didn't want to end up on the floor after the first half hour, so she took a bite of the wrap, which was oh so good.

"I'll bet you do this a lot," she said, trying not to devour the wrap in two bites once she realized how hungry she really was.

"Do what?"

"Go out. Eat. On dates."

He'd fixed one of the wraps for himself and had taken a

bite. He chewed thoughtfully, took a drink of water, then leaned back in the chair. "Well, I do eat."

She pinned him with a look. "You know what I mean."

"I do know what you mean. And no, I don't date a lot. For the past several years I've been on the night shift. There aren't a lot of women to date during daylight hours."

"You had weekends, though."

"I had night shift on a lot of the weekends, too. I wasn't exactly high man on the totem pole. You get the shit shifts when you're working your way up."

"Oh. I hadn't thought about that. Must have really screwed with your social life."

"What social life?"

"Okay. Point taken. So what have you been doing?"

He shrugged. "Sleeping. Going to the gym. Hanging out at home or going out for a beer with my friends when I do get some time off."

"Sounds about as exciting as my life."

He shot her a smile. "Minus the kids, but yeah, it's hard to have a relationship when you know you're not going to be able to take a woman out on a Friday or Saturday night, or when you know your schedule is going to be the kiss of death before you can ever get anything started."

She lifted her sake. "Welcome back to regular working hours, then, Will."

He clinked his glass of water against her sake. "Thanks. It's good to be in the land of the living again. And the same to you."

He had a point. "Thanks. It's nice to be out without the kids. I don't get adult conversation all that often."

"You should have been out well before now."

She took a deep breath. "It was important the kids had me around."

"For a while at the beginning, yeah. For two years? Come on. You don't need to sacrifice your entire life just because Vic took a hike."

She lifted her beer and took a long swallow. "Oh, how about we don't talk about Vic tonight?" Or . . . ever.

"Sure. Okay, sorry."

"No. I'm sorry." She'd snapped at him. Wasn't she turning out to be a fun date?

"You don't have to be sorry. You have a right to not want to talk about . . . that."

"No, I need to stop pretending he doesn't exist. I just wanted a nice night out tonight without thinking about my kids or my ex-husband. Is that selfish of me?"

He picked up her hand, and there was that zing again. "You have a right to have anything you want tonight."

"That's a dangerous thought."

"No, it's not."

"Yes, it is. I am, after all, with an officer of the law."

His gaze went dark. "Do you have illegal intentions?"

"I don't know. Maybe. Like I said, I don't get out much. I might want to let my inner bad girl out tonight. What if I want to go skinny-dipping in the lake?"

"I can make that happen."

She laughed. "And you'd protect me when our local law enforcement shows up to arrest me."

"I just happen to be best friends with local law enforcement. So, yes, you're in the clear."

"Good to know." Not that she'd ever do that, but it was fun to think about.

Will watched the myriad of emotions cross Jane's face.

God, she looked pretty tonight, her hair down like a dark cascade around her shoulders. And those bare shoulders were driving him crazy. He wanted to kiss them. Or at least start there, and work his way up to her neck, maybe nibble on an earlobe, then her lips.

Her mouth was distracting. She had lip gloss on tonight, calling attention to her lips, which were full and kissable. He was getting hard, probably a bad thing to do at the restaurant.

He adjusted his napkin in his lap.

She'd been so tense and nervous earlier, which was cute, because it was so obvious she wasn't used to going out on dates.

Hell, he was a little rusty, too. He wanted this night to be good for her. He wanted everything to be good for her. He wanted to make her laugh, and then later, he wanted to make her scream—in the fun way.

"So, are you ready to get naked and do your skinny-dipping now, or wait until after dinner?"

Her lips quirked. "Don't be ridiculous. It's not even dark yet. And the park is still open. Way too many people wandering around to see my naked butt."

"Okay. We'll do it after dinner. When the park closes."

Jane loved Will's sense of humor. And speaking of dinner . . . her continued buzz reminded her they needed to order. She picked up the menu and perused it. The next time their waitress wandered by, they ordered food.

She wanted this to last all night.

CHAPTER SIX

For the next hour, Jane lost herself in conversation and one of the best meals she'd had in too long to remember. By the time Will paid the check, she was stuffed, and her buzz had lessened somewhat.

"Thank you for that," she said as he held the door to the car open for her.

"It was my pleasure."

No, it was definitely hers. She'd remember this for a long time.

Figuring he'd take her home, she was surprised when they headed downtown, and even more surprised when they ended up parked across from Cain's Ballroom.

"I thought maybe you'd like some music."

"I love music."

He held her hand as they crossed the street and continued to hold it when they went inside. "There's an indie rock band playing tonight. I've heard they're pretty good, so I thought we'd give it a shot."

They were more than pretty good. She and Will were on

their feet the whole time, dancing and getting down to the band's music, which was a little alternative, a lot loud, and raucous. She had worked up a good sweat by the time the band took a break and they headed toward the bar.

"A beer?" he asked.

She shook her head and opted for a soda instead. Will did the same.

"You don't have to turn down a beer just because I'm not having one," she said.

"I'm not. I'm driving, and the drinks I had at dinner were more than enough."

And he was responsible, so unlike her ex—who she reminded herself she wasn't going to think about tonight.

They leaned against the bar. Jane took a long swallow of her drink to cool down.

"I love this band," she said. "It was so thoughtful of you to bring me."

"I'm glad you're enjoying them. A friend of mine heard them the last time they were in town and had good things to say about them, so I figured it wouldn't hurt to pop in and check them out. They're better than I thought they'd be."

"Obviously you like music," she said.

He nodded. "All kinds. And I try to get out to listen to a lot of different music whenever I can. It'll be much better now that I have my nights free. Live music is always better. I remember when Vic and I would hit these shows with the up-and-coming bands all the . . ."

He stopped. "Sorry."

"It's okay. We can't pretend he doesn't exist."

"I know you'd like to."

She shrugged. "He was a part of your life as much as he was a part of mine." It never occurred to her that Vic bailing probably hurt Will as much as it hurt her, though for different reasons. Will and Vic had grown up together, had gone through grade school and high school together.

Will had known Vic almost his entire life. And Will was

on one side of the law, while Vic was most definitely on the other.

It probably killed him to see Vic go down such a self-destructive path, and then completely disappear.

They made their way back to their seats and waited for the band to return. "Vic never talked to you about any of it?" Jane asked.

Will looked at her. "Any of what?"

"His issues. Leaving?"

Will shook his head. "I knew he battled with the drugs and alcohol. He always liked to drink, probably more than any of us. You know when you're younger, you don't pay much attention to that. The drugs didn't come 'til later, and I didn't know about it until he was heavily into it. He was good at hiding it."

She leaned back in her chair. "Tell me about it. He was so good at masking it, at appearing normal—at least for a while."

He put his arm around the back of her chair. "We don't have to talk about Vic. I know it brings you down."

She turned to him. "Actually, it doesn't. Not any more. I'm sad for my kids, of course, because they're too young to understand. But I'm over him being gone."

"Seeing me reminds you of him."

His fingers caressed her shoulders. Distracting. But good. "It does, but not in the way you think. I was wondering how you felt about it—about him. We never talked after he left. I was so self-involved, worried about the kids. I never asked how you dealt with it."

Will shrugged. "I was pissed at him for what he did—not only to you and the kids, but to himself. He had so much going for him. Great job, incredible wife and family. He pissed it all away for drugs and alcohol. I tried to talk to him, but—well, you know how it was."

She nodded. "Yes, I know. His demons were powerful and irresistible. I can't begin to understand it. I never could. But they dominated his life and he couldn't beat them."

"Seems to me he didn't even try. That's what makes me so angry. He didn't fight his addiction."

This was usually the part where she bailed, because it was so painful to talk about. No woman wanted to feel like she wasn't worth fighting for, which was why whenever anyone wanted to talk about Vic, she closed up and refused to allow the conversation. She'd lived through that hell for all those years, had begged Vic to go to rehab, had threatened to leave him. She'd done everything she could to make it clear what he stood to lose. And he'd still chosen his addiction over her and his children.

What did that say about her? She'd asked herself that question countless times over the past two years, and hadn't liked the answer. Finally, she stopped asking the question, and had refused to take the blame for Vic's failings.

"It wasn't my fault. He's the one who failed."

Will frowned. "What? Of course it wasn't your fault, Jane. Vic's the bad guy in all this. You know that, right?"

She nodded. "It took me a while to get there. For a long time I blamed myself. I tried to figure out where I failed him, until I realized he was the one who was weak. He was the one who failed. Not me. I was there for him. I'd have done anything for him. He just got so deep into that thing he loved more than me and his kids he couldn't see straight."

"I know. Believe me, I know. I can't tell you how many times I tried to talk to him. Hell, I offered to pay for rehab if he'd just go."

She shot him a look. "You did?"

"Hell yes, I did. He was my best friend. I'd have done anything to save him. He didn't want it. He laughed at me and told me he'd rather have the money for another hit."

She shook her head, not at all surprised Vic had said that to Will. But it did surprise her that someone else had to go through what she had. "I'm so sorry."

"Don't be sorry. That was a big wake-up call for me."

"Yeah, I had a lot of those wake-up calls. I stopped trying

to help him, too. You can't help someone who doesn't want the help."

The band started up again. Will held out his hand. "Come on. Let's shake it off and dance."

"Oh, I don't think so."

"I do." He tugged her hand and she went with him onto the dance floor. It only took her a few seconds of watching Will do a very unrhythmic groove for the doldrums to disappear. She laughed and started dancing with him. Soon the dance floor was crowded and she and Will were being shoved into each other. She had to move closer to him for self-preservation.

They stayed out there for the next song. Jane needed the stress release, and she liked that Will could care less that he couldn't dance. He seemed to be having a great time.

And when the band slowed things down on the following song, he pulled her into his arms and held her close. She sighed and enjoyed being held against him, the tough conversation about her ex long forgotten.

"Now this part I can do," he said, his lips close to her ear as they swayed side to side.

Yeah, he had the holding her close part down really well, her hip brushing against his thigh, her breasts against his chest and his hand clasped tight to hers. When his fingers traced that bare spot on her back, she broke out in goose bumps. And when he pulled back so he could look at her, those whiskey-colored eyes were filled with a hunger that matched her own.

"Ready to get out of here?"

She nodded. He took her hand and led her back to his car. Once inside, he took off on the highway, and she was once again struck by the care he took when he drove.

Vic had always been so reckless. Whenever they'd gone out, he usually drank too much. Which meant a battle over her trying to wrestle the keys from him so she could drive, or white-knuckling it the entire way home, hoping he wouldn't kill them on the highway. It was such a relief to be out with a guy who didn't drink too much and didn't drive too fast.

It took her a while to notice he wasn't taking her home. Instead, once they got into town he took the back road to the park. The park was closed, but he pulled into one of the parking spots in front of the lake.

"You do realize I'm not going to strip naked and go skinny-dipping," she said.

He released his seat belt and looked at her. "I can't tell you how profoundly disappointed I am to hear that."

"However, if you intended to take a dip sans clothing, by all means, go ahead. I'll watch."

"You would, huh?"

Even in the dark, she caught the gleam in his eyes. The car suddenly seemed very warm and her nipples peaked hard, her sex awakening with throbbing need.

Yeah, she had a very vivid imagination, and when Will got out of the car, her first thought was that he really was going to take off his clothes to take a dip. She wondered if he'd mind if she got a few photos to remember the occasion.

But then he came around to her side and opened her door. "Come on. Let's take a walk."

"The park's closed, you know."

"My friend Luke is a cop and he's on duty tonight. I promise you he won't arrest us."

"Are you sure?"

He pulled out his phone and punched a button, waiting while it rang. "Hey . . . Yeah, I know you're working, that's why I'm calling . . . No, nothing's wrong. My friend Jane and I are over at Hope Park, taking a walk around the lake. So if you do a drive-by and see my car, don't come and arrest us, okay?"

Jane watched as his lips curved. He looked at her.

"No, we're not going to be skinny-dipping, moron."

Jane stifled a laugh.

"Yeah, see you at the gym."

He clicked off. "Feel better now?"

"Yes. I guess it pays to have friends in high places."

"Sometimes it does."

The lake was beautiful tonight. The moon cast its silvery glow over the lake, the water so still Jane was sure she could walk on it. The night was peaceful, just the two of them wandering around there. And because she trusted Will to keep her safe, she was content to walk along the path at the edge of the lake with him. He led her to a picnic bench near the water, then set her on top of it, climbing over the seat so he could nestle his body against hers.

The only sounds were the crickets and the occasional locust. Otherwise, it was so quiet she could hear the wild slam of her heart beating double-time against her chest. Having Will close to her like this sent her breathing off-kilter. And when he threaded his fingers through her hair and brushed his lips against hers, she remembered just how long it had been since she'd felt this sense of anticipation, this wild abandon and sharp desire that threatened to steal her breath away.

Too damn long. She lightly raked her nails up and down his forearms, rewarded with his responding groan. He moved in between her legs and deepened the kiss, pulling her against him, wrapping an arm around her to drag her closer so their bodies fit together. Not exactly the most modest of positions since she had a skirt on, but frankly she didn't much care. She craved the contact of his body against hers, his tongue sliding inside to lick against hers. She heard a soft moan—hers, as his hand roamed down her back and settled against her butt. She wished they weren't in such a public place, because the closer he got, the more she realized that he was hard and she was damp, and if they had been at her place, she could get him naked and they could be having sex.

They drew apart, and she was decidedly happy that he was dragging in ragged breaths. "This—was a really bad idea."

Confused, she looked up at him. "Which part?"

"The taking you to the lake part. I have a raging hard-on and I really want to lay you out on this picnic table, get you naked, and kiss you all over. And that *would* get me arrested."

She couldn't help but laugh. "Yeah. I'm not real fond of being naked in public. Let's go to my place and get naked in private."

He scooped her off the table in record time and set her on her feet, then grabbed her hand. The walk back to the car was not the leisurely stroll they'd taken before, though Will did grab her several times and plant seriously hot, deep kisses on her that left her dizzy and so turned on she was beginning to rethink the whole naked in the park thing.

They finally made it back to his car, both of them out of breath. She buckled her seat belt, then looked over at Will, and at his very noticeable erection straining against his jeans.

"Maybe we should just do it in the car," she said.

He gripped the steering wheel, then looked over at her, pinning her with a look of pure animal hunger that seared her. "Don't tease me like that because I just might take you up on that suggestion."

She swallowed, her throat so dry it felt like sand had settled permanently in it. "Drive fast. Okay, not so fast that you're breaking any speed limits and your friend Luke has to pull you over and delay things. But let's get to my place in kind of a hurry, okay?"

"Yeah. Gotcha." He started the car and pulled out, screeching the tires just a bit as he roared out of the park. He kept it just above the legal limit, his hands tense on the steering wheel the entire time.

She figured by the time they got back to her house,

common sense would have prevailed and she'd have cooled down a bit.

Not so much. She'd clutched the armrest the entire time, and it wasn't because of Will's driving. He pulled into her driveway and she tried to be calm and rational, but she threw open the car door, her fingers fumbling in her purse for the keys. Will grabbed them from her as they hurried to the front door. With fingers more deft than hers, he unlocked the door and she stepped inside. Before she could find the light switch, he closed the door and had her in his arms, his mouth on hers.

She dropped her purse to the floor, her hand coming up to twine around his neck. She had to stand on her toes to get there, but she needed to touch him. He made it easier on her by grasping her butt and lifting her, pressing her against the door and pinning her there with his body.

Good Lord, the man was strong, holding on to her, kissing her, devouring her with his lips and tongue. His fingers dug into the flesh of her thighs and it felt gloriously, deliciously decadent. She wasn't sure she'd ever been wanted in this kind of desperate fashion, and she gave it back in kind, tangling her fingers in his hair as she kissed him with breathless abandon.

"Bedroom," he said, dragging his mouth from hers and talking to her while his lips mapped a trail across her jaw and fixed onto her neck.

She gasped out a moan. "I don't know. That way somewhere."

"We'll figure it out."

He flipped her around and started walking—in the dark, no less.

"Straight," she guided him, her mouth on his neck, that spot she'd been fixated on. She licked him and he bumped into something, letting out a curse.

"Sorry. There's an ottoman there. Take a quick turn around that and go straight past the dining room and down the hall. My bedroom's the last one."

"Got it." He stopped midway down the hall to push her against the wall and suck on that sensitive spot between her neck and shoulder. Would she have a hickey tomorrow? She didn't care because chills coursed down her spine as shivery sensation rippled through her.

He found the bedroom and held on to her with one hand while he opened the door. He made her feel light and delicate as he proceeded to the bed, making her so glad she'd changed the sheets and made the bed today—just in case.

He deposited her on the bed and came down on top of her, that delicious weight of his rocking against her as he moved his lips over her neck and lower. And when he palmed her stomach, his fingers inching the material of her top over her belly, she fluttered with awareness and need.

She toed her shoes off and he pushed her farther onto the bed, lifting her skirt.

"You smell good," he said, burying his face in her neck.

His hands were everywhere. One on her thigh, inching toward her hip, the other lifting her blouse and palming her breast. It was all happening so fast, she couldn't keep up with the sensations blasting her from all directions. And when he lifted her top over her head, all she could do was lie back and let him have his way, because she'd fantasized about this, wanted this—and oh, God, she needed this.

Right up to the point when he reached over and switched on her bedside lamp.

She lifted up on her elbows. "What are you doing?"

"I want to see you."

"Oh. Uh." Desire tamped down. "Could we maybe do this in the dark?"

Will cocked a brow, then grinned at her and pushed her shoulders down. "Not a chance in hell, Jane. You're gorgeous and I want to see all of you."

She lifted back up on her elbows. "Will. You do realize I've given birth to two children, right?"

He loomed over her, his hands planted on either side of

her. "I think you're beautiful, Jane. And yes, I realize you're not twenty anymore. Neither am I."

"Yeah, but you don't have stretch marks from childbirth."

He laughed, then pushed her back down on the bed. "No, I don't. Now relax and let me make love to you."

She looked up at the ceiling, her earlier excitement replaced with trepidation. His face appeared over hers, and suddenly he was kissing her again. Deep, soulful kisses that made her forget to be conscious of her body and its imperfections. She reached for him, slid her fingers into the soft silkiness of his hair. He laid a hand on her stomach, then over her hip, gradually pulling down her skirt. She helped him, lifting her hips until the skirt slid down her legs, leaving her in only her bra and panties.

He kissed her neck again, evoking chills, then moved his lips over her collarbone and the swell of her breasts. Jane kept her eyes tightly shut, not wanting Will to be disappointed in her. But when he removed her bra and put his mouth over her nipples, she forgot all about everything except the way he pleasured her, teasing her nipple by sucking it. Her eyes flew open and she had to watch his cheeks hollow as he took her nipple into his mouth, then flicked his tongue over the sensitive bud until she thought she might die from the pleasure. And while he plumped and pleasured her breast, he moved his hand over her rib cage and down her belly, making her breath catch as he cupped her sex, drawing out her low moan as he slipped his hand into her panties to tease and torment her.

Her back bowed as she met his questing fingers. He expertly knew right where to touch her, using his fingers to dip inside her, moistening them, and then circling her center of pleasure until she thought she might just die right there.

Taut with tension, she rocked against his hand until he brought her right to the edge.

"Come on, baby," he whispered. "Let go for me."

His words, so evocative, so dark and rich with promise, were her undoing. She burst with an orgasm she felt she'd been holding in for years, crying out against him as she thrashed in his arms. He held her as she moaned through it, using his fingers to expertly coax her right to the very edge again. And then he pulled her to the edge of the bed, removed her panties, and put his mouth on her, teasing her with his lips and tongue.

She'd been in a drought for so very long, the heat and wetness was her undoing. She came again, so quickly this time it was almost embarrassing. But Will didn't seem to think so. As she floated back down he smiled up at her, then stood, and she realized he still had all his clothes on.

She sat up. "That doesn't seem fair."

"What's that?" he asked.

"I'm naked. You're not."

"I'm about to fix that."

He pulled off his shirt, then undid the button on his jeans. She couldn't help but be fixated on that very prominent bulge that pressed against his zipper. And when he dropped his jeans and shucked his boxer briefs, she could only say, "Oh, my."

Will grinned, and she took a moment to appreciate the fine specimen of man he was. Here was someone who took care of his body. She'd seen him plenty at the gym, and he worked hard to keep his body in shape. It showed. He had strength.

Now she'd have to test his stamina, because it had been a long dry spell for her and she intended to make this night last.

She opened her arms to him and he came to her, kissing her deeply. Lord, but the man knew how to kiss a woman senseless. And to have his hard body against hers—finally— now that was definitely a dream come true. She ran her hands over his shoulders and chest, and down his belly.

"I like touching you," she said.

"Feel free to explore," he said, brushing his lips across hers.

She did, getting to know every part of him. His stomach was flat, with very fine hairs there, so soft to the touch. The only place he was soft, of course. The rest of him was covered in hard muscle.

She reached down to take his shaft in hand, rewarded with his harsh intake of breath. She began to stroke him, but he pulled her hand away.

"Too much of that and it's going to be all over with in a hurry."

"We'll save some of that exploring for round two, then."

He smiled. "I like the way you think."

He reached down to the floor and pulled a condom packet from his jeans.

"Not that I thought this was gonna happen, but I do like to be prepared."

Now it was her turn to smile. "And I like the way *you* think."

He put the condom on, and slid between her legs. He looked down at her, and she heated at the way his gaze roamed over her. And when he cupped her sex, readying her with his fingers, taking his time to smooth his hand over her, she arched her hips, pulsing and near the brink again.

It had been a while, and as he nestled between her legs, he took his time fitting his body to hers. When he was seated fully inside her, his cock pulsing, she shuddered at the unexpected emotions coursing through her.

He brushed her hair from her face and kissed her, still unmoving. She knew what it cost him to be so still while her body adjusted to him. It drove her crazy, feeling him swelling inside her, her own body throbbing with need and desire.

"Will," she whispered.

"Yeah?"

"You can move now."

"You okay?"

"Definitely more than okay."

When he finally began to thrust, it was as if her world exploded. She arched, meeting his thrusts, breaking out in a cold sweat as he rocked her world by pinning her with his body and grasping her hand to hold it above her head.

Then he showed her what she'd been missing for far too long, cupping her butt, tilting her pelvis and driving hard into her, grinding against her until she thought she might die from the sweetest pleasure she'd ever had. She squeezed his hand and cupped the back of his neck to draw him forward for a blistering kiss that was her undoing.

When she came, it was like lightning had struck her—a sudden explosion that caught her by surprise. Her eyes flew open and she met his gaze, giving him everything she had as she shuddered with the ecstasy that poured from her. He drove hard and fast into her, then growled out his own orgasm, taking her lips in a violent fury that catapulted her over the edge again, leaving her breathless and shaking.

One of them was trembling. Or maybe it was both of them. She couldn't be sure. She smoothed her hand down Will's sweat-soaked back, closing her eyes and committing every second of this to memory, because she wasn't sure it would happen again, and she needed to remember it all. Fuel for her fantasies and all that.

He rolled over to his side and drew her against him. She finally opened her eyes. He was looking at her.

"So, it's really like riding a bike, isn't it?"

She frowned. "Huh?"

"You definitely didn't forget how to do it."

"Oh." She laughed. "I guess not."

"But just in case you do forget, we should probably practice five or six times tonight."

Heat settled low in her belly, and she was shocked to find renewed desire quivering through her. One would think she'd be satiated after all that.

Apparently not.

"Yes, we probably should."

"I'll be right back," he said. He rolled out of bed and went into the bathroom.

Her cell phone rang. She frowned, and looked over at the clock on her night table. It was after midnight. No one would call her that late except Chelsea, and Chelse knew she was on a date tonight, so she'd wait until Jane called her tomorrow to rehash her night with Will.

She slid out of bed and found her phone, buried in her purse which she'd left on the floor by the front door.

It was a missed call from her mom.

"Damn," she whispered.

"Something wrong?" Will asked, coming out of the room. "I heard your phone ring."

She turned to him. "Probably. I just missed a call from my mom. The kids are there."

She punched the number, her heart pounding as she waited for it to ring. Her mother answered almost immediately.

"Jane?"

"What's wrong, Mom?"

"I don't want you to panic or anything, but Tabby got up to go to the bathroom and slipped on that rug by the kitchen and hit her head on the table."

She tried for calm. "How bad is it?"

"There's a lot of blood, but of course there would be because it's her head. But she's got a pretty good gash and I think she's going to need some stitches."

"I'll be right there to get her."

"I thought you would be. We'll have her ready."

"Thanks, Mom." She hung up and headed toward the bedroom.

"What happened?" Will asked as he followed behind her.

"Tabitha slipped on the way from the bathroom and hit her head on the kitchen table. My mom said she has a pretty good cut on her head that probably needs stitches." She started to get dressed, grabbing underwear and bra, then a pair of jeans and a T-shirt.

Will got dressed, too. "I'll drive you."

She turned to him. "That's not necessary."

"Actually, it is. You had way more to drink tonight than I did. You're likely panicked thinking about your daughter, which adds an adrenaline rush you don't need while driving."

"It's not like I have a choice. Or I can have my dad drive." Though her dad wasn't good with night driving.

"Look, you can take care of Tabitha while I drive. Plus, I know all the folks at the ER, which late on a Saturday night will be crowded as hell. I can bypass some red tape for you so you don't have to spend six hours in the waiting room."

She shuddered in a breath, realizing he had a point. And despite her wanting to do this on her own, right now she could use all the help she could get. Tabitha was her number one priority. "Okay. Thanks."

They climbed in his car and he drove her over to her parents'. The lights were blazing as she made her way to the front door. Her mom was already there. She didn't even give Will a second look, just smiled at him and nodded. "I'm glad you're here with Jane."

"How's Tabby?" Jane asked as they came through the door.

"Fine. Scared. She knows she's going to have to get stitches, and you know how she feels about that."

"I know."

Tabby was in the kitchen sitting on Jane's dad's lap with a bloody towel on her head. Nausea rolled in Jane's stomach. It was a weakness she hated to admit, but the sight of blood made her sick. She stomached it as well as she could, because she had kids and that's what a mom had to do, but she didn't deal with it well.

"Took a header into the table, did you?" Jane said, trying

to look anywhere but at the head wound and all the blood soaking the towel her dad had pressed to Tabitha's head."

Tabby's bottom lip wobbled and tears welled. Big fat drops slid down her daughter's cheeks. "I fell, Mommy. My head hurts."

"I know it does, sweetheart." She scooped Tabitha into her arms, the pungent smell of blood about to send her vaulting to the bathroom. She pulled back. "Will is going to take us to the emergency room, and we'll get you taken care of, okay?"

Tabby nodded, and Jane fell into the chair, gulping deep breaths of non-bloody-smelling oxygen.

Some mother she was.

CHAPTER SEVEN

Will took one look at Tabitha, and then his gaze crossed to Jane, who had gone pale and looked like she was about to lose the dinner they'd had earlier.

He'd monitored her drinking, and though he told her she shouldn't drive, it had been long enough that she should have been fine. She'd been drinking water and all she'd had was soda at Cain's, so he had an idea her current dilemma had nothing to do with alcohol and everything to do with her daughter's current state.

"Hey, Tabitha," Will said. "Mind if I take a look at your owie?"

Tabitha nodded and Will walked over and lifted the towel to take a peek.

"That's a pretty good boo-boo," he said. And it was. A nice gash across the top of her forehead, right near the hairline. It was going to need several stitches or staples.

"I need to use the bathroom," Jane said. "I'll be right back, Tabby."

Yeah, that's what he thought. He could see her stiffen, saw

her chin lift, and knew she was going to tough it out on behalf of her daughter, but she looked like she was about to pass out.

Jane was squeamish about blood or gaping wounds. Tough thing for a mom to deal with.

"Guess what I have in my car?" Will said to Tabitha.

"What?"

"A siren. We can use it on the way to the hospital."

That caused her shaking sniffles to stop. "Really?"

"Can you do that—I mean legally?" Sarah, Jane's mom, asked.

"Only for the most important of people that we take to the hospital," Will said, looking at Tabitha as he responded to Sarah. "And we all know how important Tabitha is."

Tabitha sat straighter in the chair, grinning as Jane came back in the room. "Did you hear that, Mommy? I'm 'portant."

"I heard. I guess we should get going then."

"Thank you for the transport, Will," Greg, Jane's father, said. "I was all prepared to take her myself."

"It's no problem," Will said. "I can get her through the paperwork a lot faster, so we can get Tabitha back home and in her bed as soon as possible."

"Since Ryan has slept through the whole thing, we'll bring him home tomorrow," Sarah said.

"Thanks, Mom. I'll call you and let you know how it goes."

"You do that. Otherwise I'll be up all night worrying."

Jane hugged her. "I know."

"Mind if I carry you?" Will asked Tabitha.

"That's okay with me." She held out her arms and his heart clenched at her trust in him.

He picked her up and they headed out the door. Once in the car, Will grabbed his first-aid kit, removed the bloody towel, and applied a loose bandage to the wound. The bleeding had stopped so he discarded the towel in a plastic bag and tossed it in the trunk. Maybe covering up the wound would save Jane from wanting to either pass out or throw up in his car.

She climbed in the backseat and buckled up next to Tabitha. Will came around to her side of the car and leaned in. "Are you all right?"

She looked a little less pale. "Yes, I'm fine."

He gave her arm a squeeze, shut the door, and got into the driver's seat. It was a short drive to the local hospital. Hope Community Hospital had a decent ER, and he knew the staff there. They weren't a huge trauma center—most of the tougher cases had to be transferred to the bigger hospitals in Tulsa. But for a simple stitch-up like Tabitha needed, the hospital in Hope would do the trick.

And as promised, he threw on his siren—though only off and on.

Tabitha giggled. "Cool."

He pulled up in front of the ER to let Jane and Tabitha out.

"I'm going to go park. I'll be right back," he said to her.

"I've got this," Jane said with a wan smile. "Unfortunately, I've been here before."

Having kids, he'd just bet she had. Probably had to do it with Vic, too. "I'll just be a few minutes."

He watched her help Tabitha inside, then he went to the parking lot. Fortunately with this being a small hospital, it wasn't too crowded, so he grabbed a parking space and headed inside. Jane was still at the front desk filling out paperwork.

"Hey, Felicia," he said to the intake coordinator as he moved up beside Jane.

Felicia looked up and smiled at him. "Hey, Will. I didn't know you were working tonight."

"I'm not. I was out with Jane and her daughter, Tabitha, had a slip and fall. She has a cut on her head." He looked over in the seating area. There were about ten people in there. "How's the wait?"

Felicia looked over the counter at Tabitha, who was leaning against Jane's leg.

"Poor baby." Then she looked up at Jane. "I've got a couple kids myself. It's never easy when they get hurt, is it?"

Jane shook her head. "No, it's not."

"We'll get you into a room and have a doctor look at your daughter's head as soon as possible."

She gave Will a nod and he smiled in thanks.

Jane handed Felicia the clipboard along with her insurance information. Felicia had it all handled with her usual efficiency, then they took a seat. It wasn't five minutes before Tabitha's name was called and they were ushered into a room in the back.

A nurse named Elaine came in, took Tabitha's vitals, and removed the bandage to take a look at the cut. Jane started looking at the monitors.

"Yeah, looks like the doc will probably want to put some stitches in. You got a nasty gash there, sweetie."

Tabitha's eyes welled with tears, the fear evident on her face. She looked over at Jane. "Mommy."

Jane got up and took a seat on the examination table with her. "It's okay, baby. I'll be here to hold your hand."

Will wondered who was going to hold Jane's hand.

"I'm going to clean up this cut and get everything ready," Elaine said to Jane, then leaned down to look at Tabitha. "This is going to sting a little when I clean up all the blood."

And Jane went pale again. But she held Tabitha's hand. She even turned to look at her, started telling her where she and Will had had dinner, and how they'd gone to listen to a band tonight and had gone to the park and seen some ducks. Will knew what looking at the wound did to her. She was tough, taking it so her daughter could be distracted while Elaine cleaned up Tabitha's forehead.

"Okay, now we're going to lay you down to get ready for the doc, okay, Tabitha?" Elaine asked.

Tabitha looked at Jane, who nodded. "Okay," Tabitha said.

The nurse got her positioned and draped. Then the doc came in.

Will breathed a sigh of relief when he saw Jeff.

"Hey, Will."

"Jeff."

"You working tonight, or just here for fun and stitches?"

Will smiled and introduced Jane. "Jane, this is Jeff Armstrong, a good friend and a great ER doctor. Tabitha is in very good hands."

"Good to know. Nice to meet you, Dr. Armstrong."

"Now that makes me sound old. Call me Jeff. And who's hiding here on my table?"

"Tabitha," came a tiny muffled voice from under the drape.

Jeff gloved up and took a peek. "Well, hello, Tabitha. My name is Dr. Jeff. I'm going to give you some awesome-looking stitches you'll be able to show off to all your friends. They're gonna be really jealous. You ready for that?"

"Sure."

Jeff walked her through the entire procedure, including the pinch from the needle. Tabitha cried a little, and even Will's gut twisted at her mournful sobs. But Jane soothed her through it with soft words and murmurs. After Tabitha's skin was numb, she was fine, though, and Jeff stitched her up, talking to her the whole time about kid's TV shows Will knew nothing about. But Jeff and Jane were laughing the whole time and talking, so Will took a step back and let them engage Tabitha, who, now that she couldn't feel any pain, seemed relaxed and even laughed.

"All done," Jeff said, removing the drape from Tabitha's head. He finished cleaning her up, then went through an examination.

"I don't think there's any evidence of a concussion."

"That's great news," Jane said.

Jeff presented a red sucker to Tabitha. "You were a good patient, Tabitha. Here's your reward."

Tabitha's eyes went wide and she looked to Jane. "Can I, Mommy?"

"Absolutely," Jane said with a sigh of relief.

"Thanks," Will said, shaking Jeff's hand.

"Hey, it's my job. And when I have cool patients like Tabitha, it's a great one," he said, winking at Tabitha, who smiled back at Jeff.

"No, seriously," Jane said, also shaking his hand and covering it with both of hers. "You made this much easier than I expected. Thank you for that."

Jeff grinned, then pushed his dark glasses up the bridge of his nose. "You're welcome." He turned to Tabitha. "No mad dashes in the dark for you anymore, princess. Okay?"

Tabitha pulled the sucker out of her mouth and grinned. "Okay."

"Take her to her pediatrician in about a week to have those stitches taken out," Jeff said to Jane. After he left, Elaine came back in with a sheet of instructions and discharge paperwork.

"We're outta here," Will said. "Are you ready to go home, Tabitha?"

"Totally," she said with the sucker in her mouth.

Will grinned at Jane, who sighed in relief. "Totally times two," she said.

He drove them back to Jane's house. "Give me a few minutes," she said, then took Tabitha back toward the bedrooms.

She came out a few minutes later. "She's restless. Wants a couple stories."

He nodded. "Understandable. I'm going to take off. I'm sure you're exhausted."

She let out a soft laugh. "It's been an eventful night."

He swept the pad of his thumb across her cheek. "Yeah, it has."

He started for the door.

"Will."

He stopped and turned. "Yeah?"

She stepped into his arms and he pulled her against him, his mouth meeting hers in a quick but deep kiss that re-ignited the passion they'd shared earlier.

Just as quickly, she stepped away. "I need to go see to Tabby."

"Yeah. You do. I'll call you tomorrow."

Her lips lifted. "I'd like that."

"Get some rest."

"Good night, Will."

He walked away and she shut the door. There was a finality to it that he didn't like.

He wanted to stay, wanted to be with her and make sure Tabitha was okay.

But he was on the outside, not a part of that family.

And that's where he'd have to stay.

For now.

CHAPTER EIGHT

For the next week, Jane focused on school and her kids. Dr. Jeff had been right. Jane had worried that Tabitha would suffer teasing from her friends at school. Instead, they'd all thought the stitches at the top of her forehead were cool. And her bangs covered what would undoubtedly be a slight scar, so she wasn't too worried.

Tabitha wasn't worried at all. She was thrilled she didn't have to suffer having to have her hair washed for several days, and she showed off the stitches like a blue ribbon at the county fair. Ryan, who'd had his fair share of visits to the ER for stitches and a broken arm, was highly jealous and proclaimed her a rock star, which nearly made Tabitha swoon since she was typically so uncool in her big brother's eyes. He couldn't believe no one had woken him up for all the blood and mayhem.

Jane was just happy to have things go back to normal, or as normal as they got in her life, anyway. Will had called the following morning, just as he'd promised, but she'd been so busy with her parents bringing Ryan home that she'd had to cut the call short. She'd promised to call him back.

And a week later, she hadn't.

"So did the date go badly?" Chelsea asked as they sipped iced tea at Bert's after school. Tabitha had gone home with a friend, and she'd dropped Ryan off at practice. One of the moms was going to bring him home later, after he ate dinner at their house. For the next few hours, she was free, for the first time in a week, so Chelsea insisted they grab a bite to eat and catch up.

"No. I already told you the date was awesome."

"Until the whole thing with Tabitha."

"Well, yeah, there was that."

"At which time he drove you and Tabs to the hospital, and got you promptly into an exam room, right?"

She rolled her eyes. "We already talked about this." Repeatedly, since Chelsea had also called her the day after her date with Will, and Jane had had to tell her about the evening, and about Tabitha's accident.

"I know we talked about this. What I'm trying to wrap my head around is why you haven't called him back a week later. Has he called you?"

She shrugged and took another sip of tea. "Yes. A couple times."

"And?"

"I told him I was busy. Which I was. You know testing is next week."

"So? Your entire life has to go on hold because of testing? You know as well as I do that changes nothing in your curriculum—or your social life. So what gives, Jane? Why are you suddenly giving Will the cold shoulder? If your date was great, then why dump him?"

She shot Chelsea a look. "I'm not dumping him. The date was fantastic. I'm just . . . regrouping."

Chelsea studied her for a minute, then sat straight up in the booth. "Oh. Now I get it. You're afraid."

"What? Afraid of what?"

"Afraid he's going to be there for you, afraid you're going to fall head over heels in love with him, and that he's going to fail you like Vic did."

"That's not it at all."

"Or maybe you're still holding out hope that Vic will come back someday?"

She frowned. "Oh, God no. And even if he did—oh, God no, Chelse. Never. Never in a million years. That door is firmly closed. Forever."

"Good to know. I'd like to give you credit for not being a stupid woman, Jane."

"I'm not that stupid. I'll never be that stupid again. I was once, but no. Never, ever again."

"So you say. But what's the deal with Will?"

She lifted a shoulder and studied her tea. "I don't know. Maybe you're right. Maybe some subconscious part of me is holding back because I'm afraid of getting hurt again."

"He'd never hurt you like Vic did."

She lifted her gaze to Chelsea's. "The logical part of me knows that. He's a nice guy and I . . . feel things for him." She felt a lot of things for him. Ever since that night, he'd been all she thought about.

And maybe that's what scared her the most. "But I feel things for him too fast, Chelsea. And it's scaring me. I'm not ready to fall in love with someone after spending one night with him. Really great sex or not, it's just too fast for me."

Chelsea reached across the table and grabbed her hand. "Sometimes love whacks you across the head and, like it or not, you have to be ready for it."

"I'd rather not be whacked across the head. I'd prefer to be eased into it."

"You don't always get what you want, honey. And you don't always get it in the way you think you want it."

"It's like someone dropped a house on me. *Bam*. There it was. All at once. No gradual realization over months of

dating that, hey, I like this guy a lot, and then, oh, wow, I
might love him. It was all right there, all at once. One date.
Mind-blowing sex. And then he was this knight in shining
armor when Tabby got hurt. And he not only took care of
her, he instantly realized that I'm squeamish about blood,
and he took care of me, too. What kind of guy does that?"

Chelsea squeezed her hand. "The kind of guy you want
to keep around forever and ever, amen, sister."

Jane shook her head. "I'm not sure I'm ready for forever
and ever. I'm not sure I'll ever be ready for it again."

"Maybe you won't be. But shutting the door on it before
it ever starts seems a little unfair, both to him and to you,
don't you think?"

"Probably." She laid her head in her hand.

Chelsea slid Jane's phone over toward her hand. "So why
don't you give him a call, and try for date two? See what
happens?"

It had been a shit kind of day. A tractor-trailer had jack-
knifed at the entrance to the Will Rogers Turnpike, spilling
its contents across both sides of the highway. Which meant
shutting down traffic going in both directions an hour before
the start of rush hour, and keeping it that way for several
hours as the mess was cleaned up. Traffic had been backed
up for miles, and had been a crap start to Will's day.

It had only gotten worse from there, as he'd dealt with
an accident on Highway 44, with injuries that could have
been prevented if people bothered to use their seat belts.
What did folks think those things were for? Decoration?

By the end of his shift, he was in a foul mood and he
needed some stress relief. He decided to head straight for
the gym. He ran off some of his agitation on the treadmill,
already logging several miles in thirty minutes.

Admittedly, as he looked through the glass into the hallway, he half expected Jane to walk by. But after she'd

brushed him off for the third time in the past week when he
called, he stopped calling.

He should stop looking for her, too. He'd been so distracted, his head filled with the events from today, that he
hadn't looked for her car in the gym parking lot. He had no
idea if she was here or not.

She'd made it clear by her lack of return phone calls that
she didn't want to be bothered. He'd grabbed a clue and
stopped calling, another thing to add to his irritation load
today. He increased his speed and started running until
sweat poured from him.

"Training for a sprint or a marathon?" Luke asked as he
climbed on the treadmill next to him.

Will didn't answer, not until he'd drained out enough
frustration that he slowed his pace to a walk, took several
long swallows of his water and could breathe again.
"Neither."

"Oh. Shitty day, huh?"

"Yeah."

"I heard about the turnpike closure this morning. That
had to blow."

He did his cooldown, walking enough now that he could
talk. "It did."

"So it's work that has you in a bad mood?"

"Mostly."

"Mostly, huh?" Luke pinned him with a look. "Wanna
talk about it?"

"Nope."

"Okay."

One thing he liked about Luke was that he wouldn't press
him until Will was ready to talk about whatever it was that
bothered him. The truth was, other than his colossally awful
day, there was a lot more that bothered him—namely Jane.
A bad day you could throw off by working out the stress.
Tomorrow would just as likely be a routine, boring day.

His issues with Jane wouldn't go away as easily.

He went to the bench press after he finished up on the treadmill. Luke joined him there not much longer after he'd started up with the lighter reps, so Luke spotted him on the heavier weights, staying quiet other than talking about work stuff. He spotted Luke and they moved over and did shoulders, then squats, working in companionable silence, just what he needed. A good workout, a great sweat, and a partner who didn't ask too many questions.

He showered when he finished and Luke met him in the locker room.

"Feel like grabbing a burger?" Luke asked.

"Sure." He'd missed lunch today and only had time for a protein bar, so he was more than ready for a good burger. They stopped at Bert's and Will ordered his with the works, along with a side salad and fries.

"Well, if it isn't two of Hope's finest in law enforcement."

And to think he'd almost made it through the entire evening. He lifted his gaze and smiled. "Hey, Chelsea. What's up?"

She pulled up a chair. "Nothing much. What are you two up to tonight?"

"Just hanging out," Luke said. "Have you eaten?"

"No. I'm doing an order to go. There's some hot reality TV at home calling my name. How about you two?"

"Eating," Will said, the evidence of that on his plate.

"Master of the obvious, aren't you, Will?" She looked over at the counter, then turned her attention back to Will. "So . . . have you talked to Jane?"

"Tried to. She won't answer my calls. But you probably already know that, so why the question?"

She shrugged. "Just thought I'd ask. Give her some time, Will. It's not you. She really cares about you."

"You should mind your own business, Chelsea, and stay out of this."

"And you know damn well Jane is my best friend, and I'm only looking out for her best interests."

"I wonder how she'd feel if she knew you were talking to me about her right now."

Chelsea frowned. "Low blow, Will. I'm also looking out for you, so don't be a dick."

Luke crossed his arms, obviously amused at the interplay between the two of them.

"Don't you have some poor kid's life to ruin by failing him or her in math?" Will asked.

She laughed. "Don't you have some poor bastard's day to ruin by writing him an unwarranted speeding ticket?"

Luke snorted. "You two should take this act on the road."

"Hey, Will knows I give as good as I'm given. And he can't rattle me."

"No, but I can tell you to go away and mind your own business."

Chelsea let out a very loud sigh. "Fine. I'll take the not-so-subtle hint and grab my to-go order and hightail it out of here. Seriously, though, Will. Don't give up on Jane."

"Seriously, though. Butt out, Chelsea." Will waved her off and dug into his fries.

"That was interesting," Luke said as Chelsea wandered off, grabbed her bag, and left Bert's.

Will finished off his meal by taking a long drink of iced tea. "Don't even ask."

"Okay, I won't." Luke took a bite of his burger, chewed, swallowed, then washed it down with milk. "Unless you want me to ask."

Will sighed. "You and Chelsea tag teaming me on this? The two of you should couple up."

Luke laughed. "Tried that for about five minutes in high school, remember? It didn't work then and it won't work now. We're more like brother and sister. "

"Yeah, I do remember. It's kind of like her and me. Surely there's a guy out there for her somewhere, someone who will rein her in and keep her from meddling."

"Maybe. Maybe not. She's kind of a free spirit. But what

is going on with you and Jane? Unless you'd like me to mind my own damn business, in which case you can tell me to and it won't hurt my feelings any."

"Honestly? I don't know. We went out, had a great time. Her little girl got hurt and I took them to the ER. Then I tried to call her the next day and she brushed me off, saying she was busy with her parents and her kids, which was fine. She said she'd call me back, and when she didn't, I called her a couple days later. She brushed me off again. I tried one more time, and got the same 'I'm really busy and I'll get back to you' speech."

Luke popped a fry into his mouth. "Maybe she's just not that into you."

Will gave him a hard look. "Trust me—she's into me."

"Overconfidence is a killer, my friend."

"No, really. We had a great night. I know she felt the same way I did."

Luke leaned back. "Then I have no idea. Women are a mystery to me, as you well know. I couldn't figure out the one I was married to."

"Yeah, well, the one you were married to was a mess."

"Don't I know it. Haven't been able to figure out women since, so I tend to stay the hell away from them. Boomer is companion enough for me."

Will shook his head. "Dude. Your dog? You have got to get out more."

Luke laughed. "You're right. I do. But I'm not the one with woman problems right now. That's you. So what are you gonna do about Jane?"

"I don't have a clue. Give her some space, I guess. I'm not going to keep calling and bugging her if she doesn't want to talk to me. I figure she'll either come around so we can talk, or whatever we had that one night was just that—one night."

"Too bad. I like her with you."

"Me, too, man. Me, too."

CHAPTER NINE

In what was an unprecedented moment of pure joy, Jane found herself with an evening to herself. She didn't have to work at the day-care center, and both kids were spending the night elsewhere. It was Friday, and Ryan was sleeping over at one of his friend's houses, while Tabitha had begged to stay with her grandparents. At first Jane had balked at that idea, considering the last go-round, but her mom had assured her the chances of Tabby's accident being repeated were slim to none. One of Tabitha's school friends lived a couple houses down from Jane's parents, and they'd made plans to play together, so Jane's mom picked Tabitha up right after school. Jane was scot-free and alone for the entire night.

Which, as a single woman, meant she could have a date if she wanted. But since she was a total coward, she had no date and no prospect for a date. Because God forbid she should grow a set of balls or some courage or whatever and call Will, who likely thought she hated him or had hated their date, when the exact opposite had been true.

Idiot. She couldn't even handle dating. So instead, she was going to make a grand attempt to work out in the gym, ignoring the women in their tight little workout pants and workout bras, and go in there with her decidedly not tight anything and do her best to not fall off the elliptical trainer.

She changed into her sports bra and T-shirt and yoga pants, tied her tennis shoes, and used her employee card to swipe her way into the workout room, daring anyone to give her the side eye. She grabbed a towel and found a vacant elliptical, read the instructions, and set a program—something easy, like baby level—then started walking, holding on to the handlebars.

Okay, so this wasn't so bad. For the first thirty seconds anyway, until her thighs started burning. If it wouldn't have been such an embarrassment, she'd have stopped the damn thing and gotten off. But since there was currently some kind of fashion model with a centerfold's body walking next to her—wait, did Jane know her? She looked familiar, but Jane couldn't place her. Really light brown hair, full lips, and small, perky breasts. Obviously she hadn't had two kids, because this woman's thighs were perfect. Everything on her was perfect. And she was working her elliptical with the ease of a gazelle, the bitch. No way was Jane going to get off after—she looked at the timer—four and a half minutes.

Jane had set her program for twenty minutes.

Twenty minutes? Was she insane?

God, she was going to *die* on this thing.

She tried to focus on the television. Something sports-related was on. Ugh. She couldn't focus. Sweat pooled and ran like a river down her back and between her breasts, and she was pretty sure she'd lost all feeling in her thighs and calves. She had no idea how she was continuing to walk. She took a quick glance over at the centerfold, who glanced back and had the audacity to smile at her.

"Jane Smootz?"

The woman knew her maiden name. "I used to be, but now it's Jane Kline. I'm sorry, you look really familiar to me."

Another smile. Not fake, but genuine. "We went to high school together. I'm Emma Burnett."

"Emma. Of course. I'd heard you were back in town." She could barely breathe, while Emma was walking along like she did this every day. Hell, she probably did do this every day. And did she have to be so damn gorgeous?

"I am. I bought out Dr. Weston's vet clinic. I've been working to get everything ready to reopen it and I've hardly had any time to get a workout in."

Right. Like it looked as though she didn't work out. "Glad to have you back in Hope."

"Thanks. I'm really excited to be here. So, you're married?"

"Divorced, actually."

"Oh, I'm sorry to hear that."

"It's okay. It's been a couple years since the divorce. But I have two great kids."

Again, that charming smile that made her look even more beautiful. Could you hate and like someone simultaneously?

"Two kids? That's awesome, Jane. Congratulations. How old are they?"

Emma continued to engage her in conversation, forcing Jane to try to work this elliptical and breathe and talk at the same time. But it did help pass the time, and before she knew it, her timer beeped and her hideous workout was finished. She moved her nearly immobile legs off the elliptical.

"I guess I should move on to the weights," Jane said while huffing and puffing. And sweating. In the meantime, Emma looked like a catalog model for perfect fitness.

"It was great to catch up with you," Emma said. "If you have any pets, I'd love to see you at the clinic once we open."

"No pets, though Ryan and Tabitha keep pestering me about a dog."

Emma grinned. "Well, kids and dogs. They kind of go together, you know."

"So they keep telling me. See you around, Emma."

Jane went and grabbed a cup of water, downed it in three very unladylike gulps, then swiped the sweat from her neck with a towel and limped over to the weight machines.

She wasn't sure she had any energy left to lift more than the towel in her hand, but she set it down and tried the chest press, keeping the weight low.

Not bad. Not impressive to anyone but herself, but at least she was doing something.

She was on her third set when she saw Will come in.

Crap.

He hadn't seen her, and he went right for the treadmill. She watched him as he stopped to greet a few people he knew, then he set his machine, plugged in his earbuds to listen to some music, and began to walk, slow at first as he warmed up, then faster, finally settling into a comfortable run.

Where she was clunky and out of shape on the machines, he seemed a part of his, running fluidly, his muscles hard with tension as he ran. She was so lost in watching his arms flex and the tightening of his calf muscles that she got lost and forgot she'd been hogging the chest press until an older man came up to her and asked her if he could work in with her.

"Oh. I'm so sorry. I'm finished here and guess I was daydreaming."

She climbed off the machine and looked around, trying to figure out where she could hide so Will wouldn't see her.

Or, she could be an adult and go talk to him instead of avoiding him like she'd been doing for the past two weeks.

She hovered around a couple machines, watching him while he finished his run. When he got off and swiped the sweat off his brow, heading for the water, she met him there. He looked surprised to see her.

"Jane."

"Hi, Will. I don't mean to disrupt your workout."

"It's okay. What are you doing here?"

She offered up a half smile. "Fumbling my way through a few of these machines."

He glanced around the room. "Need some help?"

Leave it to him to give her an out. "That'd be great. Thanks."

She told him what she'd already worked on. He took her past the machines and into the free weight room.

"I'm not sure I'm ready for these. The elliptical nearly killed me."

"Yeah, I hate that damn thing. I avoid it."

"That makes me feel better."

"We'll start with really light weights and you can do multiple reps. I don't want you to get hurt."

The way he said it, the way he looked at her, made warmth coil low in her belly. "Thanks."

He walked her through a workout that made her feel good—made her feel strong. By the time she was finished, she felt like she'd worked every body part. And he lifted alongside her, with much heavier weights of course, so she got to see his muscles flex, which was a nice bonus.

"Do you need to go pick up the kids?" he asked as they left the weight room.

"No. Actually, they're both spending the night elsewhere."

"I see. So, you have a free night tonight."

"Yes."

"That's nice."

He wasn't going to let her off the hook quite that easily. She was going to have to eat a little crow, which she deserved. "Will, would you like to go out with me tonight? If you don't have anything else going on?"

His lips curved. "I'd like that."

Her already shaky legs wobbled just a little more. "Great. I'm going to head home and take a shower."

"I'll pick you up in an hour. I don't know about you, but I'm starving."

For the first time in a while, she felt relaxed. And eager. "Me, too."

She dashed home and into the shower, then grabbed a pair of jeans and a silk T-shirt she was certain Chelsea would approve of. She slipped on a pair of fancy sandals, and was just putting the finishing touches on her hair when Will rang the doorbell.

She opened the door and inhaled his crisp, just-showered scent. "Hi."

"Hi. You ready to go?"

"Definitely."

"I thought we'd eat local tonight. There's a new Italian restaurant that opened up here in Hope and I thought we'd give them some business."

"I saw that sign go up last week. Sounds great."

New business was always something exciting in Hope. The parking lot was full because, like them, folks in town tried to check out new restaurants. There was a line waiting for tables, and the owners were enthusiastic and welcoming. And oh, the place smelled fantastic, which was a very good sign. After about fifteen minutes they were seated at a charming table by a window.

One of her former students scurried over to take their order, another girl trailing behind her.

"Mrs. Kline," she said. "How are you?"

The one thing about small towns was you couldn't escape running into someone you knew. "Hi, Melanie. Nice to see you. Are you still on school break?"

Melanie gave Will the once-over, and then grinned. "Yes, ma'am. I'll be heading back to school in about a week, but since the Serranos are friends of my parents and their restaurant is new, I'm picking up a little extra money before I go by helping them train the new staff. This is Tina, by the way. She's the trainee."

Will and Jane both said hello to Tina. Jane didn't recognize her, so she wasn't in any of her math classes.

"That's right," Jane said to Melanie. "I remember you used to work at Bert's when you were in high school."

Melanie nodded. "And I waitress part time during the semester in college."

"How's it going at Oklahoma State?"

"Great. Still making A's in all my math classes, thanks to you."

"That's good to hear. You always were one of my best math students. Have you decided on a major yet?"

"I'm in premed right now."

She always knew Melanie would go far. "Excellent. Your parents must be so proud of you."

Melanie beamed. "Thanks. What can I get for you two?"

"I'll just have iced tea."

"Same here," Will said.

"I'll be right back. Our special tonight is chicken parmesan. Gail and Orlando make the best. Trust me, you'll love it."

Melanie hurried off, and Will met her gaze. "A good student?"

"A great one," she said. "If they were all like her, my job would be so easy."

He laid his menu to the side. "Now what fun would it be if it were easy?"

She laughed. "Believe me, I'd love easy."

"So would I."

She closed her menu, too. "Did you have a challenging day?"

"I've had several. You'd think living in a small town it would be quiet and boring here. But it hasn't been that way lately."

"Hey, I drive on the highways. They're never quiet or boring."

Melanie came back with their drinks. "Have you decided what you'd like?"

"I'm going with the special," Jane said.

"Ditto," Will added.

Melanie scooped up the menus. "You won't regret it."

After she left, Jane took a glance around. The place was packed and noisy, plus there was music. There was no time like the present to clear the air between them. She'd put it off long enough.

"I'm sorry for avoiding you."

He shrugged. "It's okay. You've been busy."

"That's true. But I'm always going to be busy. That was no reason to ignore your calls. You were so nice to me and to Tabitha that night. And I was rude to you by not talking to you afterward."

"I didn't expect thanks, Jane."

"I know that." She looked down at her hands, clasped them together. "It's just that I have some issues regarding men and dating and I'm trying to work past them."

He laid his hands over hers. "I'm in no hurry. We're not running a race here, you know."

She lifted her gaze to his. "Thanks for being under-standing."

"Yeah, that's me. An understanding guy."

She sensed the undertone there, that maybe this wasn't all water under the bridge, but she let it go when their salads and bread arrived. Hunger took precedence over everything, even a pissed-off man.

After dinner, he took her to a movie. When was the last time she'd been to a movie that wasn't animated or rated G? She couldn't remember. He let her pick and she decided not to torture him by choosing the romance she'd been dying to see, instead selecting a comedy.

It was a good choice. She laughed until her stomach hurt,

clutching Will's arm during some of the really funny scenes. He laughed, too. It was a great movie and they left the theater arm in arm, talking about some of their favorite parts.

"Thanks for picking that movie," he said as they climbed back into his car. "I'd been wanting to see it."

"So you secretly hoped that was the one I'd choose."

"Yeah. I was sending you psychic vibes."

"Apparently you're good at it. I was going to choose the romance."

He made a grimace. "Really?"

"Would you have gone if I did?"

At the red light, he turned his head toward her. "Of course. Why wouldn't I?"

"Even though you would have hated it."

"I didn't say I would have hated it, but it wouldn't have been my first choice."

She laughed.

"There's a new club in Tulsa that plays country. Do you like country?"

He was being so nice and entertaining. But she wanted to be alone with him. "How about we go back to my place. I can play some country."

He gave her a look. "Yeah? You know any moves?"

She arched a brow. "I know a few."

"All right."

There was no way she wanted to waste any more time. She'd already wasted enough by being stupid and afraid. After they got to her place, she pulled out her keys and tried not to appear too anxious or in a hurry as they made their way to her front door. But her fingers fumbled with the lock. He put his hand over hers to steady her.

"That's not helping," she said, staring at his hand.

"What's not?" he asked, his body nestling very nicely against her—and her backside.

"You. Touching me."

He stayed right where he was. "So, you don't want me touching you?"

"Oh, I most definitely want you touching me."

"Then move your hand out of the way so I can get this damn door unlocked before we end up doing something indecent on your front porch."

Her lips curved at that thought, and at how scandalized her neighbors would be. She moved her hand and his deft fingers—oh, she really liked the things his fingers could do—had the key turned and the door pushed open in a few seconds, his body propelling her inside.

She flipped on the light, then turned around and took him by the hands, leading him into her living room. She grabbed the remote and turned on the TV, scrolling through until she found the music channels, selecting country.

His lips curved. "You gonna show me your moves?"

She held out her arms. "You don't really want me to line dance for you, do you?"

He swept an arm around her and tugged her close. "Hell no. Not when I can hold you against me."

They swayed together to the rhythm of the music, though she had to admit she had no idea what song was playing, whether it was a driving beat or something sweet and slow. All she knew was the length of Will's body pressed up against hers, and melting into the way he looked at her. And when he cupped the side of her neck and leaned in for a kiss, she was lost.

And all those reasons for avoiding him seemed so stupid, because she had been missing out on his incredible mouth, the way he teased her by brushing his lips across hers. He deepened the kiss and held her head with his hand, his tongue sliding in to possess.

She felt dizzy, mesmerized with each stroke of his tongue against hers. She reached for his shirt, lifting it up so she could palm the warm skin of his stomach and stroke his

rock-hard abs. They quivered under her touch and she
moaned against his lips.

Her world turned topsy-turvy when he picked her up in
his arms and carried her to the bedroom.

This was all very romantic. She couldn't remember ever
being carried to the bed before. If she knew how to swoon,
she'd be doing it right this moment.

He flicked on the light switch, then set her on the bed
and drew his shirt over his head. She took a moment to
admire that view of him with his jeans hanging low on his
hips, the dark swirl of hair disappearing into his jeans.

And as she gazed at his erection pressing against the tight
denim of his jeans, she licked her lips and lifted her gaze to his.

He moved toward her and lifted her top off.

"Nice bra," he said, teasing the swell of her breasts with
the tip of his finger.

She'd bought new underwear on the off chance they
might get to do this again. Now she was glad she did, because the look of appreciation on his face was well worth
it. And the light touch of his fingers was causing her heart
to beat faster. When he dipped his fingers inside her bra to
tease her nipples, she gasped and arched against him.

Will thought there was nothing as beautiful as the sight
before him. Jane's body was flushed with desire, her nipples
tight, hard points against his questing fingers. He flicked the
front clasp of her bra and separated the cups, baring her
to him.

She leaned back and let him pull the straps down her
arms. He leaned over her and put his lips over one crest.

She tasted sweet and soft, the sounds she made as he
covered her breast with his hand and sucked her nipple into
his mouth making his cock throb.

Everything she did made him hard. She was beautiful
and honest in her expressions, giving him everything, watching him as he pleasured her, her curiosity as natural as what
the two of them were doing.

He pushed her back on the bed and undid the button on her jeans, then drew the zipper down, his fingers brushing her soft skin as he pulled her jeans over her hips and legs.

Man, he really liked her legs. After he dropped her jeans to the floor, he lifted one of her legs and pressed a kiss to her calf, smoothing his hand over her thigh. Her eyes glazed and her lids partially closed. Her breasts rose and fell as her breathing deepened.

Yeah, he liked watching her body. All of her body, especially her eyes as he put her leg down, leaned over her, and mapped a trail over her skin with his lips. Her eyes were windows, showing everything she felt. The blue would go dark and stormy when she was mad or turned on, then bright and sparkly when she was laughing. He could get lost in her eyes—hell, in all of her. He was a goner whenever he was around her. Her skin was like silk and he couldn't get enough of touching her, tasting her, breathing in her scent. She smelled like fresh strawberries, and he put his lips on her, wanting to lick her all over. He started at her hip bone and worked his way up over her ribs. She giggled—ticklish there—but she definitely didn't laugh when he covered her right breast with his mouth and took a long, slow suckle.

She grabbed his head and held him in place while he licked and sucked. He reached down and slid his hand over her sex. Even through her panties she was damp. He caressed her, teasing her. She arched her hips against his hand, whimpering, her hands grabbing the covers.

His dick pounded in answer.

He moved down, kissing her belly, sliding his tongue in her navel, then moving lower. Here, her scent grew more exotic, sweet and musky, and he couldn't wait to taste her, to take her right to the edge and watch her fall over.

He drew her panties down and slid his tongue over her, and she cried out, spreading her legs for him, trembling as he licked her and found her clit, then put his lips around it and sucked.

"Will. God, Will, yes."

Here was where she was most responsive, and where he loved to give her pleasure. And she took it, arching against him with fervor. When she came, it was with an unabashed cry of release. He held her hips and took her right where she needed to go, loving the taste of her as she released.

He stood, enjoying the sight of her body bathed in that blush of orgasm. She sat up and reached for his zipper, her knuckles brushing his cock as she drew the zipper down.

Her eyes were dark with spent passion as she locked gazes with him while she pushed his jeans past his hips. He stepped out of them, watching her while she removed his boxer briefs and grabbed hold of his shaft.

And when she leaned forward and took him in her mouth, it was his turn to fight for breath.

He swept her hair behind her back and held it out of her way so he could watch her pleasure him. He tightened as she took him deep, his muscles tensing when she rolled her tongue over every ridge, then licked the sensitive crest of his cock before engulfing him, using her hands to stroke him.

He shuddered, right on the edge.

He pulled back, leaning over to kiss her, cradling her head in his hand so he could take the kiss deep. She pulled up and aligned her body against his.

He felt the rapid beat of her heart against his chest, the way she trembled. He felt the same way, that if he didn't get inside her soon he was going to explode.

He laid her back on the bed and grabbed a condom, put it on, then slid inside her.

She threaded her fingers through his hair as she arched upward. "Yes," she said on a gasp. "This is where you're supposed to be."

His gut tightened at her words and he thrust deep. "Yeah. Right here."

After that there were no more words because he was swept into a maelstrom of sensation, of her body taking him over, her lips meeting his in a kiss that electrified him. And as he moved inside her, he knew there was no other place he'd rather be, no other woman he wanted to be with. She fit him perfectly. Her body was made for his, and as she tightened around him and climaxed again, he went with her, groaning against her neck as he exploded with his release.

Later, when he could breathe again, he rolled to his side and pulled her to face him. He brushed her damp hair away from her face.

"Mind if I stay the night?"

Her lips lifted. "I was hoping you would."

"Good. I brought extra condoms."

"I bought a box of them. They're in the bedside drawer."

"See? This is why we're so well matched."

She grinned. "I think so, too."

It was going to be a long night, and he didn't think there'd be much sleeping.

CHAPTER TEN

In the past several weeks Jane and Will had been out as much as possible, given her schedule and his.

Her mom had been really helpful, offering to watch the kids, even during the week. Jane had balked at that at first, since school was in session. But she did want to see Will, so she allowed herself to spend at least one weeknight with him. Sometimes they went out, but usually just for a quick bite to eat, and then they'd end up at her place for some alone time before she had to go pick up the kids.

The alone time was her favorite part, when she and Will got to know each other's bodies.

He was really good at getting to know her body. And she loved worshipping his. After all, it was a great body. She could spend hours looking at it, touching it, tasting it. Those hours always seemed way too short.

But it wasn't just the two of them. And she loved that Will insisted they spend time with the kids, too.

Last weekend, Will had suggested they all go to the zoo. It had been a long time since Jane had taken the kids to the zoo. She didn't know why. Busy with stuff and other things to do, she supposed. But the kids loved the idea, so off they went.

A lot had changed at the zoo. A lot had changed in her life lately, too. Namely having Will a part of it.

Tabitha loved Will. At the zoo, she'd held his hand and dragged him to all the exhibits. Apparently Tabitha and Will shared a love of penguins, so it had practically taken an act of Congress to get the two of them to leave the penguin exhibit. Only the suggestion of lunch had pried them away.

And then there was Will and Ryan's shared love of sports. Will had talked to Ryan about baseball, and Ryan had asked if Will would like to come to one of his games, which Will of course said he definitely wanted to do.

Since tonight was the next scheduled game, Will had showed up, just as he said he would. And the third base coach had come up sick, so Will had gamely offered to pitch in and help.

Jane had to work at the day-care center, so she hadn't been there, but they'd met at the house for pizza afterward, and Ryan had given her practically an inning by inning recap. He had a definite case of hero worship. Apparently Will was an aggressive third base coach, so he'd pushed a couple of the kids to run like hell for home on a couple doubles, resulting in them winning the game by two runs against a pretty powerhouse team.

"You should have seen it, Mom. I thought Coach was going to explode. But Will was right. He had seen Henry and Brandon run, so he knew they were fast and they could sprint for home and beat the throws. It was awesome. He made the right calls."

Jane looked to Will. "And you didn't get in trouble with the coach?"

Will gave her a look, one of those supremely confident masculine ones that curled her toes. "Please. I was in charge of third base. I knew what I was doing. No way would I have waved them on if I wasn't sure they were going to be safe."

"See, Mom?" Ryan said.

"I do see. Well done, Will. And I'm glad the team won."

After pizza, Will helped Ryan with his geography home-work while Jane worked with Tabitha on her spelling. It felt like a family. Epically scary, but solidly comfortable at the same time.

She didn't quite know what to make of that.

She gave Tabitha a bath and got the kids settled for bed, then came out to hang out with Will. They watched a movie for a while.

"I hear Ryan wants to go to a camp next summer."

She paused the movie and turned to him. "Where did you hear that?

"From Ryan."

"Oh. Yes, there's a camp he wants to go to, but it's too expensive, so I had to tell him no."

"He told me that, too." Will half turned on the sofa to face her. "The thing is, I was wondering if you'd let me pay for it."

"No."

He arched a brow. "Why not?"

"Because . . . just no. Thank you, but no."

"Jane. I want to do it for him. It's a great camp. I went there when I was a kid. They have awesome activities like archery and canoeing and backpacking. It's good physical exercise and a chance to learn to work as a team. They have a great counselor-to-kid ratio, and it's reputable."

She didn't want to have this conversation about the camp—again—and especially not with Will. "I don't have a problem with the camp, I just can't afford to send Ryan there. Maybe someday, but not now."

He let the topic fall off—for about five minutes, before turning to her again. "Is there some problem with me want-ing to help out?"

She sighed. "Yes. I'm the parent. You're not. I don't need or want your charity."

"Ouch. It wasn't charity. It was a gift."

She knew she wouldn't be able to explain this right, but she had to try. "Look, Will. I appreciate it, but my kids need to learn to live within the means I can provide them without outside help. I'm the parent and I need to give them what I can afford to give them. And if I can't afford to provide them something, then they have to learn to go without. It's not like basic food or clothing or shelter. This is a luxury item."

"I get that, I really do, Jane. But I have the money and I kind of thought I was part of your life. Part of their lives. Why won't you let me do this for Ryan?"

"Because you're not his father. And you're not a part of his life."

The words had fallen out of her mouth before she'd thought about what she'd said. And now she couldn't take them back.

Will looked stricken.

"Will. That's not what I meant. Let me explain."

"It's okay." He stood.

"It's not okay. Let's talk about this."

"No, really. I understand. I'm gonna go."

She stood and followed him to the door. "Please don't leave."

He turned to her. "I appreciate and respect your independence, Jane. But at some point you're going to have to open up and let someone in, and that means sharing your life with the kids. And that means letting someone help, even financially. I know that's a sore spot for you, but—" He shrugged. "Whatever."

He walked out and she stood at the door, watching him as he got into his car and left.

She didn't know what to say. She was right to turn him down.

Wasn't she?

* * *

"**S**o you told him no?"

"I did."

"Why?" Chelsea asked as they ate lunch in the teacher's lunchroom.

"Because *I* need to provide for my children. And I'd already told Ryan that he couldn't go."

"Well, that was before."

"Before what?"

"Before you started seeing Will. You two are getting kind of serious, aren't you?"

Jane shrugged. "I don't know."

Chelsea rolled her eyes. "Come on, Jane. You're together almost every night. He does things not only with you but with you and the kids. It's obvious to everyone in town that you two are a couple, and that he loves your children. If he wants to help you send Ryan to that summer camp, what's the problem?"

She lifted her chin. "I want to be able to send Ryan to summer camp. I want to do those things for my kids. I don't want to depend on some guy to help me out."

Chelsea cocked her head to the side. "Some guy? Is that what Will is to you?"

"Come on, Chelse. You know what I meant."

"Yeah. I know exactly what you meant. Will's just some dude you're screwing around with to get your rocks off, and you want to be alone and independent the rest of your life."

"You don't understand." She picked up a carrot, then set it down again, her appetite gone.

"I do understand," Chelsea said. "I really do. You want to be able to give your kids everything you and Vic could do for them. But guess what? You're a one-person income now, so you can't and probably won't be able to until you're a two-person income again. With Will in the picture, you can do some things for the kids you couldn't do before. So if Will offers to help out with some things financially, that's a bad thing?"

"No. But what if things don't work out with me and Will? Then what does that do to my kids? They become dependent on him—and his income—just like they depended on Vic. I'm an adult. I can handle the heartbreak, but I won't have their hearts broken all over again."

Chelsea nodded. "I appreciate your fear. But you can't lock your kids away and shelter them from hurt the rest of their lives. Nor can you lock yourself away in order to protect them. You have to allow yourself to live again, Jane. Even if it means risking you—and them—and the chance you could all be hurt again."

She stared at her carrots. "I'm not sure I can take that chance."

"Then you're doomed to be alone the rest of your life. I hope you think that's worth it."

She pinned Chelsea with a look. "That was harsh, Chelse."

"No, Jane. That was the truth."

CHAPTER ELEVEN

Will thought a lot about what Jane had said the other night.

He didn't like it, but they were her kids and she had the right to make those decisions. Even if he didn't agree with all of them.

The discussion about the camp had come up in conversation with Ryan. Will had told him he'd gone to the camp when he was a kid. Ryan had been so excited about the camp, and Will thought it was something he could do to help.

It was simple. He had plenty of money. Hell, who did he have to spend his money on?

Obviously Jane didn't see it as simply as he did. Sometimes she was just damned unreasonable about things.

But, again, the kids were hers and so were the decisions. And he just needed to butt out.

He called her the next day. She answered, tentative with him. He hated that.

"I'm sorry for walking out on you," he said.

"I'm sorry for what I said."

"You had a right to say it. You're Ryan and Tabitha's mother, and you get to call the shots where they're concerned. I shoved my way in and made suggestions, and I had no right to do that."

She went quiet for a few seconds. "It's okay to suggest. I appreciate the suggestions. I just won't always say yes."

"Okay. I can live with that."

"Thank you for always being so understanding. Especially when I'm not always so reasonable."

He laughed. "So I'm forgiven?"

"Nothing to forgive."

"I'm glad you think so. Look, there's another reason for my call."

"Oh?"

"Yeah. There's an animatronics dinosaur show coming to town on Friday. Do you think the kids would be interested?"

"Are you kidding? They'd be thrilled."

"Great. How about we go out for pizza and head over to the show Friday after work? Say about six thirty?"

"That sounds perfect."

"Okay. I'll pick you all up."

They talked for a while, and when he hung up he felt a lot better about where things stood, especially when he saw Jane at the gym that night. She grinned at him and caught him in the hallway.

"Have a good day?" she asked.

"It was an uneventful one, and to me that's always a good day."

She started walking with him as he headed toward the lockers, so he veered off into one of the side hallways, grateful to see they were alone. He pushed her against the wall and kissed her. She kissed him back with fervor, sliding her fingers into his hair and pushing her body against his. He finally had to pull back and take a deep breath.

"Getting a hard-on in these shorts is going to be difficult to hide."

She breathed deeply. "I'm having the same problem."

"Yours is easier to hide."

"I can give you some tough math problems to solve," she said, her eyes bright with mischief.

"That won't help. Your body is still pressed up against mine."

She slid out from under him. "I can fix that. See you later." After a quick brush of her lips against his, she winked and waved as she hurried off, leaving him alone to think up some of those complex math problems while he breathed deeply.

Friday was a clusterfuck at work. Rain moved in, and that never boded well for traffic on the highways. The storms were intense, accidents were frequent, and to top it off, two of the patrol officers who were due to relieve his shift were sick, which meant he'd be working overtime.

Great. Just great.

He called Jane that afternoon after she got off school.

"Hey, how's your day going?" he asked.

"Just fine. The kids are really excited about tonight."

"Yeah, about that. I have some bad news. Two of our officers are sick and I have to work overtime."

"Oh, I'm sorry to hear that."

"I hate to disappoint the kids, but there's nothing I can do."

"Don't worry about it. We can do it another time. You be careful out there."

"There's another showing at noon tomorrow. How about it?"

"That sounds great."

"Good. I'll be there at eleven to pick you up."

"Perfect."

"Thanks for understanding. I need to get back to it, so I'll talk to you later."

"Okay."

* * *

Jane hung up the phone and went to the window. Thunder rolled and cracked outside, and lightning lit up the sky. Summer storms were always vicious, and this one was no exception. It had been a hard-driving storm all day.

She hoped Will was all right. She went in and told the kids Will would have to work late. They were both disappointed about not being able to go to the dinosaur show, but she explained to them how important his job was and how he was out there in the storm keeping people safe. They understood.

Good kids. She smiled and told them she'd make them homemade macaroni and cheese for dinner and they could each choose a movie to watch. The kids were excited about that.

Nothing like mac and cheese and movies to save the night.

The next morning, she got the kids up, made sure they had their breakfast and showers and were ready to go in plenty of time before Will's arrival, especially since he was typically early.

She was surprised when eleven o'clock rolled around and he hadn't shown up yet, and shocked when it was eleven fifteen and there was still no sign of him.

"Is Will coming, Mom?" Ryan asked, glancing nervously at the clock above the fireplace.

"I'm sure he is, honey, but I'll call him to make sure." She grabbed her phone and dialed his cell.

No answer. How odd. She tried again, and still no answer.

By eleven thirty and several calls, she was pissed. It was obvious they'd been stood up. No way in hell was she disappointing her kids twice in two days, especially since this whole dinosaur thing had been his idea in the first place.

"Let's go," she said, grabbing her purse and keys.

"But Will's not here yet, Mommy," Tabitha said.

"Will can't make it, so we're going without him," she said, not about to get into the intricacies of her irritation with Will with her children. She drove downtown, found the exhibit, bought three tickets and took her kids to see the dinosaur show.

Ryan and Tabitha had a great time. She stewed the entire time, her thoughts centered on Will. She turned her phone off during the show, and two hours later turned it back on.

No message from Will.

Wasn't that just great. She took the kids out to lunch and then brought them home.

Will called later that afternoon. She ignored his call, and his text messages, since they seemed like flimsy excuses to her.

Jane, I'm so sorry. My phone went dead and the charger died on me, too. Alarm didn't go off.

Jane. Please answer your phone. I promise to explain.

Jane. I'm sorry.

She didn't want to hear his excuses. All she knew was he'd disappointed her kids and stood her up. Again.

She knew the first time was work and it couldn't be helped. But really? The old "my phone went dead" excuse?

Whatever. She was over it. Relationships were entirely too much work, and she didn't have the energy for it. She spent the rest of the weekend ignoring his calls and messages.

But when he came to her door late Sunday night, she had to answer it. She stepped outside so the kids wouldn't hear him.

"I'd have come over sooner, but we have a lot of guys out sick with the flu so I had to cover another shift this weekend."

She crossed her arms. "How convenient."

He took a step forward. She took a step back.

He frowned. "You're mad. I understand, but please let me explain."

"There's nothing to explain. Your phone died or something. I get it."

"You don't believe me? You won't even give me a chance? You think I deliberately blew you off?"

"I don't know what to believe. I don't even care. I'm tired, Will."

"Seriously? I worked until almost six a.m. Saturday morning, came home, and plugged my phone into the charger. I guess a lightning strike from the storm blew out the charger and I was so tired I didn't even notice. My phone went dead, my alarm didn't go off, and I didn't wake up until one in the afternoon. I couldn't even call you because I had a dead phone. I had to run out and buy a new charger, charge up my phone, and call you."

"It's okay. I took the kids to the show."

He shoved his fingers through his hair. "I'm so sorry I wasn't there. I'll make it up to you—to them."

"That's not necessary."

"You're really mad about this. Let's talk about it."

"I don't want to talk about it. I don't want to talk at all."

"Jane—"

"I need to get the kids ready for school tomorrow. And I think we need a break, Will."

"Why?"

"Because this is too much for me."

"*This* being you and me?"

"Yes."

"Why is it too much for you?"

"Because it is."

"Because I blew one date with you and the kids because of work, and my phone died so I let you down on another?"

She wasn't going to do this with him. "I have to go."

She turned to go back inside.

"Do you know what your problem is?"

Now *he* was angry. That was awesome. She turned around. "Sure. Tell me."

"You're looking for Mr. Perfect to replace Vic."

"What?"

"After Vic fucked up so badly, you're expecting perfection, and no man will ever be able to measure up. Or maybe that's what you want?"

She narrowed her gaze. "I don't follow."

"Maybe you're looking for Vic two-point-oh, the Vic you first fell in love with before he got all messed up."

"Are you kidding me? That's not at all what I'm looking for."

"Are you sure? Are you sure that's not exactly what you want? Your life when it was perfect, before it all went to shit? Because that's not gonna happen, Jane. That's never gonna happen for you. So you might just have to settle for something a little less than perfection."

Anger boiled inside her. "You have no idea what you're talking about. I don't want Vic back, either before or after he screwed up his life—and ours. I don't want him or any facsimile of him."

"Then what do you want?"

She had no answer for him. Or for herself. She just wanted her life to be simple, and right now it wasn't.

He took that step forward, and she held her ground.

"I'm not perfect, Jane. I'm far from it, but you know what? Neither are you. Do you know what we both are? Humans who make mistakes. And I'm sorry for hurting you and the kids. I'd rather cut off an arm than hurt any of you. I'm not Vic, and I'd never hurt you the way he did. Because he was the wrong guy for you.

"So when you're ready to be with the right guy—flaws and all—you let me know. I'm willing to give you the best I've got. And yeah, I'll probably fail you now and then, but I'll never leave you, and I'll never deliberately hurt you or Ryan or Tabitha.

"Also . . . I love you. But that's got to be enough for you.

And if it isn't, then maybe I'm not the right man for you. But if I'm not, then by God, no man is."

He turned on his heel and walked off, leaving Jane staring after him, trying to soak in everything he'd said to her.

CHAPTER TWELVE

He loved her. He told her he loved her.

He'd not only told her he loved her, he'd told her off. A lot.

And she'd deserved it. All of it.

She sat in the living room with her head resting in the palms of her hands, the mother of all headaches squeezing her temples.

She'd had such righteous anger and indignation burning inside her. She was going to go it alone. She'd done it so well the past couple years. Just her and the kids, and they'd been doing just fine without a man.

Just *fine*.

Until Will had come into their lives and messed everything up by making her kids joyful and fun and filled with life and making them fall in love with him.

Just like she'd fallen in love with him.

She loved him. That's what the problem was. Because it gave him the power to hurt her.

And one simple mistake on his part and she'd cut him down and cut him loose.

Because God forbid she should ever give another man the chance to hurt her again.

Like Vic had hurt her.

Will had thought she wanted another go-round with someone exactly like Vic?

She let out a soft laugh at that. She never wanted Vic again. She never wanted to see Vic again. She hoped and prayed every day that he never came back. Vic was a train wreck.

Will had done everything right, and she'd crucified him at every turn, just waiting for him to make one wrong move so she could pounce and tear him to shreds.

So she could punish him for everything Vic had done to her.

Because she'd never been able to punish Vic.

She lifted her head, the sudden realization stunning her. Shit.

Sitting here in the darkness, everything had become so clear to her.

But was it too late to fix things?

So when you're ready to be with the right guy—flaws and all—you let me know.

He'd left the door open for her. All she had to do was walk through it.

Will paced the small confines of his apartment, too wired to sleep. Which really sucked. He dragged his phone out of the pocket of his jeans to look at the time, realizing it was after midnight and five a.m. was barreling down on him in a hurry.

"This is all your fault," he said to the phone, then shoved it back in his pocket.

He turned when there was a knock on his door. Who the hell was here this late? Probably another drunk friend of his neighbor's coming to the wrong door.

Bad night for this. He flung the door open, intending to yell at the idiot, and was shocked as hell to find Jane standing there.

"Jane."

"Hey."

"What the hell are you doing here? Do you know it's, like, twelve thirty? Where are the kids?"

"I called Chelsea to come stay with them. And yes, I'm aware of the time."

He blinked, then realized he had left her standing on the front stoop. "Come in."

She stepped in and he shut the door, still unable to figure out what she was doing here.

"Do you want something to drink?"

She shook her head. "No. I'm fine, thanks. I just want to talk to you."

They'd parted earlier—or rather, he'd left earlier—on a really bad note. It had been all he'd thought about for the past several hours.

He'd been brutal to her, had said things that, while he didn't regret them, probably could have been a little less harsh.

But he was tired of tiptoeing around her, so maybe those things needed to be said. And maybe she was good and mad and had a few things to say back.

Okay, he could take it.

"Come on in and sit down. Sorry the place is such a mess."

"It's fine. I didn't come here to critique your house-keeping."

He dragged his hands through his hair as he led her into the living room. "Good thing."

She let out a nervous laugh, then took a seat on his sofa. He sat next to her, wishing he could fold her into his arms and hold her. But since she stared down at her shoes, her hands folded tightly together in her lap, her body language told him she wasn't in any mood to be held, so he kept his distance.

He had a feeling he was about to get an earful.

He waited.

And waited.

Okay, so maybe she needed a minute to gather her thoughts.

"Are you sure you don't want something to drink?"

Her gaze lifted to his, and there were tears in her eyes. "I'm sorry, Will."

Uh-oh. That sounded like the beginning of a breakup conversation, and he was kind of hoping she would take some time to cool down, that they could still talk things out.

Maybe not. "Sorry for what?"

"For not appreciating what a great guy you are. Since we started . . . being together, you've been there for me, and for the kids. And I've done nothing but back away and hold you at a distance, because I was scared."

Okay, that hadn't gone like he thought it would. "You don't have to be sorry about that, Jane. You were protecting yourself and Ryan and Tabitha. I get it. And I was pushy. When I know what I want I'm single-minded about it, and I'll bully my way into having things my own way. Sometimes I can't see how that affects other people. It comes from being single for so long."

She looked at him. "I can see that about you. But that's hardly a character flaw."

"It makes me stubborn and bullheaded sometimes. I have to learn to look at the other side of the picture. I'm a single guy and I've never been hurt the way you have or the way the kids have. I thought I could just be in your life and it was going to be easy. I should have known better."

She frowned. "Don't make excuses for me or let me off the hook so easily."

He tried not to smile. "Okay, I won't."

"I probably fell in love with you when you mowed my lawn, or when you took me out that first night and made the most incredible sweet love to me that anyone ever has. But God, Will, you scared me, because you made me feel things that I thought I'd never feel again. You made me feel secure and cared for and you made me trust in you."

She took a deep breath and Will grasped her hand. She fought it, but he grabbed it anyway until she let him. "It's okay to be scared, Jane. I know how much Vic hurt you."

She nodded, and big fat tears spilled down her cheeks.

"I hate how much he hurt you and the kids. I'd give anything for you to not have that big hole in your heart because of what he did to you."

"The thing is, I never got to blast him for all that hurt. After he left town, our divorce was handled long-distance. So I never got to tell him to his face how much he hurt me."

She paused, looked down at her shoes again. He knew he needed to give her time to work through it all in her head, and to get it all out. So he waited.

"So I held it all inside and I stewed. And then you came into my life and gave me the outlet I needed. And I took it out on you. I put all that mistrust on you. I backed away from you and ran away from you. And that's not fair. Because you never did anything to hurt me or the kids."

"I'm sorry I let you down."

She looked at him and gave him a rueful smile. "You never let me down. You're one of the most honorable men I've ever known. You would never intentionally hurt anyone. And you were right in what you said, that there's no such thing as perfection. I'm not looking for perfection, Will. I was just looking for an opening so I could jump on it, so I could point my finger and say, 'See? See? It's going to happen again. I was right not to trust you,' when in fact, you didn't do anything wrong at all. It was stupid. I'm stupid."

He pulled her against him and kissed the top of her head. "You're not stupid. You were protecting your heart and your children. I love how fierce you are about keeping them safe."

She pulled back and gazed up at him. "I was afraid to give my heart to you, because I was in love with you. And that gives you the capacity to hurt me."

Hearing her say the words back to him made his heart squeeze, made his throat go tight with emotion that he'd never felt before. He swallowed. "I'll make mistakes with you, Jane. I know I will. But I'll never hurt you. I promise."

She finally lifted her gaze to his. "I know. I believe you. I believe in you, Will, because I love you."

His hopes soared. "We can make this work, you know. And we'll take it slow. We won't rush things. The kids need to get to know me better."

She swept her fingers across his jaw. "My kids love you as much as I do."

He brushed his lips across hers. "We'll still take it slow, because you all need that. And we have all the time in the world. I'm in no hurry, and I'm not going anywhere."

Jane sighed and fell into his arms. Will wrapped his arms around her and sealed the deal with a kiss that curled her toes inside her tennis shoes.

She felt foolish for being so reticent, so stupid for hurting him. And he'd been so easily forgiving when she didn't deserve it. She didn't deserve him, but she'd spend as long as it took making it up to him, and proving to him that she could make him happy.

When he finally broke the kiss, she was lying across his lap.

"Do you have to go home?"

She shook her head. "Chelsea said she'd stay the night, because I told her I might be here with you—talking—all night long. Or at least that's how I hoped it would go."

His lips curved in that devilish smile that never failed to

make her stomach flip. "Well, you can stay the night, Jane, but I don't think there's going to be a lot of talking."

She reached up to pull his head down to hers. "I like the way you think, Will."

PERFECT STRANGER

A Serendipity Novella

CARLY PHILLIPS

To all my readers who love the town of Serendipity and the people who live there. This story is for you! Thank you for buying my books, reading my stories, and writing to tell me how much you enjoy them. Alexa's story is for you.

CHAPTER ONE

Joe's Bar. Familiar stomping grounds for Alexa Collins, yet everything about the night felt off to her. First, the bar's owner and his new bride were on their honeymoon, so Joe wasn't serving. Alexa's normally happy friend Cara Hartley sat morosely stirring her drink, staring into the glass for answers, but the man who'd caused the problems was nowhere to be found. Alexa couldn't relate to guy issues considering she lived an extremely busy life, spent hours in the hospital ER, and had no time for a relationship, let alone hot, stress-relieving sex—something she could definitely use. For the last couple of weeks she'd been suffering from a definite case of the blues, and the strain of her life was beginning to wear on her.

No wonder she was in a funk.

The music now blasting through the speakers gave her a jolt akin to a caffeine kick, and Alexa perked up at the sound. Rising from her barstool, she glanced at her friend.

"I feel like dancing," Alexa announced.

With a disinterested sigh, Cara shook her head, but Alexa

wasn't taking no for an answer. Cara needed to have fun and forget about Mike Marsden, the man who'd broken her heart.

She jerked her head toward the dance floor. "Dance. Now."

Cara groaned but complied, standing up on command.

Alexa looked to the third woman in their trio. "Liza?" Liza and her husband, Dare Barron, had joined them for a night out along with some other friends who mingled around the bar.

Liza swayed her hips in time to the beat of the music. "Why not? I could use some letting go."

Katy Perry's upbeat tune reverberated around them as they headed to the dance floor near the jukebox. "Teenage Dream" began the set, which segued into "Firework," one of Alexa's favorite songs. She closed her eyes and allowed herself to get lost in the moment, her body moving to the beat, her entire being consumed by the tempo and the sounds pulsing around her.

When she opened her eyes, she noticed she wasn't the only one attracted to the upbeat music. The crowd had grown in size, everyone on the floor pumping their fists, swiveling their hips, and dancing as if they were shooting across the sky as the lyrics suggested.

Dare had joined Liza, wrapping himself around his wife in a heart-melting embrace. Alexa looked away to avoid the obvious intimacy between the couple and her gaze met that of a man who sat alone at a table near the dance floor. A sinfully sexy man with shaggy, sandy blond hair and an unwavering stare.

He watched as she danced, his heavy-lidded scrutiny focused on her as he sipped at his beer. His demeanor seemed casual but his stare was anything but. Thinking of how down she'd been lately and how great this music made her feel now, she was unable to resist the impulse to crook her finger his way.

A glance told her that her best friend wasn't watching, which was a good thing considering Cara wouldn't know what had gotten into Alexa. And she would be hard-pressed to explain. All she knew, all she felt, was a bone-deep loneliness that reached into her soul, and this man's intense and interested stare provided her heart with a jump she hadn't felt in too long.

A slow smile lifted his lips and her pulse skyrocketed as he stood and made his way toward her, his swagger indicating a self-confidence that was rare. Alexa experienced that same kind of self-assuredness in medical settings, but she normally fell short in other areas of her life. Still, she'd called on that confidence when beckoning him over, and she was glad she hadn't stopped to think it through.

He joined her on the dance floor, immediately picking up the rhythm. He danced close enough for her to smell his woodsy cologne that both surrounded and aroused her. As they moved, their bodies spoke for them, their synchronicity startling for two people who'd never met, let alone danced together before. And when the music turned sultry, he was all too willing to join her for some dirty dancing. He ground his hips against hers, the swell of his erection pressing deliciously against her stomach, too intimately for strangers. But too good to deny.

So she didn't.

Instead she let the heat of desire crackle and spark between them, and fire licked at her veins as a result.

Cara eased closer and looked from Alexa to her partner, her eyebrows raised, a concerned expression on her face. Alexa ignored her. She needed this sense of freedom, the release this man provided. She hadn't realized how badly until now.

Pure enjoyment and fun.

When was the last time she'd allowed herself the luxury?

Her dance partner's hands slid to her waist. She'd worn black leggings and a cream cardigan, which she'd unbuttoned to show both cleavage and the barest hint of her lace cami underneath. She reaped the benefit of her clothing choice now, as he slid his hand beneath the layers, and she trembled at the rasp of his calloused palms caressing her sensitive skin.

A sexy grin lifted his lips and he continued the dance along with the erotic assault on her senses. She could have lingered in their intimate embrace all night, but from the corner of her eye, Alexa caught sight of Cara's ex-boyfriend, Mike Marsden, the man who'd broken her best friend's heart.

He strode up behind Cara and wrapped his arms around her. She jumped in surprise but soon settled into the embrace. Alexa figured Cara thought it was one of her guy friends joining her for a dance, because no way would she allow Mike that kind of privilege. Not without him doing some serious groveling first. Worried about her friend, Alexa kept an eye on the couple, prepared to step in if needed.

"You okay?" her dance partner asked in a Southern drawl. It was the first time she'd heard him speak, and the sexy voice fit him perfectly.

She nodded and smiled at him, her gaze roaming over his handsome face, which had dimples on either side of his perfect mouth and full lips and a faded scar above his left eyebrow. But even as she admired the view, she never lost sight of Cara, knowing her friend would do the same for her.

Mike pressed his front against Cara's back in a more intimate touch. Before Alexa could even wince, Cara whirled on her ex with a surprised then furious spark in her eyes.

The music was too loud for Alexa to hear much so she inched closer, remaining vigilant and on call.

"What are you doing here?" Cara asked, her voice tinged with the pain Alexa knew she'd suffered ever since Mike's abrupt departure.

"I'm back." His gaze never left Cara's.

"Good for you," she said with deliberate sarcasm.

He appeared as worn and ragged as Cara had earlier, before Alexa had forced a dance session on her friend.

Cara perched her hands on her hips. "And you thought

you could wrap your arms around me and pick up where we left off?" she asked, her voice rising.

Oh, go girl! Alexa thought, stopping short of clapping, because Cara wasn't greeting Mike with open arms. As a cop, Cara could handle herself in any situation, but as a woman, she was more fragile. Yet she wouldn't let any man, including this one, walk all over her. Alexa was proud of her friend.

Serendipity, New York, was a small town, and Mike was the former police chief whose sudden departure had sparked many wagging tongues. Add the now loud discussion between exes and, sure enough, Cara and Mike were attracting stares from the crowd. Alexa knew they needed closure, but they didn't have to do it in front of an audience. Time to put an end to the show, Alexa thought.

Figuring she'd buy her friend some time to handle this on her own terms, she tapped Cara on the shoulder. "Are you okay?" Alexa asked.

"Yeah." But the hurt in Cara's blue eyes told another story.

"Can we go somewhere and talk?" Mike asked her.

"Seriously?" Cara blinked in obvious shock. "Let's get something straight. I don't know why you're here or for how long and I don't care. But I will not be your booty call every time you come back to town."

Alexa stifled a grin.

Behind her, she sensed her former dance partner was still there, watching the scene unfold, and Alexa spared a moment's regret for having to ditch him this way. But he was a momentary diversion, while Cara's friendship was forever. And no self-respecting woman abandoned a friend in need for a man.

"Cara—" Mike reached for her but she pushed him away, shoving at his shoulder.

"No." Cara jerked out of his reach.

Alexa moved closer. "I'm going to the ladies' room," she

said, tipping her head toward the back of the bar. The silent *Do you want to join me?* was implied. She wanted to give Cara options before dragging her away.

Mike whispered in Cara's ear, something Alexa couldn't hear, but Cara shook her head.

Alexa turned, shooting a regretful glance at the man she'd never actually meet. "Sorry. Friendship calls." She smiled at him, wishing they'd had more time.

He nodded in surprising understanding and gestured with a sweep of his hand. "It was a pleasure," he said, the words dancing along her nerve endings, similar to the way his touch had branded her skin.

She held his stare for a few more precious seconds before breaking eye contact and focusing on Cara, who, though torn, would thank Alexa later for stepping in.

"Let's go," she said to her friend, and steered them through the crowd toward the restroom, leaving her sexy dance partner behind.

Lucas Thompson watched his dance partner walk off, her hips swaying, her delectable derriere displayed to perfection in her tight black leggings. He liked what he saw. Hell, he'd liked what he'd felt even more. She wasn't too skinny, like the NFL groupies who usually followed him around back home; her waist felt soft and generous in his hands.

He groaned and headed to the bar. A cold drink would cool him off before he went to his buddy's house somewhere in this small upstate New York town. Luke was here for a visit but his ex-teammate Sawyer Rhodes wouldn't show up till late tonight. He was busy getting his father settled into an assisted living facility today. Sawyer's plan was to stick around, fix up his father's house, and put it on the market. Since Luke was in Manhattan for meetings with his agent, he'd taken Sawyer up on his offer to stay with him instead of in some sterile hotel room in the city. As pro football players, they both had enough of that when they were on the road. He'd help Sawyer out for as long as he was in town.

Luke had pulled into the parking lot, planning to grab a beer and maybe some wings at Joe's Bar. Dancing hadn't been on his agenda. Then again neither was the russet-haired woman who'd captured his attention. She'd been a surprise in many ways, the most pleasant being that she hadn't recognized him as the tight-end of the Texas Titans. Either she wasn't a sports fan or she was more into her hometown team, the one to which Sawyer had recently been traded. Which meant her invitation to dance had been based purely on mutual attraction. Even before he'd seen her up close, and taken in those sea green eyes and the smattering of freckles on her nose, his gut told him the woman was more wholesome than any who'd crossed his path in way too long.

He'd been watching her shake those hips with undisguised interest, and when she'd crooked her finger his way, his cock had jumped in delight.

"Want to keep a running tab?" the bartender asked as he set Luke's soda on the counter.

He shook his head. "I'll settle now." He'd already had a long day of meetings. Between his agent and the potential sponsors he'd lined up for Luke to meet with, then the hours' drive up here, Luke was beat.

Before taking off, he looked around for *his woman*—he chuckled at the term; he hadn't learned her name so it seemed to fit. He found her standing on the other side of the room, deep in conversation with the same guy who'd been hassling her friend earlier. Her friend, a pretty brunette, was nowhere in sight. Apparently Luke's dance partner was mediating a dispute between the two.

Luke shrugged, tamping down the disappointment. At a glance, she didn't strike him as a one-night-stand kind of woman, although considering the way she let him grind against her on the dance floor, who knew where the night would have ended if they hadn't been interrupted.

Unfortunately, he'd never know.

He set a twenty on the counter and waited for the bartender to make his way back to his end of the bar, which took a while since the place did a steady business.

Finally, Luke got his change, left a tip, and started for the door at the same time someone ran inside shouting. "Alexa! Get out back now. Cara needs a doctor!"

To Luke's surprise, his onetime dance partner turned and bolted toward the rear exit.

A doctor. Something about the information made him grin.

Luke couldn't stop the impulse to follow the crowd out back. Alexa—he knew her name now—knelt by her friend, the woman she'd been so protective of.

"What happened?" he asked the man next to him.

"Cara was attacked." The guy, who appeared about the same age as Luke's almost thirty, suddenly eyed him warily. "You're not from around here, are you?"

He hailed from a small town himself, where everyone knew everyone else, so this man's distrust didn't surprise him.

Luke shook his head. "No, sir. Here to stay with a friend." He wasn't about to mention Sawyer's name, not wanting to draw any attention to himself as a pro athlete while he was here. "But I was dancing with Alexa earlier," Luke said, more to reassure the man that he wasn't a part of whatever had gone down here.

"I see." The man nodded slowly, seeming to take Luke at his word. "Well, she's the best doctor we have. She'll be running University Hospital one day when her father steps down." Before the man could continue, a siren sounded in the distance, the noise growing closer and making it impossible to continue the conversation.

The paramedics arrived and things got even more hectic. They loaded Cara onto a stretcher and Alexa went in the ambulance, after insisting the ex-boyfriend meet her there with his car. Alexa had been too preoccupied to even realize Luke was in the group of people surrounding them, and soon the ambulance doors slammed shut and the vehicle sped away. The crowd slowly dispersed, the fun gone from the night.

Luke climbed into his car and turned on the engine. The directions to Sawyer's place were in his GPS, yet instead of turning it on, he picked up the southern route on the highway he'd taken here, and exited at signs for the hospital. The same exit he'd passed on his way to Serendipity.

He parked near the emergency entrance and scratched his head, asking himself what the hell he thought he was doing. The woman was a stranger to him but she intrigued him on a level no woman ever had. And that was saying something, considering the smorgasbord of choices laid out for him over the years. He'd enjoyed it when he was younger, but he'd be thirty next month and he was over the lifestyle that came with the fame. The booze, the women, the occasional bar fight. So. Over. It. His teammates called him an old man. So be it. Luke knew he could take each one in a fight and still have energy left over. He just knew there was more to life than partying and he was ready to find it. Whatever *it* was.

Right now, *it* was Alexa.

He'd first seen her as a sexy woman with haunting green eyes and a hot body that Luke was damned attracted to. She'd transformed into a loyal friend who'd given up a sure thing—since Luke couldn't see himself turning her down if she'd wanted to hook up—in order to look out for a pal. Then later, she'd morphed again, this time into an in-control doctor, capable of putting away her emotions and treating her unconscious friend.

In the span of thirty minutes, Luke discovered Alexa was

not just beautiful but multifaceted, and as a result, she'd captivated him completely. He couldn't leave without finding out if her friend was okay and how she was doing after the night's crazy events.

Although, as he walked through the sliding ER doors, Luke had to ask himself if he wasn't a little crazy himself, pursuing a perfect stranger he'd never really met.

CHAPTER TWO

Once Alexa checked Cara over and had tests run, she diagnosed her friend with a concussion and a bruised trachea. The abusive bastard who'd attacked Cara had done so because he'd blamed her for his wife leaving him, not only because Cara was a police officer but because she was a human being who'd cared enough to take the woman under her wing. Now he was behind bars and denied bail, so Cara was safe from the man. As for Mike, Alexa had stuck around to make sure his presence didn't upset Cara, but with the sedative, she was out cold. And Mike had sat by her bedside all night, never leaving. Alexa snoozed in the on-call room, waking up to check on things before allowing herself more sleep time. By the time eight A.M. rolled around, she'd all but forgiven Mike, knowing he would do anything to repair his relationship with Cara. Alexa had no more reason to stay.

She stopped by the nurses' station and wrote down discharge instructions, then ran through them with the nurse assigned to Cara's room. "And now, I'm leaving. Call me if something urgent comes up, otherwise I'm indisposed."

She stretched her arms over her head and yawned. "I need a good meal and a couple of solid hours of uninterrupted sleep." Though at this point, she didn't know which would happen first. She might fall facedown before she ever ate.

Emily, an older nurse who'd been on staff when Alexa's father was first starting out, shook her head. "Honey, you need more than that if you're going to get a glow back in those cheeks. Do you even know what the word *vacation* means?"

Alexa laughed. "Not really. The chief of staff here drives me pretty hard, you know."

Emily frowned. "That father of yours is going to work you into an early grave, and for what? To keep a Collins in charge of this hospital?" A buzzer sounded, distracting the older woman, and she glanced down. "That'll be Mrs. Evans in two eleven. I swear she better need more than her pillow fluffed or I'm going to scream."

Alexa laughed as Emily walked away, but her words lingered. During these weeks of Alexa's discontent, there had been many issues she couldn't verbalize, even to herself. There were simple things in life that other people took for granted, things that Alexa just didn't have time for, like a regular social life, dating, or even a relaxing night with a friend.

She gathered her jacket and purse, and headed for the elevator. With her mind clear of worry about Cara, Alexa's thoughts immediately strayed to the sexy stranger who'd danced with her last night. The man who'd given her more in thirty minutes of dancing than she'd had in years. Her body tightened at the reminder of that too short carefree moment. Serendipity didn't get many strangers passing through, so chances were she'd never see him again. The sad fact was, even if they did cross paths, Alexa had no time for sex. But if their chemistry was any indication, he'd be so worth her making the time for.

Which brought her thoughts full circle. No time for sex, no time for a future. That was what she'd been trying so hard not to dwell on. But the sad truth was, the longer she accepted her father's mantra, that *a Collins puts work first always*, along with his plans for her future, the less likelihood there would be of her ever getting married. Having children, a family. And Emily was right about working herself to death, even if the other woman didn't mean it literally.

There were some days Alexa barely remembered crawling into bed at night because she was so exhausted from being on her feet at the ER.

Exactly how she was feeling now.

She stepped out of the elevator and pushed through the doors of the waiting room that led to the exit, when she heard her name spoken in a sexy drawl that could only belong to one person.

One man.

"Alexa," he repeated.

She turned to stare into a pair of golden brown eyes, which were once again focused on her. "You're here," she said, sounding as shocked as she felt. "Are you sick?"

He shook his head. "Just waitin' for you."

She blinked in surprise.

He grinned. "I was beginning to think you'd gone out another door but the guard there assured me you'd have to pass this way." He folded his arms across his broad chest. "So I waited."

"You're here for me?" A wave of pleasure rolled through her that was so strong and unique, she almost didn't recognize it.

"Are you the pretty lady who danced with me last night?" he asked with a wink.

A hot flush rose to her cheeks and she managed a nod.

"Same one who ditched me in favor of a friend?" he continued teasing her. Before she could reply he added, "I admire loyalty, by the way."

"I—"

"I'll take that as a yes, that was you. And by your scrubs, I'd say you're the same woman who turned out to be one hot doctor. Which means, yes, I'm here for you."

Alexa felt flattered and steamrolled all at the same time. "Why?" Why would he stick around all night and wait for her this morning?

"Been asking myself that same question in between Z's. The best I can come up with is that you intrigued me, we clicked, I wanted to know if your friend was okay—"

"She is." And he was sweeping her off her feet with very little effort. "You cared about my friend?"

"I cared about you." He shook his head. "Yeah, I know. Short time, crazy thing. I'm guessing after pulling an all-nighter you need breakfast?"

Whatever exhaustion she'd been experiencing had since disappeared. "That would be great," she said. "Breakfast, I mean."

He grinned, obviously pleased. "Since I'm not from around here, you're going to have to recommend some-place."

There was only one diner in Serendipity. "There's a place called The Family Restaurant on the edge of town." Unfortunately, she'd left her car at Joe's, and though she wanted to have breakfast with this man, she didn't think getting into a car with a stranger was all that smart. "Listen, I don't really know you so I'm not going to get into your car."

He immediately extended his hand. "Luke Thompson."

"Alexa Collins," she said, noticing how much smaller her hand was as she placed her palm against his. Instant awareness sizzled along her nerve endings at their handshake, telling her that last night's electricity hadn't been a fluke.

They were chemically compatible. Now, if she could make sure he wasn't a serial killer or stalker, she'd be all set, she thought wryly.

"I'm a friend of Sawyer Rhodes. Does that help?" he asked.

A small town was a small town. "The football player," Alexa said, nodding.

"I'm staying with him for a couple of days to help clean out his father's house."

She recalled her father mentioning something about recommending retirement homes. "Did Mr. Rhodes move to assisted living?"

"Yesterday," Luke confirmed. "So you know them?"

"I know the family," she murmured.

"Good enough of a reference for me to drive you to breakfast?" he asked.

She couldn't stop the smile he inspired. "Well if you're a friend of the Rhodeses, I guess you're safe enough."

He let out a laugh. "Darlin', I don't know many people who'd call me safe."

And with the way his hot gaze devoured hers, she couldn't say she felt safe, either. The Alexa she'd become didn't take chances, didn't date, and she certainly didn't give up sleep for a meal. She didn't crook her finger and invite a sexy stranger to grind with her on the dance floor, either. But the Alexa she was around this man apparently did all those things . . . and looked forward to doing even more.

Luke liked a woman with a healthy appetite, something he rarely saw unless he was home with his mother and sisters. Alexa ordered a serious meal: scrambled eggs, two pancakes, bacon, a large glass of orange juice, and coffee. He wasn't sure what he enjoyed more, eating his omelette or watching her devour her breakfast. She didn't seem the least bit concerned about what he might think, and by the time they'd finished their food, he had yet another reason to like this woman.

"Oh my God, I was starving," she said, wiping her mouth with a napkin and finally coming up for air.

He grinned. "Feeling better?"

She nodded, eyes sparkling. "Definitely got my second wind."

Her words hit him in the gut. He could think of a lot of things they could do to make use of that newfound energy. Instead, he did the unexpected, even to himself, and settled in to get to know her better. "So your friend's okay?"

Alexa's gaze softened. "Yes, thank God."

"And things better with her guy?"

"Probably not yet, but if Mike has his way they will be." Alexa spent the next few minutes explaining to him how Mike had what she called "sticking" issues, but that she'd never seen him so intent on making things right. "So I'll give him that chance. But if he hurts her again, I'll remind him I'm an expert with a scalpel."

Luke made a mental note to remember that, too. "Blood-thirsty?" he asked.

"Just not squeamish. I've been around medicine since I was born. My father's a doctor, too."

He nodded, enjoying this glimpse into who she was. "And you followed in his footsteps?"

"It was mandatory," she said, taking a sip of her freshly refilled coffee. "Especially after mom died and I had no one to stick up for what I might want," she admitted.

"How old were you?"

"Ten."

He winced, unable to imagine his sisters getting through their teenage years without their mother's steadying influence. "I'm sorry."

"Thanks. How about you?" she asked, clearly deflecting. "Parents? Siblings?"

"Hmm. Both parents still alive and married, and three sisters."

She opened her mouth, then closed it again. "And you came out a jock anyway?" she asked, laughing.

He grinned. "My dad was the high school football coach and I was the oldest. All pretty much worked in my favor." His mom got her girls to fuss over and his dad worked hard kicking Luke's butt and nurturing his talent.

"You were lucky," she murmured.

"Yeah, I was."

"Did you always know you wanted to play football?" she asked, leaning closer, clearly interested in his answer. Interested in him.

He nodded. "Pretty much. It came naturally and I always loved it. Still do. Not just the playing but everything about the life. How about you, Doctor?"

"The idea of being a doctor? Yeah, that I wanted. A lot. The reality?" She shrugged. "It's been a lot tougher than I thought."

"The actual work? The hours? Or what?"

She leaned back in her seat with a full-blown sigh. "I love medicine. I love to treat people, kids especially. But my path hasn't been pediatrics. Ever since I came back to town, my dad pulled me into his practice, his hospital, grooming me to be his successor as chief of staff. So I work the ER, I help out with the administrative duties, I oversee doctors and nurses and shifts and OR schedules. And because I don't want to lose touch with medicine, I keep hours at the office with patients."

"Doesn't sound like you have much time left for you."

"You caught that, huh?" She laughed.

Even knowing her less than twenty-four hours, Luke knew the sound was forced. "You were out dancing last night."

"That was an effort to get Cara out of the house so she'd stop thinking about Mike. I had to get someone to cover for me in order to do it."

"Doesn't the hospital have enough doctors to give you more normal hours?" he asked, understanding that the weariness in her expression obviously came from more than being up all last night with her friend.

"Not if I don't want someone else to usurp the position my father's been grooming me for."

He noted she didn't say it was the position *she* wanted. But it wasn't his place to point that out. She was a big girl and if her life made her unhappy, she'd change it. "You looked like you were enjoying yourself last night. Before the excitement went down," he amended.

"I made time to go out for Cara's sake but once I hit the dance floor, I realized how much I needed the break. And then I caught sight of you." Her voice dropped, the slightly breathless hitch catching him off guard, in some ways as reassuring as it was sexy.

She studied him intently, making Luke wonder what was going on in that beautiful head of hers. And she was beautiful. Even without much sleep, little makeup, and in hospital scrubs, Alexa Collins, with her gleaming chestnut hair, creamy skin, and intelligent eyes, stood out. But it was more than her looks, though he liked staring at her. He enjoyed talking to her, too. And thinking back on their dancing had him itching to get his hands on the body he'd barely touched the night before.

"What happened when you caught sight of me?" He pressed her to continue because she'd invited him onto the dance floor with her. Because she'd let him get close enough to turn them both on. And because she'd agreed to have breakfast with him this morning.

The waitress had just set the check on the table and Luke knew where he wanted them to end up next. He just wasn't sure she'd be on board. Then again, she'd been staring at him on and off throughout the meal, her interest as obvious as his. The chemistry was still there, alive and brewing with an intensity he'd never experienced, not in an ordinary setting like this diner. Hell, not in any place at any time. Something different was happening between them, and he wondered if she felt it, too.

She bit into her lower lip, making him wonder if that fleshy portion was as soft as it looked. If she'd taste sweet like the maple syrup on her pancakes.

"When I looked at you, everything around me disappeared," she said softly, her words more sugary than he'd hoped.

She reached out and placed her hand over his. "Come home with me?" she asked.

He hadn't expected her to be so blunt, but she'd described her life as hectic and without much time for herself. If she wanted something, she'd have to reach out and take it when she could. She obviously viewed him as her break, an escape from daily life, and the irony of it was, that was exactly what he wanted to give her.

"Darlin', there's nothing I'd like more."

CHAPTER THREE

As a grown woman, Alexa knew what she was doing when she invited Luke home. She just couldn't believe she'd done it. She blamed her lack of sleep and the fact that he'd gotten her to talk about herself, her career, and her lack of personal time. Not only had her guard been down, but she'd been reminded of all that was missing in her life. Sitting across the booth from the hottest guy she'd seen in her lifetime, one who looked at her like she was something special and wanted to eat her up . . . how could she not allow herself this one indulgence? She certainly wouldn't be working today whether or not Luke Thompson, pro football player, joined her in bed.

Although she hadn't changed her mind about her invitation, she experienced a twinge of awkwardness as she gave him directions to her house, a small three-bedroom she'd bought from the bank when the owners foreclosed and moved out of state. She might not spend much time there, but it was home and she'd done all she could decor-wise to make the house her own. Having grown up in one of the larger mansions in the wealthier part of town, in a place her father had turned into an art showcase after her mother died, Alexa focused on homey touches instead. White walls, lavender trim, and real plants that needed watering, which was something she made time for each week.

As Luke followed her into her house, Alexa was acutely aware of him taking in his surroundings.

"Pretty place," he said as she placed her bag and keys onto the foyer table.

"Thanks." She didn't turn to face him, wondering if she should invite him up to her room. Or into the kitchen for a drink first. Her gaze fell to the clock on the wall.

Ugh. It was ten A.M. No drink.

She'd been at the hospital all night and felt grimy. How could she have thought to ask him here? And now that she had, how did she begin? Did she just jump him in the hallway? Dating a colleague, she'd done that on occasion. Bringing men home? Not ever. She was so out of practice at this sort of thing it wasn't funny. Her thoughts were all over the place, as were her nerves. And now she couldn't stop her mind from going a hundred miles an hour.

Suddenly she felt him step up behind her, his body heat warm against her back as he pushed her hair off her shoulders. "Relax," he said in a deep voice that melted her bones. "We've got all day and you're wound tight. Why don't you go up and shower. I'll still be here when you're through."

How did he know exactly what she needed?

"Okay," she said softly.

"It's going to be so good," he promised, then settled his lips settled against her neck and nibbled on her skin.

She curled her hands around the edge of the table and bent her head forward, giving him better access. He nipped, licked, and soothed with his tongue. Nerves forgotten, she trembled, desire licking at her from the inside out.

"Better go," he said, his hand cupping her behind. "Unless you want to start this right here."

With a pained groan, she stepped aside. "Meet me in my bedroom." She ran for the stairs and headed up to shower.

Luke watched Alexa walk up the few steps in her split-level house, his eyes on her ass. Her body was well hidden in the generous scrubs, yet he found her appealing anyway. With a groan, he shifted his gaze and looked around, not surprised the woman he'd begun to know had an honest to goodness house with a white picket fence. The color scheme was a soft white and light purple, and the whole place radiated warmth. She was everything—and nothing—like he'd expected, and unraveling her layers was as exciting to him as a new playbook each season.

Speaking of plays, giving her time alone had been a strategic move designed to make her more comfortable. Yeah, she'd have time to think too much, but she'd also be able to pull herself together. And he sensed a woman like her needed to feel good about herself in order to get into bed with a man. He had sisters, and though he refused to think about them having sex, he still knew how nice girls thought. Alexa reminded him of his sisters, girls willing to take a walk on the wild side, but who didn't do it often. Good girls.

The kind he'd want to see again.

And now he was getting ahead of himself. So with a last look around the house, which was pretty but was missing personal touches like family photos—which his mom filled both her house and his apartment with—he headed up to find her bedroom.

The sound of running water alerted him to the right room, and he stepped into an ultrafeminine area, draped white curtains, too many frilly pillows, and, of course, purple touches everywhere. He grinned at her consistency. When the shower water shut off, his groin immediately hardened. The next thing he heard was the sounds of her moving around, picking things up, putting them down. He kicked off his shoes and settled onto her bed.

He didn't have to wait long. She stepped out of the bathroom. A scent he didn't recognize but would forever associate with this moment seeped out of the bathroom along with the humid air. One look at her and his breath literally fled. Her hair, which had been pulled back earlier, was now damp and fell around her face in tangled waves. When wet, the long strands appeared darker, her green eyes standing out against her pale skin even more. She wore a deep purple robe—no surprise—but the rich silk material clung to her curves and parted in a seductive vee that showed more than a generous hint of cleavage. It ended mid-thigh, and he realized she had long, toned legs. Sexy legs. And her pretty, makeup-free features gave him his first glimpse of the real woman beyond the seductress from the dance floor and the competent doctor who'd taken over in an emergency.

A woman he wanted beneath him immediately.

He extended his hand and she walked forward, no hesitation in her step, though he definitely saw nerves flickering in her eyes and she paused by the foot of the bed. "C'mere, darlin'."

She eased herself onto the edge of the mattress. "Your Texas accent's stronger when you turn on the charm."

"I'm not turning on anything. I'm already there," he said, hiding nothing in his words. And if she looked at his jeans, she'd have proof. Very hard proof.

Her lips parted on what sounded like an eager sigh. Taking that as his cue, he reached out, hooked an arm around her waist, and rolled her on top of him. She felt good and smelled better. He positioned her over him, her legs draped around his hips, her body above his, ripe and ready for taking. He wrapped his arms around her waist, which had the added bonus of her pressing her warm heat over his aching erection.

Her eyelids fluttered closed and she arched her back,

rocking once, then twice against him, her entire body trembling like she was already on the edge.

Damn.

"Need something?" As he asked, he thrust his hips upward.

She whimpered something he couldn't understand.

"Say it again," he managed, gritting his teeth and forcing himself to hold on to the last shreds of his control, and it wasn't easy. Not since high school had a woman gotten him this hard, this fast, ready to go off while still fully dressed.

She opened her eyes but didn't meet his gaze. "It's been so long for me," she said, her cheeks pinkening at the admission.

He swallowed hard, not wanting to think too deep on that. "Then I'd better make it good for you," he said, before finally kissing that gorgeous mouth.

Her lips touched his and immediately parted, the kiss going from zero to one eighty in seconds. She fit against him perfectly, kissed like a dream, and drank from him like she'd been starving for a taste of him for years.

He held her head in position and took everything she was willing to give. And she gave plenty, her tongue twirling against his, her lower body in motion, and soon they were going at it like kids in the backseat of a car. He slid his hand beneath her robe, expecting a silken barrier. Instead he found heaven. Warm, moist heat greeted him and he slid his finger inside her wet sheath.

She groaned and kissed him harder, her hips grinding in insistent circles against him while he thrust his fingers deeper. She stiffened and cried out, coming apart around him, over him, and completely overwhelming him with the intensity and swiftness of her orgasm.

Her body trembled for a while after, and he held on until she rolled off him, propping herself up on one elbow.

Her gaze was soft on his. "That was amazing."

"Glad you liked it." He made quick work of the robe,

peeling the silk off her shoulders, revealing her body to him for the first time.

Luke might be a jock but he was never at a loss for words. This glimpse of her did it. Pale from lack of sun, her skin was porcelainlike in sheen, gleaming with a mixture of dampness and moisturized beauty. "Perfect," he said, stroking his finger over one dusky nipple.

She moaned and he dipped his head for a taste. Her fragrant scent surrounded him, providing an added sensual high, as if he weren't already feeling enough. Luke's tongue swirled around her nipple, laving over her breast. The tiny bud tightened and a shudder hit her hard. So damned responsive, he could watch her come over and over again without getting bored.

Alexa had never felt so much. A lick, a touch from Luke, and she felt the pull from her nipple to her core, becoming fully aroused all over again.

Wonder overwhelmed her and she arched against him, seeking more. She was a one orgasm a night—or in this case day—kind of woman. Normally she didn't think much of it, but the steady beat between her thighs made her hope that, just maybe, she wasn't finished yet. She liked the thought.

She also appreciated that he'd made her come first, which had the effect of relaxing her and making her more comfortable around him. And completely ready. She wanted more of him, wanted him inside her. But she wasn't selfish. Aware he was doing all the giving, Alexa levered herself up onto her knees.

"Your turn," she said in a husky voice she barely recognized. "Undress."

His golden brown eyes met hers. Without hesitating, he sat up and pulled off his shirt, giving her a glimpse of tanned skin, muscles that showed how hard he worked on his physique, and a sprinkling of light brown hair that covered his sexy chest.

She swallowed hard, her gaze never wandering as he reached for the button on his jeans. He stood, shucked them off, and returned to bed gloriously naked, completely erect, and so very, very male.

He took her breath away and, hesitantly, she reached for him. He grasped her wrist and placed her hand against his chest. His heart beat out a rapid rhythm that she knew was all for her. She added her other hand, soaking up his hard heat.

"It's your turn," she said again, trailing a path downward with her hand.

"I'm not keepin' count. That said, I'm not going to argue, either." He pulled her against him and she got lost in another kiss that shot her ability to think to high heaven.

He surrounded her with his lips, his body, his scent, and when he eased her down to the bed, all she could do was feel his strength—and his impressive erection at the juncture of her thighs. She sighed at the brief contact, flesh against flesh, the tip of him merely grazing her most sensitive parts.

"Condom," she managed.

"Shit." He raised his head. "I was going to buy them in the hospital store but I figured you'd think that was too cocky."

"I have some," she murmured. But not for the reasons he probably thought. "I sometimes guest at the high school, teaching sex ed. Gotta have condoms if you want teenagers to get the safe sex talk."

He tipped his head back and laughed. "Damn, I'd have liked to learn sex ed from someone who looked like you." He chuckled some more before sobering. "Where are they?" he asked.

"My purse." She pointed to the dresser across the room.

He rose and returned in a flash, handing her the bag. She reached inside and handed him a foil packet. He tore it open and sheathed himself by the time she'd tossed her purse onto the floor. Then he was back, his big body over hers, staring into her eyes at the same time he thrust deep, penetrating her hard and fast.

She sucked in a breath and he stilled.

"Breathe, darlin'. And relax." His warm voice reverberated through her.

"It's been a while," she said, repeating herself.

He stroked her cheek with the back of his hand and she responded instantly, her entire body easing, growing accustomed to him.

"That's it," he murmured.

Just the sound of his voice had her relaxing, and soon he was able to move inside her easily. His eyes darkened and he picked up rhythm, gliding in and out as if he were made to be there, arousing her body with every perfect thrust until the sensations took her back to the peak of pleasure. She met his eager thrusts, sought harder, deeper penetration, and he complied.

His hips pumped faster, hitting just the right spot, and just as he groaned and came hard, Alexa joined him, sparks flying as she came—again—harder than she ever had in her entire life.

Luke woke up in an unfamiliar place. He took stock and realized immediately he wasn't drunk, thought back to yesterday and grinned. He was in Alexa Collins's bed in her pretty purple bedroom. Normally, waking up in a one-night stand's house would bother him, but Alexa wasn't his typical hookup. In fact, she didn't feel like a one-nighter at all.

They'd spent the day in her bed, ordered in Chinese for dinner, ate, and had more sex in her living room, followed by another round in her bed, before he fell asleep with her cuddled into him. He woke up this morning feeling pretty darn good. Luke didn't understand it, probably because he'd never experienced anything like it—anyone like *her*. He might not get it, but he knew one thing for sure—he wasn't finished with the good doctor just yet.

He rolled over, only to find the other side of the bed empty.

He patted the sheet and groaned. Not just empty. Cold. She'd obviously been up and gone awhile. Well, wasn't that a kicker. The first time he wanted more from a woman, she obviously didn't care enough to wake him to say good-bye.

He rose from the bed and discovered a note on top of his clothes, which Alexa had folded and placed on her dresser.

Thanks for last night. Emergency at hospital.
Let yourself out. A.

Well damn.

CHAPTER FOUR

"**A**re you sure your father wasn't a hoarder?" Luke asked Sawyer, as they lugged yet more boxes of admitted crap from the basement out to the curb.

Sawyer dropped his box with a groan. "No comment."

The day had dawned sunny and hot for a July morning in New York.

"You know what's in these things?" Luke asked as he wiped the sweat from his forehead with the back of his arm.

"Fishing magazines. Now can we talk about something else? Like where the hell have you been?"

"When did you become my Goddamned mother? I called to tell you I wouldn't be here till later this morning."

"You also said you met someone. Then you walked in here and not a word about it. Serendipity's a small town. Chances are I know her. So tell me more."

Luke had no intention of standing around and gossiping like a girl. Ignoring his buddy, he headed back to the house for another load of trash.

"Was she any good?" Sawyer asked, pushing for answers.

Not that Luke blamed him. In the past, they'd never hesitated to share information if they picked up a hot chick after a game or out of town. Thing was, it'd been a long while since Luke had been on that path. The same for Sawyer. So maybe that explained the other man's interest.

"What's wrong? Dry spell so bad you have to live vicariously through me?" Luke asked as Sawyer caught up to him inside the house.

Sawyer opened the fridge and tossed Luke a vitaminwater, then took one himself and chugged it down before meeting Luke's gaze. "Touchy and secretive about a hookup with a tramp who doesn't mind doing you not twenty-four hours after meeting you."

Luke clenched his teeth and silently counted to ten, reminding himself that this was Sawyer's way of provoking him into replying. Sawyer wasn't Mr. Sensitive, but he wasn't a jackass about women, either.

"Not going there," Luke said.

He wasn't in the right frame of mind to talk about Alexa. Truth be told, he was pissed she'd left him alone in her bed. The least she could have done was wake him before she headed out. Sad thing was, he'd done it to many women in the past, never thinking how shitty it would feel to be on the other end. And maybe some women could handle it. Hell, if certain females had left his bed before he woke up he'd have been one happy man, not that he'd tempted fate by letting them stay. He knew better than to set up expectations. And maybe that's why he felt so crappy now. One-night stand or not, he liked her enough to see her again. Clearly she didn't feel the same and that sucked.

"Hey. I'm serious. Who is it? Obviously she got to you, and if I know her, maybe I can help." Sawyer hopped up on the counter.

Now that Sawyer realized Luke was really bothered, he'd

cut the bullshit. And that was the friend Luke would talk to. "Alexa Collins," Luke finally said.

Sawyer's mouth opened wide. "No shit? The doctor?"

"One and the same."

His friend let out a slow whistle. "You don't mess round. Class all the way. No wonder she got to you."

Luke downed half the bottle of vitaminwater and let it stand as his answer. Sawyer was right. Alexa *had* gotten to him and he didn't know what to do about it. "Do you know her?"

"Her dad's my father's doctor and he spent a lot of time with my old man over the past couple of months. When I was around, I picked up some things."

"Like?" He propped a hip against the counter and waited.

"She's an all work, no play kind of woman. Doesn't seem like you'd have much in common there." Sawyer raised an eyebrow.

"Then you'd be wrong." They'd hit it off. Everything about her interested him. "From her perspective it sounded more like her father had pushed her in the career direction she took. It's expected of her but I'm not sure she's that happy with the end result."

"Her old man says she's taking over as chief of staff at University Hospital when he retires. She's a shoo-in with the board. And to keep herself there, she has no playtime. Hell, man. I don't think she knows how to play."

"Oh, she knows how," Luke muttered.

Sawyer laughed hard at that. "I take it you would know."

"Not goin' there," Luke repeated.

"Yeah, protective and silent. She got to you. So what are you going to do about it?"

Luke tipped his head back and stared at the ceiling. "If I were smart? Nothing."

"Why the hell not?"

"I live in Texas, man. She's from here. I ought to leave it as a one-night stand." The thought made him want to puke. That right there was a sign.

"But you won't."

Luke shook his head. "No, I won't."

"Got a plan?"

Only what had been kicking around in his head since Sawyer told him Alexa was known as an all work, no play kind of woman. Luke shrugged and replied, "I'm gonna teach her how to have fun."

A fter the night she spent with Luke, Alexa bounced through her rounds of patients in the morning and her meetings after, and she was still bouncing on a high when her father caught up with her right before lunch. Her body still tingled in all the best places. Long-neglected places. Places that were now happy and thanking a certain football player for making them come alive.

"Alexa, what's this I hear about you treating children at the youth center downtown?" Alan Collins was a good-looking man, with dark brown hair that had only a hint of silver, and distinguished features. Unfortunately his perpetual scowl and all-business attitude turned many people off and prevented them from seeing some of his finer qualities.

He'd raised her alone and though he'd directed her life, she'd never doubted that he loved her. She'd certainly seen those qualities when she was a child; she just hadn't been the recipient of them recently. Her father had lost his ability to enjoy life, something else he was trying hard to pass onto his daughter.

"Well?" he asked, when she didn't answer right away.

She placed the stack of folders down on the top of the counter at the nurses' station.

She should have known he'd get word of her activities last weekend. "Strep was going around, some of the kids weren't feeling well, and I offered to take a look."

"Did you use hospital supplies to do it?" he asked.

She straightened her shoulders. "No, I did not. I paid for those supplies with my own money, and how dare you suggest otherwise."

"Did it not occur to you that you could treat paying patients with your time?"

A steady pain began to throb in her temple. "Then sick children would go untreated."

"Their parents could take them to their pediatrician and pay there."

Those same parents sent their kids to the youth center so they could work, even on the weekends, not that her father would understand. "I don't have to account to you for my time off." She turned to the nurse behind her, who was blatantly eavesdropping. "Can you please make sure you mark down all the medication changes I made so my patients get their correct doses?" She patted the charts she'd finished with.

"Yes, Dr. Collins." The other woman picked up the folders and walked away.

Alexa turned back to her father. "Now, as I was saying—"

"If you have enough time to treat gratis, perhaps I should give you more hours in the ER."

She clenched her jaw and breathed in deep, deciding to ignore his bluster and call him on his complete lack of emotion when it came to the important things in Alexa's life. "Did you happen to hear who I spent the night before last treating?"

Her father blinked. "I haven't checked the roster of patients."

"What about town news? Did you hear that Cara was attacked?"

"Cara?"

"Hartley. My best friend," she reminded him.

Since Alexa was from the wealthier side of town and Serendipity kids tended to run in cliques, Alexa hadn't grown up hanging in the same circles as Cara, and she was a few years older. But when she'd returned to Serendipity after med school, she and Cara had become reacquainted and grew close. Not that her father paid attention to his daughter's friends.

"An abusive asshole almost strangled her behind Joe's. I spent all night treating and worrying about her, and all you can talk to me about is that I treated sick *children*, as if there's something wrong with that?" Alexa asked, her voice rising.

"Alexa, darlin', glad I found you," a familiar voice said. Luke.

She glanced away from her father only to realize Luke must have come over while they were arguing and she hadn't noticed. She'd been too busy making a spectacle, something that Luke, from the pissed-off look in his eyes, had obviously noticed.

"Am I interrupting something?" he asked.

"Who are you?" her father eyed Luke warily.

Alexa swallowed over the answer that came to mind. *Dad, meet the hot guy I picked up at Joe's, took home for wild sex, then left sleeping in my bed this morning.* She had no doubt what Alan Collins would think about the way his daughter had chosen to spend her day off yesterday. Or the night that followed.

He wouldn't appreciate her choice any more than she'd figured Luke would appreciate the note she'd left him, one she'd deliberately kept brusque enough that he wouldn't think she was a clingy female. She'd tossed in a little white lie about having an emergency so she'd have an excuse for slipping out and avoiding the awkward morning after. Her plan seemed sound, since she hadn't expected to see Luke again. Even if she'd thought about running into him, it wouldn't have been here in the hospital, and definitely not so soon after the best, most explosive night of her life.

"Luke Thompson," he said, extending his hand toward her father.

"Dr. Alan Collins." The two men shook hands. "Which still doesn't answer my question. Who are you and what do you want from my daughter?"

Alexa groaned. She was almost thirty-one years old and her father was acting like he had a right to ask. Jesus. "Dad, Luke's a . . . he's a friend." She caught his sizzling gaze and was happy he accepted that description and kept his mouth shut. "And we're going to talk. In private."

"You have patients to see," her father said, inserting himself into the conversation.

"No, I have lunch to eat."

"Great! Because I came to take you out. I have a picnic basket in the car," Luke said, having no problem interrupting and disagreeing with the other man.

"It's chilly outside!" Alexa whipped her head toward him and looked, really seeing him for the first time. He wore a cream sweater that made his tanned skin even more appealing, and his golden eyes sparkled as if he had some plan in mind.

"My daughter's right. And she doesn't go out for lunch, she eats in the cafeteria so she can be around if she's needed."

Luke scowled at her father. "I know it's cold, darlin'. I'm freezing down to my Texas bones. But if I've learned anything in the last twenty-four hours, it's that you need to loosen up and have fun. So we're getting out of here and having a picnic lunch somewhere private. Then you can come back and work."

Her father stared at Luke as if the man had lost his mind.

Alexa was sure she'd have been doing the same thing—if she wasn't so tempted by both his offer and the man himself. He hadn't been put off by her note. He'd sought her out. Planned something special. And then there was the little fact that the vein in her father's head began throbbing—the one that pulsed harder when she did something he didn't agree with.

The devil on her shoulder wanted to stick it to Alan and do something that Alexa wanted for a change. But more important, the woman inside her that Luke had awakened last night wasn't going quietly back to sleep.

She glanced at Luke, hoping to convey both her gratitude and the desire he'd reignited in one quick look. "Let me get my coat," she said.

His grin—and the fire in his eyes—assured her he definitely shared her underlying desire.

"Alexa, we aren't finished with this conversation," her father said.

She straightened her shoulders. "I'm sure you're not, Dad. But I am. At least for now." But one thing she knew for sure: the argument and his pressure would be waiting for her when she returned.

Now Luke knew what Alexa was up against when it came to her father and her career. The man was a bastard, and though she stood up to him, it was no wonder she had no time for a social life or any kind of fun. Which made his mission all the more worthwhile. Sawyer thought Luke was insane but he'd recommended a place where he could take Alexa for privacy. He agreed that The Family Restaurant was the best place for him to pick up sandwiches and chips. Luke had a plan. He was in town for a couple of days, and he intended to make good use of them with Alexa.

He drove her out to the lake at the far edge of Serendipity. He parked the car and led her to the cabin on the lake that Sawyer's father owned. The Rhodes men used the place for summer fishing but Sawyer assured him all he had to do was turn on the heat and the boiler would kick in.

Alexa had been silent on the drive and he had no doubt she was angsting over leaving work, the argument with her father, and now being alone with him. He hopped out and headed to her side in time to help her out of the high truck.

"Thank you." She glanced over her shoulder at the rustic cabin behind them. "Whose place is this?"

"Sawyer and his dad's." Luke clasped her hand and led her toward the door. "Let's get inside, I'll turn the heat up and go back out for the food."

"You really thought this through," she murmured as he toyed with the thermostat and, thankfully, the loud rumbling noise indicated they were in business.

"You left me with plenty of time to do it," he said, referring to the time after she'd abandoned him in bed.

"I had an emergency," she said, rubbing her hands together, but not meeting his gaze.

"Did that emergency involve getting the hell out before you had to face me?" He wanted to clear the air before the lie went any further. Luke was a light sleeper, and if her phone, beeper, cell, or whatever had gone off, he'd have heard it. If she was scheduled to be at work, she'd have just said that. She hadn't. Besides, Luke had used deception often enough in similar situations to recognize it.

He wanted to think *they* were different than any old one-night stand, and right here, right now, he intended to find out if he was right.

CHAPTER FIVE

Luke called her on her deception and Alexa reared back in shock. No man had ever questioned her motives or truthfulness before, not in a relationship and not on the job. In fact, she was so used to people respecting her word—well, everyone except her father, and because he respected nobody's word, he didn't count—she couldn't believe this man had seen through her and called her on the lie.

It humbled her.

It embarrassed her.

She forced herself to face him. "You may be a pro at one-night stands, but I'm not. I thought it would be easier on both of us if I just left."

He blinked, obviously startled that she'd opted for the truth without trying to bluster through.

She taught her interns that if they made a mistake, it was better to own up to it and face the consequences. She could do no less in her personal life.

His eyes darkened. "I may have been a pro at it once, but it's been a long time since I pulled a stunt like that."

It was her turn to blink. "Really?"

He grinned. "Yep. You're not the end of a long line, darlin'. Not by a long shot."

"At least not lately."

He laughed. "Exactly."

She wondered why not and decided not to ask. "Yet despite my leaving, you came after me." She bit down on her lower lip, pondering that fact.

He'd done a lot more than just come to talk, too, she thought, taking in the bags filled with food on the counter and the cabin he'd appropriated the keys for.

"You're an eye-opener," he said, answering her unspoken question. "I've been on the doing end, never on the receiving end of waking up alone, and I didn't like what I learned."

She winced. "I'm sorry."

"Don't be. I'm a man who likes to learn a good lesson. And if I thought you left 'cuz you weren't interested, I wouldn't be here now."

She couldn't stop the smile his words inspired. "So you think I'm interested."

A dimple formed in one cheek. "Don't think it. I know it."

"Cocky." She liked the hint of ego in him and figured it fit his sports persona. Oddly, the display of conceit made him even more appealing.

Not that she'd let him know it so easily.

She folded her arms across her chest, and narrowed her gaze. "Whatever gave you the impression that I'm still interested?" she asked.

"I could either count the orgasms you had or point out the pink flush in your cheeks when I showed up to ask you out today. Your choice."

She just couldn't bring herself to be offended and burst out laughing instead. "Okay fine. You win. So what's in the bags?" She swept her arm out toward the packages he'd brought in from the car.

"Don't change the subject. I want to hear you say it." He

stepped forward and she inched away, the dance continuing until her back hit the wall.

"Say what?" she managed, this despite the fact that he loomed over her, a large, imposing, sexy male who smelled as good as he looked. At his nearness, her breath hitched and memories of him surrounding her in other ways rushed through her.

"I need to hear you say you're still tempted. By me," he said, his mouth hovering over hers.

She caught the hint of mint on his breath and sighed into him. He had her and he knew it. "I'm tempted," she murmured.

A pleased gleam flickered in his gaze at the admission, but he still didn't move, studying her instead of kissing her senseless like she wanted. Needed. Craved.

"I only have an hour or so for lunch," she reminded him.

He muttered a soft curse and sealed his lips over hers. He swirled his tongue with hers in a way that had her body heating, which was saying something since her jacket already had her roasting. And she kissed him back for all she was worth, wrapping her arms around his neck and getting lost in the moment.

Until he broke their connection with a harsh groan.

"What? Why?" she asked, disappointed and bereft.

"Because you only have an hour or so and you need to eat." He stepped back, shrugged off his jacket, and began to unpack the bags. "Is there any chance I can convince you to play hooky this afternoon?"

She looked into his hopeful gaze, and for the first time in her adult life, the thought of doing something other than work was actually tempting. "I wish I could, but I have a meeting with the parents of one of my younger patients." Disappointment filled her and she wished her afternoon consisted of something cancelable.

"But you considered it." He stared at her for a beat, his expression . . . pleased. Then he turned and began to unpack food, pulling out plastic-wrapped sandwiches on plastic plates, complete with chips. Real silverware came next, followed by two large thermoses.

"What's in those?" she asked.

"Hot chocolate."

"Oh, yum, my favorite!"

"I know."

She wrinkled her nose. "How?"

"I made friends with Gina Donovan, pumped her for your favorite orders and asked her to pack everything up for me." He shrugged and began to peel the wrapping off the food.

She ought to help, but remained frozen in place, stunned by the lengths to which he'd gone to make this picnic, as he'd called it, special. For her.

No one had ever considered her favorite foods, or gone out of his way to make her feel important. She hadn't had her mom to do it. She barely remembered her mother, and her father's mother, who'd moved in to help him out, had about as much of a soft streak as he did. Forget the men in her life; even the ones she'd dated on occasion knew she didn't have time or wasn't giving them one hundred percent, and so they didn't bother with an attempt to win her heart anyway.

In an insanely short time, Luke Thompson had made her feel cared for and treasured. And she didn't know what to do with that.

"Luke?" She softly called his name.

He turned from his task. "What's up?"

She swallowed over the lump in her throat, the words escaping before she could think them through or stop them. "I can't play hooky this afternoon, but can I have a rain check for tomorrow?"

When Alexa asked him for a rain check, elation had soared through Luke as strong as after any touchdown he'd scored. He knew how difficult it must have been for her to convince herself that she could take time off from work. That she'd do it to be with him, well, it blew his mind.

"You've got yourself a date," he'd promised her.

Afterward, they'd enjoyed their lunch at the cabin, cleaned up, and made out a little bit. He grinned at the memory of them sitting on the old, beat-up couch, kissing and groping. He'd ended up aroused to the point of pain. She'd ended up grumpy and annoyed, but he'd left her hanging, too, reminding her that good things come to those who wait.

Then he'd driven her back to the hospital, walked her to the big sliding doors at the entrance, kissed her in front of he didn't care who, and sent her back inside with a goofy grin on her face. Not that he'd told her that. He figured Dr. Alexa Collins wouldn't appreciate knowing she'd returned to work well kissed.

Laughing, he'd driven back to Sawyer's and helped his buddy, who'd rented a Dumpster to get rid of the garbage his father had accumulated. That night, he and Sawyer had shared a couple of beers and watched a movie, and now, the next morning, Luke was implementing the next phase of teaching Alexa how to have fun.

"Where are we going?" she asked as he helped her into his truck.

He glanced at her, discovering yet another facet to her personality. She looked like a happy young woman, not a sexy siren, an uptight doctor, or even the tense daughter he'd seen yesterday. Today she had on a pair of jeans with boots over them and a light sweater, her long hair pulled into a ponytail. She was, in a word, breathtaking.

"It's a surprise," he said, controlling his emotions.

She clapped her hands together in excitement, and again he experienced a wave of passion so strong it nearly drowned him. He'd given her that rosy flush in her cheeks from just these plans alone.

"Another picnic?" she asked.

"Among other things," he said, deliberately vague and

teasing. It wouldn't do to reveal his intentions. Part of having fun involved spontaneity, something else he sensed she hadn't had much of in her well-organized, routine life.

"How about a hint?" She curled her legs under her and turned toward him as he pulled out of her driveway.

He laughed. "How about not?"

Her phone rang and she pulled it out of her pocket, glanced down, and hit send. The next ten minutes consisted of her talking to someone at the hospital about medications and various patients.

He clenched his jaw and tried not to let his annoyance get the better of him. He respected her job. Hell, who wouldn't? But they'd planned for this. He didn't have a huge temper but he was finding he was impatient when it came to anyone or anything cutting into his limited time with Alexa. He had to head home tomorrow for his niece's birthday party on Saturday. He had only this limited time with a woman he wanted way more from—he knew it already.

Most people would call him crazy. Most, but not his mother, who'd met his father and called it love at first sight. He'd romanced her, she'd fallen hard, they married quickly and stayed together happily. Besides, it wasn't like he was a child. His sisters were younger than him and they were all married with kids. He'd been through dating and living enough to know Alexa was the one he wanted to test some serious waters with.

How they would do that, with her living in New York and him in Texas, he had no idea. But for now, every minute counted.

He stopped the car down the street from his ultimate destination, not wanting to ruin the surprise, and parked.

By the time Luke climbed out of the truck, Alexa waited by the trunk for him to open it up and reveal his surprise. She hopped up and down, excitement filling her, wondering what he had planned for them today.

"I can't imagine what you're like at Christmas," Luke said, chuckling.

"Christmas was never like this," she spoke, more to herself than to him.

He turned, one hand propped on the trunk door, eyeing her with a serious look on his face. "Talk."

She sighed, knowing that, once again, she'd be revealing something more about herself and, oddly enough, wanting to share with him. "Dad didn't have time for a tree, his mother didn't care, hence . . . no tree."

Luke stiffened. "No tree." He sounded appalled, his expression disgusted.

"Okay, now you know. I come from a family of Scrooges." She ducked her head and avoided his gaze. "So if the bloom's off this rose, you can take me back home now," she said, wanting to give him an out.

"Hey." He touched her arm. "I wouldn't take you home just because you never had a Christmas tree! What kind of jerk do you think I am?"

She managed a laugh. "I was more worried about what you thought of me. But I can assure you that *I* have a Christmas tree. Even if I'm not home much to enjoy it, I make sure I have one." She was rambling from embarrassment and changed the subject. "So what's in the trunk?" she asked too brightly.

He stared at her for an uncomfortable minute. It was probably just a second or two but it felt like a full sixty seconds. "Something else I'm now thinking you didn't get to experience." He reached into the trunk and pulled out a pair of ice skates.

Brand-new, shiny white skates with purple laces.

"Oh my God." She didn't know what got to her more, the gesture or the purple laces. "My favorite color." The lump in her throat grew bigger, her awareness of just how deep this man went dawning on her.

He just laughed. "Can you skate?" he asked.

"I used to go with a friend when I was younger. Until my

dad found out and made me stop because it was too dangerous. *What happens if a blade cuts your hand? How will you
ever operate? Or be a doctor?*" she said in a perfect imita-
tion of her parent.

"How old were you?" Luke asked, his voice gentle.

A bigger lump swelled in her throat. She swallowed
hard. "Fourteen."

"Son of a bitch." He slammed a hand against the truck.
"You should have been out having fun with your friends,
not worrying about a future I'm sure you didn't even think
you wanted."

Her eyes misted. "Did you know what you wanted at
that age?"

"Yeah."

"You did?" she asked.

A grin took hold and a wicked gleam lit his gaze. "Yep.
I wanted to get my hands up Lucy Granders's shirt."

She chuckled, softly at first, then harder. "You are too
much!"

"I'm also deadly serious. I played, but wasn't thinking
about pro football when I was fourteen. And you shouldn't
have had to think about medicine." He held her hands in his
larger ones. "Now, do you want to go ice-skating?"

"Will you hold on to me until I get the hang of it?"

His eyes darkened. "Oh yeah, darlin'. I'll hold on to you."

She rolled her eyes at him. "You're still that fourteen-
year-old boy at heart, aren't you?"

"God, I hope so."

She grasped his shoulders and pulled him close. "Me,
too," she said, and settled her lips on his.

Sparks ignited immediately. She curled her fingers into
his jacket and pressed herself into him. She might have
started the kiss but his low groan gave her fair warning he'd
be taking over. And he did. His tongue delved deep into her
mouth, possessing her, marking her in a way she'd never

forget. She loved his taste, the hint of mint and the dark flavor that was all Luke. Add in the sweet part of him and the impossible was happening.

She was falling hard for this man. Too bad all they had was a few days of time. Because when all was said and done, nothing in her life had changed, her time for a relationship was zero, and Luke Thompson was a good man who lived in the state of Texas.

CHAPTER SIX

Luke didn't have to guess what Alexa wanted or how she was feeling. She wore her heart on her sleeve, her feelings on her face. And when she reached for him, he knew he was a goner. If he let the kiss go on, they'd end up on the ground, not on the ice. As much as he wanted her, he had plans for her first.

With more willpower than he thought he had, he broke the kiss. "Skating, darlin'."

Eyes glazed, she looked up at him and nodded. "Skating."

"You gonna be steady out there?" he asked, his hands on her forearms, keeping her upright.

"No, but you already said you'd hold on to me." She grinned and stepped back. "Do I get to try on my skates now?"

He nodded and walked with her to the ice rink, already knowing that they fit. This time he'd had to go to the source, her best friend, Cara Hartley, a Serendipity police officer who Luke found at her home. And it hadn't been easy to get her address. When he got there, she looked him up and down, placed her hands on her hips, and divulged Alexa's shoe size. "I have a gun and I know how to use it," she then said. "Break her heart and you'll answer to me."

"Message received," he told her. "I like how you two look out for each other." He inclined his head. "Well done. And glad to see you're feelin' better."

The big bad cop's expression softened. "Thanks."

"Also glad your man came around," Luke said, pushing his luck a little further.

Her eyes narrowed.

"And now I'm getting out while the getting's good." With a wink, he'd taken off, heading next to the small store located in the skating rink in the next town over.

Sawyer joined him for the ride, laughing all the way there—and back. Luke ignored him, figuring he'd have some chuckles of his own when the other man found his woman.

Now, Luke turned back to *his* female and watched her lacing up the skates.

"They fit!" she exclaimed, her excitement like that of his niece's on Christmas.

"But they're new, so you'll probably end up with blisters," he warned her. "We'll take it easy." He stood and held out a hand, which she readily grabbed.

A few minutes later, they were on the ice. He wished he could say she was a natural. She wasn't. But what she lacked in skill, she more than made up for in both enthusiasm and a willingness to keep getting back up—no matter how many spills she took. And unfortunately for her, she took plenty. Her ass was going to be sore tomorrow, which meant he'd have to give her some TLC today.

No big chore.

On what felt to Luke like her hundredth tumble, he caught her before her butt hit the ice. "And we're all finished for today," he said.

"I can go more," she said through chattering teeth.

He wrapped his arm around her waist and steered them

toward the edge of the rink. "If you won't admit to freezing your ass off, I will. I'm cold and I need your body heat to warm me up."

Her eyes darkened, but she didn't give up that easily. "One more circle around the rink."

At that moment, Luke cursed her father for instilling that need to prove herself in his daughter. "No. You're freezing and your butt cheeks hurt like hell, but I'll bet you've never given up on anything in your life. If I don't call it a day, we'll be out here while you try to prove something to me you don't have to prove. This was supposed to be fun, remember?"

She blushed. "I . . . yeah, I remember. And I did have fun!" From the sparkle in her eyes, he couldn't help but believe her.

"Me, too. Now just a short drive away, we have a cabin all to ourselves where the heat's pumping and the bed's warm. So you tell me, do you want to keep on bruising your pretty behind, or let me ease those aches and pains in a way that I promise you'll like?" His own blood pumped faster at the notion. He raised an eyebrow and waited for her to decide.

"Well, when you put it that way . . ." She grasped his hand. "Last one to the truck is a rotten egg." She took off, but Luke wasn't about to let her fall again, so he grabbed her around the waist and carried her off the ice, listening to her shrieks of *put me down* the entire way.

Alexa had a blast on the ice. Sure, she sucked at skating. Who knew that it wasn't like riding a bike, easy to pick up again? Not that her father encouraged that either—*Concussions are dangerous, Alexa*. But Luke never lost patience, he just held out a hand, helped her back onto her feet, and off they went again, him holding her tight in his strong arms until she was ready to try going solo again. She inevitably fell onto her butt again.

By the end, her feet hurt like hell, she probably had those blisters he'd mentioned, and the cold was setting in, and he'd still had to drag her off the ice. "Luke?" she asked, as he drove them from the rink to the cabin.

"Yeah?"

"I loved every minute," she said, wanting him to know exactly what kind of gift he'd given her.

"Yeah?" A smile pulled at his lips.

"Absolutely."

He parked in front of the cabin and cut the engine, got out, and met her on the passenger side, opening her door.

Before she could hop out, he braced a hand on the roof over her head. "You know you didn't need to prove anything to me. I didn't care if you could skate or not. I just wanted you to enjoy the day." His serious gaze told her he was worried she'd pushed herself too hard.

"I did. Every last minute. Even when I fell on my ass," she said with a grin.

He scowled at her comment. "You won't be feeling so generous about that tomorrow."

She smoothed the frown lines on either side of his luscious mouth with her fingers. "I will if you take care of me like you promised," she said, her voice deep and husky.

Next thing she knew, she was back in his arms as he carried her to the front door. He smelled delicious, a combination of outdoors and sexy man, and she tangled her fingers in his hair as he somehow worked the key, never putting her down as he let them in.

"What'd you have to promise Sawyer to get this cabin again?" she asked as she kicked off her shoes and let them fall to the floor.

He laughed, the deep sound rumbling through her. "Just my firstborn." On his kidding words, his gaze snared hers and her breath caught at the intensity she saw there.

Luke and kids. The idea, once planted, no matter how lightly, buzzed around her brain. Alexa loved kids, worked with them when she could, because as patients, they were far more fun than cranky adults. Hence her youth center hours and free medical care for them. She was beginning to think she'd never have a family of her own. With one joking comment, this man caused a yearning deep in her soul.

"Alexa? Lex?" Luke asked. "What's wrong?" He laid her down on the bed and eased next to her.

She blinked and deliberately cleared her mind. "Not a single thing," she assured him.

Fanciful thoughts and feelings about a man she'd known a few days were ridiculous. What he was giving her in this precious time, the chance to experience *life* and to live all she'd been missing, was priceless. When he was gone, she knew she'd have choices to make about how she wanted to go forward from here.

But right now, she had him.

And just like he taught her, she intended to live in the here and now. So she unzipped her jacket, shrugged it off, and tossed it to the floor, then reached for his zipper and did the same to his.

He wore a fitted long sleeve thermal in a chocolate brown that brought out the gold in his eyes and accentuated the muscles in his chest and arms. With her mouth watering, she tugged at the bottom of the shirt, pulling it out of his jeans and working it up and over his head. With a targeted toss, the shirt hit his jacket on the floor.

"Hey, I thought I was going to take care of you?"

If that's what the man wanted, that's what he'd get, Alexa thought. "Go for it," she told him. "I'm all yours."

With a low growl from deep in his throat, he raised himself up on one knee and began divesting her of her clothes, piece by piece. Her jeans, damp from her many falls on the ice, took some effort, but finally he'd bared her to him, except for her lacy underwear and matching bra.

"You take my breath away, darlin'."

Her breath caught and her throat swelled. "You do the

same to me. But more than that, you make me feel good. Special. I'll never forget that." She glanced away, embarrassed that she was revealing so much, yet unable to hold back the words.

"You *are* special."

Not according to her father. *Surgeons like you are a dime a dozen, Alexa. Try harder. Do better. Give more of yourself or you'll never stand out.* God, she was so sick of his words tormenting her. She'd taken the full day off, covered her patients with a reliable doctor, and deliberately not checked in with her service or looked at her phone. Yet the pressure remained, a subtle heaviness in her chest and that damned voice in her head.

"Lex," Luke said in a concerned tone.

"I'm here." She smiled into his warm eyes, liking how he shortened her name. It was special.

"You weren't."

"I am now," she said, with what she hoped was a seductive smile. She had no desire to get into where her mind had wandered. Not when she had such a sexy specimen in front of her.

But she was coming to know Luke, and if she didn't distract him, he'd push her for answers and kill the mood. She refused to let that happen. She reached for the front hook of her bra and released the clasp, then slowly lowered the straps over her shoulders and down her arms. The cups eased down, one catching on her nipple, and Luke grinned at the sight.

"Let me help you with that." He bent his head and, using his teeth, he gently pried the material away from her breast.

The material fell away and Luke's mouth quickly replaced it. One lap of his tongue and Alexa's head fell back against the pillows, the sensations so strong and startling, she let out a moan. He licked again, nipped harder, and she began to tremble.

* * *

Luke had never had a woman be so open and genuinely responsive. There was no pretense, no artifice, everything she felt, she showed, and knowing he could take her so high so fast gave him no small amount of satisfaction. She'd been starved, not just for sex but for affection, and he wanted to give her everything he could in the time he had.

While he kept up the friction on her breast with one hand, he used the other to slide her panties off her body. He cupped her mound, feeling the heat emanating from her, and stifled a groan as his cock let him know exactly how much he liked what he was feeling.

"Luke." She sighed his name, parting her legs. He took advantage, slipping his finger into her slick opening.

Her hips jerked, sucking his digit in deeper. He grit his teeth and slid his thumb over the tiny knot of nerves, rewarded when she arched her back, her head thrashing from side to side.

"Beautiful," he muttered, watching the flush on her cheeks as she lost every inhibition she possessed.

Her body shook, her lashes fluttered up and her eyes locked on his. "I need—"

"I know what you need." But she wasn't coming alone or without him inside her. He rose and quickly shed the rest of his clothes, pausing only to grab a condom from his pocket before returning.

Taking him by surprise, she plucked the packet out of his hand, ripped it open, and managed to roll the latex over his straining erection.

She grinned at the results. "Now hurry."

He swung a leg over her and positioned himself at her entrance. She whimpered, the sound inflaming his need, and he braced a hand above her shoulder, looking into her beautiful eyes as he thrust deep. Thrust home.

Her eyes widened, then rolled back slightly before she managed to focus on him once more. "Oh, God."

"That's not God, darlin'. That's you. And me." And damn they were hot and wet.

He pulled out, slid back, the slick sounds of sex surrounding them along with Alexa's whispered pleas of *harder*, *faster*, and *oh, God*, nearly making him come too soon. He held on, gritting his teeth as she bent her knees, taking him deeper. Then, without warning, her body gripped his, clamping on tight as she came.

Her orgasm released his tenuous hold and restraint. He pumped into her, feeling more than he ever had, knowing in his gut this was so much more than sex, and he accepted it and reveled in it as he came.

It took a while for them to catch their breath, and finally Luke rolled off her. "You okay?" he asked.

She met his gaze, her eyes glazed and dreamy. "Never better."

"Glad to hear it." He kissed her nose, then pulled himself up and headed for the bathroom.

He returned to find her staring at the ceiling, a satisfied smile on her face and a healthy, happy glow on her cheeks. One he'd put there, Luke thought, grinning, too.

"Roll," he said to her.

"Hmm?"

"Roll over." He lightly patted her hip.

She groaned but turned over as he asked. He glanced at her bare bottom, white smooth skin with hints of pink and more than a few scrapes. He frowned at the sight. "Hurt?" he asked, rubbing his hand over first one cheek then the other.

"A little sore," she admitted, her words muffled in the pillow.

"Sorry, sugar. I never meant to cause you pain." He pressed a kiss to her cheek and she giggled.

"I'll live," she assured him.

"I hope so." He massaged her skin and she sighed in contentment.

"When do you leave?" she asked, the question muffled. She didn't peek out from where she'd buried her head in her arms.

The question was long overdue. "I have to be home for my niece's birthday party on Saturday." He pulled in a deep breath. "So my flight's tomorrow."

Silence surrounded them, the mood broken as reality intruded.

"You'd really like my nieces," he heard himself say. "Cute little things. Girly girls, with bows in their hair and cowboy boots on their feet." He continued to speak, unsure of how to bring them back to before, when it was just Luke and Alexa in the cabin. Not Luke from Texas and Alexa from New York.

He heard what sounded like a hiccup. Or her choking back tears.

Shit. Shit. Shit.

"Take the weekend and come with me to Texas," he said.

She popped up in bed and flipped over. Her eyes were red as they zeroed in on him. "Say that again?" she asked.

The suggestion came out unexpectedly but the sentiment was heartfelt, he realized. "Come to Texas. Meet my family. You'll have fun and they'll love you."

Her eyes opened wide. "But . . . work. The hospital. My patients." Her father. That last one went unsaid.

"Will all be here when you get back." He didn't know what he hoped for out of the request. He only knew he wasn't ready to be apart from her.

The rest he'd figure out.

If she said yes.

CHAPTER SEVEN

Alexa sat up in bed, the sheets pulled up over her breasts as she stared at Luke. *Come to Texas*, he'd said, and boy was she tempted. She'd never wanted to chuck the responsibilities in her life and take off for the weekend, but she did now.

Unfortunately, the reliable, dependable side of her spoke louder in her head and took over. "I can't just pick up and go when the whim strikes me." She winced, knowing she sounded more like her father than herself.

And the hurt on Luke's face confirmed it.

"Luke—"

"I get it. You have to work." He'd been sitting on the edge of the mattress and now he reached down and grabbed his pants off the floor.

She wasn't ready for their time together to end, especially not like this. "No, you don't get it. I want to go with you. I really do."

He paused in the middle of pulling on his jeans and glanced over his shoulder. "It's not as hard as it sounds. I'm guessing you have plenty of vacation time built up, and since you managed today, I figure you also have people to cover for you. Hell, knowing you, half the hospital probably owes you a favor."

Her cheeks burned because he was right and he'd figured her out in a very short time. "I want to go," she repeated, needing him to hear her and believe. "But I can't leave without giving any notice."

He secured the button on his jeans before answering. "Lex, I'm not gonna lie to you. These past few days weren't just unexpected, they were fucking amazing," he said, letting loose with his language for the first time.

She grinned but said nothing, mainly because, a) it didn't bother her, and, b) she agreed. Their time together had been exactly that.

He hooked his fingers in the loop of his jeans, his chest bare, his gaze level on hers. "Nobody respects discipline and routine more than me. I wouldn't be where I am in my career if I didn't dedicate myself one hundred and ten percent during the season and stick to some kind of schedule on the off-season. And if I thought you were saying you couldn't come because you wanted to work or it would affect your career, I'd never push. But that isn't it, is it?"

With every word he spoke, her defenses rose higher. She stiffened her shoulders until her neck hurt, and she glared at him, but he clearly wasn't finished. "Tell me what you think it is," she said, folding her arms across her chest, protecting herself from whatever he would say next.

Which was ironic since, five minutes ago, she wouldn't have thought she'd have to protect herself from this man—ever.

"You don't want to tell your father you're taking more time off. You don't want to disappoint the old man or lose the legacy he's so carefully prepared for you. But, darlin', I'm asking you straight out to be sure that's the future *you* yourself want."

Her mouth ran dry. As quickly as her anger had grown

at his words, it deflated with his further insight. She wasn't sure about her life and he knew it. And he didn't want to hurt her; he wanted her to be happy.

His gaze softened. "If I could stay longer and be with you, I'd do it. Give up a meeting or two, miss a practice if I thought I could work it out. But the one thing I won't miss in life is a family event because those happen only once. I can't get back a missed birthday or the look in my niece's eyes when she sees that power-charged Barbie car I bought for her that'll be waiting in the driveway."

Oh my God. He was killing her. Alexa didn't even know the little girl he spoke of, but she suddenly had a whole new vision of Luke Thompson, and it took her breath away. His words sliced deep because how many of her birthdays had her own father missed because of work, while Luke wouldn't skip his sister's daughter's special day?

She'd thought this man was something special. Something real. Now she knew for sure.

Her cell phone suddenly rang inside her purse, the ringtone the one she'd programmed for her father. She cringed at the interruption.

Luke glared at her bag. "That him?" he asked.

Alexa nodded. Unable to help herself, she reached for the purse and pulled out the ringing phone. At least half a dozen missed calls, all from her father. "I didn't tell him I was taking off today." She glanced at Luke but found no understanding in his gaze.

"How long are you gonna let him run your life?" he asked.

"He doesn't—"

Luke pinned her with a knowing gaze. "Give me more credit than that. He does."

The cell stopped it's incessant, annoying ring, and another missed call and voice mail notification popped up on the screen. Disgusted, she threw the phone onto the bed.

"Get dressed," he said, more gently than she'd have

expected. "I'll toss the sheets into the washer. Sawyer said there's someone who comes in and does laundry, so she'll finish up what I start."

Nodding, she rose, feeling self-conscious that she was naked and he wasn't. In silence, she looked for the clothes she'd shed and realized her jeans were still damp. She pulled on her underwear and shirt, her back to him.

"Do I have time to dry these for a little while before I put them back on?" She turned to find him right there, in her personal space, and she sucked in a shallow breath.

He braced his hands on her forearms, his thumbs rubbing lazy circles over her shirt. "I don't want to end this with an argument." He met her gaze, those warm eyes communicating real regret.

Her stomach twisted nervously. "Me neither." She didn't want to end it at all, but he'd made the gesture and she'd turned him down.

Alexa knew she had a lot to process, but she couldn't upend her life in a heartbeat. She'd always been a thinker, someone who processed first and acted later. During this time with Luke, she'd enjoyed spontaneity, but a lifetime's worth of habit wouldn't be broken quickly.

"Give me your jeans. I'll toss 'em in for a bit," he said.

"Thanks." She handed him the damp denim, then helped him strip the linen off the bed and pillows.

They worked in somewhat comfortable silence, but the atmosphere between them had changed. No longer sexually charged or light and playful, a pall had fallen over them, because they both knew they'd reached the end of *this*.

Whatever this was.

And Luke was right. It had been fucking spectacular.

Luke drove Alexa home. He walked her to her front door, wrapped his arms around her, and kissed her. She knew it was good-bye, even if he didn't say the words. Even if he'd programmed his phone number into her cell phone, she sensed the finality in the kiss.

Alexa entered her house, wanting nothing more than to be alone. She didn't return her father's calls. He could damn well wait until she returned to work on Friday before she dealt with his anger. Instead she gave herself time to grieve. As insane as it sounded, that's what she did. She grieved for a relationship she'd walked away from before it began. For a man who'd given her more in three days than anyone else had given her in a lifetime. And she grieved for the lonely years she'd spent growing up and the frustrating time she'd spent trying to please a man who couldn't be satisfied.

Suffice it to say, Alexa held a pity party complete with ice cream and phone calls to her best friend. By the time she fell into a fitful sleep, she did so with the knowledge that this time tomorrow, Luke would be gone.

And she had some harsh decisions and choices to make about herself, her life, and her future.

A lexa dressed in her navy power suit, the outfit she saved for board meetings and arguments about changing the status quo with the so-called powers that be. The same board headed by her father. She slipped on a pair of high heels, not her usual choice for the hospital, but one that made her feel in control. Like she could handle anyone and anything— the way she felt when she was around Luke.

Makeup in place, she climbed into her car and drove to University Hospital, then parked and entered the building that had been home since she was a little girl. She listened to the click of her heels as she made her way down the halls to her father's office, and realized there was a lot wrong with that bit of truth. But truth it was, and she was finally ready to confront it—along with the man who'd created her reality.

She knocked on her father's office door.

"Come in!"

She poked her head in. "Dad? I need a word."

"I'm busy," he said, not looking up from his paperwork. The one thing she'd always dreaded about the chief of staff job was the massive amounts of paperwork and the resulting lack of interaction with the patients.

She took a deep breath and stepped inside anyway. "I'd appreciate it if you made the time, it's important." She shut the door behind her, not planning on leaving until she'd had her say.

With a resigned sigh, he put his pen down and gestured to the chair in front of his desk.

She opted to remain standing, needing all the leverage and power she could muster.

"Well? I don't have all day."

She clenched and unclenched her fists. "Are you happy?" she asked her father.

He blinked, then looked at her with a frown creasing his forehead. "Excuse me?"

She'd thought long and hard about how to approach him, what she wanted to say. This was rehearsed and she knew it. "I asked if you're happy. In your life? Your job?"

"Alexa, I'm a busy man. I don't have time for philosophi-cal conversations."

"Well, I'll say it again. I'd appreciate it if you made the time. This is important to me."

Hands on his desk, he met her gaze. "Fine. I don't think about happiness."

Her heart seized at the admission she'd expected. What she hadn't anticipated was how much the knowledge hurt. "Did you ever? Think about it, I mean." To hell with power. She lowered herself into the chair, needing support. "When you were younger? When you met Mom? When you fell in love?"

That last question was a stretch. Alexa had no idea if her parents had been in love. Or not. She didn't remember them interacting and her father never spoke about it.

His scowl deepened. "What's going on with you? Are you ill?"

She drew a deep breath. "I'm taking a leave of absence." She said the words slowly and deliberately, not rushing through them the way she was tempted to do.

The only way he'd take her seriously was if she sounded firm, didn't back down, and stood her ground. All things Alan Collins respected. Unless it involved going against his directives or wishes.

"Okay, now I know you're sick. What the hell do you mean, you're taking a leave?" He leaned forward in his seat, talking at her like she was just an employee, not his only child.

"In the last couple of days, I've had time to think about what I want out of life and—" She pulled in a deep breath. "This isn't it. I don't want to be a paper pusher for this hospital. I don't want to follow in your footsteps, I want to create my own path."

"You want to create your own path," he mimicked her. "Don't tell me. This has to do with that football player," he said in disgust.

"You know he plays football?" She said the first thing that came to mind.

"The nurses couldn't stop whispering about it. I thought you'd be above that sort of thing. At the very least I thought you'd get that little rebellion out of your system and return to work fully focused."

She blew into her hands in an attempt to calm down. "Well, you thought wrong. And that little rebellion you mentioned? It's been a long time in coming. These past few days may have shown me what it's like to really live and enjoy life and be happy, but the discontent began long before and has been brewing for years."

"Alexa, not many people get the opportunities you've had," her father said, too slowly and patiently, as if he were talking to a misbehaving child. "Not many people have the avenues available to them that you do."

She held up a hand. "Stop right there. I'm grateful for each and every one, but did you ever think that maybe I don't want the same things you did?"

"And what is it you think you want?"

There it was again, that patronizing tone. She knew then he'd never get it, never understand. Her stomach hurt because he was her father, but he wasn't her daddy. He never had been. "I know that I want to enjoy my job. My days. I'm not naive. Life isn't always easy or fun, but I want to wake up in the morning knowing that, at the very least, I'm doing something of my choosing. Not yours."

His hands bunched in frustration, his knuckles turning white. "That's not gratitude; that's disrespect."

She cocked her head to the side. "I beg to differ. I did everything you ever asked or wanted. I tried things your way. Now I'm going to try my own."

His face turned red, his cheeks flushed, and anger vibrated from him. "I raised you."

"Which is what you do when you have children. What you don't do is direct and manipulate them into being what you want, envision, or need. I love you, Dad. But I have to live my own life."

"Are your giving up medicine?" he asked.

She shook her head. "I just want the time to figure out what kind of medicine I want to be in." She'd wondered if she should add this, and then decided she'd come so far, might as well go all the way. "I also need to figure out where I want to practice it." Hospital, private practice, more pro bono work at the youth center. Alexa didn't know but she wanted to figure it out.

He cleared his throat. "You might want to reconsider. The world keeps moving. In other words, your job may not be here when you want to come back."

Her own father wouldn't hold her position for her. She hadn't anticipated that, but she managed to hide the pain of his betrayal. "I'll take that chance," she said.

"Your choice. Now, if you're finished, I have work to do." Without meeting her gaze, he picked up his pen and looked back down at his papers. If not for the slight tremor shaking his hand, Alexa would think him completely unaffected.

"One more question," she said softly.

Maybe it was her tone of voice but he glanced up. "What is it?"

"What did we do for my fifth birthday party?"

His gaze narrowed once more. "I don't remember."

"Tenth?" she asked.

He clenched his jaw. "Same answer."

Alexa nodded. The only birthdays she recalled were the ones she spent missing her mother and hurting that her father chose to work instead of staying home.

"The sad thing is, I wish I didn't remember them either," she said, fighting to speak over the lump in her throat and the tears threatening to fall.

Something flickered in her father's gaze. Or maybe Alexa just wanted to see emotion there. She didn't know. "Bye, Dad," she said.

But when she looked over, he'd returned to his work and didn't reply.

CHAPTER EIGHT

Family gatherings at Luke's parents' house were always huge events. With three sisters—all married, all with kids—cousins, neighbors, and friends included, the noise level was high and the privacy factor nil. Usually Luke loved these events. Not today.

Today his heart wasn't here, it was back in the small town of Serendipity, New York. A place he never thought would leave a mark on him, much less impact him so strongly. He couldn't get Alexa out of his mind.

They'd said good-bye on Thursday. Today was Saturday. He'd programmed his number into her cell and hoped she'd use it. With the way they'd parted, Luke giving her his unasked-for opinion on how to live her life, he wasn't holding his breath.

In order not to focus on himself, he looked around to see which sibling he was in the mood for and his gaze settled on Ashley, the youngest of his three sisters. She had two kids, having married right out of high school to a guy Luke hated. And Luke considered himself an easygoing guy who got along with most people, but not her jackass husband.

"Hey, sweet cheeks," he said, using his nickname for her.

"Hey, yourself."

He sat down next to her on the picnic table bench and she immediately laid her head on his shoulder. Warning bells went off in his brain. "I was only gone a week. What happened?"

"I left Todd," she said, her voice cracking.

Luke held in his cheer, more concerned about his sister's feelings than his own. "Why?"

"He was cheating on me with Mandy Stone." The whispered words came with a wealth of hurt, Luke knew.

"Mandy Stone whose daddy is Todd's boss?" Luke asked through gritted teeth. The same Mandy Stone who felt it was her civic duty to hit on Luke at every town event he attended, and had done so since Luke accepted the scholarship to University of Miami to play football for the U.

"I think Mandy was just the most recent in a long line. He never liked being tied down."

Luke stiffened, wanting to beat the crap out of the other man. "Then he shouldn't have gotten you pregnant the summer before college."

She sniffed but ended in a laugh. "Takes two to be stupid, Luke. And I wouldn't trade my kids for anything."

"What will you do now?"

"The kids and I moved in with Mom and Dad. I need some time to work out a plan."

He kissed her temple. "You will. And I'll be here to help you."

"Thanks."

"Anything for you, sweet cheeks. You know that." He loved his sisters even when they were being pains in his ass.

She sighed. "I do. And I love you for it. So how was your trip east?"

"Business was good, got some solid endorsement deals lined up."

"Just for Men? Erectile dysfunction meds? Hemorrhoid cream?" She nailed him in the ribs with her elbow.

He rolled his eyes. "This is when 'sweet cheeks' changes to 'brat,'" he muttered. "How about Ford Broncos and my own cologne?"

She let out a Texas whoop. "I'm proud of you! So what else did you and Sawyer do? Pick up any hot chicks while you were there?"

Luke weighed just how much to tell her, then decided to go for broke. He needed to talk about it and Ash needed the distraction from her own life. "Cleaned out Sawyer's dad's house, though I think he's gonna do some work on the place and keep it instead of selling. And, yeah, I met someone."

Ashley sat up and turned in her seat, her eyes slitted as she stared at him.

"What?" he asked, uncomfortable under her narrowed gaze.

"I asked if you and Sawyer picked up any hot chicks. You countered with *I met someone*. Big difference. What gives?"

Luke glanced up at the cloudless sky. "Been asking myself that same question since I laid eyes on Alexa."

"What makes her special?"

Luke could list a million things, but the ones that came to mind were too personal for him to share, even with his sister. Like Alexa's stunning vulnerability. For a doctor who held lives in her hands, she'd been manipulated her entire life and didn't know her own self-worth. He'd tried to give her that in a few short days, then he'd invited her out here, and when she didn't jump at the chance like the other women in his life—the women who meant nothing to him and who he easily left behind—he threw those insecurities in her face and told her she needed to figure out what she wanted.

Nice of him, he thought, with no small amount of regret and an even healthier dose of self-directed disgust.

"Oooh, silence," Ashley said with a grin on her previously sad face. "You're in deep and you can't even say why.

You've fallen hard!" She clapped her hands in glee, suddenly back to being the sister who liked to tease him when they were kids. "I want to meet this girl."

No chance of that, Luke thought, frustrated. "Cool it," he muttered, instead of letting her in on what he'd done.

"Sorry." Ashley settled back in next to him. "What's she like?"

"She's a doctor. Busy. Not sure she loves the work situation she's in. She's loyal, saw her step up to take care of her best friend when she was attacked, then stayed overnight at the hospital to look after her. Pretty. Auburn hair—"

"Brown with reddish highlights? About my height? Does she ever wear her hair in a ponytail and would she look uncomfortable at a Texas barbecue?" Ashley asked, a too-big grin on her face.

Luke jerked his body around and there she was. Dr. Alexa Collins, walking across his parents' big Texas spread, talking to his *mother*, as she led Alexa to where Luke and Ashley were sitting.

"I'll be damned," he muttered.

"Since I always know everyone at these shindigs, I figured that had to be her. What's she doing here?" Ashley asked.

"I invited her," Luke said, stunned.

"What? You didn't tell me she was coming!" Ash punctuated this with a shot to his shoulder.

"That's because she said no." Luke rose to his feet as the women approached.

"Lucas Thompson, you didn't tell me we were having a guest!" His mother, Louise, who ruled this ranch along with her family, glared at him like he'd committed a crime.

"He didn't know, Mrs. Thompson." Alexa spoke softly.

"He invited you. That means you're important to him, and that means he should have told me."

"Ma!" Luke knew he'd better call her off before she scared Alexa away.

Alexa grinned and, man, Luke had missed that smile. "It's fine," she assured him.

Luke shook his head. Nothing about his mother's form of torture was fine. "Alexa, this is my sister, Ashley. Ash, this is Alexa."

His sister jumped up and shook Alexa's hand. "He was just telling me all about you!"

Luke rolled his eyes. "God save me from the two of you," he muttered. "Ash, take Mom away, would you? Go eat. Drink. Something." He met and held Alexa's gaze. "We need to talk."

"We're going," Ashley said, understanding in her tone despite her earlier teasing. "Come on, Ma. You can talk to Luke's girl later."

"Ash!" Luke's voice vibrated with annoyance, but to his surprise, Alexa's eyes were lit with amusement as she obviously held back her laughter.

"At least someone finds them amusing," he muttered to his mother and sister's retreating backs.

"You have no idea how lucky you are," she said, staring after his family, a wistful expression on her face.

Luke didn't know what she was doing here, but he had to assume it boded well for him that she'd come. He hooked his arm in hers and led her away from the yard and around the side of the house to his mother's special place. When Luke was born, she'd insisted she needed a place of her own and his father had put up a gazebo in the most private corner of the yard, right off the side door to the house.

They settled in the swing chair. "I take it getting away wasn't easy?" he asked.

"That would be an understatement."

Her pretty green eyes told the painful story. He wouldn't push her for an explanation, sure it would come when she was ready. "Yet you're here."

"I hoped the invitation was still open," she said hesitantly.

There it was, that vulnerability he'd been thinking about before she materialized in front of his eyes. In her blue jeans and white lace tank, with a light denim blouse tied around her waist, she looked like she belonged here on the ranch. Yet everything about her screamed her uncertainty, something he never wanted her to feel around him.

"Invitation's always open, darlin'."

She released a long-held breath. "Well, that's good, since when I took a leave of absence from work, my boss informed me he wouldn't be holding my position open." Her jaw set tight at the admission.

That bastard. "Your father said that?"

"It seems he didn't appreciate the idea of me finding my own path."

He wasn't sure what surprised him more, the smile she gave him or the fact that she'd listened to his advice and was taking time to figure out what she wanted, despite the consequences.

"I think that's great," he said, grasping her hands, thrilled down to his bones that she'd come to him. "So you're here for a while?"

Alexa shrugged, wondering that herself. "I'm here. How long? I thought we'd figure that out together. See if we still like each other and all." God, she sounded like an unsure idiot, Alexa thought. It was a wonder she'd survived the plane ride, not knowing what awaited her here.

She'd gotten Luke's address from Sawyer Rhodes, who swore his friend would be happy to see her and encouraged her to surprise him with the visit. Since she wasn't in any hurry to have Luke turn her down if he'd changed his mind, she'd agreed and hopped on a plane.

"See if we still like each other?" Luke chuckled. "I don't know about you, but what I feel for you is a lot more than *like*, darlin'." Luke brushed his finger down her cheek, his golden eyes sparkling with reassurance as he dipped his head in close.

His heat reached out to her, his familiar scent settling the butterflies deep in her stomach.

"I started falling hard for you the second we met," he continued. "Having you come down here, unsure of your welcome but taking that chance on me? That just cemented the deal. I can't see us going anywhere but forward from here."

"Me neither." She swallowed hard, her heart pounding in her chest, everything inside her screaming this was right. "I've never felt anything like this before."

"Same. And I sure never thought I'd want a woman with me, by my side, not talking about leaving any time soon, but that's how I feel about you. So let's take this time to get to know each other better, and help you figure out what you want to do with your career." His eyes held hers. "And while you're thinking on what you want, maybe you'll reconsider where you do it. Assuming things keep on . . . keeping on."

He grinned, and Alexa knew everything would be all right.

"Would you like that?" he asked.

"A lot," she whispered.

"Good. Did I say I'm glad you're here?" Before she could answer, he said, "I'm glad you're here. Good play, darlin'."

She grinned. *Not a good play*, she thought, as he closed his lips over hers. *A perfect one.*

THE LEGEND OF JANE

JESSICA CLARE

CHAPTER ONE

The weirdest calls always came late at night.

Hank had learned to dread those two A.M. phone calls, because they would inevitably lead to something strange. But that was to be expected when you worked the night shift.

"Bluebonnet PD," Hank answered the phone.

"That you, Hank Sharp? You working the late night shift?"

"I am," he said. "What can I help you with?"

"There's a girl in my cow pasture," Don Tatum said into the phone, and he sounded both tired and baffled. "With a video camera. And she's talking to herself. I think she's a cow tipper."

A cow tipper? Of all the crazy, ridiculous things. "One of the high school kids?" Hank asked. They were usually the culprits, too stupid or drunk—or both—to realize that cows slept lying down, and cow tipping was just a myth.

"Nope. Older." He paused a minute. "Definitely a cow

tipper. She just ran up and tried to push one from behind. You want me to get my shotgun?"

"No, Don," Hank said, getting the keys to his squad car off the hook in the tiny Bluebonnet Police Department. "You stay inside. I'll take care of this."

"All righty," Don said mildly, sounding more perplexed than annoyed. "You might want to make it fast, Hank, before she gets herself kicked in the face."

"On my way," Hank said, and hung up the phone. He left the office and climbed into his patrol car. He could have driven out to Tatum's small farm with his eyes closed, but he observed every stop sign and streetlight along the way regardless. It wouldn't do for a police officer to break the law, after all.

And Hank came from a long line of police officers. The rules had pretty much been driven into his brain from childhood.

He slowed his patrol car along the farm road, looking for a parked vehicle. There was not a single building along this stretch of road, which meant that if he found a car, it'd likely belong to his tipper. Sure enough, his high beams lit upon an out-of-state license plate. Florida. He pulled up behind the car and made note of the license plate number, then grabbed his flashlight to give the car a quick inspection.

No one home. Definitely his cow tipper. Hank clicked the flashlight off and headed for the barbed wire fence. He examined it and the hot pink scrap of material stuck to the fence. His cow tipper didn't know much about barbed wire, it seemed. Bending the wire down, Hank squeezed between the lines and entered the field.

Though Tatum owned several acres, it wasn't hard for Hank to find the girl. All he had to do was look for the cows. Sure enough, they were all clustered in one of the north fields close to the house, and they were lowing as if something bothered them.

"Stupid cows," he heard a voice growl in the distance. "Go to sleep already! I'm not going to sing you a lullaby!"

Hank glanced in that direction and saw a pinpoint of red light. That would be the camera, all right. What kind of fool woman was out there in the middle of the night trying to tip cows and film it? With his fingers hitched to his belt, he strolled forward to confront the tipper.

And paused when she began to speak again.

There was plenty of moonlight thanks to the full moon, and he was able to make out the shape of a rather tall some-one in the field. She was leaning in front of the camera and speaking. He didn't see a light on it except for that red one, so he wasn't exactly sure what she was taping.

"Okay," she told the camera on the tripod, her hands on her knees. "We're going to wait about fifteen minutes and look for another sleeping cow. Then, it's tipping time. You wouldn't think that cows would be so freaking difficult, but these are the least tired cows I've ever seen in my life. It's two in the morning. You'd think they'd be ready for a little nap at least."

She sounded disgruntled. His mouth twitched with amusement.

"All right," she said to the camera again, then glanced behind her. "One of the cows is standing pretty still. I'm going to give it about two minutes to go to sleep, and then we commence tipping." She rubbed her hands in front of the camera, and then adjusted the tripod.

Time for him to step in. Don Tatum was right. She was going to get kicked in the face. Hank clicked on his flash-light and shone it right in her face.

"Police," he drawled. "Don't move."

She froze, squinting her eyes closed and throwing her hands in the air.

With the light on, he was able to get a better look at her. She was pretty, despite her face being scrunched up. Her hair was pulled into two crazy ponytails atop her head, and her hot pink athletic tank top had a rip down the front that matched the scrap he'd pulled from the barbed wire. She also wore bright pink lipstick and lots of glittery eye makeup. She looked like she was heading to a rave instead of a cow pasture. He let his flashlight travel down her legs. She wore bright pink and green striped knee-high socks and very short black shorts and combat boots.

What the hell was she doing, exactly?

"It's not what it looks like, Officer," she said, keeping her hands in the air.

Hank glanced at the field, then at the crazily dressed woman before the camera. "Looks kind of like a cow tipping to me."

One eye squinted open to regard him. "Okay, then it *is* exactly what it looks like." She put a hand in front of her eyes to block the light from his flashlight. "I don't suppose you know the proper procedure for tipping a cow?"

"No, ma'am," he said. "I do know it's against the law to trespass on private property, though, and this is definitely private property."

He waited for her response. Most people he knew would immediately start apologizing or making excuses, anything to get out of trouble.

She sucked in a breath, and then let out a squeal, doing a happy little bounce. "Oh my god. Does this mean you're going to arrest me? Hang on! I have to make sure I have enough juice."

"More . . . juice?" His brows drew together.

She turned to her camera and yanked it off the tripod, checking the settings. "Battery life. Looks like I'm good. This'll totally work. I can get two weeks of footage instead of just one. Awesome." She fiddled with the camera, not even looking over at him. "If I resist arrest, will it make things look more convincing?"

"More convincing, ma'am? I didn't say I was going to arrest you. I just want you to leave Mr. Tatum's property."

She looked over at him, crestfallen. "You're not going to arrest me?"

"No."

She gave him a shrewd look. "Then I'm not going any-where."

He sighed. Damn it. Of course he'd get stuck with a crazy woman. "Turn that camera off so we can have a real discussion."

"No. Absolutely not. I need the camera."

Now she'd gone from perplexing to downright annoying. Time to scare her a little. "We're about to move straight into resisting arrest territory if you don't start listening to me, ma'am." A little white lie never hurt anyone. She wasn't really resisting arrest—just not listening—but maybe the threat would make her pay attention.

"Perfect," she said, setting the camera back on the tripod. She glanced at it one last time, and then turned back toward him, her hands outstretched. "Cuff me, baby."

Definitely crazy.

To her vast disappointment and loud complaints, he'd turned off her camera and hadn't cuffed her. He had, how-ever, put her in the back of his vehicle and taken her down to the station to book her for defiant trespassing, since she wanted to be booked so damn bad. He'd have been just as happy sending her on her way. That was how things were done in a small town. You showed up, put a little fear into the trespassers, and sent them on their way.

This crazy woman didn't seem to figure that out, though. She *wanted* to be arrested. She'd been fascinated by the process, too, asking him all kinds of questions and if he could "play" the police siren for her.

He'd refused.

Now she was sitting in Bluebonnet's lone jail cell (which was not in use all that often), waiting on someone to come and pick her up. Hank busied himself with completing one of the computerized "smart forms" required for any processed police case. Of course, "smart form" was a figure of speech, because the damn computer was acting up. Damn thing ran slower and slower every time he turned it on. He wasn't much good with computers. Didn't have time to fuss with them. No one at the station did.

Hank examined the woman's mug shot. She'd posed for it, vamping for the camera even as she held the plaque in front of her. When he'd finished snapping it, she'd asked to have it retaken so she could "pick the best one."

He'd declined.

She'd been excited to be fingerprinted, too, and even more excited when he sat her in the jail cell.

Strange woman.

He'd noticed a logo on the back of her pink tank top—www.thelegendofjane.com. And of course, he couldn't help but wonder about it. After wrestling with the slow office computer to get her picture and prints uploaded, he poured himself another cup of coffee, and then decided to check out the website. Immediately, his screen filled with a few flashing ads and a big, splashy logo screamed THE LEGEND OF JANE at him, followed by I DO STUNTS SO YOU DON'T HAVE TO. A video immediately began to play.

The Legend of Jane, it seemed, was a blog. A video blog. Made by his crazy woman. In the video, she was chatting to the camera. She wore the same glittery eye makeup and the same ridiculous outfit, her hair pulled in identical pigtails. It seemed to be some sort of costume for her.

"This week, we're in the woods of East Texas in search of the infamous Bigfoot! There's a farm here where they claim to have seen Bigfoot multiple times on a regular basis, and they state that he swings by to steal their chicken eggs. How can we resist? I asked, and they've allowed the Legend of Jane to stop by and film. Let's go say hello, shall we?"

Bigfoot? What the heck? He paused the video and looked at the prior week. A haunting at an old Louisiana plantation. He flipped back a bit further. Jersey Devil hunting. Another date was her and a friend eating Pop Rocks and enormous quantities of soda and laughing hysterically.

That did it. Jane was insane. And she wanted to tip cows just to get more fodder for her blog? Is that what she'd been up to? He shook his head and went back to booking the charges. And as he did, he glanced down at her driver's license. Luanne Allard.

It seemed his legendary "Jane" was more of a Luanne.

Right around dawn, before the day shift showed up, Emily Allard-Smith arrived at the police station, dressed in sweats and with her dark blonde hair pulled into a ponytail. She wore no makeup, which was surprising to Hank, given that she was normally dolled up.

He knew Emily, of course. The entire town did. She'd bought the old Peppermint House and was trying to set it up as a bed-and-breakfast. And she was convinced the place was haunted. She'd called the cops multiple times for every rattle that the old place made. The other cops were convinced that nice Emily Allard-Smith was just scared to live alone in that big house.

But Hank was starting to wonder if the ghost thing was just her crazy sister at work.

She grimaced at him, seemingly embarrassed to be at the station. "Hi, Hank. I heard you have my sister here?"

He stared at her thoughtfully. "I don't know if you noticed, Emily, but your sister's a loon."

"Be nice. She's not crazy."

"You sure about that?"

Emily sighed and placed a container of breakfast muffins on the counter. That was another reason that everyone at the station kept showing up at the Peppermint House. Emily was a damn fine cook, and generous. "I brought you some blueberry muffins. Was Luanne much of a chore?"

"Did you girls grow up in the city?"

Emily nodded, perplexed. "Why?"

"Your sister thinks cow tipping's real."

"Oh no." Emily clenched a hand. "She didn't."

"She did."

"It's that stupid blog. She's convinced it'll—" She stopped abruptly, then shook her head. "Never mind. I'm here to bail her out."

"No bail, ma'am. Just a citation." At Emily's surprise, he shrugged. "She wanted to spend the night in jail. I obliged her and left her in the holding cell."

And here Emily said her sister *wasn't* crazy. Love was blind, because that Luanne gal was nuttier than a pecan pie.

Luanne drummed her fingers on the cold metal bench she sat on.

All right. So jail? Not that much fun. Not that she'd expected it to be fun. But it would have been worth the trip if she'd gotten some decent footage for her blog. She could have turned a jail visit into a really fun series of videos and milked it for weeks.

Unfortunately, Officer Hotness had confiscated her camera and hadn't wanted to play along. Spoilsport.

She supposed she couldn't fault the man. She was trespassing. She *had* been saying crazy things. But put the camera on her, and she thought of nothing but the footage.

Heck, she knew cow tippings weren't real. The thing was, her audience didn't *know* that she was well aware of it, and so it made good, easy footage for her blog. And that was the trick. As long as she kept entertaining them with her wacky stunts, they'd keep coming to her website. And traffic to her website meant money in her pocket.

A key rattled in the door, and Luanne jumped to her feet. Officer Hotness was the first one through the door, his tall, broad form so big that he practically had to stoop to enter the cell.

She noticed things like height on a man. Luanne figured that at six foot tall in flats, it narrowed the dating pool down for her quite a bit. When someone came along that was just the right height, her ovaries tended to perk up and pay attention.

And those ovaries screamed at her every time Officer Hotness came through the door.

He wasn't the most good-looking man she'd ever seen. His features were a little too blunt and unsmiling to make him handsome. But he was incredibly tall and had big shoulders, and had an ass that wouldn't quit in that uniform.

Hotness, indeed.

Officer Hotness gave her a disapproving look as he entered the cell, and he was quickly followed by her sister, Emily. Luanne smiled brightly, ignoring her sister's chagrined expression. "Hey, Em! Glad you could bail me out."

"No bail," Officer Hotness said, and handed her a paper. "A ticket. Be mindful of other people's property in the future, Ms. Allard. I don't want to see you in here again."

"Yes, Officer," she said in a sweet voice. "Can I have my camera back?" Maybe if she was nice to him, he'd let Emily film some action shots of Luanne leaving the jail cell. She could supplement what footage she had with a few well-staged clips.

"You can have it back once you leave."

Luanne sighed. So much for that.

Five minutes later, they had left the police station and were heading back to Emily's house. Luanne clutched the ticket in one hand, her camera in the other. "My car's still on the side of the road, Em."

"I gave Officer Sharp your spare key. He's going to pick it up and drop it off for you later today. I'm guessing he doesn't want you hanging around Mr. Tatum's farm again."

"Gee, Officer Sharp sure is trustworthy," Luanne said sarcastically. "Like a big golden retriever. I can't believe you trusted him with my keys."

"That's how things are done around here," Emily said with a small shrug of her shoulders. She put on her blinker and turned into the driveway of the house. "Small towns are a little weird, I know."

More than a little weird, if you asked Luanne. But no one did.

She stared up at the red and white monstrosity of a house that her sister had purchased. The Peppermint House, as it was known about town, was an eight-bedroom Victorian. It was the first house built in Bluebonnet, and had the distinction of also being the biggest eyesore in town. At some point, some fool had thought it would be "cute" to paint the house bright candy red and the trim and shutters white. It looked like a big ugly candy cane.

But Emily loved the damn place. And she was determined to run a bed-and-breakfast, even though she'd never actually run a bed-and-breakfast. She'd also never renovated a Victorian home, either, and she was doing that as a solo project as well. Luanne normally stayed out of Emily's business because she was pretty sure Emily didn't want to be second-guessed on her new career path. And Luanne could respect that.

They slid out of the car once it was parked, and Luanne glanced up at the lacy curtains fluttering in an upstairs window. "You really ought to let me do a feature about this place on my blog, Em. Haunted hotels are really big right now. I'll fake some noises on camera to make it seem legit. You'll be crawling with customers in no time."

"No, Luanne," Emily said firmly, heading to the front door. "I don't want to be on your blog. I want normal customers, not ghostbusters. Plus, I'm still renovating."

She pushed open the front door and stepped inside. Not locked. That was another thing that wigged Luanne out about small towns. No one locked their doors.

"Why not?" Luanne dropped her camera on the foyer table and headed into the kitchen to grab a drink. She was thirsty. Officer Hotness hadn't offered her a drink while she'd been in jail, which was a shame. It was almost as if he hadn't liked her. "You need the money."

"I don't need the money yet," Emily said. "And your blog attracts weirdos. This is a small town. I like the small-town vibe. No one wants any kooky stuff." Her sister gave her a prim look. "Except you."

"Kooky stuff pays the bills, Em," Luanne said, swiping a bottle of Dr Pepper from the fridge and moving to a barstool. "Last month's ad revenue was double what I normally make. My traffic's gone through the roof. You got any of those muffins left over?"

Emily bustled past Luanne, pulled a plastic baggie of muffins out of the fridge, and set it before Luanne. "Yeah, and the stalkers went through the roof, too. That's why you moved here, right? Because someone followed you home once?"

Luanne shrugged and pulled a muffin out of the bag, peeling the paper from it with great interest and avoiding her sister's direct gaze. "The Legend of Jane is popular with men."

"It's because you're dressed like a nut while you do these stunts." Emily complained. "You should get a real job, Luanne."

"No one will hire an investment broker with an expired license and bad credit, Em. You know that." She bit into the muffin. "Jane's all I've got right now. In another month, I'll have the last credit card paid off. I can't fix my credit, but I figure if I get enough money in the bank, it won't matter. Then I can see about setting up a business. A real one. But for now, the Legend of Jane rides on."

Emily sighed and shook her head, then grabbed a muffin for herself. "I just worry that you're going to get in over your head, Luanne."

"Pfft," she said. "I've got it all under control. It's not like I'll get sent to jail . . . Oh, wait," she teased.

Emily threw a muffin at Luanne. "You're horrible."

CHAPTER TWO

Luanne trailed a finger along a shelf in the hardware store, yawning to herself as she thought. This small mom-and-pop place wouldn't carry what she needed for her next stunt, seeing as how they didn't have lumber. But since she was already here, she might as well check out the rest of the store. She lifted her finger and shuddered at the dust coating the tip. Clearly cleaning supplies were not high on the hardware store's list.

She needed props for this weekend's stunt. Even though she had her cow tipping episode (however botched) and the subsequent arrest on tape, she liked to have a few episodes filmed ahead of time.

Plus, she was working a lot because she was bored. Since she'd just moved to Bluebonnet, she didn't know anyone other than Emily, really. And all her friends were currently at their day jobs and couldn't text or chat on the phone. So to pass the time, she was prepping for her next stunt. This upcoming one would be crop circles. She'd driven past a long, flat field while heading down to Bluebonnet, and it had given her the idea. Apparently you could make crop circles by using rope and boards and pushing the grass down in circles. Luanne had watched some videos and she figured she could make a reasonable attempt at it. And hey, if she failed, that made just as good an episode as the successful ones.

With a length of rope tucked under her arm and two spools of duct tape over her wrist (one never knew when one would need more duct tape), Luanne headed for the checkout counter. She paused, waiting as the ancient man behind the cashier's desk slowly rang up the items for the man in front of her. When they paused to discuss whether the right size nuts were being purchased, Luanne stifled her laugh and glanced out the windows to the street.

Downtown Bluebonnet was kind of cute, she had to admit to herself. There was a homey, quaint feel to things and the shops that lined the street were cheerful, even if they weren't much to her city-girl eyes. Her gaze drifted over to the Mexican restaurant—the only one in town, mind you—the coffee shop, the beauty salon, and an antiques store that looked more like an overfed yard sale. There was a cute little gazebo in the center of town, and on the other side of Main Street were a few more small shops. Two streets down, and she could walk back to the Peppermint House, which made Main Street rather convenient for her. But since the hardware store didn't carry lumber, she'd have to borrow Emily's car and head into the city, since her car was still with the police.

Speaking of the police . . . her eyes narrowed with dislike in the direction of the city hall-slash-utilities-slash-library-slash-police building. That darned cop was probably in there, telling stories about how he'd kinda-sorta arrested "Jane" from the Legend of Jane website. She hoped she never saw his ass again. Then she paused. His ass was actually pretty hot. She wouldn't mind seeing *it* again. She hoped she just never had to talk to the owner again. But not being able to stare at an ass that hot would seem like a waste of a perfectly good ass.

The customer in front of her finally finished, and Luanne set her rope and duct tape on the counter with a smile. "Morning."

The old man gave her a toothless grin. "Morning to you. Did you find what you were looking for?"

Why, what a grand opening. Luanne grinned at him and fished a printout from her purse. "Not really, but I wanted to ask you two things."

His brows wrinkled together. "I'll help if I can."

He seemed like a sweet old man. She smiled and unfolded the printout, showing it to him. "Have you seen one of these around town?"

The old man stared at the printout and then frowned at her. "That's an ugly dog."

"It's a chupacabra," she told him, and moved ahead with her lie. "I talked with a farmer the other day who said he saw one off of the highway. You ever seen one?"

"Chupa-whattah?"

"Chupacabra," she repeated, and patted his hand. "You can keep that printout. I'll pay two hundred dollars to interview an eyewitness that's seen one."

His eyes widened. "Mind if I post this by the register?"

"That would be lovely," she said sweetly. When he finished hanging it, she beamed at him. "I was looking for wood planks this morning. About five feet long. Two inches thick. And a drill."

"This here's the hardware store."

"Yes, I know. Some hardware stores carry wood. You don't?"

He scratched his chin, thinking. "Lemme go to the back and check." He began to shuffle out from behind the counter.

He moved at a snail's pace, and the morning was half gone already. "It's okay. I can go somewhere else."

"No, I don't mind. I'll go look."

"It's really not necessary," she continued, watching his plodding steps and wincing at his speed.

He waved her off, disappearing down one dusty aisle.

Lord, she was going to be here all day if he was going to check in the back for a plank of wood for her. Luanne sighed and hopped up on the counter to wait, dangling her feet. She glanced out the dirty window back to Main Street . . . and froze.

Officer Hotness was passing by the window.

She groaned. *Don't come in here. Don't come in here. Don't come in here.*

He glanced through the window, squinted . . . and his steps slowed.

Damn it.

He headed for the door of Merle's Hardware.

Just her luck. Luanne straightened, pinning a smile to her face. The best defense was a good offense. Maybe if she came on hot and heavy, he'd skedaddle right away. It was as good a plan as any.

The officer entered the hardware store, and she noticed he ducked a little when he went through the door. Maybe it was because she was a six-foot amazon, but that simple motion seemed irresistibly sexy somehow. This was a man she wouldn't have to wear flats to go out on a date with, she realized. This was a man she wouldn't have to hunch down next to in photographs. This was someone she could relax around. And that was incredibly, unbelievably appealing to someone as tall as she was.

She didn't have to fake the purr in her voice as she smiled at him. "Why, hello, Officer Hotness."

He stopped in his tracks and glanced behind him.

"I'm talking to you."

He wore mirrored sunglasses, but she was pretty sure he was blushing underneath them. "Officer Sharp," he corrected.

"I'll say," she added with a wink. "How's it hanging?"

Yep, he was definitely blushing.

Officer Sharp moved to her side and pulled a set of keys out of his pocket. "These are yours. The car is parked in front of the station."

"That's very thoughtful of you," she said, swinging her feet and staring up at him thoughtfully. "How are the cows?"

"The cows?"

"No worse for the wear despite my visit?"

A hint of a smile curved his mouth, and she saw hints of sexiness in his rugged face. "No. They're fine." He looked her up and down, noticing her plain jeans and white T-shirt. "No Legendary gear today?"

"Afraid not," she said with a smile. "Jane only comes out to play when I'm filming. The rest of the time it's just plain old me."

He leaned on the counter next to her, and his arms crossed over his chest. "I'm not so sure about the 'plain' part, Miss Allard."

He remembered her last name. And he said she wasn't plain. Officer Hotness was flirting back with her. How . . . fun. Luanne tilted her head at him, staring up at her reflection in his glasses. "That's sweet of you. I bet you say that to all the crazy trespassers."

A flash of white teeth shone. "Just the pretty ones."

"So where would a trespasser like me go to get a drink around here, Officer?" She was inches away from batting her eyelashes at him like an idiot. The man was definitely stroking her ego.

"Only one place in town serves alcohol. You like Tex-Mex?"

He must have been talking about the hole-in-the-wall Mexican food place she'd been avoiding since moving here. Figured. "Don't suppose you'd like to get a drink?"

His grin widened. "I . . ." His voice broke off and his smile disappeared.

"What?"

He reached past her and snagged the flyer that Merle had put on the register. "What's this?"

"Oh, nothing," she said lightly. "Someone's looking for a—" She leaned over the paper and made a show of reading it. "Chupacabra, looks like."

Officer Sharp stared at the flyer, his mouth thinning. Then his face turned toward her again. "If I call the number at the bottom of this flyer, is your phone gonna ring?"

Luanne swung her feet. "Maybe."

Just then, Merle appeared from the back storage room, his steps shuffling and slow. "The only wood I have is on the mops," he pointed out, unscrewing a mop and then waving the handle at her. "It's not a flat board, but will this do?"

"No, I need flat," she told him quickly, hoping he wouldn't dismantle any other mops on her behalf. "It's okay. I'll head into the city and go to one of the big lumber stores. No big deal."

"I'd like to help," Merle said, staring at the headless mop and then offering it to her. "You sure?"

"I'm sure."

"I'll just ring you up, then."

It got quiet as Merle shuffled back behind the counter. Luanne hopped down and peeked over at Officer Sharp. His arms were crossed over his chest, the chupacabra flyer discarded on the counter and forgotten.

"What's with the do-it-yourself kit?" he finally asked.

She'd been rather hoping he wouldn't. "Just a project."

"A Jane project?"

Luanne fidgeted as Merle began to ring up the duct tape and rope. "It might or might not be for making crop circles."

"Luanne," he said in a warning tone.

So they'd moved beyond "Miss Allard" and "Jane" on to Luanne. And now he was using his disapproving cop voice

on her. Gone was Officer Hotness. Officer No-Fun had
returned.

"It's just stuff," she told him. "Don't worry. I'm going to
crop-circle outside of your jurisdiction."

He said nothing as Merle gave her the total, and she
pulled out a wad of cash and paid him. But when she picked
up her purchases and headed out the door, he followed her.

Damn it. She paused on the sidewalk outside of the hardware store, glancing down the street. He'd parked her car
on the side of city hall, she could see now. She could go
there and pick it up, but Officer Hotness would probably dog
her footsteps every inch of the way. Or she could run like a
chicken and head down the street back toward the Peppermint House.

A tall shadow fell over her, blocking out the light, and
Luanne squinted up at the cop. It was rather novel, having
to squint up at a man. This must have been how regular-
height women felt. "There a problem, Officer? Is buying
rope and duct tape illegal now?"

His lips thinned as he regarded her upturned face. "I
don't like what you're doing. This is a quiet town. You don't
need to get everyone riled up about chupacabra or crop
circles or cow tippings. You're just causing trouble to cause
trouble, and I can't have that."

"Are you giving me a lecture on being naughty? That
seems unfair, considering I pretty much asked you out and
you just turned me down." So she was fudging the facts a
little. She was still a little disappointed that they'd gone from
sexy flirting to Jane-is-a-bad-bad-girl.

That expressive mouth fell open, just a little. "Asked
me out?"

She rolled her eyes. "I asked you where a girl has to go
to get a drink around here. Hello? Classic pickup line."

She could have sworn his ears turned just the slightest
bit red. "I see."

"I'm a big girl," she told him. "No height joke intended. You can just say no without lecturing me. I won't cry."

He took the sunglasses off in the next minute, and she realized just how very green his eyes were. How striking. A hint of a smile curved his mouth again, and she felt a flare of attraction between them again. "I don't think I want to say no, Miss Allard. What time should I pick you up?"

CHAPTER THREE

For some reason, Luanne was nervous. She smoothed her black dress in the mirror, then sighed and tore it off, tossing it on the bed with thirteen other outfits. This was just a stupid date. It wasn't even supposed to be a date. She should just think of it as dinner with a friendly stranger who happened to be a guy. That's all.

But she kept thinking of the appreciative way he'd looked at her—Luanne, not wacky Legend of Jane—and for some reason, she wanted to get this right. So she changed clothes again, slipping on her favorite pair of jeans that made her ass look fantastic, and a silky top with no sleeves and a loose neckline that displayed some cleavage she was rather proud of. Much better. This outfit said that she was interested but not invested. The dress said a little too much. Jeans were perfect.

Luanne dug through the bottom of her closet and triumphantly pulled out a bright red pair of heels. They were four-inch stilettos and gorgeous. She loved them. She never wore them, though, because they made her tower over every man she'd ever dated, or made her look like a flagpole when she went out with her girlfriends.

Tonight, though? Tonight she had a date with a man who was easily six inches taller than her, and she could put on stilettos. And that was something she was definitely going to take advantage of.

With that in mind, she headed to the bathroom to put the finishing touches on her makeup.

When the doorbell rang, she nearly stabbed herself with the mascara wand she was wielding. Instead, she smeared black under one carefully lined eye. Drat.

"I'll get it," Emily called from downstairs, and Luanne hastily fixed her eye makeup. He'd seen her fully kitted out as Jane, and she wanted to avoid that tonight. Just a bit of eyeliner, some mascara, and some nude lipstick. Nothing fancy. Nothing that screamed Jane. Her hair was down and hung in soft, natural waves around her face—another change from Jane.

She hoped he liked it and wasn't disappointed. It seemed like every guy she'd gone out with in the past year wanted to see Jane instead of Luanne.

But when she came down the stairs in her tight jeans and red heels, she knew she'd chosen wisely. Officer Sharp— Hank, she reminded herself—was chatting with Emily and doing his best not to loom over her. Lucky Emily was on the shorter side of five foot and hadn't inherited their father's height like Luanne had. He glanced up when Luanne landed on a creaky step, and a slow smile spread across his face as he looked at her, clearly approving.

Of her. Not Jane.

This evening was already off to a great start. Luanne smiled back down at him.

They walked to the restaurant, since it was only a few blocks away and the temperature was surprisingly pleasant and cool for June. They'd made small talk about the weather, the conversation stilted and awkward. Silence eventually fell and they walked quietly toward the restaurant.

She looked pretty tonight, Hank thought. No, more than pretty. Downright gorgeous. Her hair fell around her shoulders in light brown waves, and she wasn't wearing that ridiculous glittery makeup. Her face was appealing, and her legs seemed like they went on forever in those jeans.

She was way out of his league. He was just a too-tall unexciting country boy with an average face. He knew what ladies looked for in a man, and Hank Sharp wasn't it. His dating record in Bluebonnet consisted of more strikeouts than home runs, and everyone in town seemed to think he was a devoted bachelor. And he was, except it wasn't by choice. Most women didn't show a lot of interest in a man almost a foot and a half taller than them.

But Luanne? She was tall. Gorgeously tall.

After a few moments of uncomfortable silence, she glanced over at him. Hank cleared his throat. "You been here before? To eat?"

She shook her head, smiling at him. "I just moved in with Em two weeks ago. I haven't really had a chance to do much around town."

Nothing much, except a cow tipping, a trip to the police station, and planning crop circles. He didn't bring that up, though. "It doesn't look like much, I know. It's an old house that was converted into a restaurant."

"Really?" She wrinkled her nose like she didn't approve. "That's strange. I'm not sure if I'm keen on sitting in a stranger's living room and eating."

"It's a family-owned business," he explained, as if he needed to somehow defend the town to her. "Food's excellent."

Luanne glanced over at him and smiled. "Then you're going to have to tell me what's the best thing to order."

"I can do that," he agreed, opening the door for her and waiting for her to step past. He ducked inside and noticed they were getting a few looks. Not surprising, because he was tall and she was, well, gorgeous. She seemed a little uncomfortable at the attention, though.

"Officer Sharp," one of the waitresses said with a smile, passing by the host booth and grabbing a pair of menus. "Want your regular table?"

"That'd be great," he said, putting a hand on the small of Luanne's back to steer her forward.

Luckily for him, his regular table was at the back of the restaurant. Usually it was so he could scarf his lunch while keeping an eye on everyone else in the restaurant out of habit. Tonight, though, it meant privacy for him and his date, which was nice. He pulled the chair out for Luanne and she sat down gracefully.

"You have a regular table here?" she asked him, unfolding her napkin and placing it in her lap as he sat down.

"Only restaurant in town." He didn't add that the owner was friends with his father the police chief, so any man in uniform got a free meal. Then that seemed like an insult to the restaurant, so he added, "Food's good."

Luanne gave him a curious look, and then examined her menu. "So what's your favorite?"

He told her, and they ordered the same thing, along with a pair of Coronas. Silence fell over the table again, and Hank inwardly winced. He sure was botching this. He should talk about something. Anything. Nothing was coming to mind, though. He was one big blank. Damn it. If she didn't speak up and break the awkward silence in the next minute, he was going to start sweating.

"So," she began, and he almost sighed with relief. "Have you always wanted to be a police officer?"

"Yup." Hank picked the lime out of the top of his Corona and set it on his napkin, then took a swig. "Runs in the family."

"Really? Who else in the family is a cop?"

"My father's the police chief. His father before him.

There have been Sharps in Bluebonnet ever since Bluebonnet was founded."

Her smile widened. "The family business. I could see that. You seem like the type."

"And what type is that?" He wasn't sure if that was an insult or a compliment.

"You know, the good son. The loyal man. All that." She waved a hand in the air and then stuck a finger on her lime, shoving it into the neck of her Corona before she took a drink. "You look as if it's written in your DNA."

Hank frowned. She made him sound like a giant Boy Scout. Not exactly date material. And yet . . . she pretty much had him pegged. He was the good son. He did join the force because it was what Sharp men did. "You make it sound like it's a bad thing."

She shook her head and grinned at him, her beer still tilted close to her lips. "Women say they want a wild man they can tame, but most would probably prefer to have a nice guy . . . as long as he's sexy."

Well, considering that women weren't beating down his door to date him, he was guessing that she was wrong on that account. Still, it was nice of her to try to make him feel better about it. He knew most women wanted a bad boy, and that wasn't Hank Sharp.

And yet, Luanne was here, and she was smiling at him, so that was something. "What about you?"

Her smile faded just a little and she set her beer down on the napkin. "What about me?"

"Your sister lives here in town, right?"

She brightened, as if the subject had skirted something she was afraid to talk about. Interesting. "Yes! Em has always wanted to run a bed-and-breakfast. I thought she was crazy when she told me she bought a fixer-upper out here, but the place is interesting, even if it's a little garish with the red and white paint and all."

"She thinks it's haunted. Calls the police station about once a week for us to come and check on something."

Luanne rolled her eyes. "I've been there a few weeks and haven't seen or heard a thing, and I've been in a few haunted houses."

"As Jane?"

"Yup. I'm pretty sure it's not haunted. And if it was, she could make a killing by letting me do a little filming, but she refuses."

"Not everyone wants to be on camera," Hank told her, keeping his tone as mild as he could.

She frowned at his reproach and they lapsed into silence again.

Damn. He really wasn't good at this dating thing.

After chips and salsa were dropped at their table, Luanne plucked one and sighed at him. "This is really awkward, isn't it?"

"Yeah." Disappointing, too.

That impish smile crossed her face again. "You probably would have been more comfortable if I showed up as Jane, huh?"

"No," he said, almost too quickly. He liked Luanne. He didn't much cotton to her Jane persona. "She kinda stands out in a crowd."

She looked surprised, then laughed. "The clothes and makeup? I guess so. It's just armor, anyhow."

"Armor?"

"I got the idea from roller derby girls," she said. "I watched them in Austin once. Saw a few girls head through the back entrance, looking sweet and mild as could be. When they came out on the rink, though, they were totally different. Like banshees. It was crazy. Wild hair, wild makeup, wild uniforms. I realized that it was like putting armor on for them. You put on the costume and you get your game face on. So that's what I do, too. It's all about putting on a good show and getting into the zone." And she winked at him. "Like you and your hot cop uniform."

Great, now he'd gone from being awkward to blushing. "You flatter a man."

She wiggled her eyebrows at him and ate another chip. "You show a lot of ladies your nightstick?"

Her playful attitude was catching. It was hard not to play back, so he didn't resist. Instead, Hank leaned forward. "Most of them run away as soon as I break it out. I think they're scared of the size."

She clapped a hand over her mouth, laughing. Her eyes sparkled in the low light of the restaurant. "I thought they were collapsible?"

"Not mine."

"So it's hard all the time?"

He ate a chip slowly so he wouldn't have to answer her.

"You realize that your ears turn the cutest bright red when you get shy?"

Hank cleared his throat, pretty sure that his ears were probably turning redder. "You're really forward, aren't you?"

"Being a shy, retiring flower gets me nowhere. Being forward got me a date with a hot cop, so I can't complain."

Neither could he.

After the initial awkwardness, they had a great time at dinner, or so Luanne thought. Hank was just like he seemed—easygoing and laid-back, with a country boy charm to him. She suspected he really was as nice as he appeared to be. Sort of like the Southern version of Dudley Do-Right. And she loved that little blush of his. She was crazy attracted to him.

He was funny, too. Rather quiet, she noticed, but it seemed to be because of a habit of people-watching rather than any shyness. He was extremely observant, remembering small details about their run-ins that she thought he would have missed. And he told her all about the town, the history, the gossip, the scandals (such as they were). Each story was told with that same dry humor and clever observation that made him so attractive. And when he told her a story about the first "cat" he'd been called out to rescue out of a tree, only to find out it was a possum? She thought she'd never stop laughing.

A laid-back, incredibly tall, sexy cop who had a good heart. Good lord, they grew them well here in Bluebonnet, didn't they.

The date went by almost too fast. She'd drank only two Coronas and switched to water, not wanting to miss a moment of conversation because of a beer buzz. She'd noticed that he'd only drank one beer and done the same. Not much of a drinker, then, her officer. And that was okay, too. He didn't seem like the party boy type. More like the responsible one who swooped in and rescued the party boy from himself.

When the check arrived, he swiped it without even asking and paid. And then he'd walked her back to the Peppermint House, keeping carefully at her side but not reaching for her arm or draping one over her shoulders. Instead, his hands were stuffed in his jean pockets. Did that mean he didn't even want to try to get a little more cozy with her?

It had been a nice date. But was it just that? Nice? Or was he interested in more? She wasn't sure she could tell. Most guys sent signals that were easily read, but not Hank. He was a closed book, and it was driving her crazy.

As they walked up the steps of the oversized front porch of the Peppermint House, Luanne stole another peek at him. He looked different out of his cop uniform. Not in a bad way, either. Despite the warm summer weather, the shirt he'd chosen to wear was a clean-pressed black shirt with long sleeves. One or two buttons were open at the neck, revealing a dark undershirt. He didn't seem to mind the heat, either. He wore long jeans that were tight across the ass (in a fabulous way) and boots. She was pleased there was no chewing tobacco circle imprinted on the back pocket of his jeans, either. His close-cropped hair looked just as appealing now as it did with his cop uniform on.

In sum, he was Officer Hotness even out of the uniform. She totally wanted him. Her fingers were practically curling to dig into the front of his shirt and pull his face down to her, but she didn't want this to be one-sided. She didn't want to be that crazy out of town woman who threw herself at the local cops.

They paused in front of the door and she gave him an expectant look.

His hands remained stuffed inside his front pockets, and he gave her a faint smile. "Had a nice time tonight, Luanne."

This was good. This was leading up to something, hopefully. "I had a great time, too."

Hank smiled. "Well, all right, then." And he turned to leave.

What the hell?

He was just going to turn around and leave? What was this, grade school? Would they have to pass notes for a year before she got a kiss or something? Ridiculous. Luanne frowned at his retreating shoulders as he hopped down a step. "Can I ask you something?"

Hank turned to look at her. Moved back up a step. "Yes, ma'am."

Yes, ma'am? That sounded overly formal and polite. Like they hadn't had a cozy dinner together. "Is there something wrong?"

"Wrong?"

"Yeah. I'm standing here on the porch staring at you and you didn't even try to kiss me or get grabby. Do you not find me sexy?"

His mouth thinned and he took another step toward her, looking almost irritated at her confrontational tone. "Why would you think that?"

She put her hands under her breasts and bounced them.

"Because I've been jiggling in this top all night and you haven't looked at the girls once. And I'm wearing jeans that make my ass look fabulous. And fuck-me pumps. And you're treating me like a nun. So I'm just curious. Is it me? Is it my height? Is it Jane? Because if so—"

He crossed the last foot or two of the porch, silencing her rambling. His hot, hard mouth pressed over her own, and she felt the prickle of a five-o'clock shadow rasp against her chin. He moved his lips until they parted slightly, and he began to ever so lightly suck on her upper lip.

Luanne's knees went weak. Such a simple caress and she was melting like an ice cream sundae. His arms went to hers and he was bracing her while still continuing that soft, slow sucking on her upper lip. It was the most sensual kiss she'd ever received, and her lips parted from the pleasure of it. He must have taken that as a sign to continue, because his lips parted over hers even more and she felt his tongue skate between her lips and into her mouth. A soft moan escaped her throat, and when his hands slid to her ass and tugged her against him, she went easily, wrapping her arms around his neck.

His height was . . . perfect. For the first time, she was kissing a man who was built just for her. There was no awkward leaning or hunching to kiss him. No jokes about how she towered over him in her heels. Instead, they fit as if they were made for each other, and her breasts pressed against his chest even as his big hands kneaded her backside and his tongue continued to sweep against hers in a deliciously intoxicating kiss.

When he finally broke away, she stared up at him, dazed. His mouth was gleaming from kissing her, and that made her want to lick him and start the kiss all over again.

"If I didn't look at your jiggling, Luanne, it's because I didn't want to rush things on a first date," he said in a low voice. "But I noticed your ass. And your fuck-me pumps. And your breasts. I noticed all of you. I stared so hard at you at dinner that I thought I might scare you away. But I'm not the kind of guy to maul a woman, no matter how incredibly sexy she looks. I have self-control. I was raised that you don't do that to a woman you want to date. You move slow."

"Well, Officer Self-Control," she said in a breathy voice, smoothing his collar. She might have rumpled it a little. "There's a difference between moving slow and moving glacially. We're adults. And from now on, if you want to kiss me, you just up and kiss me—"

His mouth swooped over hers again, the kiss harder and more demanding now. No more politeness this time, she guessed with an inward sigh of delight. This kiss lasted so long that her toes were curling, and when he broke free from the kiss, she wobbled in place.

"That was better," she gasped.

A smile curved his mouth. "Yes, it was. When can I see you again?"

Her fingers toyed with the nape of his neck. "I'm free tomorrow."

"I'm working overnight." He leaned in and pressed another light kiss to her mouth. "Early dinner?"

It turned out that she saw him again the next morning on the way to the post office. She was walking down to the town square to buy a book of stamps when a patrol car pulled up alongside her.

"Morning, ma'am," a familiar voice drawled.

She looked over and grinned at the sight of Hank in his patrol car, mirrored sunglasses on over his eyes. With a little hop in her step, she moved to stand next to the car and glanced down at him admiringly. "Nice outfit. Those glasses part of the uniform or do all cops shop at the same place?"

"We all shop at the same place," he said easily.

She grinned. "I knew it."

"What are you up to this morning?"

She waved a hand at the central building that was

Bluebonnet's post office slash police station slash city hall. "Heading to get some stamps. You off to arrest some perps somewhere? Living a life of danger?"

"Not at nine in the morning. I was going to go set up behind a sign and see if I can catch some people speeding through a school zone."

"How naughty of you."

"How naughty of them."

Ooh, he was flirting back with her. Her stuffy cop had a sense of fun after all. She liked that. "So from what I'm hearing, you're going to stop people from being wicked? That's no fun."

"Why, are you planning on being wicked?" There was definitely a flirty look in his eyes.

"I might. There's a field or two out there just dying for a crop circle."

She said it in a playful way, but his face immediately changed. Gone was the frisky look. In its place was a grim, disapproving smile. She'd apparently said the wrong thing.

He glanced down the street, then back at her. "Luanne, you can't be pulling those stunts around town."

"Well, I wouldn't do it in town," she said lightly. "I'd have to do it in a field."

"You know what I mean. If I catch you, I'd have to arrest you. These Jane stunts are dangerous and you shouldn't be doing them."

She rolled her eyes. They were not dangerous. "Remind me not to tell you about them, then."

He looked like he wanted to protest, but bit it back.

They stared at each other for a long minute, and Luanne felt awkward. Man, mention one crop circle around a guy and he got all stiff and unhappy. It was like he hated her job. But if that was the case, then why was he going out with her? Did he even want to go out with her?

She had to know. "I had fun last night," she said, drawing the conversation back to safer topics.

The smile returned to his mouth. "Me, too. We still on for dinner?"

"I thought you were working tonight?" She trailed a finger along the door of the squad car. "How come you're working now?"

"Picking up an extra shift. I didn't lie to you."

She laughed. "Of course you didn't lie to me, silly. I was just curious."

His ears flushed a little, and her heart melted just a tiny bit. "Of course. I'm sorry. In my line of work it's just . . . well, honesty is really important. That's all."

She winked at him. "I'll keep that in mind. And I'll see you tonight?"

"I'll be there."

One week later

As was her habit, Luanne woke up early, grabbed a coffee, and then opened her laptop. She went immediately to her web page to check her page hits. She scanned her traffic statistics—up from last week. That was good. She'd uploaded the first cow tipping video last night, and she scrolled through the comments. No surprise, it was a hit. It seemed the more ridiculous the situation she put herself into, the more popular the video was.

Check out the hottie in the uniform, one of the commenters said. *What city is this in and can I get myself some of that man meat?*

Sorry, ladies, she thought. *Officer Man Meat is claimed.* She sipped her coffee and then clicked on the video, fast-forwarding until Hank came into frame. She paused it and studied his intense frown and his big body for a long moment with pleasure.

They'd seen each other every day this past week. He'd moved a few shifts around so he could take her out for dinner, and when he hadn't been able to do that, they'd met for breakfast instead. He had the day off today, so they were going fishing. Which sounded absurd to think about—one didn't go fishing on a date, after all—but she was looking forward to it a bit too much for her own good. There was just something about Hank and his good-natured country boy attitude that appealed to the city girl in her.

Plus, she was pretty sure she could come up with some sort of fishing stunt to use for her video blog. Just what, she wasn't exactly sure yet, but given time, she'd come up with a good concept that was sure to bring hits. She was good at that.

She hadn't had much time to work on her blog this week, she realized with surprise. She set aside her coffee mug and picked up her favorite jeans from the floor, scrutinizing them for a moment. With a shrug, she slipped them on and reached for her favorite tank top. There hadn't been one single call about chupacabra—which was unusual, given the small-town nature of this place and the two-hundred-dollar reward she was offering to talk to an eyewitness. Surely there had to be a town drunk somewhere who was willing to make up a good, credible story. She'd put out more flyers last night on a few telephone poles just in case. She could always hire an actor or pay someone, but she preferred "real" eyewitnesses. Mostly because they were much better liars on camera than a buddy who was reading woodenly from a script.

Luanne tugged her hair into a ponytail and checked her face. No makeup. Ah well. It was just fishing, and last night he'd kissed off all of her makeup when they'd made out in his truck, so this would do. Just thinking about kissing Hank made her flush with pleasure. For a tall, lanky country boy who modestly claimed he hadn't dated much, the man could kiss like a fiend.

She really couldn't object to a talent like that, especially when she benefited from it.

Sliding on a pair of sandals, she tucked her ID and a few

bucks into her jeans pocket, along with her cellphone. As soon as she picked up her phone, however, it buzzed with an incoming text.

Gonna be late, Hank sent. Dad can't figure out how to work one of the new computer programs again. I'm heading there first and I'll be over in about a half hour.

A smile curved her mouth. Another station computer emergency? They seemed to have one daily. Luanne thought it was ironic that the police station employed five men, and not a single one seemed to know how to do a thing with a computer.

I'll meet you there, she sent back, and headed down the stairs of the house.

Emily glanced up at her from a chair in the living room, still wearing her robe and fuzzy slippers. A large wallpaper sample book was perched in her lap, and she glanced at the clock when Luanne headed for the front door. "Where are you going so early?"

"Hank's taking me fishing."

Em snorted and flipped a page. "You sure have been seeing him a lot. Aren't you supposed to be blogging? Doesn't that take up all your spare time?"

Luanne looked at her sister guiltily. Okay, she might have mentioned that editing the video blogs was time-consuming (a lie) so she could get out of going tile shopping with her sister. But really, tile shopping? Boring. "I still have two weeks' worth of videos to post before I run out. There's plenty of time to edit up the next video."

"Mmm-hmm."

"Really. Plenty of time. I'm rounding up witnesses for my chupacabra segment as we speak."

"Uh huh."

She lifted her chin. "And if you know of someone that's willing to shave his poodle and have it guest star on a grainy video as a chupacabra, you let me know. Tell him I'll pay well."

Em rolled her eyes. "Yeah, I'll get right on that."

Luanne grinned at her sister. "What? It's good money."

"It sounds crazy. Your entire job *is* crazy, Luanne," Emily said, an argument that Luanne had heard a jillion times before. "I'm surprised that police officer you've been dating approves of your stunts."

She shrugged. "Hank hasn't said that he minds them," she lied. He just had an enormous, silent scowl on his face every time her job was brought up. That wasn't exactly *saying* that he minded.

"Ha. Likely. Sharps are law-abiding citizens, through and through. That man probably goes the speed limit in school zones and has never met a red light he didn't come to a complete stop at. I'm surprised he hasn't taken it upon himself to keep you busy just so you can't stir up the locals." Emily waved her fingers at Luanne in a shooing motion. "Have fun and try to catch dinner."

"Hope you're hungry for minnow," Luanne called as she opened the front door.

"Yum yum," her sister called back before the door shut.

Luanne bounded down the porch, smiling at her sister's teasing. Em came across as a cranky older sister, but the teasing was simply affection. Em was a motherer, and since she'd gotten divorced a while back, Luanne figured that she didn't have anyone to mother but her. She began to walk to the police station.

And frowned to herself, just a little.

It seemed ludicrous that Hank would insist on taking her out every night just to keep her busy and out of trouble . . . didn't it?

"Lord 'a mercy," one of the cops drawled as she walked through the door. "It's the Legend of Jane."

Hank's head shot up over one of the computers in the back, a scowl on his face.

Luanne sighed. So not a good sign. But she pasted a

bright smile to her face and greeted the cop at the front desk who was staring at her with obvious delight. "That's me."

"My kids love your blog!" The man took off his baseball cap, wiped his forehead, and then replaced his hat with a grin. "That time you went cliff diving to try and get a bald eagle egg? We all laughed our asses off. It was terrific. You're one wild girl. Where's your glitter makeup today?"

She smiled at him, feeling a bit weary of the attention. "I don't wear it unless I'm filming." Like she normally trotted around town in glittery pink eye makeup?

He looked crestfallen. "Oh. I'd love to get a picture with you for my kids, but I don't know if they'll recognize you without your getup. You're a tall one, though." He whistled and stared up at her. "Don't look nearly so tall on camera."

"Maybe we can do pictures some other time," she said, still smiling, though it was a bit more forced now. "I'm here to see Hank."

"He's trying to show his dad how to use the computer," the man said with a grin. "New forms from the county, and everyone's all thumbs trying to figure them out."

She knew Hank wasn't exactly a computer guru himself. She could only imagine how bad his father was if he was trying to show the man how to do something on the computer. "Thanks. Can I head back?" At the man's nod, she slipped past the front desk and moved to the back desks where Hank and a tall, lanky man with a grizzled white beard both squinted and leaned over a computer.

"Go to the next field, Dad," Hank murmured. "You have to fill out all the fields in red."

The older Sharp frowned and moved the mouse a little, then clicked slowly. Then clicked very slowly again.

"No, Dad, when it says you double click, you have to click two times."

"I did. You saw me."

"You have to click two times fast."

"That's what I did."

Hank sighed and glanced over at Luanne. "We might be a minute."

"It's okay," she said, leaning over to glance at the computer screen. "Anything I can help with? It looks like a pretty simple Access database template."

Both men turned to look at her.

"Database . . . template?" Hank said slowly.

"Yes," she said, smiling. She gestured at one of the fields. "You enter in the information and I'm guessing you press this calculation button and it'll pull in additional information from a database of some sort. Is that right?"

They continued to stare at her.

She laughed. "You don't have to look at me like that. I was pretty good with computers in my former life."

The elder man gestured at the computer and got out of his chair. "Be my guest."

Luanne slid into the seat and took the scribbled notes that they handed her. Within a few minutes, she had the ticket logged into the county database, and showed them how to move around in the database itself. They nodded understanding, but she was pretty sure they'd forget as soon as they needed to enter something in again.

The older Sharp clapped a hand on her shoulder as she finished. "We should fire one of these boys and hire you here at the station."

"Not funny, Dad," Hank said in a low voice.

"I wasn't being funny," he said. "Stewart falls asleep on patrol all the time."

"He's seventy, dad."

Just then, Luanne's phone buzzed with an incoming text. She glanced at the screen and checked the message. Hi there. I got this number off of a flyer. Were you asking about a chupacabra?

Score! She pocketed the phone and smiled brightly at both men. "I don't need a job. I have one. We ready to go, Hank?"

"Sure, give me just a second to wrap up here."

She nodded and slipped away, pulling her phone back out to send a hasty text. She knew if Hank saw the message, he wouldn't approve. Better not to share it with him. Instead, she headed out to the parking lot and leaned up against her car, thumbs flying over the keyboard of her phone.

Busy right now, but can I call you in a few hours? I really want to talk about the sighting.

Hank emerged a minute later, smiling down at her, and she hastily hid her phone, sliding it into her back pocket. "You're my hero," he said in a low voice, his hand sliding to her waist. "I might have been there for an hour trying to show my dad how to use the computer."

"It was my pleasure," she said in a husky voice, smoothing her hand over the tan collar of his uniform. "I'm always eager to be a help, Officer."

A smile tugged at his mouth. "Now that doesn't sound like the Luanne I know."

For some reason, that hurt her feelings. He made it sound as if she was a nuisance. Worse, a menace. And she didn't like that. So her job was a little off the rails. So what? A girl had to get paid. Luanne slipped out of his grip and opened her car door. She ignored his questioning look and sat down, closing the door and buckling her seat belt.

Before she could pull out, Hank folded his long body into the car in the passenger seat. Damn. She should have locked the door. Instead, she glared at him.

"What'd I say?"

She jammed the key into the ignition and stared out the windshield. It was still early, the sun barely shining from behind the trees in the distance. Hank had been up all night on an evening shift, but he'd wanted to spend time with her. She, on the other hand, was fully rested. So why was she so prickly?

Her phone buzzed in her back pocket, reminding her.

She hated sneaking around. It made her feel like she was doing something wrong. She glanced sharply over at Hank, who was just as tall and physically attractive as could be. It was a shame he was Dudley Do-Right in the flesh and would disapprove of her job at all turns. And it made her somehow feel like she was embarrassing him. As if she were doing something wrong.

Which was stupid, really. It was a harmless, slightly off-the-wall job that just happened to bring in money.

Unless Emily was right and he was just spending time with her to keep her out of trouble. But that seemed silly. Didn't it?

So she looked over at him. "If I'm such a pain in the ass, why are you dating me?"

He slid over, and for the first time, she wished her stupid sedan had bucket seats. His thigh pressed up against hers and there was a too-cocky grin on his mouth. "Did I hurt your feelings?"

"No one likes to be told that she's a huge obnoxious pest, Hank Sharp."

"You're not a huge pest," he told her in a soft, low voice. "You're a pest that's sized just right for me."

She shoved at him. "That is not funny."

He grabbed her hand, forcing it to remain against the center of his chest, and he grinned down at her scowl. "I was just teasing you, Luanne. You know I like you."

"Yes, but you don't like Jane. And Jane seems to be all that anyone remembers, so how do I know that you really do like me? What exactly is it about me that you like?"

He tucked a lock of hair behind her ear—it had slipped out of her ponytail—and she shivered at the small touch. "You really want me to list it out?"

"Yup," she said flatly.

"Well, you're tall—" he began, and cut off with a chuckle when her glare intensified. "I'm kidding. I like a lot of things about you."

"So many that you possibly can't name them all, obviously."

Hank ran a hand down his face and sighed. "Luanne, I'm not great with this sort of thing."

"Which is ironic, because I am."

"And that's one of the things I like about you," he told her quietly. "You're fearless."

That sounded like a compliment and not like *Luanne, you are a scourge on mankind.* "Go on."

"You're funny," he said in a low voice, sliding a bit closer to her in the car. "You're really smart and you know a lot about computers. You're friendly and open to everyone. You're always willing to try new things." At her skeptical eyebrow lift, he grinned, his arm looping around her shoulders and tugging her close. "I might have watched a few videos of the Legend of Jane on my phone while I was on speed patrol late last night."

She settled into his arms, feeling a little better about things and less like a leper. "Now you're just trying to flatter me."

He laughed. "I'm not. I promise I'm not. It's just that . . . the things I like about you are the things that I wish I was more like. I wish I was smarter with computers. I wish I was fearless like you. I wish I was as outspoken and friendly and willing to be adventurous. I'm just a small-town cop who wouldn't know how to be adventurous if it bit him in the ass. It's not how I was raised." He leaned in and pressed a feather-light kiss to her temple. "But it doesn't mean that I can't appreciate it in you."

Her breath caught in her throat at that faint graze of his lips against her skin. She closed her eyes and tilted her head back, raising her mouth to him in a not-so-subtle gesture.

Hank's lips grazed against hers. "Am I forgiven?" he whispered.

"You were never in trouble," she said in a light voice, twisting so she could wrap her arms around his neck. "I just like hearing the compliments."

"You're pure evil, Luanne Allard."

"You love it. You eat it up."

"I think I just might." Hank wrapped her hair around his big hand and tugged on her ponytail, tilting her head back, and he began to lightly feather kisses along her throat. "And I'd rather eat you up."

A jolt of pleasure rocketed through her body at his words. They'd been dating for a week, but they'd done little more than kiss and flirt. To hear him be so brazen with a suggestion, well, it made her toes curl with anticipation. And then his tongue trailed a line from her chin to her ear, and she forgot just about everything.

A low moan rose in her throat when he took one of her earlobes between his teeth and nipped, then tongued it to take away the sting. Her fingers dug into the collar of his uniform. "My ears are really sensitive."

"So I see," he murmured. "I find that very interesting. Another thing I happen to like about you." And he lightly bit down on her earlobe again.

Luanne whimpered, her hips rocking in reaction to the pulse of heat that flared once more. When he gently licked her earlobe again, she thought she'd go mad with the sensation. Of course, that was before he moved to the shell of her ear and began to trace it with the tip of his tongue. Her nipples were rock-hard in response to his touch, and she arched her back, pushing against his chest.

"Touch me, Hank. Touch me everywhere."

His hand left her ponytail and she felt his tongue slide against her ear again just as his other hand slid under her tank top, resting on her belly.

That wasn't good enough. Luanne moved a hand to rest over his and directed him to her breast, sighing with relief when he cupped her through her bra.

"You feel so good in my arms, Luanne," he murmured into her ear, then sucked on her earlobe again. His thumb grazed over the tip of her breast, teasing her nipple. "Maybe you believe me when I say that I'm crazy about you."

"I . . . might need more convincing." The words gasped out of her as he pinched her nipple through the fabric, and she ruined her ballsy statement with another low moan. "Oh my god, Hank. You—"

Footsteps sounded on the pavement a few feet away. They broke apart like guilty teenagers, Hank quickly sliding over to the far side of the car just as Stewart knocked on the car window and peered down at them.

"Everything okay?"

Luanne gave him a thumbs-up, sure that her face was bright red, and hoping desperately that her nipples weren't visible through her tank top.

He motioned for her to roll down the window, so she started the car and then jammed a finger on the button until the window went down. And then Stewart passed her a print-out of a photo of her in her Jane gear. "Can you sign this for my grandkids?"

She took the Sharpie he offered her and quickly signed, handing it back to Stewart with a smile. The moment with Hank was gone, which made her sad. Now that the picture of Jane had come up, she didn't know how he'd react. And she didn't look over at him until Stewart was gone.

Hank's ears were bright red. "I didn't realize we were in front of the station house still."

A distracted Hank was sexy. She grinned and ran a finger lightly under his collar. "You say you're not adventurous, but you almost got to third base in front of the police station. I'd say that's pretty adventurous."

"Third base? Since when did third base become your breast?"

"Who said we were stopping at my breast?" She winked at him and put the car in reverse. "But I suppose you want to go fishing now, right?"

"Who the hell is thinking about fish at a time like this?"

She grinned.

*   *   *

They only fished for a few hours before Hank began to nod off, exhausted from his night of work. She drove him back to his house and tucked him into bed, tugging off his boots and turning off all the lights before she left. He'd tried to drag her down into bed with him for a cuddle, but she'd resisted, though it was sweet of him.

Truth was, she had too much to accomplish, the perfect time to do it was while Hank was asleep.

CHAPTER FOUR

"Thank you again, sir, for volunteering to be on camera."
Luanne wiped a stray bit of glitter out of one eye and
adjusted one of her striped kneesocks, camera clutched
firmly in hand. "You've been a great help."

The kid—Bobby—pocketed the money she'd given him
and smiled in a way that he probably thought was seductive,
except for the fact that he was seventeen if he was a day.
"I'm glad I can help. I'm a big fan of yours."

"Thank you. That's sweet."

"I mean it. You ever need anything else done around here,
you just call me. I'm happy to guest star."

She paused, thinking. She was already all dressed up as
Jane and had a willing volunteer. The sun was just now going
down, and she had footage for her chupacabra episode that
included a "trail" and sightings, and an in-depth interview
with a kid who was clearly lying through his teeth but made
for a good video segment. She could shoot a chupacabra
"encounter" with her night-vision camera some other night.

But for tonight, if she had help, why not kill two birds with one stone? She checked the amount of battery life in her camera—still good. And she had the planks and rope in her car. Luanne glanced over at Bobby. "Don't suppose you know anything about crop circles?"

"I don't," he said eagerly. "But I know a dude with a sorghum field just a few miles away that's totally ready to be mowed down."

Perfect. "Lead on, then."

H ank was just getting out of the shower when his phone rang. He yawned and headed to the receiver, peering at the caller ID. The county sheriff's office. Damn. What now? He picked up the phone. "This is Hank."

"Hank? It's me, Rick Brannan. Sorry to be bothering you."

"It's okay. It's my day off." He scratched his still-damp chest, yawning. Hell. Just the person he didn't want to be talking to today. Rick sometimes called him to take a speed patrol shift on the highway when he was short a guy for the weekend, and Hank always covered for him. Except, tonight he didn't want to. Tonight he wanted to see Luanne's smiling face again. Maybe they'd go out for a late dinner—or an early breakfast. "Just woke up. You need me to take a shift or something? Because I don't know—"

"Ain't calling about that."

"Oh?"

"Well, we had a weird incident tonight."

His blood went cold. "What?"

"You ever heard of crop circles?"

He groaned. "Don't tell me. There's a tall woman with a pink shirt on and she's in trouble."

"We brought her and a boy into the station. She says she knows you."

"She's my girlfriend," he said flatly. Who exactly was the kid she was with? What the hell was Luanne thinking, dragging in someone else? Damn it. He'd told her to knock the crazy shit off, and as soon as he went to sleep, she went ahead and did it anyhow?

The man on the other line chuckled. "That's what she was saying. You—"

"I'll be there in a half hour." And he hung up before he could hear any more.

This was going to get around town. Hell, it was going to get around the entire county. And he liked Luanne, but this was thoughtless and foolhardy of her. He couldn't have a girlfriend who was constantly getting into scrapes and then posting them online. Because then if she got away with something illegal, people would start to look at him and wonder what he was letting her get away with. *It's mighty convenient for a lawbreaker like Luanne Allard to have a cop for a boyfriend,* they'd say. *Probably turns a blind eye to everything she does.*

And as much as he liked her, he couldn't afford that in his life. If people thought he was just a bit crooked? In such a small town? He was done.

If she kept going with her career, she'd ruin his.

They'd have to break up, or she'd have to quit her job. There were no two ways about it. And he knew that wasn't a conversation that would go down well.

Mouth grim with anger, Hank shoved his legs through a pair of jeans and dressed.

When he arrived at the sheriff's office, Brannan was smirking at him knowingly. "You come to retrieve your girl?"

Of course that was why he was here. Like he'd be here for anything else. But he only glared at the man and gestured for him to lead on.

Brannan led him back to the holding cells, and opened the door to the first one.

There, sitting on a metal bench and looking very guilty, was Luanne, dressed in her Jane gear. There were grass stains on her kneesocks and her normally perky blonde pony-tails were drooping. Glitter was smeared on her cheeks. And she looked up at him with a faint smile. "Surprise."

He didn't smile back. Instead, he glanced over at Brannan, waiting.

"The farmer decided not to press charges. The boy that was accompanying her was underage so he's been sent home with his parents."

Hank nodded, not looking at Luanne as she got to her feet and moved to his side. "I'll drive her home. Thank you, Brannan. I appreciate it."

"You sure I can't do anything else for you?" Brannan said with a knowing smile.

"I'm sure." His voice was flat and cold. He put a hand to the small of Luanne's back, all but shoving her out of the station.

They didn't speak until they got into the parking lot. Luanne put a hand to the door of his squad car and then gave him an impish look. "You want me to sit in the back because I've been naughty?"

He glared at her.

"Okay, clearly someone doesn't have a sense of humor today," she said under her breath as she slid into the front passenger seat.

He said nothing. He simply waited until she got into the car and buckled up, then he started the engine and turned onto the highway.

Silence reigned for a few minutes. Then, she glanced over at him. "Are you going to talk to me at all?"

He bit down the sigh that threatened to escape. "What is there to say?"

"I don't know," she began. "How about a 'I'm really mad

at you, Luanne. You can't keep pulling this shit.' And then I'll say something like, 'You're not my dad, and I'm allowed to do what I want.' And then we'll argue for a bit longer and then fall into this backseat and make love like two wild and crazy people."

"I'm not your father," he agreed as he exited the highway, heading for Bluebonnet. Almost home. "And it's clear that I can't stop you unless you do something illegal. Which means that I'll probably have to choose between you and my job."

"No, you don't—"

"Yes, I do. I'm a police officer, Luanne. How do you think it would look if I sat back and let my girlfriend do all kinds of illicit activities and then post them online for the world to see? What do you think that would do to my job?"

"Crop circles aren't against the law—"

"No? That field belongs to a farmer who depends on those crops for a living. From what I hear, you went in and trampled almost a quarter of an acre. That's money that comes out of his pocket. That's money that you're taking out of his kids' mouths. That's trespassing, Luanne. That's trespassing and willful destruction of another person's property. I don't know about where you come from, but it's illegal here. You're lucky he didn't press charges. At the very least, you owe him an apology."

She was silent. She was silent for so long that he finally glanced over at her. Her mouth was set into a mulish line, and glitter streaked from the corners of her eyes.

"But I guess it's different when you don't know the people, right? I guess it's different when it's just funny stunts for your blog." His tone was biting and cold as he pulled the car down the long driveway to the Peppermint House and parked.

"You don't understand, Hank. This is how I make a living. It's not because it's fun for me. It's just something I do.

And the wilder the stunt, the easier it is for me to pay the bills."

"You're right, Luanne. I don't understand. It's how you make a living. But doing illegal things isn't the right way to make a living."

"Not everything I do is against the law." Her arms crossed over her chest in a defensive position. "You make it sound like I'm a bad person. Some sort of dangerous criminal. I'm just a video blogger."

"I don't think you're a bad person," he said quietly. "I just don't think you're thinking of anyone but yourself."

A small laugh escaped her and she gave him a sideways glance. "Who else should I be thinking about?"

"Me."

The look she gave him was incredulous. "What do you mean?"

"I mean that I'm a police officer, Luanne. This is a small town. What you do reflects on me." When she shook her head, he continued. "I can't have you doing stunts around here and not do anything about it. It means that if I know about it, I have to arrest you. So it's better that I don't know about it." He paused, and then continued. "And it's best if we say good-bye here."

"Good-bye?" She seemed shocked. "You're breaking up with me over a stupid crop circle?"

"No. I like you, Luanne. Really, really like you. You're the perfect woman for me in all ways . . . except one. Our jobs just aren't compatible. And if we're together, one of us has to give up their job. I can't ask you to give up yours, and you can't ask me to give up mine, so it's best we go our separate ways."

She stared at him.

"I'm sorry, Luanne."

"I'm sorry, too," she said furiously, shoving the door open and pushing her way out of the car.

Damn it. He'd hurt her. He'd tried to do this gently, even though he felt like shit about it, but she was still hurt. Hank turned off the car and opened his door, unfolding his long body to his full height. "Luanne," he called after her.

She ignored him, stomping her way to the front porch. Her back was stiff, and she wouldn't turn around.

He'd definitely hurt her feelings. But hell, what was he supposed to do? Turn a blind eye to her antics? She was posting them online, for crying out loud. Hank ran a hand down his face and got back into the car. He stared at the dash without seeing it, even after she slammed the front door of the Peppermint House and the front porch light went off.

For some reason, he already missed her.

"**E**xplain it to me again?" Emily said, grabbing a cup of coffee and sitting down at the dining room table. She frowned at Luanne. "Your mouth was full and I couldn't make out what you said."

"I said," Luanne gritted between a mouthful of cereal, "that Officer Stick Up His Ass broke up with me." She hugged the punch bowl full of cereal closer to her chest. Some people drowned their sorrows in ice cream. She drowned hers in Cap'n Crunch. "He said my job was stupid and reckless."

"Well, it is," Emily said.

That got her a glare from Luanne.

"Oh, come on. If it wasn't stupid and reckless, no one would go to your website to see it. There are a million cute girls on the Internet. Only a few special idiots go cow tipping dressed like a hooker."

"Not a hooker," Luanne protested, her voice rising an octave. "This is a freaking roller derby costume. Jeez!"

Emily waved a hand. "My point is, you dress up like a

nut, you perform nutty antics, and you post them online in the hopes of driving traffic to your website so you can make money from the ad revenue, right?"

She shoved another spoonful of cereal into her mouth and crunched for a long moment. "Yeah. So?"

"I can't imagine that a straitlaced cop like Hank Sharp would ever have a problem with that," Em said in an innocent voice. "He must have misled you about who he is. Perhaps it was all the piercings? The tattoos? The Harley he drives? Oh wait, I'm wrong. He drives a police car and never puts on anything that isn't starched to regulation first."

"You make him sound like a dweeb, Em," Luanne protested, and then wondered why she was defending the jerk. After all, he'd dumped her. There was no need to defend anyone anymore. "He's not like that."

"He's not? What's he like, then?"

Luanne crunched for a long moment, thinking. And then she sighed. "He's really fair."

"Fair?"

"Yeah, you know." She waved her spoon, sending milk droplets splashing across Em's antique table. "He's a good guy. He listens to people when they have problems. Gets kittens out of trees. He likes to help people and do the right thing."

"He sounds like a horrible jerk," Em said in a laughing voice, plucking a paper towel from the countertop and wiping up Luanne's mess. "Thank goodness you're free of him, huh? I bet he was always telling you what to do and how to act, too."

Luanne was silent. Truth was, he'd never done that. He'd appreciated the way she'd dressed. He liked the way she talked. He loved the way she carried herself. And when she was a bit brazen? He liked that, too. She was the opposite of him, but instead of him trying to tamp her down and force her to behave, he seemed to love watching her just be herself.

The job was the only sticking point. She chewed slowly, thinking. "Something like that."

"Probably for the best that you two broke up. You love your job, right?" Her sister's voice was mild.

She gave Emily a scathing look and took another large bite of cereal. Em knew that Luanne hated the Jane schtick. It was a lot of work. It was obnoxious. She had stalkers, for crying out loud. People wrote her daily asking her to take her top off in videos. It was tiresome. The last three guys she'd dated had wanted her to "stunt" with them on dates. They'd wanted Jane and not Luanne.

And all Hank had ever wanted was Luanne.

She groaned, laying her head on the table. "This sucks, Em. This really, really sucks. Why is it that I find a good guy and he has to be Officer Straight and Narrow?"

"Is that so bad?"

"It is when he dumps me over my job."

"So give up your job. It's ridiculous. You can find something else."

"I can't just give up my job! It pays the bills, Emily. And you know I have a lot of bills." Luanne frowned. "Had a lot of bills."

"I thought they were all paid off?"

"Almost." She stabbed at the bowl of cereal again, watching the Crunch Berries in her bowl drift to the edges. "I'm not quitting just because he wants me to. That's crap. What am I supposed to do instead? Sit around and knit doilies for a living?"

"Maybe you get a real job like the rest of us," Em said. "Or you could, I don't know, help your sister run a bed-and-breakfast."

Luanne sighed and shook her spoon at Emily. "I told you. I'll design you a website but that's where I draw the line. Home renovation is not my gig."

"Whatever you do, I'm sure you'll do it with a glaringly loud and obvious style, Luanne," Emily said with a grin, and reached over to pat her hand. "Why don't you call Hank and tell him you want to talk to him?"

Luanne thought for a minute, and then shook her head. "I want him to come to me first. I'm not crawling back to the man and begging for a second chance."

Emily sighed.

One week later

"**T**hat's right, Officer. I'm pretty sure I heard voices in the upstairs room." Emily Allard-Smith's voice trembled on the other end of the line. "I'd appreciate it if you'd come by the house and check it out."

Hank stared out the dark window of city hall and sighed. "I'm the only one at the station right now, Ms. Allard-Smith. The next shift doesn't come in until midnight. I—"

"I baked some cookies," she said hopefully.

Like cookies were going to be enough to draw him out to the Peppermint House? Although, they probably were enough of a lure for his father. "Ms. Allard-Smith, I—"

"Please," she said in a soft voice. "I'm really scared. I'm positive this place is haunted."

And he was positive that all she had were a few squirrels in the attic and an overactive imagination. "I'll see if I can send someone out."

"Oh good," she said in a grateful voice. "Luanne and I are so scared. She really hasn't been herself this week and this is just the icing on the cake."

Luanne was scared? He sat up straighter, thinking hard. She hadn't been herself that week? Was she missing him? Like he was missing her?

Bright, vivacious Luanne seemed to make everything in his life more exciting, more fun. He'd noticed in the week that they'd been broken up that even the normal dull routines seemed . . . well, they seemed just a tad bit duller than usual.

It was like all the light had gone out and he was just going through the motions.

Which was silly. But then he thought of her wild little smile, and thought maybe it wasn't so silly after all. Maybe she was just as good for him as he was for her.

Except that neither one of them were good for each other's jobs. It just couldn't be. Didn't mean he couldn't stop thinking about how it might have been, though.

"I'll be there in five minutes," he told Emily in a tired voice.

"Perfect," she said, and sounded almost excited.

CHAPTER FIVE

Emily met him at the front door, dressed in a pink sweat-shirt and a pair of jeans with the knees ripped out. She smiled brightly at him, seemingly unafraid. "Thank you so much for coming by, Officer Sharp."

He stepped into the house, scanning the living room. Things were a mess, the furniture covered by white sheets. But then again, things were always a mess in this house since Emily was renovating it single-handedly. No sign of Luanne, either, but that wasn't surprising—even if it was disappointing. She'd likely heard that he was coming over and ran out the door. He suspected she was avoiding him, which he wasn't thrilled about. He kind of wanted to see her again. Wanted to see if she missed him like he was missing her, or if he was the only dumbass messed up over their short relationship. He cleared his throat and looked down at tiny Emily. "Have you had any more incidents since you called me?"

"Incidents? Oh, no. No, I haven't." She put a hand to his

arm and began to push him toward the stairs. "Let me show you what room I heard it in."

He allowed her to lead him, and they climbed up the stairs of the large Victorian house. Though there were some areas that clearly needed repairs, it wasn't a bad house. Just a run-down one.

She paused in front of a door, and her voice dropped. "It was in this room. I think you should check it out."

Hank nodded and put his hand on the door handle. He heard something, all right. It sounded like rustling. With a frown, he pushed the door open.

And stopped in surprise at the sight of Luanne in yoga pants and an old T-shirt, her hair pulled into a haphazard bun. A magazine was open in her lap.

Her jaw dropped and her gaze went to Emily, accusing. "What is he doing here?"

To his surprise, tiny Emily gave him a surprisingly strong shove, knocking him into the room—Luanne's bedroom. "You," she said, pointing at Hank. "Apologize to my sister for breaking up with her and hurting her feelings. And you." That pointing finger swung to Luanne. "Tell this man what you really think about your job and why you do it."

They stared at her.

Emily gave a firm nod and then one more warning look at them. "I don't want to see either one of you come out of here until this is settled. Understand me? You can have cookies when everything is back to normal." And with that, she slammed the door shut behind her, leaving Luanne and Hank in the room alone.

There was a long pause, and then Luanne stifled a giggle. She gave Hank a rueful look. "I think Em missed her calling as a schoolteacher."

He relaxed a little, her smile melting away any irritation he might have had. "Does she treat everyone like they're seven?"

"Pretty much," Luanne said, and closed her magazine, staring at him with wary eyes.

Hell. He had hurt her feelings. And here he'd been trying to go about it the right way. Hank shifted on his feet, uncomfortable. Wasn't it better to break up with her before he had to arrest her? But judging from the wounded look in her eyes, he was guessing he'd messed this up anyhow.

And he shouldn't have cared, but he did.

He crossed his arms over his chest and glanced at the door. It remained shut. He looked back to Luanne and she gave him an expectant look.

"Well?" she said. "Are you here to apologize to me?"

Actually, he was here looking for Emily's ghosts. But now that he was here, he couldn't stop thinking about Luanne. Couldn't take his eyes off of her, either. She was real pretty tonight, her skin flushed with emotion, her face devoid of makeup, her hair in a loose bun atop her head. Tendrils framed her cheeks and he wanted to brush them aside with his fingers, trace the lines of her face, and oh-so-carefully kiss that wary frown off her mouth. He opened his mouth, but the words didn't come out. Hell. Hank wasn't one for fancy words anyhow. He didn't know what she wanted to hear from him.

So he decided to start with the truth. He scrubbed a hand over his jaw and sighed. "I thought I was doing the right thing, Luanne. You know it's going to be a problem between us."

"You didn't have to just drop me off on my porch and wave good-bye, though," she said, and there was all that hurt again. "I mean, if you don't want to date me, just tell a girl, will you? I can handle rejection just as well as the next person."

"But I do want to date you. I just . . . I can't. Do you understand why?"

To his surprise, she nodded and got to her feet, her long legs unfolding. "I do. I just wish you'd talked to me first instead of deciding it right away."

"I wish you'd talked to me before you went off chasing chupacabra!"

"Actually, I was chasing crop circles." A hint of her impish smile returned and she moved to his side, standing in front of him, inches away. "Everyone knows chupacabra's just a myth anyhow."

Hank sighed.

She ran a hand up his chest and rested it against his heart in that possessive, admiring way that always made his cock get hard instantly. "It's okay. I forgive you."

"And?" he prompted.

"And?" she asked, looking up at him innocently, her fingers playing with the first button on his shirt.

"Your sister said I should apologize and you should tell me the truth about your job." He leaned closer to her, inhaling her fresh scent. Damn, she smelled sexy. "Way I see it, I kept my side of the bargain."

Her playful look instantly disappeared and her hand dropped. Luanne's expression became guarded, almost anxious, and she twisted her hands.

Whatever it was she had to tell him, it made her nervous. Unhappy.

He didn't like that. He liked the fearless Luanne. Frowning at her anxious look, he moved to sit down in the chair she'd vacated and pulled her down into his lap.

She fell into his arms, hers going around his neck. "I don't know if I should be sitting in your lap, Officer."

"If you're my girlfriend, I don't see why not."

Luanne stilled and looked at him with a serious, almost hopeful gaze. "So am I?"

Was he going to regret this later if she didn't give up her job? Probably. Did he care? Not at the moment. "I don't want anyone else."

She leaned in and kissed him lightly, her lips brushing over his, the smile returning to her face.

Hank deepened the kiss, leaning in and stroking his

tongue against her parted lips, letting her know that he wanted her. She made a sexy whimper in the back of her throat and then her mouth opened for him, and she pressed her breasts against his chest as she kissed him.

When they finally broke the kiss, both were breathing hard. Luanne looked dazed.

"And?" he managed to say. "You were going to tell me about your job?"

Luanne dropped her gaze. "You sure you want to know the sordid truth?"

"More than anything." Well, almost more than anything. Right now he wanted to kiss the hell out of her again, and possibly see what she looked like without those clothes on. But he'd settle for her snuggled up on his lap, her ass pressing down against his erection.

Luanne sighed. "It's not that I want to keep doing the Jane stuff. It's that I don't have any other options."

"What do you mean?"

She paused for a long moment, and the room got so quiet that he could hear a nearby clock ticking. Then, she blurted out the truth. "I was stupid over a man." When he said nothing, she looked over at him. "I told you I have a master's in finance, right? I also had investment certifications. I am eminently qualified to sell and trade stock and handle investments."

That sounded totally foreign to someone like him. "I see."

"The problem is, when you're working in investments, your credit rating is of the utmost importance. After all, you can't really be trusted with other people's money when you can't handle your own, right?"

Realization dawned on him. "And your credit's bad?"

"My credit's awful," she admitted, a tiny, forced laugh escaping her. "You see, about two years ago, I had a live-in boyfriend who stole my mail and ran up a bunch of credit cards in my name. And then he left me and ran off to the West Coast to find his inner self or some crap. I didn't even know he'd run up all the cards until a few months later, and the banks would only let me dispute some of it. My credit was shot to hell, and I was laid off from my job for an unrelated reason, only to find out that I couldn't get another because my credit was hosed. I went through all of my retirement savings paying off debts and trying to fix things."

He rubbed her back, letting her know that he supported her. He didn't interrupt, just let her talk.

Luanne twisted her hands and continued. "The Jane thing started as a joke. A friend took me skydiving to help me forget my problems, and it was the most ridiculous thing ever. We both dressed in absurd getups and cracked jokes the entire time to hide the fact that we were about to pass out with fear. And it turns out they record videos of your dive and sell them back to you, right? Well, she posted the video online and the next thing I knew, it had a hundred thousand hits and more people demanding stunts and suggesting them."

She shrugged her shoulders. "One thing led to another, and I started doing stunts because it was an interesting way to pass the time while I was job hunting. I got an offer to host ads on my website, and it seemed harmless, so I gave it a shot and then forgot about it. The first check was for four figures. It startled the hell out of me to get that out of the blue, and then after that, I was addicted. I was putting up videos constantly, and cultivating an audience, blogging, everything. I've made a small fortune from Jane and have sunk it into paying debts back." She looked over at him and smiled weakly. "But it's not what I want to do with my life. The thought of jumping out of helicopters or eating strange stuff just to get video hits got old about a year ago, except I can't turn the money down. I'm unemployable in my field. I do Jane stuff because Jane's the only thing I'm good at."

He was surprised. Stunned, actually. "I thought you liked it."

She gave him a brittle smile. "Kind of hate it at times, actually. No one wants to talk to *me*. They only want to see

Jane perform some wacky trick. I've gone out with guys who want me to turn into Jane the moment the lights are off. I've had waitstaff spill plates of food on me in the hopes that I'm filming and they'll get into the next shot. I've had stalkers waiting at my car."

His hands tightened around her. "You can find another job if you hate it. One that's safe. One that's quiet."

Luanne shrugged. "Sometimes it's just easier to be Jane and let the money roll in, though."

"I have money," he said quietly. "Do you want to borrow some?"

"God, no. The last thing I want is to owe someone else. I pay off my last credit card next month. Then it's only five years or so until my credit's fixed." She gave him a weary smile. "See, you thought I only played a train wreck. Turns out I am one in real life, too."

"I don't think you're a train wreck," he told her, continuing to rub a soothing hand on her back. "I think you trusted the wrong guy and got burned, and you fought your way out the only way you could. That doesn't change what I think of you. If anything, it makes me like you more." At her skeptical look, he grinned. "Underneath that rakish, devil-may-care exterior, Luanne Allard's a completely responsible stick-in-the-mud. Just like her boyfriend."

She leaned in so close that her breath fanned against his cheek. "There are worse things than being like my boyfriend," she murmured.

"Mmm. Such as?"

"Being lonely," she told him, and slid her hand between his legs, cradling his erection. "I missed you."

"Missed you, too, baby," he said, leaning in to kiss her. And then he groaned. "Hell. I have to get back to the station. I've been gone too long already and I'm the only one there tonight."

She wiggled on his lap in a way that made his eyes want to cross. "Can I come with you?"

"Only if you promise to distract me."

"Deal."

Hank got to his feet and set her down, letting her long body slide against his equally long one. She felt so good against him. "I think you should walk in front of me when we leave."

"Why's that?"

He rubbed his chin, grimacing. "I don't feel like showing your sister my nightstick, and right now I can't seem to put it away."

"Naughty officer." She gave him a lascivious grin and rubbed her hand along the front of his pants again. "I'll do you one better. I'll distract Emily and let you sneak out."

They made it back to the station in record time, and as soon as they hit the door, Hank left her side and moved to the switchboard, checking the phones. He exhaled a sigh of relief. "No calls."

Luanne grinned at him "So very responsible."

The smile that curved his mouth was slow, and incredibly sexy. "It turns you on."

"It just might," she agreed, sauntering over to his side. She stood over the edge of his desk, but he grabbed her by the waist and dragged her into his lap again, which she loved. Hank was the only guy she'd ever dated who she didn't tower over, and his manhandling of her? It made her feel small, petite, and utterly feminine. She was eating it up.

At least, she was until he logged in to a web portal on the computer. "Oh my god, what is that?"

He frowned at her. "What?"

She took the mouse from him and clicked backward. "That website you were just on."

"That's the Bluebonnet city website."

A giggle escaped her throat. It looked . . . awful. Like if

she scrolled down, she expected to see glittery unicorn gifs at the bottom of the page. An obnoxious picture of the city's symbol was set as a repeating, blinding wallpaper, and dear god, was that Comic Sans they were using as the font? "Please tell me it doesn't play music."

"We couldn't figure out how to get it to play," he admitted.

She gave him another horrified laugh. "Did you put this together?"

He nodded, a grin slowly curving his mouth. "Told you we were shit with computers."

"Oh, honey . . . it's so cute." And awful. "You want me to fix you a new website?"

"If you do, you have to promise to show my dad how to use that Access thing again."

Luanne curled up in his lap, wrapping her arms around his neck again and nuzzling him. "Do the big bad po-po need a little woman to come and straighten out their computers for them?"

"I think they do," he said in a husky voice. "This can be your community service."

"Community service?" She raised a teasing eyebrow at him. "Am I under arrest for something, Officer Hotness?"

"Concealment of a deadly weapon," he said quite seriously, and then squeezed her ass.

"That is so lame," she told him with a mock groan. "Seriously. If those are the best lines you have, Officer Sharp, it's no wonder you've been single for so long."

With his hands still on her ass, he stood up, hefting her into the air and carrying her across the room. "It's true, ma'am. You're under arrest."

"What ever will you do with me, Officer Hot Stuff?"

"Well," he drawled, and then gave her an appraising look. "I think I should search you and then take you into a private room for further . . . questioning."

"That sounds so sexy."

"Doesn't it?" He continued walking to one of the back rooms and then set her gently down on a long wooden table.

Luanne glanced around the room in surprise. It was tiny, with only one mirrored window and two chairs. Nothing hung on the walls. As she sat on the edge of the table, watching Hank, he moved to the outside of the door and returned a moment later.

"Where'd you go?"

"Turned off the camera for the interrogation." He leaned in and kissed her. "Unless you felt like showing the world how Jane gets out of an arrest?"

She stilled. His deliberate stress of the word "Jane" told her everything she needed to know. If she wanted to continue to be Jane, well, he'd live with it. "You don't mind?"

"You're an adult, Luanne. I can't make you do anything. And I just want you to be happy. We'll figure something out."

Affection swelled in her chest and she had to blink back sudden sappy tears. "I don't want to show anyone how Jane makes love to Hank. I want to show everyone how Luanne makes love to Hank."

Hank paused, watching her for a long moment, and then his hand slid up to cup her cheek. "You want to make love to me, Luanne?"

She nodded and gave him a cheeky grin. "Actually, I'd prefer if we kept the cameras off, though."

"That, I can do." He leaned in to kiss her. "You sure you want to take this step?"

"Absolutely. I keep throwing myself at you but you're playing hard to get."

He raked a hand through his hair, looking frustrated. "I don't have a condom."

"It's okay. I'm on the pill and clean. As long as you're clean as a whistle, we're good."

"I don't think my whistle's ever been dirtied much," he admitted ruefully.

She grinned and undid the first button on his shirt. "We can fix that for you, lickety split."

He groaned. "Don't say the word 'lick' or I might lose track of my thoughts."

"Can I show you instead, then?" She leaned in and popped the second button of his uniform, then pressed her mouth against the vee of skin revealed. "Mmm, delicious."

"You're the one who's delicious."

"We can both be delicious." She pulled him closer, settling the weight of him between her spread thighs and smiling up at him. Then one hand slid to cup his ass and she tilted her head, as if judging the quality. "Nice and tight. I approve of your butt, Officer."

"I thought this was my interrogation."

"Looks a bit like I've turned it into my exploration." She slid her other hand between two more buttons of his shirt, and pouted when she discovered a white undershirt instead of bare skin. "You are wearing entirely too many clothes."

"And here I thought women liked a police uniform."

"Oh, they do." She squeezed his ass again. Lord knew that she sure liked looking at him while he was in uniform. It did naughty things to her insides. "I'm thinking you should keep it on."

His smile was slow and sexy. "Were you planning on getting me out of it?"

"Parts of you." And she moved her hand from his ass to his cock, testing his reaction. Of course, her own reaction was one of surprise . . . and then pleasure. "Oh my. It seems my officer's packing quite a lot of heat in his uniform."

Hank groaned as her hand rubbed up and down his shaft in a slow, exploratory way. "You're a tease."

"I'm not," she said playfully. "A tease implies that one is going to be left unsatisfied. And that's not part of my plans at all."

"You have this all planned out, do you?" His hand slid

to her calf and then he raised her leg, hitching it around his waist.

Now she was reaching directly between them to stroke his cock. If she pulled her hand away, he'd be pressed up against the apex of her thighs . . . and she rather liked that thought. The low pulse of desire coursing through her veins began to centralize in her hips.

"I do have it all planned out," she admitted, her breath coming in quick little pants. Actually, she didn't have anything planned, but he seemed mesmerized by her boldness, and she was taking that ball and running with it. She liked that he let her take the lead. It was just another thing in their relationship that felt so very right. "First, I'm going to take off my top and amaze you with my breasts. And then I'm going to strip off my pants and amaze you with my long, sexy legs. And then I'm going to lie back on this table and unzip this monster out of your pants."

And she stroked his cock once more.

Hank groaned again, and leaned in to kiss her, hitching her legs tighter around his waist. It pressed his cock against her hand hard, squeezing both between her thighs. His tongue plunged into her mouth and he kissed her with a brutal, fierce kiss that spoke of all kinds of need and left her breathless.

So much for her taking the lead in bed. Screw that. Him getting all fierce with her? Just as sexy and just as exciting. She wiggled on the table, looking up at him, breathless, waiting to see what he'd do next.

Hank leaned down and tugged on her lower lip with his teeth, playing with the soft flesh and then slicking it with his tongue. She whimpered in surprise at that. He felt delicious. "If you take off your own shirt, Luanne, you'll deny me the pleasure of doing it for you."

"Who am I to rob you of such things?" she said in a light, playful tone that seemed just a bit shaky. "Be my guest."

His hands tugged at the hem of her shirt and then he

pulled it over her head, revealing the gray sports bra she wore underneath and had forgotten about. She grimaced up at him. "I swear I have sexier lingerie. I really do. I just wasn't expecting you tonight."

A chuckle escaped him. "You look incredibly sexy in this. Don't sell yourself short."

"I'll look better without it."

His eyes narrowed and she could tell that turned him on. "Show me, then."

She tugged her sports bra off as gracefully as she could—considering it was a slip-on sort of thing, it wasn't all that graceful. But the look in his eyes when he saw her bared breasts made her forget all about grace and elegance and things like that.

"You're gorgeous." His hand cupped a breast, hefting the slight weight of it as if stunned by the feel.

She arched against his hand, pressing her breast against his palm. "Touch me more, Hank. Please. I want your hands all over me."

He obliged her, one large hand continuing to caress and stroke her breast while the other began a leisurely exploration of her bared torso. The backs of two fingers trailed lightly down her rib cage and then over the flat length of her stomach, stopping briefly at the dip of her navel.

She shivered in response, the light touch sending shockwaves of response through her, her nipples hard and aching. Luanne glanced up at him, but he was staring down at her bared skin with an intense look of concentration on his face. As if she were the most important thing in the world at this moment.

And that was a heady feeling.

His trailing fingers moved to her side and then around her back, lightly tracing up and down her spine in a soothing, rubbing motion that made her want to come out of her skin. When she looked up at him again, he was gazing back at her, his eyes heavy-lidded with desire.

"For a rather tall woman, you sure are small and soft in my arms, Luanne."

Her hands went to his shoulders, pulling him close again. "You say the sweetest things."

They kissed once more, the kiss a bit more intense and urgent. His hand went to her shoulder and he gently pushed her onto the table.

She leaned back until her skin touched the cool surface of the table, and her head leaned over the far side, her tousled hair spilling over the edge. She felt like a platter to be devoured, which was rather exciting all in itself. His large hands smoothed over her belly and paused at her hips, and as she stared up at him, he began to tug down the rest of her clothing.

A moment later, she was bare and sprawled on the table before him, her long legs hanging over the edge. Hank groaned at the sight of her and then leaned down to press a light kiss to her belly button. "So beautiful."

For once, witty comebacks escaped her and she shivered with expectant excitement on the table.

He hovered over her belly for a long moment, pressing light kisses there, and just when she was about to turn blue in the face from holding her breath, he slid a bit lower and pressed another kiss to the top of her mound. Her breath exploded from her lungs, causing him to look up with a grin. "Too much?"

"No," she breathed. "Keep going."

Hank did, sliding a bit farther down and kissing his way until he reached the slick lips of her sex. He ran a finger along the seam, and she moaned in response. She was completely wet for him. When he continued to tease her, she lifted her hips, trying to encourage him to go deeper, to slide a finger home and help her ease some of the tension in her body.

But he only continued to tease her, stroking back and

forth as she twisted on the table, raising her hips repeatedly.

"Hank, please," she panted, desperate with need.

Just when she thought she could stand it no longer, he relented in the torture and she felt his thumb stroke along her wet slit one last time, and then sink deep to touch her clit. She moaned at the fierce bolt of pleasure that rocketed through her. Oh god, that felt so good. Her moan turned into whimpers when his thumb remained in place and began to lightly stroke, back and forth.

"Haaank," she moaned, her fingers digging into his shoulders, her hips bucking against his thumb. He was driving her mad with desire. "I'm going to come if you don't stop—"

"So come," he said in a low, husky voice.

She shook her head. "I want to come with you inside me."

He groaned then, showing her that he didn't have nearly as much control as he seemed to. He paused in his stroking, and then his hand lifted. She almost cried out in disappointment, but instead, she heard the sound of his buckle coming undone. She lifted her head and leaned back on her elbows, watching as he removed his belt and slowly unzipped his pants. He shoved them and his boxers down to his knees, and then she was staring right at his rather impressive erection.

"Good man," she told him with an appreciative purr. Luanne was rather pleased that he was big all over. There was nothing small about Hank Sharp. Thank God for that.

He leaned his big body down over the table to kiss her, and she was pinned between him and the unyielding wood, and the sensation was delicious and naughty. She wrapped her legs around him, wriggling underneath him at the feel of his scalding flesh pressed against her own. And as they kissed, he slowly rubbed up and down against her until she was panting with need.

"Inside me," she whispered.

"You're a bossy woman, Luanne Allard," he murmured against her lips, but she felt him slip a hand between them. In the next moment, she felt his cock poised at the entrance of her sex.

"You like that."

"I do," he said, and with a surge, he buried himself deep inside her.

Luanne gasped at the jolt. It had been a while since she'd had sex, and the feel of him inside her came as a bit of a surprise to her body. A pleasant, delicious surprise, she decided, her toes curling with desire. She could feel his big length inside of her, filling her, his weight on top of her, and the waves of desire threatened to overwhelm her. "You feel so good."

"You feel better," he murmured, rising up until he loomed over her. She imagined how decadent it must look from his point of view, her spread on the table before him, pinned to his body by their joined hips. He grasped her hips and pulled her a bit farther down on the table, and then slowly pulled out, then thrust deep again.

The walls of her sex were so slick with need that the swift stroke sent little pulses of delight echoing through her. "More."

He obliged, thrusting deep again, and then began a slow and steady rhythm of thrusts that had her reaching backward and clinging to the lip of the table. Each thrust seemed to fill her perfectly, to hit all the right spots inside her. They were made for each other.

His hands gripped her hips tightly and he continued to thrust, the motions becoming rougher and fiercer the longer he pounded into her, and the slow burn of desire began to turn into a raging inferno. Before long, she was crying out his name and demanding that he fuck her harder, and every time she begged for more, he gave her more. Soon, the table was rocking with the force of his attentions, and her legs were curling around his waist, locked tight, and she was babbling his name, incoherent with pleasure.

Her release took her by surprise. She was just about to suggest that he reach between them and touch her to bring her off, when his next stroke sank deep and seemed to rub against something inside her that made her body go off in a jillion fireworks. She gave a small scream, clenching around him, her body spasming with her orgasm. Over her, she heard him swear and then his thrusts became erratic. She felt him spill inside her, his hands clenching her hips tight, and then he slowly fell down over her, pillowing his head on her breasts as he panted and tried to get his breath back.

Her hands went to his hair and she played with it a little. God, this man was sexy. She was a lucky, lucky woman.

After a long minute of cuddling, he pulled away from her body, grabbed some tissue from a nearby box on a desk in the corner, and handed her a few. "Should probably clean up. I'm sorry I don't have anything better than this."

"That's fine," she said, noticing how bright red his ears were. So cute. He was embarrassed now.

Hank hitched his pants back up around his waist and gestured at the door. "I should, uh, check on the phones to make sure that I didn't miss a call. It'd be bad if it rang to one of the on-call officers and he showed up at the station to see what was going on."

"That would be bad," she agreed in a blissful voice. "And then you'll be back?"

He stared at her, dazed. And then a slow grin spread across his face. "And then I'll be back."

By the time they'd been dating two months, Hank and Luanne were a definite couple. Emily joked that they were joined at the hip, and most in town figured she was probably right.

After all, it had only taken a week or two of Luanne's help around the station before Officer Sharp (senior) decided that they needed an office manager to help run the small police station. Someone who was good with computers and spreadsheets, had ideas for how to make things easier, could run the website, and could keep the place running smoothly while the officers went out and did their jobs instead of being bogged down with technical stuff.

It was the perfect job for her, really. It didn't pay anything close to what her investment jobs had, but that was okay, too. She was happier than she'd ever been, and living with Hank meant that they didn't have to bring in a ton of money anyhow. Rent was cheap in Bluebonnet, and they carpooled to work. People joked that they acted like an old married couple, living together, working together, and maybe they did. Maybe that was boring to most people, but to Luanne and Hank, it was pretty damn nice. They even went fishing together on a regular basis, and Luanne helped Emily continue her renovations on the Peppermint House, even if she didn't see the appeal in hanging wallpaper or things like that. She just liked spending time with her sister.

Everyone was content. And if Hank tended to murmur a few "I love yous" over the police scanner when he knew Luanne was listening, the other officers just pretended not to hear them. Or her somewhat risque responses that were designed to make Hank's ears turn red.

As for the Legend of Jane, well, Jane posted a few more videos and then quietly went away. As attention spans were always short on the Internet, it wasn't long before the world pretty much forgot about a crazy stunt blogger and her ridiculous ideas. The hits on her webpage slowly trailed off to a trickle, and when the money went away, Luanne took down her page. She thought she might regret it and the loss of income.

But instead, all she felt was an overwhelming sense of freedom.

The only person she ever had to be again was Luanne Allard. Boring, plain, too-tall Luanne Allard. And that was just fine with her. After all, boring, too-tall Hank Sharp liked her just the way she was.

ICE PRINCESS

ERIN McCARTHY

CHAPTER ONE

"I'm going to break an ankle. Or a wrist. Or my face. I must be insane to try skiing." Chelsea Carruthers was clumsy on a good day, downright dangerous on a bad day. She sighed and opened her eyes, the steam from the sauna clearing her nostrils. "Hello, is anyone listening to me?"

Nope. Not a soul was paying her an ounce of attention because her two best friends were making out with their boyfriends on the bench across from her. Really? Like it didn't suck enough to be the only single one on this weekend jaunt, now she had to be a fifth wheel to their interpretation of episodes of *The Bachelor*? Matt's hand slid in between the bare legs of her friend Lacey, right on under that towel.

Okay. Time for her to head back to her hotel room. Even though she was wearing a bikini and a towel herself, Chelsea felt there was just a little too much steam and near nudity going on in this sauna for her personal comfort level. "Yeah. I'll see the four of you tomorrow."

Amy broke off from tongue twirling with Sam to put up a weak protest. "You don't have to go, Chelsea."

Because it would be so much fun for her to stay.

"I most definitely do. Before I decide to get mischievous and record both of you and put it online." Which she would never do, but cracking a joke was better than crying about it, which was tempting. She should have canceled her room for this weekend when she and Eric broke up, but she had wanted to prove she was above all that single girl misery.

So here she was, being miserable.

Good plan, Chels. Top-notch. She mentally rolled her eyes.

"You would never do that. If you want to grab a drink we can meet you in the bar," Lacey said. "We just need to go change."

Like Lacey and Matt would reemerge in under an hour if they went and stripped their clothes off to change. It was a sweet gesture, though, and Chelsea appreciated it. She did not, however, want to sit by herself in the hotel bar on a Friday night. It was a resort. No one was alone at a resort unless they were a serial killer. Or a fifth wheel. And she did not want to meet either one of those. Being the latter was awkward enough. Forced small talk with a sociopath over vodka tonics while her friends had orgasms back in their rooms was not her idea of a good time. She'd much rather read a book under the covers with her gas fireplace cheerily spewing ethanol into her hotel room.

"No, thanks. You guys have the rest of the night off from Chelsea-sitting. I'm going to order room service and drink alone."

Amy laughed. "You're always such a good sport. I don't think I could make jokes if I were the one flying solo."

Which was why Amy had never, in the ten years Chelsea had known her, been without a boyfriend. Chelsea, on the other hand, was holding out for a hero. Eric had turned out to be more fire-breathing dragon than anything else, but that was a minor misstep on the rotting rope bridge of life. Being alone didn't bother Chelsea for the most part. Just when she was stuck in a sauna with the merry make-out maids.

"I'll see you in the morning when I most likely will die a horrible death, impaling myself with a ski pole or some other equally impossible fatal accident." Chelsea had no delusions about her ability to participate in high-speed sports. But she was willing to give it a shot. Once. "Please don't let the mortician put red lipstick on me for my funeral. I don't want to look Goth in death. It's too cliché."

With that, she waved and exited the sauna. After a brief stop in the locker room to pull on a sweatshirt and yoga pants, Chelsea was heading back to her room with damp hair and an even more dampened attitude. She was trying to hang tough and be cheerful and embrace new things, like skiing and winter. Generally speaking, she and winter didn't get along all that well because she was a klutz and there was ice. Slippery ice. But here she was in Lake Placid, prepared to go all snow bunny, and there was no one to appreciate it.

Or to give her an orgasm. That was really the main problem. She hadn't realized how addictive regular sex could be until it was taken away. Now she was starting to feel like she might climb out of her skin if there wasn't a penis inside her sometime soon. Exacerbating the issue was the fact that everywhere she turned people were paired off, snuggling and holding hands and mocking her with obvious indications that they were getting laid. Even as she walked through the halls of the hotel, there were two giggling teens crawling all over an ancient bobsled, and each other, in the lobby. She saw young honeymooners fresh from the Jacuzzi, staring into each other's eyes. An older couple was sucking face by the elevator. Studiously trying not to stare at them as she waited for the doors to open, Chelsea glanced to the left.

For the love of God. There was even a vacationer's husky giving it to his female companion in the manner named after his species, right there in the front of the stone fireplace, all casual-like. Like it was doggy date night. Weren't there health codes? Laws about dogs in public places? This little dirty business was obviously part of the reason why there were No Dogs Allowed, yet in the brief time she had been in Lake Placid, Chelsea had seen dogs in restaurants and stores.

Though until now none of them had been making it like a seventies porno. She checked the fireplace mantel for wine-glasses, expecting a slow R and B tune to start playing any second now. Sheesh. It was so not fair.

The teenagers noticed the dogs getting it on and shooed them apart, laughing as Chelsea stepped onto the elevator. She felt a little better. She shouldn't be the only one suffering from sexless-itis. That was the medical term for it. She should know, being a nurse and all. It was a valid condition experienced primarily by hormonal teenage boys and thirty-year-old women who broke up with their lame boyfriends and refused to date online.

It hurt.

That was the bottom line.

Chelsea found herself hoping the shower jet was fairly substantial as she keyed open her door. A little water therapy might do her good because the sauna certainly hadn't helped relax her.

Unfortunately her room was about a thousand degrees, rivaling the sauna for heightened temperature. "Oh, my God." She didn't like to be cold, but this was like walking in New Orleans in a wet suit. Turning the thermostat down ten degrees, Chelsea tossed her wristlet and the room key on the bed and went for the sliding glass door that led to a small balcony. She cracked it open a foot and stuck her head out into the night air.

Better. She could breathe again. Her room overlooked Mirror Lake and she was surprised to see that there were people out on the ice. She wouldn't trust that ice not to give way, but there were two girls cutting a clear path across the lake on figure skates, and a man running a dogsled team. Intrigued by the beauty of the moonlight on the ice, Chelsea stepped outside, a shiver rippling through her as the crisp winter air hit her overheated body. It felt good actually, and that surprised her. Normally she didn't like to be cold, but this felt refreshing.

Maybe there was something to this embracing-winter thing after all. These people looked like they were having fun. All day long, men, women, and children had looked like they didn't mind wearing goofy hats with flaps and boots that were virtually impossible to walk in as they strode around town. It was almost like they enjoyed it. Very interesting.

Worried she was going to cool her room down too much, Chelsea closed the door behind her and leaned over the balcony railing, the snow crunching beneath her elbows. She'd never been to Lake Placid before, and she never would have been the one to pick it as a destination, but the irritation she'd been feeling disappeared as she watched the graceful glide of the skaters, their skates cutting across the ice with a sharp sound that resonated in the silence of the mountains.

But it was cold, no denying that.

Feeling better, she turned and went to open the door, blowing on her hands to warm them.

Only it wouldn't open.

Yanking it harder, Chelsea felt the stirrings of panic. "Holy shit." It wasn't locked, that was obvious. The door was stuck in ice on the runner. Bending over, she tried to scrape it away with her fingers, which promptly turned beet red and went numb. The door still wouldn't open.

She pulled as hard as she could. She rocked it back and forth. She kicked the doorjamb. She blew on it, hoping to melt the snow. Nothing worked.

Great. She wasn't even going to make it until her first ski lesson before she died.

Peering over the railing, she gauged the distance to the ground and decided this wouldn't be happening if she had a sex life.

Brody Durbin stepped out into the cold night and took a deep breath. His sister meant well, but her pointed questions were driving him insane. He only saw her a few times a year since she trained for the pro alpine circuit in Utah, so why did she have to spend their time together grilling him about his knee injury, his future career plans, and his lack of a girlfriend? It would be nice if they could just sit and talk. Shoot the shit. Instead he felt like a presidential candidate being interviewed in the middle of a national crisis.

So he'd lied and said he had to go in to work early, and he'd ditched the hotel bar where Tracey was staying. On impulse, he'd ducked outside for a calming glance at the lake before he went home, and he felt like a jerk for leaving on such a dumb excuse. He didn't want to hurt Tracey's feelings. But neither did he want to explain that he was spending the majority of his time growing facial hair and studiously ignoring the Black Diamond trails, even when he wanted nothing more than to have a good run. A big middle finger to the doctors on a ride down the slopes. Which he never did, because it would be stupid.

With a sigh, he went down the sidewalk, intending to walk the circle around the lake that the skaters had cut with their blades before heading out to the parking lot and his truck. He loved Lake Placid, was born and raised right on the side of the mountain, and the lake held special memories of pickup hockey games and dogsled races from his childhood.

But most of his time had been spent skiing. That had been his love, his passion. He'd never loved anything else with that kind of intensity, not even a woman.

The moon was out and a few skaters were fooling around, but other than that it was quiet. He enjoyed the relative silence as he breathed deeply.

Until he heard a muffled, "Help."

It sounded more breathless than urgent and he glanced around for the source, not overly concerned. He felt his eyes widen when he saw that a woman was dangling from a second-floor balcony, her arms wrapped around the railing, her sweatshirt riding up so a sliver of her back above her waistband was exposed.

"What the hell are you doing?" he asked, totally baffled as to why anyone would be hanging there like beef jerky in the smoker. She was only wearing one shoe, and a glance down showed the other in a drift below. The lack of coat, hat, and gloves concerned him a bit, too. It couldn't be more than twenty degrees outside.

"I got locked out of my room so I figured this was my only option." She darted a glance at him. "But I misjudged the distance. Can you catch me?"

Of course he could catch her. She was petite and dangling in midair and he'd be a complete a-hole if he didn't rescue her. But he wasn't sure he trusted her not to freak out and drop with flying elbows and feet and knock out his front teeth.

"Why don't you try to sit on my shoulders first?" He moved in behind her. Even stretched out like she was, she didn't appear tall, and her tight stretchy pants indicated she was in shape. Nicely in shape, if that heart-shaped ass was any indication.

Brody cleared his throat, suddenly aware that he had just suggested she wrap her legs around him. And that he had avoided relationships and sex as avidly as the Black Diamond trails. But he maintained this was still the most logical way to get her down despite the unexpected direction his thoughts had just taken.

"What do you mean?" This was punctuated by a tiny shriek as she almost lost her grip.

Brody reached out, not willing to watch her plummet to the ground and break a bone. "I'm touching your legs, so don't freak out. Or kick me." He ducked his head between those same legs and stood up, so that he took the slack and relieved her arms. She wound up seated on his shoulders, still clinging to the decking of the balcony. "Better?"

"Yes." She sighed. "Holy crap, I thought I was going to fall and split my skull open. Or freeze to the railing." Her thighs clenched his head, giving him earmuffs of sorts. "Would it be weird if I said I'm grateful your head is so warm? Even my cooter is numb."

Brody almost dropped her. An erection sprang to life at the thought of warming up her so-called cooter. He could definitely think of a better head to handle that particular project than the one that housed his brains. Or lack thereof, given that he was getting horny and he hadn't even seen her face yet. But there was something about her voice. Her ass. Her warming cooter.

Damn, he needed to get her on the ground. "Okay, let go of the balcony. I've got you."

"Are you sure?" she asked suspiciously.

"Positive."

She let go, not tentatively, but both hands simultaneously, throwing them up in the air like she was on a roller coaster. Brody wanted to laugh, except she had thrown him off-balance, and he spread his feet quickly apart so they didn't both go down. His knee didn't act up often, but he'd really hate for this to be the moment it crapped out on him.

"I'm going to bend down and you can just walk off my shoulders." He did it as carefully as he could but she still sort of tumbled off the front of him, sliding on the ice, her arms flailing.

Brody stood back up and reached out to steady her. She turned and swiped her hair out of her eyes. Oh, man, Brody didn't know whether to be grateful or horrified, but she was gorgeous. Like *eat your fucking heart out, boys* kind of beautiful. Everything on her was . . . perky. From her breasts to her smile, to her hair to her eyes. She radiated beauty and a healthy appreciation of the ridiculousness of the situation.

"That was a close one. I cannot believe I didn't break anything. Or pee my pants." She winked at him. "Bet you're glad about the last one."

No, golden showers had never been an interest of his. But he could think of a whole lot of other things he would clearly enjoy doing with her. "This could have all gone horribly wrong. You could still be hanging there if I hadn't decided to come outside. But all's well that ends well."

"Good point, Pa. You got some chewing tobacco to go with that?"

The words might have sounded harsh, except she was smiling. Smiling the kind of smile that made Brody's pants too tight. She was flirting with him. Ten seconds out of a potentially disastrous fall and she was moving on. He respected the hell out of that. "No, I quit. Ma and Doc Jones say it's no good for me. But I think its horse puckey." He could play, too.

She laughed, her breath puffing out in a vaporous cloud in the cold air. "But disaster hasn't totally been averted, since I strongly suspect my sock is freezing to the ground as we speak."

Geez, he'd forgotten she was only wearing one shoe. Brody stripped off his jacket and handed it to her. "It's nice and warm. Like my head. Put it on."

She did, looking like she was considering a comment or two, her mouth turned up in a smirk. Before she could respond, Brody bent over and picked her up at the waist, lifting her straight up in the air. Her worries proved accurate because her sock stayed on the ice, its wet heat clearly refreezing at contact. She made a sharp sound, a shiver rushing through her.

Without bothering to explain his actions, figuring they were obvious, Brody headed for the back door of the hotel.

"Thank you," she said. "This would suck a lot harder if you weren't around."

For some reason, he felt ridiculously pleased by that odd compliment. He was glad he'd been around, too. "You're welcome. Glad I could help."

"I dub you Sir Liftsalot."

He laughed as he pulled open the door and heat rushed over them. "I'm no knight in shining armor. I just happened to be in the right place at the right time."

"Shh. Don't ruin my fantasy. You've saved me with your muscled haunches, and now you should gaze at my flowing golden locks for ten seconds before a fire-breathing beast sends us running again."

Brody fought a grin. She wasn't exactly like any other woman he'd ever met, and he found her sense of humor very amusing. "Well, there is a husky behind you, does that count?"

"Yeah, that'll do." She slid down the length of him, his waterproof jacket swallowing her. "Though I don't really feel like running. With one shoe on. I'd much rather go to the bar and get a hot toddy. Care to join me? My treat in thanks for your chivalry."

He'd love to. Except that his sister Tracey was probably still in the bar. Did he risk it? Besides, this woman was in snow-soaked yoga pants and one sock. He thought fast and with his libido. "Why don't you go to the front desk and get a new key, then go up and put some warmer and drier clothes on? I'll order your drink for you."

"Oooh. You'll be waiting in the bar for me with a hot drink? You *are* my hero." She batted her eyelashes in an exaggerated way.

Brody snorted. "Overkill. I no longer believe your sincerity."

She laughed. "Okay, I'm off. My foot feels like cracked glass, and while I'm in no danger of hypothermia, I pretty much want to marry a wool sock right now."

"How did you end up locked out anyway?"

"Well, I opened the door for fresh air and went outside.
Then I closed the door. Then I tried to open the door, only
it was stuck on the track and it only opened a grand total of
two inches. And even sideways I am more than two inches.
Clearly. So I was stuck."

"And you decided to jump down off a two-story balcony?" he asked, amazed that she had seen that as her first
solution.

"Well, what else was I going to do? Freeze to death?"

She had him there. "Call for help?"

"I did. And you rescued me. All's well that ends well."
She smirked.

What he had on his hands was a smartass. He liked it. "I
can't argue with that. Okay, see you in a few minutes."

He moved with her to the elevator, then suddenly realized
he was missing an important piece of information. "What's
your name, by the way?"

The elevator doors opened. She got on and turned to face
him. "Chelsea."

"I'm Brody. Nice to meet you, Chelsea." It was very nice.
He felt the stirrings of a deep sexual attraction. Hell, it was
a goddamn whirlpool of chemistry swirling between them.

It just might be time to dive back into the dating pool.

Or at least get his feet wet.

Sometimes it paid to be a dumbass.

As the elevator doors closed on the burning hunk of
mountain man in front of her, Chelsea collapsed against the
wall with a fair amount of feminine swoon. Holy crap, the
man was hot. What were the odds of her being discovered
by a hot guy? One in a million, surely. It most likely should
have been an old dude who couldn't sleep or was out walking
the shih tzu one last time for the night. A family man who
was checking to make sure his teenagers were truly playing

hockey and not playing hide the stick on the lake. A hefty maintenance man prepared to fire up the Zamboni.

Not super hottie single guy with a strong jaw attractively covered by a devil-may-care smattering of facial hair. At least she assumed he was single. There was no ring on his finger—she'd checked—and he was waiting in the bar for her. That said single. If not, then he was a douche bag and she was going to be highly disappointed. But that was negative thinking and she didn't subscribe to that. She was just going to spend a minute reveling in the fact that this crapfest of a night had turned around.

When the elevator dinged on her floor, she remembered one little fact. She didn't have a room key. Crud. Pressing down, she rested her bare foot on the other one, trying to warm it up. She wondered if she had time to take a thirty-second shower to warm herself up. Probably not. She wasn't sure how much patience Brody had. Then again, if he was impatient, he would probably be lousy in bed, and that would be no fun.

Not that she was intending to sleep with him. Not tonight, anyway.

Reminding herself not to overcomplicate things, she explained what had happened to the front desk clerk, who promptly put on a mask of grave concern.

"Oh, no, well, let me send up a maintenance staff member to fix the door for you."

"It's not a big deal. They can take a look at it tomorrow."

"No, it's no problem at all. I'm sure the room will be really cold if we don't address it promptly. It's eighteen degrees outside."

Chelsea didn't disbelieve that. Her ass was still defrosting. But she was still going to protest, only the clerk was already on the phone.

"Here's Mike. He'll go straight up with you." She gestured behind Chelsea.

Turning, she spotted Mike, the maintenance man. He clearly moved at the speed of sound. "Thanks," she said, not really feeling thankful at all.

She really wasn't feeling gratitude twenty minutes later when Mike was busily thawing her doorjamb with a hair dryer. "Happens all the time," he told her. "French doors would be better."

"Uh-huh." Chelsea had changed in the bathroom, door firmly locked, and she was eyeing the back of Mike's head, pondering how well she could trust him in her room alone with her panties. He seemed legit, but her iPad and her cell phone charger were on the desk, along with a five-dollar bill she'd flung there when she'd been digging in her purse for ChapStick. If she went over and gathered it all up, she'd look like she thought he was a thief. If she left it and headed downstairs, he could be a thief. It was a dilemma, and the whole time she calculated the cost of her belongings, she was thinking about how freaking cute Brody was and how strong he had been. He hadn't dropped her. He hadn't even been breathing hard when he'd set her on the ground.

She didn't want to miss out on that.

What she really wanted to do was sop him up with a biscuit like a rich creamy gravy. Finger-lickin' good.

That was a surge of heat and moisture in her panties. Yes, indeed. Trying not to pace in her jeans, her feet in very cute argyle rain boots, Chelsea was about to say the hell with it, scoop up her iPad, and run downstairs, when Mike triumphantly showed her the door could open and close just fine, thank you very much.

"Wonderful. Thank you."

"I don't recommend opening it again though. Just in case."

"Safety first," she told him. "Got it."

"Have a good night, then."

"I'll head down with you. I'm meeting a friend for a drink." A Mr. Sexy-Pants friend.

Only when Chelsea got to the bar and looked around, there was no Brody. She glanced at her phone. It had been more than thirty minutes since she'd parted ways with him. Damn. "Have you seen a tall guy with a bit of five-o'clock shadow?" she asked the bartender.

"Yeah, he left like five minutes ago. Are you Chelsea?" The bartender was a smiling woman in her fifties.

"Yes." Maybe he had left his phone number. Hopefully.

"This is for you. He said he had to run."

A Bailey's Irish coffee was placed in front of her.

That was not a phone number. "Thanks. What do I owe you?"

"Oh, he paid for it."

Which meant she might as well drink it.

Since it was going to be the only thing warming her up that night.

Brody glanced at his phone for the tenth time. Chelsea was either doing weird stuff like emergency flatironing her hair, or she wasn't going to show. It had been half an hour and he'd already sucked down a beer in record time. Flagging the bartender, he made arrangements for Chelsea's drink, just in case she showed, because it was time for him to leave. He had spotted his sister wearing a bathing suit and clearly on her way to the hotel pool.

He was busted.

"Brody?" She waved enthusiastically.

"Hey." He thanked the bartender and headed Tracey off before she charged into the bar in nothing but a bikini, her towel loosely tied around her waist. "Isn't the pool closed by now?"

"A guy I went to high school with, his dad owns this resort. They gave me permission to do laps after-hours."

"Cool." Tracey was a hometown girl made good, poised to compete on the ski team in the next winter Olympics.

They would be happy to accommodate her. It didn't hurt that Tracey was sweet and what most men would consider gorgeous. Brody just thought of her as a kid. He couldn't help it. There were eight years between them.

"I thought you left like a million years ago."

"I forgot my credit card at the bar," he lied, making that the second time in one night he'd been full of shit with his sister.

"Oh, bummer. See you tomorrow, right?"

"Yep." Tracey was planning to ski Whiteface Mountain and Brody was working there. "Good night."

With one last glance back, hoping to see a small blonde with a grin pop up behind Tracey, he stepped through the automatic doors and out to his truck.

It was a rather deflating end to an unexpectedly interesting night.

Chances were he'd never see Chelsea again.

Now if only his dick would deflate as quickly as his hopes. Otherwise he was going to find himself spending the rest of his Friday night spanking the monkey. Which was not exactly where he'd pictured himself at thirty-two years old.

CHAPTER TWO

"I can't believe you got yourself locked out of your room," Lacey said.

"Are you kidding? This is Chelsea we're talking about," Amy added.

Chelsea was fortunately too concerned with figuring out how to carry ski boots, ski poles, and skis, all while preventing her goggles from falling down onto her lips, to be offended. "Last chance for you both to buy life insurance on me."

"It's just lucky that someone heard you yelling for help."

"Why, yes, it was." Chelsea dropped a ski pole. A glove fell after it. There was too much equipment for skiing. She felt like a swaddled newborn in the pants and jacket she'd borrowed from Amy, who was something of a jock. If she could get away with crying like a baby, she would, but she doubted her friends would have much sympathy. But damn it, she was uncomfortable, and walking through the ski center, she felt like she'd been ushered into an alien world. With big goggles and even bigger boots on, everyone tromped

around, inexplicably looking like they were enjoying themselves.

"It's too bad he wasn't cute, because that totally sounds
like something that would happen to you. I'd get a troll
rescuing me and you'd get the hottie."

Chelsea had no idea where Lacey would get an idea like
that, and she found herself unwilling to admit that was exactly what had happened. Or that she'd screwed up her shot
at a little Lake Placid sexy time. Somewhere, in a dark room
that smelled like cheese, her ex Eric was laughing at her.

Picking up her pole and glove, Chelsea nodded. "Yeah,
it's too bad. Now will someone show me how to put these
boots on so I can experience the joy and exhilaration of
flinging myself down a hill on tiny sticks?"

"We're almost to the ski school station. Just hold your
horses. We'll drop you with your instructor and she can show
you how to put the boots on."

"I hope she has an endless well of patience, cuz she's a
gonna need it." Chelsea shoved her goggles back up. They
promptly fell down again.

"Chelsea Carruthers," Lacey told the desk clerk. "She
has a beginner lesson at nine."

"Great. Your instructor is right here." The older woman
gestured to her right. A tall man was bent over, snapping
his boots closed.

Chelsea's view was partially blocked as she shoved the
goggles up for the ten millionth time. "Thanks."

The instructor started to stand. Oh, hell no, it could not
be . . .

"Hi, I'm Brody Durbin." His eyes landed on her as he
stood to his full height. "Chelsea?"

"Yep, it's the one and only," she said, her heart suddenly
starting to pound from more than fear of snow down her
pants and the ski lift. Fate had planted Brody in her path
again. How kind of Fate. She'd have to send it a fruit basket.

"Of course it's you. I'd recognize those flowing golden locks anywhere."

She officially came in her ski pants. He'd remembered her absurdity. He was continuing it. Be still her sarcastic heart. "Are you and your muscled haunches going to teach me how to ski?"

He was struggling not to grin, she could see it. The desk clerk was eyeing them curiously. She didn't have to turn to know that her friends were doing the same. "In a manner of speaking," he told her. "But you're going to have to put your boots on first."

"Uh, Chels, aren't you going to introduce us?" Lacey asked pointedly.

She'd rather not, but manners won over. "Lacey and Amy, this is Brody. We met last night when he caught me dangling off my balcony. Poor man." She studied him as he reached out and shook her friends' outstretched hands and smiled. He was so masculine, his jaw strong, his nose straight and narrow, his forehead high. But then he had the most deliciously luxurious eyelashes framing those deep blue eyes, and she suddenly wanted to run her lips over the abrasive stubble on his chin, then over the softness of his lashes. "And now, by a horrible twist of fate, he has to teach me how to ski. I think he must have pissed off karma in a bad way."

"I think it's called a coincidence," he told her. "Now sit down and put your boots on."

Bossy. Yeesh. She wondered if he'd be bossy in bed. She shifted uncomfortably as she sat down. It was hot inside and she was wearing too many layers. She had been guarding against the possibility of being cold, so she was wearing two layers of Under Armour, a turtleneck, two pairs of wool socks, and the ski pants and jacket. But she hadn't anticipated hanging around inside, nor had she expected to encounter Brody, who with one smile could shoot her temperature up a good ten degrees.

He was so damn distracting. So sexy. And he was

supposed to be teaching her to ski. This had all the makings of a spinal injury.

"Are you going to be okay?" Amy asked, suddenly showing solicitous concern.

"I'm fine." She sat on a bench and waved her friends off. They hadn't exactly been worried about her until they'd seen her ski instructor. She called shenanigans.

"By the way, I'm sorry I missed you at the bar last night," she told Brody. "The maintenance man was determined to defrost my door one frozen flake at a time. I think I must have just missed you. But thanks for the drink." She wanted to make it clear she had not blown him off.

"You're welcome. Maybe another time."

Was he serious or was that just him being polite? Fighting the urge to ask, Chelsea ignored Brody and stared at her boots. These were no rain boots, honey. There were all sorts of tabs and Velcro and snappy things. She tried to put her foot in and it got stuck halfway. She pushed a little harder. Nothing happened.

"I don't think these fit."

"Are they your size?"

"Well, yeah, but my foot won't go in."

Brody knelt on the ground in front of her and picked up the boot. "Don't be delicate. This isn't a glass slipper. Shove your foot on in."

This could have been romantic except he sounded impatient and she wanted to bean him with a ski pole for making her feel like an idiot. "I am! My ankle is going to break."

He used his other hand to grab her ankle. He pushed the boot and her foot simultaneously, and wouldn't you know it, her foot suddenly popped into place. She tested it. Yep, it fit. "Huh. That's weird."

Brody gave her a wry look. "Told you."

"Well, at least you're understanding about it." She looked down at her foot. "Now what?"

In a flurry of activity he strapped her into her boot, then

did the other one. It was like foot origami. She half expected to look down and see a couple of paper swans for feet. "So I guess you've done this before."

"A time or two."

"It's intimidating, you know. This is like a cult of the Snow God. Everywhere I look there are weird compartments and equipment and a secret language. I feel totally out of my element."

"That's hard for me to comprehend. I was skiing at two years old. But no worries, no one expects you to know everything, and by the time you've been out for just a couple of hours, you'll be getting the hang of it."

"Your confidence in me is charming. I'm glad you're a regular guy, instead of like some former pro skier turned instructor who resents that he missed the Olympic team by one inopportune fall ten years ago. Teaching me would be like the seventh circle of hell for a guy like that." Not to mention wildly intimidating.

Brody put his hand out to help her stand. "Oh, I don't know. So far I'm not minding it all that much. But we haven't hit the slope yet."

Say what? Chelsea looked up at Brody in horror as she stood, wobbling on her boots. "Are you saying that you were a skier who missed the Olympics by a fall and now instructs idiots like me? Or are you just saying that you instruct idiots like me?" Please let it be the latter. They were still holding hands, or at least she was still clutching him, afraid she was going to fall over as she rocked precariously in her boots. From a distance, this probably looked charming. From where she was standing, it was rapidly sliding into horror territory.

"I was on the US alpine ski team for three years. I competed in the Super G and was set to go to Torino in 2006 when I fell and tore my knee up." He winked. "So now I instruct idiots like you."

Oh, my God. "Excuse me while I shove this ginormous

ski boot in my mouth. I'm so sorry. I didn't mean that to sound like it did." Her mother had always told her that her sarcasm was going to bite her in the ass, and it had seriously just bitten. If she could stand independently she would rub its soreness.

"It's okay. I'm glad I can still ski." Even if he couldn't do the Black Diamonds anymore. Brody was glad he hadn't been forced to completely give up his love. But poor Chelsea looked so stricken that he almost laughed.

There was no doubt in his mind that she hadn't meant to be insulting, but he also suspected that on more than one occasion she had found herself in hot water as a result of her wit.

Her look was chagrined, and she spoke around the goggles that had slid down over her mouth. "I may be beautiful, but I'm not very smart. Please forgive me."

Brody laughed. He could honestly say he hadn't met anyone quite like her before, and he was intrigued by her. Attracted. If anyone else had made a joke about his injury, he probably would have spent the next hour feeling sorry for himself in that dark place he had frequently gone to after he'd realized his dreams were shattered. But maybe Tracey was right. Maybe he needed to get out more, spend less time brooding.

"So what do you do for a living, Chelsea?"

"I'm a nurse."

He imagined her patients loved when she blew into their room, a cheerful whirlwind of activity. It suited her. "Good. So you can patch yourself up when you fall."

Her face contorted into a grimace.

"Kidding. I'm kidding. I've never had a student get injured. So let's go."

Watching Chelsea walk was one of the funniest things he'd seen in a while. He'd seen three-year-olds with better balance in boots than her. She looked like she had weights on her feet, not ski boots. When her goggles fell again,

Brody reached over and yanked them off her head. He tightened the strap and handed them back.

She put them on and they stayed. "Oh, look at that. Much better. Thanks."

It was lightly snowing and bodies were moving in all directions, heading up the beginner hill, skiing down it, lining up for the gondola to take them to the top of the mountain where the most advanced skiers would blaze down the trail. Brody led her to the ski rack, where he collected his skis and dropped them onto the ground and snapped them into place.

"Is that what those things are? I've been hauling my borrowed skis around this joint for no reason?" She looked put out.

"Yep." He took her skis out of her hand and dropped them to the ground.

"Don't you worry they'll get stolen?"

"No. Now stop stalling and step into your skis. Bend your knee and just click your boot into place." He figured that Chelsea would talk her way out of two-thirds of the lesson if he let her.

She attempted to follow his instructions, but somehow the ski just slid out from under her and fell back two feet. "Shit."

Brody retrieved it for her and held it while she struggled to snap it on, her arms flailing. He started to think she might prove to be his greatest challenge yet. He actually loved teaching beginners to ski. Seeing the moment when they got it, when they understood why skiing was just freeing and amazing, was very rewarding to him. It was like convincing someone to try your favorite ice cream flavor and watching how their face lit up as they bit. But the woman in front of him might be a challenge, on more than one level.

"Okay, you're in."

"I feel trapped. Its claustrophobic."

"Claustrophobic?" He'd never heard anyone describe skis that way before.

"Yeah, I can't just take off. I'm stuck in these. So, like, if a killer was after me and I wanted to run, I couldn't. I'm stuck."

"If a killer is after you—which seems a little unlikely on a Saturday on Whiteface with hundreds of people around— but if he is and you're on skis, you can just ski away from him." It seemed a bit obvious to him. "Skiing is faster than running anyway."

"Oh." She made a face like she thought he was a know-it-all. "You just don't get it. What if I need to go up to get away from him?"

Brody was again amused. He wondered if she would talk in bed, or if she would just let him lick and touch every inch of her without a word. Would she cry out when she came? He suddenly really wanted to know. "So let's walk up the hill. Just turn sideways and dig your ski in. Right, left, right, left, see, you're walking. That's how you go up."

"I'm walking." Chelsea sounded out of breath already. "And why am I walking, exactly? There's no way I could out-walk a killer at this speed."

"Let's not worry about killers, okay? You just need to get familiar with the skis. The basics are walking and stopping. So we're going to go up a few feet, then we'll have you practice how to stop."

Chelsea wasn't any better at stopping than she was walking. Brody kept saying, "Make your V," like he had shown her and she kept not doing it.

"I am!" she yelled as she slowly glided down the small incline, unable to stop, not making a V.

Brody physically moved her skis together behind her. "Like this."

"Oh."

There was a lot of "oh" in their lessons, but while she had zero natural ability Brody had to admit she had

stubbornness in spades. She dragged herself up the hill time
after time on pure determination, not skill.

"Okay, let's go get on the lift."

Her face froze and she swiped at her hair. "Are you sure
that's wise? I could fall off the lift."

"I'll have them slow it down for you. We're just going up
the beginners hill, no big deal. We can see the top from
here." He pointed with his pole. "Don't worry, I'm going to
be in front of you when we go down, and you're going to
hold on to me."

It was clear she was suspicious. It was also clear that she
should have pulled her hair back and tucked it under her hat.
Her blonde hair was soaked with fat, wet flakes of snow. He
reached out and twirled it, then shoved it under her hat. He
figured her thighs had been wrapped around his head, so
touching her hair couldn't be off-limits.

But the contact jarred them both. He saw it in her eyes
when she glanced up at him, startled, and in the way she
licked her lips for no reason. He was close to her, too close,
and he wanted to kiss her with a hot urgency. But he was at
work and she was off-limits. At least for the next thirty
minutes.

"Come on. Just stand in front of the chair and then when
it touches you, sit down. Leave your poles here."

"Why?" The thought seemed to panic her. "Don't I need
those?"

"No, we'll use mine." Prying the poles out of her death
grip, he urged her in front of the lift after indicating to the
attendant he needed it slowed down.

He managed to get her on with only one squawk from
her, but she did clutch the side of the chair desperately. "Has
anyone fallen off this thing?"

"No." He didn't really know that for sure, but it seemed
like the right answer to reassure her. "So where are you
from?" Maybe if he distracted her, she wouldn't be so
nervous.

"Albany. Where I spend all winter pretending it doesn't exist. How about you?"

"I was born and raised here. I went to Utah to train for a while, but I came back in '06." His plan had been to beat out the Austrians and Swiss and win gold, but it hadn't worked out that way. Though, as he rested comfortably in the chair crawling up the side of the beginner's hill, with Whiteface sprawled out in front of him, Vermont just over the other side of the mountain, he realized this was where he was meant to be. Maybe the thrill of winning and the rush of competition had been exhilarating, but he couldn't imagine still being on the circuit at this point in his life. He was digging his roots deep in Lake Placid.

"It was a cool place to grow up. I think I was actually conceived during the Olympics of 1980 when they were held right here in town. My mom was a speed skater, and she and my dad celebrated her accomplishments with sangria and no birth control. Not that they'll admit to that, but it's my personal theory."

She laughed. "So sort of like the blackout babies when all the electricity on the East Coast went out, you're an Olympic offspring."

"Something like that."

"Do you have a husky?" she asked. "Everyone here seems to have a husky."

"German shepherd. They're less whiny." His dog, Mabel, was the only woman who slept in his bed these days, and he had a feeling she wouldn't be too thrilled with any competition for her side of the bed.

"I have a Newfoundland," Chelsea told him. "Everyone said I was insane and maybe a little selfish, because I live in an apartment. But I couldn't resist his sweet face and all that fuzzy wuzzy fur."

Her voice took on a tone that made him wish she were rubbing his jowls. If he had jowls. Which he didn't.

"What's his name?"

"Grape Ape. I just call him Ape. He'd love it here with all this snow."

Brody laughed. "Your dog's name is Grape Ape?"

"What's your dog's name?" she asked defensively. "Something boring like Sam, I bet."

"It's Mabel." Though he was tempted to screw with her and say it was Sam.

"Mabel?" She looked surprised. "How vintage of you."

"If you haven't noticed, this is kind of a vintage town." Brody lifted the bar off their laps and into the air as they approached the drop. "Now just step out of the chair and move away when we slow down, okay?"

She made a panicked sound, but managed to get herself off and away from the next incoming chair. He'd been a little worried she'd get clocked, but she did alright. Gutsy chick, that was for sure.

Ten minutes later, he was reevaluating that statement. Chelsea was clinging to his pole like a baby monkey and pleading with him not to let go.

And he knew that he was in trouble, because he thought it was the cutest damn thing he'd seen in years.

CHAPTER THREE

Chelsea fought against the urge to close her eyes and begged Brody not to make her do it. "I'm going to die. I will hit a tree and die. If a Kennedy and Sonny Bono died while skiing—oh, and Liam Neeson's wife—why would I survive? This is stupid. Pure stupidity." She had just managed to get the hang of walking and stopping and gliding a couple of feet, and now he wanted to hurl her down the side of a mountain.

Amy shot past her on her snowboard, totally at ease, recording Chelsea on her phone. Despite wearing thick gloves, she flipped her friend off. No one needed to see this moment. Ever. But then she regretted letting go of the pole when her ski started to move. It was the damndest thing. These effing skis kept moving.

Brody had his pole up between his hands and was facing her. She was clutching his pole. The plan was for him to ski backward and for her to go forward, his pole keeping her steady. But that plan required her not freaking out, and so far she hadn't managed it.

The man was a picture of patience. He was still watching her calmly, and told her, "It's okay. I won't let go. You're in the middle of the hill and if you feel like you're losing control, just make your V."

If she survived this, she was going to show him what he could do with her V. And it wasn't going to involve snow.

Resigned, she decided the sooner she did this, the sooner she could go sit by the fireplace. So she nodded. "Okay, let's do it."

Brody pushed back and she started to move, immediately picking up speed. "Bend your knees. Lean forward. Bend your knees," he said, looking perfectly in control.

So not fair. She tried to follow all his instructions, and in a minute, they were down at the bottom. Thank God. It hadn't been too bad.

"Over to the lift. Let's go again."

Did the onslaught never end? Chelsea wished she could check her phone, because as charming as Brody's company was, she was getting a headache from the fierce concentration not breaking every bone in her body required. "Can't we practice walking again?"

"Nope. Back up."

Three times they went up, twice they came down. On the third run, Brody insisted she go it alone. Without poles, which supposedly gave her greater balance. Which clearly didn't work, because Chelsea realized almost immediately she was going too fast and she started to panic. "Brody!"

"Make your V! You're doing fine."

But she was going so fast he was actually suddenly kicking his own movement into gear to catch up with her, and she tried to do the whole V thing, she swore to God, she did, but before she could even register what was happening, she had left the trail, skied over some brush and a boulder, and dropped to an unceremonious landing on her ass. Heaving in and out, she gauged how close she was to the copse of trees. Too close.

Game over. She was out of here.

"You okay?"

"No. And the only thing that will fix it is me in the bar in the lodge. I want hot chocolate with marshmallows and a cookie." Not to be a baby about it or anything.

Brody helped her up. "You did great."

"I skied over a rock. How is that great?"

"It's your first time. Our hour is up though."

Thank you, baby Jesus.

"But we can keep going for another hour. You're really making great progress. Another lesson and you'll really gain some confidence. I definitely recommend it."

"No, thank you."

"Really? Are you sure?"

Why did he look so bewildered? Had he not just seen her windmilling her way sideways down the hill? It didn't seem that shocking to her that it was time for the goggles to come off.

"Does a chicken have a pecker?" Chelsea dusted her ass off. "This is very stressful for me, all this concentrating and worrying and knee bending and leaning and whatnot. I need a break."

"Okay. Sure." Brody smiled. "Last time down, then. And, yes, you can hold my pole."

Without thinking, her eyebrows shot up. Did he have any idea how much she'd like to hold his pole? It seemed he did, because immediately he seemed to realize what he'd said. His eyes darkened and there was a strangled sound that came from the back of his throat.

"Is that a promise?" Chelsea asked him, unable to resist.

But Brody didn't back down or pretend to not understand what she was referring to. "Yes. But only if you really, really want to."

If the excess saliva pooling in her mouth and the throbbing wetness in her panties was any indication, she wanted to. She moved in closer to him, willing herself not to fall on her ass. "I can't think of anything I'd rather do, actually."

She was certain if they weren't wearing goggles and skis and it wasn't snowing and he wasn't at work and they weren't on the side of a mountain—okay, really more like a hill where they were—that he would absolutely, one hundred percent kiss her.

"Grab on," he murmured, lifting his ski pole up between them. "And in case you're still around later, I get off at four."

It was tempting to make a joke about that choice of wording, too, but she restrained herself. "Oh, yeah?" she said brilliantly. This was the tricky part. She wasn't chasing after him. It wasn't her style, and she had learned the hard way that if you chase, they run. Or they let you catch them, but then you had to work for everything through the entire relationship, always giving, never taking. She wanted a two-way street, even in a weekend fling. She was not going to be the vacationer who threw herself at her ski instructor.

So the question was, if he didn't expand on that piece of information, what did she do?

Play it cool. "I'm off now. This was exhausting."

"You're going back to your hotel?" He looked disappointed.

Or so she'd like to think. "I don't have a ride back, but as soon as my friends are done, yeah. But I'll be in the coffee shop until then."

"Do you and your friends have plans tonight?"

"Probably something awful like dinner where I have to watch them flirting with their boyfriends."

"Well, if you want to grab a beer, I'm available."

Yep. There it was. Come to mama. "Is that so? Mabel won't miss you?"

"She can manage alone for one night." Brody gave her a smile. "Do you like beer?"

"Does the pope wear a funny hat? Now do I have to stand here holding your pole all day or are we going to move?"

His jaw dropped before he quickly recovered. "Keep a tight grip, smartass."

"Is that how you talk to all your students?" she managed to say before she let out a shriek. "Holy crap!"

Brody didn't hold back. He was pulling her forward at what was surely death-defying speeds. She was going to crash. She was going to fall. She was going to wind up flat on her back with no hope of an orgasm whatsoever. She was going to . . . wind up at the bottom of the hill. Well, whatta ya know.

She'd made it.

Sucking the cold air in and out, she was about to deliver a scathing setdown that would clearly show him who was in charge.

Only she wiped out. Just fell flat on her ass for no apparent reason, her skis slipping between his open legs. She wound up facing the front of his ski pants, both the wind and her sass knocked right out of her.

Brody hauled her to her feet. "Good run," he told her. "Your best yet."

Now who was the smartass? "I have snow up my back and I don't like it."

"Snow's cold. You kind of have to expect that." He bent over and popped her boots out of her skis and picked them up for her. "Let's go inside and warm you up."

She had no sarcastic response to that. Grateful for the freedom of being on solid ground, walking erect, instead of sliding hunched over on surely one of man's weirdest inventions, Chelsea asked Brody, "Who invented skis? I mean, really, who thought this was a good idea?"

"Humans have been skiing for five thousand years, but only for recreation in the last one hundred years or so. The first downhill ski race was in Switzerland in 1911." Brody opened the door for her. "But maybe that was a rhetorical question."

"It was," she assured him, pulling her goggles off. "But I feel well informed for final Jeopardy! now."

He laughed. "Toss your boots in the boot dryer and give

me your phone number. I have another lesson starting in ten minutes."

As Chelsea looked around, wondering what in Sam Hill a boot dryer was, she recited her number for Brody, liking the challenge he suddenly presented. Not a challenge in terms of getting his interest—she knew she had that—but a challenge in that he wasn't turned off by her sense of humor, nor was he a puppy-dog type. That's who she usually attracted, and while Lacey had once told her it was like she carried a penis in her purse, wanting to be the man in relationships, it wasn't something she had intentionally sought out. She'd much prefer a manly man. Just one who treated her as an equal. It wasn't her fault that normally only wimps were attracted to her.

"That's a boot dryer," Brody told her, pointing to where boots were lined up. "It dries your boots."

"Of course it does," she scoffed. Duh. She would have figured that out eventually. In a year or two. Which was how long it would take her to actually get the boots off.

Brody was a manly man. She couldn't wait to see just how manly. There was no way to tell anything in ski pants, but she was hopeful she wouldn't be taking a spin around the short track later that night.

"Your skis are in this rack." He put the poles in after. "And I'll call you when I get off work, okay?"

"Sure," she said breezily, because that's who she was, Chelsea Breezy, independent woman and master of nonchalance. She had skis and poles and looked damn good in these tight pants thanks to that insane hot yoga Amy had insisted she try. She was sexy and seductive and hair-flipping flawless.

"Don't try to jump off any balconies in the meantime," Brody said. "Or fall in a snow drift." He gave her a cocky grin and left.

If she didn't want to have sex with him so badly Chelsea would be annoyed. As it was, she was more than slightly irritated. This was her fantasy, and he really should respect the fact that in her own mind she should be entitled to be perfect.

Really, men could be so obtuse. Chelsea wondered, not for the first time, how exactly Snow White had managed to live with seven men without murdering at least one of them.

Mind-boggling. It really was.

After five unsuccessful attempts at removing her boots, Chelsea figured the hell with it all and went to the lounge where she ordered an Irish coffee and a brownie the size of her head.

Brody made it through two more lessons by rote, and fortunately his students were a little quicker to learn, and a little slower to argue than Chelsea. Which was good, because he was distracted, already thinking ahead to later that night when he could take Chelsea out for a beer, then take her home for something a whole lot more fun. Maybe it was presumptuous to think she would sleep with him on a first date, but hey, a guy could be hopeful.

Because there was something about her . . .

She made both his blood boil and his heart lighter. She amused him in a way he hadn't been amused in a very long time.

Maybe his sister was right. He'd gotten too serious over the last few years.

He was meeting his sister after his last lesson and he stripped off his outer layer and tossed it over the back of his chair as he sat down next to her in the coffee shop. Brody noted immediately there were at least four lovesick guys hovering around watching Tracey and trying not to be obvious. Given her local notoriety and her write-up in *Sports Illustrated*, along with a sexy photo of her wearing only her ski jacket and boots, it was no wonder she had a trail of horny twenty-year-olds behind her at any given moment.

But she seemed completely oblivious to it, just like she had expressed surprise at Brody's and their parents' outrage at her partially clothed photo shoot.

Tracey didn't strategize and she trusted everyone. She just wanted to ski and wasn't really aware of how pretty she was. Brody had been the opposite. He had navigated the pro world with intense distrust. The irony was, who had ended up happier? Not him.

"You have a captive audience," he told her now as he sat down and shoved her helmet out of the way.

"What?" Tracey glanced around. "What are you talking about?"

That she could actually look around and still not see it amazed him. "Never mind. How was your run? Are you having fun?"

Technically, she was home on vacation.

"Yes. You know I love being here. So much less pressure. Though I don't know why Mom and Dad had to move to Florida. It would be nice to see them."

He shrugged. "Snow can be tiring when you get older."

Her eyebrow shot up. "Brody, sometimes you sound old yourself. Will you please promise me that you'll at least attempt to have some fun?"

That made him instantly defensive. He wasn't boring. He just wasn't a partier. Nothing wrong with that. He was thirty-two. Partying at his age was unnecessary. "I'll have you know I have a date tonight."

Tracey leaned forward on the table, the sudden gleam in her eye scaring him. "Really? Who is she?"

Right then Chelsea came into the coffee shop with the brunette she'd been with earlier, laughing and tossing her hair out of her eyes. The kick of lust he felt was unmistakable. He wanted to unzip that pullover and uncover every sexy inch of her. He wanted to have her legs wrapped around his head again, but in a totally different way.

"As a matter of fact, she just walked in. She's one of my students." Brody nodded in her direction.

Tracey turned.

If she was seeing what he was seeing, it was that Chelsea had spotted him and her laugh had died out. Her animated expression had been replaced by one of pure sexual interest, her tongue sneaking out to swipe her bottom lip. Brody shifted in his chair and raised his hand to wave at her. God, he wanted her. He couldn't remember ever wanting a woman with this sort of base lust. It was uncomfortable. Yet exhilarating. Like doing the giant slalom. It banged you on impact, but it was the most satisfying of any course.

"Oh, well, she's cute," Tracey said speculatively.

Chelsea waved back and came over. "Done torturing beginners for the day?" she asked wryly.

"For now. There's always tonight."

Her jaw dropped a little before she recovered and gave a sexy laugh. "Some things I'm no beginner at."

Damn. He had walked into that, and now he had an erection with only a small table between him and his sister and a roomful of people. Awkward.

Chelsea turned to Tracey. "I'm Chelsea, by the way. Nice to meet you. And this is my friend Lacey."

"I'm Tracey, Brody's sister. It's wonderful to meet you, too. He was just telling me about you."

Oh, God, seriously? Brody shifted in mortification. He hadn't been telling Tracey about Chelsea. He'd said he had a date. Now she'd made it sound like he was gushing over Chelsea, like he never interacted with women at all. Like one little date was noteworthy in some way.

Which maybe it was, considering it had been about a year since he'd had one. But he didn't want to advertise that.

"Really?" Chelsea looked downright delighted. She grinned at him. "Did he tell you how he rescued me from certain death?"

"No."

Now Lacey was smiling, too, and Brody felt like a complete idiot. "I'm sure you would have managed without me."

"Probably," Chelsea agreed.

Nice.

"But then I would have twisted my ankle and I wouldn't have been able to experience the joy of skiing, and where would the fun be in that?"

"That would have been disappointing for both of us," he told her with a healthy dose of sarcasm. She was a handful. He couldn't wait to silence her with a kiss. Or twelve.

Chelsea laughed. "See you later. I'm on my second brownie of the day, so after we grab some coffee we're heading out."

He wasn't sure why a second brownie meant imminent departure, but with Chelsea, he figured there was no telling. "Cool. I'll call you."

She gave him an exaggerated double thumbs-up and made a weird face, then left, her hips swaying enticingly.

He wanted to nail her to the wall so badly it was becoming painful.

Tracey gave him a look. "Wow. I think I just may have met the woman who can crack your crusty exterior."

Brody gave her a black look. "Crusty exterior? Don't piss me off."

Tracey just laughed. "You need a distraction from your brooding."

"I don't brood," he said, now thoroughly exasperated. "Can't I live a quiet life? Is that a crime?"

The look she gave him told him exactly what she thought of the nonsense he'd just spouted.

Hell, hearing it out loud, even he knew it was nonsense. He had been brooding.

Maybe that was about to change.

CHAPTER FOUR

Chelsea walked into the bar and grill where she was meet-ing Brody and scanned the room. She was wearing jumbo boots and a hat with flaps. It had taken everything in her to be practical and dress the way she had, but the reality was it was flipping cold and she didn't figure she'd be very sexy shivering uncontrollably, so she'd gone with the winter wear. She shouldn't have worried. Everyone in the entire restaurant was dressed like she was, layered up in wool and fleece.

Brody had offered to pick her up, but she had declined, feeling like it was just a little cooler to show up on her own. Besides, she didn't really know him, and getting into his car didn't seem too bright. He could have her cut up in minutes. The whole town was as cold as a meat locker. He could stash her anywhere and she wouldn't rot until April. There was a cheery thought.

But better safe than sorry. That was something those chicks in fairy tales never caught on to, and look what hap-pened to them—there was a witch/troll/wolf around every corner. Chelsea figured the smart-girl thing to do was meet Brody in a public place.

What she didn't anticipate, however, was just how public it would be. The restaurant was a throbbing, undulating mass of bundled human bodies, with one whole corner of the restaurant consumed by young boys. It looked like monkey island at the zoo, with squawking and climbing and in-your-face confrontation occurring every which way. Scary. That was some seriously scary shit.

Brody was at the bar and he stood up, waving to her.

Chelsea took the seat next to him. "What is going on here? Why are all these kids out of the house so late?"

"It's eight o'clock. I don't think that's generally considered late for ten-year-olds on a Saturday. But I'm getting the impression they just won their hockey tournament. There's a lot of high-fiving and many rounds of Dr Pepper."

"Oh, I guess that explains all those hockey sticks leaning against the wall." Chelsea sat down. "Why did they bring them inside anyway? It would seem like it'd be easier to leave them in the car."

"They're expensive. They like to keep them in sight."

"But you trust your skis outside in a ski rack?" Chelsea dropped her purse to the floor. "None of this makes sense to me."

"You have a point. Can I get you a drink?"

"Yes, I'll take a dark beer. Whatever their specialty is." She couldn't stop staring at the kids, who appeared to have zero parental supervision. "Why are they all wearing those hats?"

Almost every kid wore a bright colored hat with fleece tentacles popping up in all directions. A couple had what looked like felt mohawks springing up from their skulls.

"It's just what's in style right now. They wear them skating and skiing. It's fun to see those crazy hats come flying down the mountain."

"I don't think I want to wear one of those."

"Well, you're not a ten-year-old boy, so I think you're safe from the fashion trend."

One of the boys tackled another, and they both let out yells before crashing against the wall. Yeah, she was glad she wasn't a ten-year-old boy, thank you very much. A woman three tables over stood up and yelled, "Boys, knock it off!" before taking a sip of her beer. Chelsea couldn't confirm she was their mother. For all she knew, it was some random lady because, honestly, no one looked willing to claim these boys.

"This is definitely a happening place."

"Sorry, maybe this wasn't the best choice." Brody flagged down the bartender. "Would you like to go somewhere else?"

And look like a total diva? No, thanks.

"No, this is fine. I like that it's lively. Good people watching."

But after one beer each and repeated shouts of "what?" to each other as they tried to converse over the melee, Chelsea was starting to rethink her response.

Brody frowned at her. "Did you just call me a twerp?"

Chelsea laughed. Maybe she wasn't the most demure of women, but even she didn't usually call her dates twerps. Not on the first date anyway. And then it would probably be something more R rated. "No, I said I was thinking about ordering dessert."

"Oh." He laughed. "How about I take you somewhere quieter for dessert? Do you like ice cream?"

"Does a bear shit in the woods? Of course I like ice cream." Ice cream was arguably what made life worth living.

"Wow, no hesitation there." Brody tapped his temple. "I'll make a note of that—loves ice cream."

Chelsea wondered if he had any idea how badly she wanted to lick him from head to toe. He was so smoking hot. She didn't get to do hot men. Never. She got men who were addicted to video games who thought an athletic moment was thumb wrestling. She wanted to touch those muscles she was sure were hiding under that sweatshirt. In fact, she wanted to eat her ice cream off his pecs. She wanted to skip straight to the real dessert—him.

But there was such a thing as being too honest, so she kept her thoughts to herself. Preoccupied with thoughts of his beard tickling between her thighs later, and how she might arrange that as quickly as possible, Chelsea just smiled. She probably looked vapid, but hell, she felt vapid. Women could be ruled by their hormones, too, and hers were cracking the whip saying she needed to get some of *that* ASAP.

"Want to head to the scoop shop?"

Was there anything cuter than going to the scoop shop together? Suddenly her hormones were overcome by a twinge of teenage girl. That sounded so romantic she couldn't help but feel her heart quiver just a teeny tiny bit. If they could get some woodland animals to accompany them they'd really be in fairy-tale territory. "Perfect. Are they still open?"

"Only one way to find out. You don't mind walking, do you? It's just a block." Brody stood up, passing his credit card to the bartender.

"I don't mind walking." Much. She was grateful she'd gone with the Eskimo boots. "But I think it's my turn to buy."

He just shrugged. "You can buy my ice cream if you really want to."

"Deal."

As they walked down the sidewalk, boots crunching on the snow and ice, Chelsea was surprised that she wasn't freezing. It was amazing what the appropriate gear could do. She was also surprised that she was enjoying herself. The air was clear, the sky filled with stars, the mountain rising in the distance, the town huddled at its basin in post-card perfection. There were skaters cruising around the speed-skating track, the Olympic rings posted prominently above it.

"It's very cool here," she told Brody. "Not generic like the suburb I grew up in."

"Yeah, I like it here. It has a small-town feel. People are friendly enough, but at the same time, not too friendly. Plus if you love winter sports, you're in the right place."

"Well, we know how much I like winter sports," Chelsea stated, tucking her mitten-clad hands in her pockets.

Brody laughed. "Exactly. You'd fit right in here."

Actually, despite the fear of dying skiing had brought, Chelsea wasn't finding the whole weekend as miserable as she expected, and that wasn't just due to Brody's company. It was amazing what the right clothes could do for a situation. Normally she would be whining about how cold she was, but walking now, layered up, she felt fine.

"I've always hated winter, truthfully, because I fight against it. I want to wear cute shoes and skirts and don't want hat hair. Plus I've never done any winter sports at all, as you could so clearly tell, so for me, the whole winter is like a waiting game for spring." Which sounded like such a huge waste of time and energy now that she said it out loud.

"How come you don't move south?"

"Because all of my family is scattered around upstate New York, and my friends, too. I don't want to leave them." She adjusted her hat. "But maybe I should give winter a chance. I'm kind of having fun here."

"I'm glad to hear that. You could be a respectable recreational skier with some more practice. But if that's not your thing, you can try skating, or cross-country skiing. Ice climbing, ice fishing. Tubing. Ice sculpting. Snowmobiling. There are all kinds of things you could do to have fun while passing the winter."

"Ice climbing? Does that sound like a good idea to you?" Chelsea laughed at the image of her scaling the icy side of a rock. Good God. "But you're right. I should find something to do to try and enjoy my winters."

Brody pulled the door of the ice cream shop open for her. "How about dogsledding? You ever been?"

"No. Though that actually sounds really fun. I love dogs. And the driver just gets to stand there. That's perfect for me." It was a sport designed for her, honestly.

"We could go now if you want. I have a buddy who has a team and they're out on the lake training."

"Right now?" Though she shouldn't be surprised. Dogs seemed to party in this town. They had a more active schedule than Chelsea.

"Yep."

"Sure." They went up to the counter and Chelsea gazed at all the flavor options. "It's like picking one child over another. How do I choose?"

Brody laughed, watching Chelsea as she peeled her hat off her head and clutched it, her blonde hair tumbling around her cheeks. There was a wave to her hair, somewhere between straight and curly, and it suited her. It was carefree, just like Chelsea.

When he'd been younger, and was featured in *People* magazine as part of an Olympic hotties issue, he had been the object of many a girl's desire, and they'd thrown themselves at him. He had taken, because, well, he was just shy of twenty-six and they were offering. But he had never really stopped to ask himself what kind of woman he liked. What mattered beyond a pretty face. Then his career was over and the interest dried up and he hadn't ever really answered that question.

It was clear to him now that he appreciated a woman with a sense of humor.

"Have two scoops."

She looked at him, astonished, her eyes lighting up. "You're a genius. Of course I should have two scoops."

As they walked out a few minutes later, with Chelsea licking that cone in a way that had him jealous, he asked her, "Is that good?"

"Is a frog's ass watertight? Hell yes, this is amazing. Peanut butter and chocolate together in one cone, a perfect pairing that changed the world. It's orgasmic." Her eyes fluttered in ecstasy.

Brody clenched his own cone so tightly he almost broke it. Did she have any idea of how sexy she was and how badly he wanted to have her repeat that same look, naked, in his bed? He could let the comment slide. But he didn't. "Oh, do you come that easily?" he asked in a low voice.

Her gaze shot up, the corner of her mouth turning up in a tempting little smile. "Why, Brody Durbin, I can't believe you just said that."

"Oh, did I shock you? Somehow I doubt it. And you didn't answer the question."

"It depends on the circumstances," she told him, her tongue flicking across the creamy surface of her treat as they strolled down the street. "And the partner. If he knows what he's doing, I don't think I'm that tough of a nut to crack."

"Good to know." If she dove into sex the same way she enjoyed that ice cream, Brody knew he wouldn't be disappointed. Quite the contrary.

"What's it to you?" she asked slyly, her tongue making another slow pass across her cone.

"I could crack your nut," he told her, figuring he had nothing to lose. She was just as attracted to him as he was to her, he'd bet money on it. So why pretend otherwise, especially since she was only in town for the weekend?

"Is that a promise?"

He gave her a slow smile back, knowing exactly how to play this flirtation with Chelsea. "That's a threat."

She laughed, a low, husky sound that made him want to lean over and kiss her, right there on the sidewalk.

So he did.

She knew it was coming. She didn't back away. Instead, her head tilted and her lips parted in a clear invitation.

That's what he was talking about. Brody covered Chelsea's mouth with his in a soft, teasing kiss. Her lips were warm, sticky, and sweet, and she tasted like chocolate. Delicious. Putting his hand behind her head, he pulled her a little closer, wanting another one of those. He liked how she didn't resist, how when he paused, she picked up his slack, so that they were dueling with each other, attack, retreat, a sparring of their mouths, their desire evenly matched.

Brody liked that Chelsea wasn't shy. When they finally broke apart, drawing in breath, she didn't look around and express concern that someone might have seen. Instead she grinned.

"Maybe we can defer that whole dogsled thing for another time. I'm cold and I have a Jacuzzi in my hotel room. Care to join me?"

Hell yeah, and then some. "Is the sky blue? Not as clever as your sayings, but you get the point. Yes."

She licked her ice cream. Temptress. "No bathing suits allowed in my Jacuzzi."

"That's good because I don't have one."

"Then why are we standing here?"

"Because I'm trying to be a gentleman and wait for you to lead the way."

"That's very polite of you." She started walking. "Please don't be polite in bed with me."

God, she was killing him. He was going to die from anticipation before they even got there. Spontaneous sexual combustion. Backed up, well . . . he just needed to walk faster. "I thought we were getting in your Jacuzzi. Because poor little Chelsea is cold. You never said anything about your bed."

"Oh, I love it when you act like me," she said, biting her cone hard and making a satisfying crunching sound. "It's really exciting to me that you get my sense of humor. Almost no one ever does."

"You mean, they think you're actually serious about fairy tales and your overdramatic pronouncements?" He had only spent three hours with her and he could tell when she was being serious, which wasn't often, and when she wasn't, which was mostly. Her ability to laugh, and make him laugh, was something he really dug about her.

"Yes. Stupid people. But you're clearly not stupid, Brody, and I applaud you for that."

"Give me an hour and you'll really be clapping for me." He nudged her with his elbow and gave her a grin.

"Don't try to be as funny as me. You'll never succeed." But she was fighting a grin. She popped the remains of her cone in her mouth. "Can I have the rest of yours?"

"No." Brody guarded his own cone closely. If he wasn't careful, he suspected she would just steal it. She was a wily one. Lousy on skis, but there was no telling what she'd do on solid ground. Honestly, he couldn't wait to find out. "So what kind of nurse are you?"

"That sounds like the first line of a joke. But the answer is, I'm a geriatric nurse. I love taking care of the seniors. They have great stories. Plus, they don't mind that I talk too much."

"I bet they appreciate conversation. And someone treating them with respect. I'm sure you're good at it."

"I enjoy it." Chelsea paused and looked up at her hotel. "This is a big hill. And the sidewalk looks icy."

"It's fine." It didn't look that bad to him and it was the only way to the hotel unless they went back for his truck.

"Don't you have a knee injury?"

Brody fought the twinge of annoyance that rose in him. "I can walk up a hill. Didn't you see me skiing down a hill yesterday? I just don't have the ability to compete professionally, that's all. But I'm not handicapped." And how was this conversation at all sexy? He regretted bringing up her job, because it had led her to bring up *his*. Or rather that damn sidewalk had. He sighed. There probably hadn't been any way to avoid this awkward moment. Awkward for him, that is.

"Okay. I didn't realize. I was just trying to be considerate."

"I understand. Thank you."

Now they were being polite and reserved. But at least they were already halfway up the hill she was so concerned about.

"If I grab your junk will it make this less awkward? Will you forgive me?"

Brody laughed. "I'm not sure, but you can give it a try. And for the record, there's nothing to forgive. I'm not so super sensitive that concern offends me." At least not for longer than a few seconds before he pulled his head out of his ass.

Her hand snaked over and caressed his thigh as they were walking. Of course she would really carry through with her outrageous pronouncement.

"You're in the right area, but you're missing the real junk," he told. "The good stuff. A little to the left."

"Good junk? Is there such a thing?"

"Well, you know what they say. One man's junk is another man's treasure." Just to help her along, and because those light teasing strokes were making him insane, he moved her hand, firmly pressing it onto the front of his jeans and his very painful erection.

She stopped walking. He stopped walking. She turned toward him, her hand stroking firmly up and down. "I think I just struck gold."

He wasn't sure he was capable of speaking.

CHAPTER FIVE

Chelsea watched Brody's eyes darken right before her. His lips were ground together and his fingers gripped her wrist painfully. He wanted her as much as she wanted him. Which was evident in the erection she was stroking so brazenly through his jeans. It was a good thing it was freezing outside, because they were mostly alone. There were probably people who could glance out their hotel windows and see them, but they would just look like they were standing on the sidewalk talking, given their bulky coats and gloves.

No one would guess how naughty she was being.

"I wish you weren't wearing gloves. I wish I wasn't wearing pants," he said, his voice ringing with so much sincerity Chelsea wanted to laugh.

"We're almost there. I'm reminding myself that I am fully in my fairy tale rights to take you up to my room. I mean, come on. Snow White lived with seven little men. Cinderella didn't know the Prince's name and yet she totally made out with him. Sleeping Beauty was diddling the guy in the woods. And Ariel gave up her voice after like a thirty-second glimpse of Eric on the boat. So really, what I'm doing isn't the least bit objectionable."

"I have no objections, that's for sure. We're adults. We're having fun." He shifted away from her touch, but he did lean over and kiss her again. "I have no idea who Ariel and Eric are but they're not coming to bed with us."

"*The Little Mermaid*," she murmured between kisses, letting her head drift back so he could nuzzle her neck.

"Your Disney knowledge is scary."

"I have a lot of nieces and nephews. My siblings are older. I was my dad's midlife crisis. Most forty-year-old men take up golf or buy a sports car. My dad got my mom knocked up."

He chuckled. "Now that's the gift that keeps on giving."

"Well, he said I came out making noise and haven't stopped since." Brody's hand attempted to brush across her chest but there was no way he was going to find her breast through all those layers. He'd need a scalpel to penetrate all that down and fleece. "Okay, it's time to go inside."

"So eager. And I'm not even a prince." Brody urged her to continue on the sidewalk toward the hotel.

"I have a confession. I'm not really looking for a prince charming. Because that is, in fact, a fairy tale."

"What are you looking for?"

A nice guy who would love her dog and put up with her. A guy who would think she was funny and who would open the door for her and her mom when she came over. A guy who liked children to crawl all over him at family events and a guy who could build a bonfire. But she wasn't going to say all that to him, because they'd just met and that would be weird.

"The beast. That's what I'm looking for."

Brody laughed. "Minus the fur, I'll see what I can do."

The automatic doors of the lobby opened for them. Chelsea had to ask something before they got into her room and caution and intelligence went out the window. "Do you, by chance, have condoms?"

He made an enigmatic face but he just said, "Yes."

"Cool." Chelsea studied him, enjoying the way he didn't quite look at her. "Did you go buy some after work?"

"Yes."

She hit the button for the elevator and laughed. "I'm flattered. And grateful."

"I was hopeful, what can I say? And unlike in my younger days, I'm not exactly in high demand so I don't carry them with me."

"The old man isn't getting any, huh?" Chelsea rolled her eyes. "Please. You could get laid every Friday if you wanted. Maybe even Saturdays, too, if you put some effort into Friday."

Brody rolled his eyes right back at her. "Thanks, I think. But I'm okay."

The elevator door opened and fortunately no one was on it. They stepped in and Chelsea pushed the button for the second floor. "Should I show you you're in high demand? Should I throw myself at you?" She followed up her teasing words with unzipping her coat and sidling up to him.

"I don't have a problem with that," he told her, the corner of his mouth turning up.

"Oh, Brody, you're so hot and fast on your skis," she said, using a breathless voice, pulling down the zipper of his jacket so she could spread her hands across his chest. "I want you so."

She had expected him to laugh, had expected herself to laugh. But what she saw in his eyes killed anything but desire.

He took her by her upper arms and turned her, shoving her up against the wall. Oh, my. The beast had come out. He kissed her, a hot, thrusting kiss that had her clinging to his chest like a simpering virgin. It wasn't even really possible to kiss him back, it was more like a full-on assault of her senses, his tongue sliding in and doing tantalizing things to hers. Somehow he managed to tug her undershirt out from her waistband and move his hand up over her bare skin to her bra. She hadn't even had time to take her gloves off and he had snuck his off when she wasn't looking. Tricky.

His other hand was on her backside, pulling her firmly against him. When the elevator dinged and he pulled away from her, she almost fell off the wall, breathing hard, her nipples tight and her inner thighs aching.

Note to self: Brody made a bad-ass beast.

She liked it.

He held the door open. "You'd better hurry up or I'll take you in the hall."

Oh, my. She may have created a monster.

Thank God.

For the most part, she did not take her sex with sugar. She wasn't into sweet.

Digging in her pocket for her key as she walked, she told him, "I'm guessing people know your face around here. You might want to be discreet." He hadn't told her much about his pro days but she knew enough about sports and small towns to figure he was known by the locals. Not that she was hip on doing it in the hallway, but if he kept looking at her that way, she might be tempted to throw caution to the wind.

"So your balcony is out then?"

Yes, and it had nothing to do with protecting his reputation. "Yes. Because there is no way in hell I would remove any of my clothes in these temperatures."

"You were outside in your socks and no coat last night."

"That was unintentional." She unlocked her hotel room door and tossed the key card onto the console. She was peeling her coat off when Brody helped her along by yanking off the sleeves.

His was already off and on the floor. When the hell had he done that? He plucked her hat off and threw it, then he came into her space and completely filled it up with a whole lot of sexy man.

"You won't get naked outside for me? You won't let me bend you over that balcony and do wicked things to you until you scream?"

"When you put it like that . . ." She pulled his shirt out of his jeans and ran her fingers over the warmth of his flesh. "Still no."

He gave a low laugh. Then he kissed her until she was breathless. Until she was irrational and no longer thinking of anything but him and the feel of his body against hers. Until she thrust her hips at him in a silent request, and her fingers dug into his shoulders.

She hadn't been that blown away by plain old kissing since she was sixteen and making out with a nineteen-year-old in her mother's minivan. Only then she would have never let the guy whose name she couldn't remember put his hand down her pants. When Brody popped the snap on her jeans, she was thinking it was about damn time.

Without hesitation he took her zipper down and maneu-vered his hand inside, his finger gliding with unerring ac-curacy right into her panties and deep inside her. "Holy crap," was her opinion on that.

Sagging against the wall, she gripped him harder, afraid she was going to fall. Afraid she was going to come.

"Oh, my God, you're wet," he murmured, his voice stran-gled, eyes hooded.

"I can stop that if you'd like," she said, because somehow he made it sound like a bad thing. Though she wasn't sure she really could stop her desire at this point. He'd turned the faucet on and it wasn't about to run dry anytime soon.

"Now why would I want you to do that?" He stroked inside her while nuzzling her skin, stretching the neck of her sweater to get as close to her breast as possible. "Where would the fun be if I couldn't make you soaking wet for me."

That was a good question. One she had no answer for because she was rocking her hips forward to meet the rhythm of his finger. "Well, I don't know about soaking," she said, because she felt the social pressure of a required response.

It was the wrong thing to say because he completely pulled his finger out of her and held it up for her to see how it was glistening with her sticky sweetness.

"Soaking," he told her again. Then he peeled his shirt off.

Hello, Most Amazing Chest Ever. Chelsea checked the corner of her mouth for drool.

But before she could express appreciation, he picked her up and didn't lay her on the bed so much as he threw her. Chelsea was still bouncing up and down from impact when he ripped her boots off her feet and sent them flying. Then he yanked down her jeans and panties with one swift motion, and before she could say *oral sex*, he was between her thighs, his mouth on her, his fingers squeezing her legs as he held them apart.

Looking down at the top of his head, with his knit hat still on, his beard stubble rough against her tender skin, and his tongue doing laps across her clitoris, Chelsea took a deep, shuddering breath and let the pleasure wash over her. She was immensely grateful she'd gotten locked out of her room and that Brody had been walking by at that precise moment, because this was some seriously good shit going on between her legs.

Gripping the bedspread, Chelsea couldn't keep her eyes open or her mouth shut. She was letting out rather loud groans of ecstasy as he licked up and down with slow, painstaking strokes. It had been a while since she'd been with a guy, and even then, Eric had considered oral sex punishment. She'd only gotten it on special occasions and with zero enthusiasm or skill. Brody was eating her out like he was a starving man and she was a muttonchop. Or something sexier than mutton. Like she was a truffle.

It had her bursting in a full-fledged orgasm in about ninety seconds.

"Oh my God." If it didn't feel so amazing she might

actually be embarrassed at how quickly she'd come, but it did, so she didn't. Instead, she just lay there and enjoyed the ride.

All the tension left her body and she released the bedspread she'd been holding hostage as the spasms settled and she regained the ability to speak. "Brody . . ."

Before she could even finish her sentence, he was stripping off his pants and sheathing himself in a condom. She tried to sit up to offer assistance, or at least take a look at the penis she had only stroked and never seen before, but he pushed her back down onto the mattress. Then he took her hands and moved them up over her head, pinning them together with a tight grip.

Chelsea was startled, but not in a bad way. She liked the way he took charge. She liked the impatience. With his free hand, he popped her bra open and dragged it down her arms with his teeth, the tip of his tongue forcing goose bumps to rise on her flesh. Covering her breast with his mouth, he sucked lightly, drawing her nipple into his mouth.

"Yes," she said, because she wanted to encourage him to continue doing that. There was something about the tingling tug that caused her still-simmering desire to boil over again.

The fact that he stopped would have been disappointing, except he was nudging at her still very wet opening with the head of his erection. The anticipation was killing her as he teased, dipping slightly in then out again, his finger brushing over her swollen clitoris.

"Do you need an invitation?" she asked.

"You already gave me one when you invited me up to your room."

Yeah, she wasn't one for subtle most of the time. "Then I won't waste my breath with another one."

"Am I making you impatient?" Brody was dying himself, desperate to plunge into her welcoming heat, but he enjoyed teasing her, wanting to hear what she would say, how she would urge him on.

He'd never met a woman like Chelsea, and she hadn't been the least bit intimidated by his aggressiveness. He had always liked his sex a little on the rough side, but he'd held that in check, because most women in their twenties didn't roll that way, or at least not the ones he'd met. The only time he'd really gotten down and dirty was with an older woman, but Chelsea hadn't even blinked when he'd torn off her clothes and tossed her on the bed. In fact, she'd clearly liked it. She wasn't lying—she wanted the beast.

Which he was more than happy to give her.

"No, I'm fine," she said, clearly lying through her teeth. "I'm in no hurry."

Under other circumstances he would have laughed. And he did appreciate her sense of humor and bravado. But here, in bed, with his cock throbbing and his balls tight with need, her legs spread for him, he felt a surge of desire, a need to prove that she wanted him. "No?"

That very well might be her plan. He was aware of that. He was also aware that his reaction was a testosterone-laden Pavlovian response, but knowing it didn't stop him from having it.

"I can wait all night," she told him, licking her bottom lip, her breasts bouncing slightly with the rapid rise and fall of her chest, her fingers trembling beneath his iron grip.

The fucking hell with that. She was going to take it now.

Without saying a word, Brody thrust deep into her.

"Oh!" she said, her eyes widening.

Desire pooled in his mouth, and he gritted his teeth against the sensation of her body wrapped around him. He didn't pause, didn't hold back, just pounded into her, needing to feel that release he'd been careening toward for twenty-four hours. It wasn't pretty. It wasn't delicate. It was a hard, base need that had sweat beading on his forehead and his knuckles whitening as he held her hard against the bed.

The expression of surprise on her face faded away as her eyes drifted closed, little soft moans of pleasure escaping her mouth. She was a beautiful woman, her nose pert and cute, her eyes intelligent, her lips sensual and full. Both days he'd seen her she'd been wearing minimal makeup, her skin glowing with health, her cheeks pink. The skin above her breasts was splotchy from desire, and Brody would have called it an out-of-body experience except that he was so damn aware of his body it hurt.

But as he sank in and out of her, his muscles tense, the urgency so desperate it almost scared him, he realized he'd never experienced anything quite like this, certainly not with a woman he'd just met. He didn't want to think about it, or analyze it. He just wanted to feel it.

If the way her body tightening around his was any indication, she felt it, too. Her inner muscles started to quiver.

"Don't stop doing that," she breathed, her eyes opening to lock with his. "If you change the rhythm I will kill you."

"Why, are you going to come?" he asked her, knowing the answer.

"Oh, yeah."

"I guess you couldn't wait all night."

He grinned down at her, loving the way a flash of annoyance crossed her face at the same time she squeezed her inner muscles, gripping him like a vise, her orgasm sweeping over her.

"I guess not, Brody."

It was spoken in a way he'd never heard his name. It was soft yet aggressive, shaky but controlled. It was his name on the lips of a woman who knew exactly who she was and what she wanted. What she wanted was him. And she was shattering beneath him.

Sexy as hell. That's what she was. Brody had never felt so tight, so hard, so completely inside a woman, and her orgasm sent him rushing into his.

Normally he kept his thoughts and his enthusiasm to himself, but he couldn't contain it this time, not with Chelsea so honest and straight up, her pleasure so obvious. He let out a deep groan through gritted teeth and let himself go. He didn't just let his body go. He let himself go as well, just fell into the moment and took it for all it was worth.

It was the best orgasm he had ever had, and when it was over, he just stared down at her for a second, panting. She stared up at him, panting. They stared at each other.

"Well," she said finally, while Brody was still trying to assemble his thoughts. "That didn't take us long, did it?"

"No." Brody forced himself to pull out, even though he would have loved to have just taken up residence inside of her permanently. "I think we both needed that. To take the edge off." He knew he had. "What do you say we jump in your Jacuzzi then go again, a little slower this time?"

She pushed her hair back off her forehead and moistened her lips, giving him such a sexy, speculative look that he felt his dick give a jump of approval.

"Sounds good," she said. "As long as slow doesn't mean gentle. I like the beast."

Yeah, she was going to kill him. He honestly didn't think he'd ever met a sexier woman.

Brody shifted closer and kissed her. Then bit her lip. Hard. "I think I can manage that."

CHAPTER SIX

Chelsea followed Brody to the bathroom, naked and still a little stunned from how hot and fast things had gone between them. She had expected that she would enjoy herself, but that had been intense. It was easy to blame celibacy for why they had both been so hungry and so quick to orgasm, but she knew it wasn't that simple. Chemistry was either there or it wasn't, and it was clearly there between the two of them.

Walking behind Brody was a beautiful thing. She had known in theory, of course, that a man's ass could be that tight, with that much muscular definition, but she'd never seen it in person. It was awe-inspiring. He glanced back and caught her staring. She just raised an eyebrow and dared him to say something. He was the one walking naked. She had every right to look.

But he didn't say anything. His eyes just smoldered. It was ridiculous. He had brooding, sexy alpha male down pat. Chelsea wanted to bottle him up and take him home.

"How hot do you like the water to be?" he asked as he turned the faucets of her jetted tub on. "We should have brought some wine or something with us."

"I like it a shade shy of scalding. And a beer would be nice but I'm not going to the store like this." She gestured to her lack of clothes, thrusting her shoulders back in the universal female trick of making her breasts look bigger and her stomach flatter.

Brody just nodded. "Too cold."

Damn, he had a good poker face. "It's hard to get a rise out of you, isn't it?"

Which actually made him laugh. "Oh, I think you're doing just fine getting a rise out of me." He gestured to his erection, which was back, full sail.

Nice to know she was appreciated. "Good pun. Six points."

"We're keeping score?" Brody turned the water on and plugged the tub. "Hop in. I'll figure out how to turn the jets on."

"I think there's a button on the wall." Chelsea stepped into the tub and eased herself down into the warm water. "Ahh, that feels good. And I guess we shouldn't keep score because I would win. Hands down."

"Well yeah, because you're the one doling out points." Brody hit the button for the jets.

Chelsea wasn't prepared for the intensity of the spray, and it knocked the bar of soap she had just picked up right out of her hands. It pummeled her breasts and her knees and hit her in the face. "Ahh! I can't see anything, turn it off. Turn it off!"

Brody did.

She wiped her face, blinking, stunned. "Oh my God."

He was clearly fighting the urge to laugh, unsure of her reaction. But Chelsea was no diva. She started laughing herself. It was funny.

"Now you can really say you got me wet."

Brody handed her a towel to wipe her face. "I had no idea that would have so much power. Are you okay? I think I can turn it down."

The jets started again, a more gentle rush of water this time. After scrubbing herself dry, she found herself at eye level with his penis. "Uh, yeah, I'm fine. What were we talking about?"

Without waiting for an answer, she reached out and stroked the length of him, enjoying the sharp exhalation of air from his mouth. His penis was as attractive as the rest of him, long and thick and shiny. She didn't imagine a man wanted his penis called pretty, but his was. There were no imperfections, no changes in skin tone, no curve to the tip. It was just a perfectly pretty penis, and Chelsea decided she was going to suck it.

With the tip of her tongue, she started at the top and worked her way to the end, enjoying the anticipation and the way his fingers were suddenly pressing into her shoulders. Then she fully enclosed her mouth around him and drew him deep.

"Chelsea, damn."

She didn't really have a response since she was busy, but she figured actions spoke louder than words anyway. Gripping the base of his shaft, she picked up the pace a little, pulling him in and out, letting her saliva lubricate her strokes. With her other hand, she cupped his balls gently, her feathery touch causing them to draw up tighter. Then, because she could, and because she wanted to touch such a tight ass for herself, just to say she had, Chelsea continued until she was gripping the firm muscles of his backside.

The sound he made was gratifying. It was somewhere between a groan and a hiss. Chelsea started to shift restlessly in the water, her inner thighs aching anew, her nipples puckering as they brushed against the cold porcelain as she leaned over Brody. The decreased jets were hitting in very pleasant places and the room was steamy, Brody's body warm. Glancing up at him, she gave him a smile, then stopped moving her head, using her hand to guide him forward to rock onto her mouth.

At first he let her control the movement, but then he started thrusting, filling her deep. Chelsea thought about how it had felt to have him thrusting inside her, and she shifted in the water, the ache of desire blooming into an unbearable burn. She wanted more.

He seemed to understand because he suddenly pulled out, his hands on his hips as he breathed hard. Then again, maybe he hadn't been thinking of her, exactly. Given the way his jaw was working and his cock was jumping, he had been on the verge of an orgasm. Chelsea wanted to preen at how satisfying that was. She had brought him to the edge.

Feeling a little arrogant, she leaned back against the tub and put her arms on either side, feet crossed at the bottom, closing her eyes to further the effect. "Ah. This is nice. Very relaxing."

When he didn't answer, she opened her eyes again.

It seemed to take him some effort to speak, his hand hovering over his erection like he wanted to stroke it himself and stop the agony, but he finally said, "Scoot up."

"Sure," she said lightly, moving forward so that she was hugging her knees. Brody stepped in behind her, sloshing the water over her breasts.

"Keep going."

"Go where?" She glanced back at him. Uh-oh. His expression was downright fierce and he was unwrapping a condom. He wasn't going to lie back and soak in the tub. She actually shivered a little in excitement, her inner muscles quivering with anticipation.

"On your knees. Hold on to the edge."

Yep. That's what she thought he was going to do.

Lifting her backside, she shifted her legs as far apart as they would go and braced herself both on the wall of the tub and on the ledge in front of her. Brody grabbed her hips, and then he was sliding inside her. It was glorious. He was the perfect size for her and he instinctively knew that she liked to stick with one rhythm. Sure, he was a little high-handed, but she had asked for that, and unlike some women, she found it hot. She might like to get in the last word, but that didn't mean she wanted to be the aggressor in the bedroom. Or in this case, the bathtub.

Plus, she liked being on her knees. It gave her a huge sense of freedom and heightened the tension in each thrust. She really liked it when he reached around and tweaked her nipples. It made everything feel tight and hot and anxious in the best way possible.

"Harder," she urged him.

"Harder with what? Your nipples? Or fuck you harder?"

Why should she have to choose? "Both."

There was a brief pause when she suspected she had shocked him. Or excited him. Hell, probably both. But then he complied quite nicely, pinching her nipple harder and pounding her exactly the way she had requested. Chelsea held on to the edge of the tub for dear life and closed her eyes as the pleasure washed over her. She might have actually met the man who could satisfy her.

He moved his touch from her nipple to her clitoris, tweaking the swollen bud. Oh, yeah, he could satisfy her. She let out a deep low groan as she came hard, a tight, quick orgasm that left her breathless with its intensity.

Almost immediately he shuddered and found his own finish.

And again, all she could say was, "Wow."

Her knees suddenly made themselves known as she realized they were smashed against the sides of the tub, and her hips gave a creaky protest when she started to shift her legs together, but it was worth it. So worth it.

"You're right, this is a relaxing bathtub." Brody pulled out of her with a deep sigh.

He settled back against the wall, and with a lot of legs in the way, and a pull that wasn't exactly graceful on her part, he managed to get her between his legs and leaning back against his chest.

It was such a firm chest. As good as the wall, but warmer. Chelsea gave her own sigh. "I told you. I have good ideas."

"Damn straight."

Chelsea watched her legs float in front of her and marveled at the pleasant ache in every inch of her body. She liked this. She could get used to this. Except that she lived in Albany and this was truly the epitome of a one-night stand.

It was a bit of a bummer.

"You're leaving tomorrow?"

It seemed he was remembering the very same thing, though she couldn't tell if he was disliking the idea of her leaving as much as she was.

"Yep."

"So do you mind if I stay over?" Brody said. "We could have breakfast before you shove off."

Waffles with Brody had a very large appeal. As did waking up next to him and having one last tumble in the sheets. If this was it, she might as well take all she could get.

"Of course you can stay over. That way you can wake me up with oral sex."

He gave a short laugh. "Do you want me to cook for you, too, while I'm at it?"

"If I had a kitchen, I'd say yes. I hate to cook."

"I actually love to cook. But there's a great breakfast place that's two minutes away. I love their pumpkin pancakes."

Chelsea shifted a little, gripping his thigh to stabilize herself. It was strange to feel so at ease with someone she had just met. Yet she did. A little feeling was starting to burble up inside her, an idea that she found both fascinating and annoying. The idea that maybe she and Brody could actually date and have some sort of relationship.

Which was ridiculous. It didn't work that way. One-night stands did not turn into happily ever after, and long-distance relationships never worked. It was a fairy tale. An urban legend.

She knew that, one hundred percent.

Yet she still felt that if given half the chance, she might just decide to captain this ship of fools.

Give her a jaunty cap and see how long it would take to go aground on a sandbar.

She stood up, splashing water on Brody's legs.

"Where are you going?"

"The water's too hot. I need a drink."

And a big old reality check.

Brody watched Chelsea grab a towel and head back into the hotel room, still naked, still wet. He had the uncomfortable feeling that he didn't want her to go. Not into the other room. Not back to Albany. But those were the breaks, weren't they? It would be next to impossible to pursue dating when they lived 120 miles away from each other.

It figured. He met the first woman to really secure his interest in years and she was leaving forty-eight hours after he met her.

That was life, he supposed, and he could whine about it, or he could just enjoy it. She probably wouldn't want to date him anyway. She was a nurse with a snarky sense of humor who hated winter. He was a ski instructor who'd spent two-thirds of his life in the snow and the other third sleeping. They weren't a good fit.

Yet there had been nothing wrong with their fit ten minutes ago.

Brody stood up and wrapped a towel around his midsection, and padded across the cold tile floor to the main room.

Chelsea was standing in front of the door to the balcony, and he could already tell that she had opened it. And that it was stuck again. Her backside jiggled a little as she tried to discreetly close it.

"Did you open the door?"

"Yes. I was hot."

Brody wanted to laugh, but at the same time he wanted to wait until she was away from the backlit glass door. "Yeah, you're definitely hot. I can't argue with that. And probably anyone out on the lake can see that right now, too, since you're standing naked in front of an open door."

She may not be his, but he didn't want anyone else looking. At least not tonight.

"The door is stuck," she said begrudgingly, glancing at him over her shoulder, her hair even curlier than usual from the humidity of the bath.

"I know." Brody took her by the arm and shifted her out of the range of curious eyes. Behind a thick curtain. "I was debating asking why you would open a door that got stuck just last night but I figured it was a moot point at the moment."

"I thought, what are the odds of it happening twice?"

"When something gets stuck, the odds of that being repeated are actually pretty high." Brody tested the door. Yep. Stuck. Fortunately, she'd only cracked it open an inch, and while the wind was cold enough to shrink his balls, under the blankets in bed it probably wouldn't matter.

"You're a know-it-all."

"And you're impulsive." Brody took off his towel and crammed it into the open doorway to block some of the air. Then he yanked the drapes closed and figured that was the best he could do at the moment.

"It's not a dirty word." She was sitting on the bed, goose bumps all over her flesh, her nipples taut.

"No. *Fuck* is a dirty word. Which is what I'm about to do to you."

"Again?" She glanced down at his dick, which increased its burgeoning erection. "Yes, please."

"I fully appreciate your impulsiveness," he told her, and moved toward the bed. The night wasn't over yet.

CHAPTER SEVEN

Chelsea tried to ignore the pounding on the door but it wouldn't go away. Stumbling out of the warm bed, she pulled on a T-shirt and pajama pants from her open suitcase and rubbed her eyes. Brody didn't even move, his mouth open on a soft snore. They had spent half the night playing hide the salami, and whoever was at the door better have a damn good reason for knocking so early because she was tired. Worn out. Sexually exhausted. Orgasmed into a coma.

It was Lacey, who gave her a look of pure astonishment. "Why aren't you dressed?"

"Because I was sleeping."

"Chelsea, it's ten. We're leaving now."

"Now?" Was Lacey insane? "It's like *dawn*. Even the roosters aren't up. If my day was the history of the world, this is the Jurassic period. Humans don't exist." Though now that she was standing, Chelsea really wanted a cup of coffee.

"It's not five in the morning. It's ten. We're leaving in twenty minutes because checkout is at eleven and Matt wants to stop for gas."

"So why can't we leave at eleven?" And why the hell hadn't she driven herself here? "I need to take a shower." Because she smelled like sex. "And I want to eat breakfast." With Brody.

"Twenty minutes. We'll eat when we hit the road."

Lacey looked so perky and put together in her jeans and thick wool sweater that Chelsea was afraid to look in the mirror. It wasn't going to be pretty. She had cottonmouth and felt like she'd slept on damp hair, which she had. One side of her hair was flat, the other sticking up. Maybe she should be grateful Lacey had woken her up while Brody was still sleeping. Now she could sneak into the bathroom and do some repair work.

"Who is it? Is it housekeeping?" Brody's groggy voice came from the room behind her.

"No, it's my friend," she called back to him.

Lacey's eyebrows shot up. "Who is that?" she whispered. "Is that your ski instructor?"

She nodded.

"Oh, my God. I'm jealous."

"So you'll tell Matt to hold his horses for an hour?"

"Well, no, I can't do that. When he has a plan, he can't be talked out of it. Sorry."

How accommodating. "I'll be there," Chelsea told her, annoyed beyond belief that she wasn't going to get one last ride on the naked merry-go-round. Chances were she was never going to see Brody again. She had been looking forward to waking up with him, having slow, easy sex, then going out to breakfast.

It wasn't going to happen.

She closed the door and went over to the bed. "My friends are making me leave in twenty minutes. I didn't drive, so I don't have much of a leg to stand on."

Brody rubbed his chin and yawned. "For real? That sucks. But I get it."

"I'm going to jump in the shower, and no, you can't join me or we'll never make it downstairs."

He grinned. "Good point. Alright, I'll behave myself."

She was bitter about it, but thirty minutes later Chelsea was down in the lobby, her suitcase rolling along behind her, Brody carrying her floppy winter hat. When they stopped in front of the electronic doors, he put it on her head and tugged the two dangling strings.

"I had a great time, Chelsea."

"I did, too." Her thoughts were crowding together, her heart urging her to do something, say anything, to open up the possibility of there being more than one night, but they had only just met. If they lived in the same town, she would suggest coffee or a drink another day, but given the distance between them, suggesting any of that would make her a stalker. Or at the very least, look desperate.

She glanced around. "I don't see my friends." But she did see a couple of huskies sniffing around each other. It might have been the couple from Friday night, but she wasn't sure. This town seemed to be Club Med for huskies.

Chelsea wanted to say something brilliant about the strange rarity of true physical attraction, about how she wanted to chuck her suitcase into the back of Brody's truck and spend a lazy Sunday in his bed. In his arms. But she didn't.

She just gave him a smile and said, "Thanks for the ski lesson. Every time I make my V, I'll think of you."

Brody laughed. Right up until the end, Chelsea amused him. He stared down at her, wanting to kiss those pink lips until she moaned. How weird would she think he was if he suggested she come back the following weekend? Too weird for him to say it out loud.

"It was my pleasure. No, really, it was." They were both smiling at each other. Neither of them was making a move to leave. Brody felt ridiculous and excited and deflated all at the same time. He'd met someone he could really like and he had to walk away. He was in uncharted territory here, so he bent over and kissed her softly.

"If you're ever in town, give me a call."

Which was a stupid thing to say. It meant don't call if you're not. Which wasn't what he wanted to say. But he had wanted to hint at a future meet up in some way, and he didn't mean as a casual hookup. Frustrated, he jammed his hands into his pockets.

"Sure." Chelsea saluted him. "Catch you on the flip side. Keep on keepin' on. Have a good one. Over and out."

"My thoughts exactly." Brody added, "Have a safe drive back."

Then he left before he said something completely pathetic.

But after letting Mabel out and playing in the snow with her, he found himself driving to Whiteface and strapping on his skis.

He rode the gondola up to the top, determined to conquer his fears about his knee, determined to live a whole life, not a half one. So he wasn't going to compete on the pro circuit. That didn't mean he couldn't ski just for the sheer joy of it. If he fell on his ass, so be it. Chelsea had fallen on her ass. Hell, she'd dangled from a balcony rather than sit around and wait to be rescued.

If he fell, he'd just get back up.

But he didn't fall.

And when he reached the bottom of the mountain, he was so exhilarated he texted Chelsea.

If I was in Albany would you go to dinner with me?

Her answer came before he could even tuck his phone back in his pocket.

Does Dolly Parton sleep on her back?

Brody shook his head, a grin splitting his lips. Where the hell did she come up with these?

She followed up with a second text.

Yes. When are you going to be in Albany?

To hell with worrying about looking too eager. Brody was going to throw it out there.

Whenever you're free.

He almost got nailed by a snowboarder, so Brody un-clipped his skis and moved toward the lodge.

Next Sunday? Since it's both our days off.

Sure.

It looked like he was going to Albany for the day.

You can bring Mabel.

Oh, yeah. He was making the right choice.

CHAPTER EIGHT

Chelsea leaned into Brody's warm arms and sighed, tucking the blanket tighter around her as the sled slid across the ice behind the dogs. She was lying sideways, so that she could see his face and talk while his friend Dan guided the dogs as they ran. "I can't believe it's taken us a whole year to finally get out on the lake for a sled ride."

"Well, we spent half of our time in Albany. Then there was summer. Then fall. Now here we are."

Chelsea rolled her eyes in the dark. "It was a rhetorical statement."

"I know."

She knew he knew. She also knew that she and Brody were a perfect fit for each other. A year of dating had proven that. He was steady and reliable, sexy and romantic, and he had an endless well of patience. He loved her dog. He opened doors. He never failed to give her an orgasm. He took her teasing and he gave it right back.

"I don't know why I put up with you, honestly." She gave a fake sigh.

"Because you love me."

She did. "That I do." She was cuddling against him, and she ran her fingers across the stubble on his chin. She loved him in ways that still surprised her, every day. "I love you like the desert loves the rain."

"Wow." Brody kissed her roaming fingertips, his lips cold in the quiet night. "I love you, too. Like a dog loves a bone."

It wasn't Byron, but she'd take it. "How would you feel about being able to love me more frequently?"

"I definitely would like that, but what do you mean?"

"I mean I've been offered a job at an assisted living facility. Ten minutes from here."

"Really? That would be awesome. I'd love for you to be here, but I don't want to pressure you. I want you to want to move. Do you want to move?"

"Does a hobbyhorse have a wooden dick?" Chelsea kissed Brody, hard, feeling breathless and excited and in love. "Yes. I want to be with you."

"Can you move in with me? I don't want you to get your own place. I want you curled up next to me every morning."

Chelsea was so glad she'd held out for a hero. "Yes. Yes, I'll move in with you."

Brody kissed her back as they slid across the ice, the wind whistling around them.

"I am standing right behind you, you guys do know that?" Dan asked. "And I'm feeling very uncomfortable right now."

Brody glanced back at Dan, too happy to feel embarrassed. Chelsea was moving in with him. They were going to have a real future together and he was ecstatic. She still couldn't ski her way out of a paper bag, but she made him laugh every day, and she was kind and generous and loved his dog. She was the woman for him, no doubt about it.

"Maybe you can take us back in. I think we'll save the full circle of the lake for another night."

"With another sled." Dan pulled the reins and turned the

dogs. "With a driver you don't have poker nights with. This is awkward."

"Sorry." But the truth was, he was too excited to really feel a huge amount of remorse.

Brody wrapped his arms firmly around Chelsea. Now that he had her, he wasn't letting go. He leaned over so only she could hear. "Want to practice making your V? In bed?" He would never get tired of the enthusiasm she displayed during sex.

"Sure. I never get it right. Maybe because out on the slopes, you're always telling me knees in, and then in bed you're always telling me knees out. It's confusing."

"I'll show you what I mean."

"Such a gentleman."

If he were really a gentleman, he wouldn't have his hand between her legs, stroking against the seam of her jeans. But then he wouldn't have the satisfaction of seeing her lips part in arousal either. They were only twenty feet from the edge of the lake.

"Dan, we'll walk from here."

"Thank God."

He gave Chelsea a nudge to get her moving, then he took her hand as they walked across the snow-dusted ice. Chelsea slipped, of course, but he held her up. "I may not be able to protect you from a fire-breathing dragon, but I can keep you from breaking your neck."

She laughed. "That's all I ask. Save me from free-falling off balconies and give me great sex. You are totally my Prince Charming."

They were probably more like Jack and Jill, but the truth was, to him, she was absolutely a prize to be won. "Hey." He pulled her to a stop. "I love you, princess."

Her laugh disappeared and her eyes softened. "I love you, too."

Then she promptly fell on her ass.

And they lived happily ever after.

Erin...the good girl
Cole...the bad boy
The attraction...off the charts!

From *New York Times* Bestselling Author

CARLY PHILLIPS

Perfect Fling

A SERENDIPITY'S FINEST NOVEL

Assistant District Attorney Erin Marsden, is Serendipity's quintessential good girl. The only daughter of the ex-police chief, she has never made a misstep, content with her quiet, predictable life...or so she thinks.

After years of deep undercover work in New York City, Cole Sanders returns to Serendipity to help his aging father and to find his moral compass once more. Not to get involved with wholesome Erin. Even as a rebellious teen, he knew a girl like Erin was off-limits and that hasn't changed. But neither one of them can resist their off-the-charts chemistry, and a one-night stand brings complications neither Erin nor Cole expected.

"Carly Phillips has me addicted!"
—*Joyfully Reviewed*

carlyphillips.com
facebook.com/CarlyPhillipsFanPage
facebook.com/LoveAlwaysBooks
penguin.com

M1262T0213

Once passion ignites, you can't stop the flames…

From *New York Times* Bestselling Author

JACI BURTON

Hope Flames

Emma Burnett once gave up her dreams for a man who did nothing but hurt her. Now thirty-two and setting up her veterinary practice in the town she once called home, she won't let anything derail her career goals. But when Luke McCormack brings in his injured police dog, Emma can hardly ignore him. Despite her best efforts to keep things strictly professional, Luke's an attractive distraction she doesn't need.

Luke knows the only faithful creature in his life is his dog. After an ugly divorce that left him damn near broke, the last thing he needs is a woman in his life. Fun and games are great and, as a divorced man, the single women in town make sure he never lacks for company. But there's something about Emma that gets to him, and despite his determination to go it alone, he's drawn to her feisty spirit and the vulnerability she tries so hard to hide.

PRAISE FOR JACI BURTON AND HER NOVELS

"Jaci Burton's stories are full of heat and heart."
—Maya Banks, *New York Times* bestselling author

"Passionate, inventive…Burton offers plenty of emotion and conflict."
—*USA Today* Happy Ever After blog

jaciburton.com
facebook.com/AuthorJaciBurton
facebook.com/LoveAlwaysBooks
penguin.com

M1260T0213